Patricia yearned to be a writer after reading Enid Blyton and Carolyn Keene and even wanted to be Nancy Drew when she grew up. She has now grown up (she thinks) but the closest she's come to Nancy Drew is writing crime!

In 2009, after her husband died, she retired from her job and started writing seriously. Fascinated by people and their quirky characteristics, she always carries a notebook to scribble down observations.

Patricia also loves to paint in watercolour and lives in the Irish midlands with her children.

ALSO BY PATRICIA GIBNEY

The Stolen Girls
The Lost Child

THE MISSING ONES

PATRICIA GIBNEY

D.I. LOTTIE PARKER BOOK ONE

sphere

SPHERE

First published in 2017 by Bookouture, an imprint of StoryFire Ltd.
This paperback edition published in 2017 by Sphere

3 5 7 9 10 8 6 4

ISBN 978-0-7515-7218-6

Printed and bound in Great Britain by
Clays Ltd, St Ives plc

Papers used by Sphere are from well-managed forests
and other responsible sources.

Sphere
An imprint of
Little, Brown Book Group
Carmelite House
50 Victoria Embankment
London EC4Y 0DZ

An Hachette UK Company

www.hachette.co.uk
www.littlebrown.co.uk

For Aisling, Orla and Cathal
My life, my world.

PROLOGUE
31st January 1976

The hole they dug was not deep, less than three feet. A milky white flour bag encased the little body, firmly tied with the strings of a soiled, once white apron. They rolled the bag along the ground, even though it was light enough to lift. Reverence for the deceased was absent as one of them kicked it into the middle of the hole, squeezing it further into the earth with the sole of his boot. No prayers were said, no final blessing, just the shovelling of damp clay quickly covering the whiteness with darkness, like night descending without twilight. Beneath the apple tree, which would sprout white buds in spring and deliver a flourishing crop in summer, there now rested two mounds of earth, one compacted and solid, the other fresh and loose.

Three small faces watched from the third-floor window, eyes black with terror. They knelt on one of their beds, cushioned with rough-feathered pillows.

As the people below picked up their tools and turned away, the three continued to look at the apple tree, now highlighted by the crescent of the moon. They had witnessed something their young brains could not comprehend. They shivered, but not from the cold.

The child in the middle spoke without turning his head.

'I wonder which one of us will be next?'

DAY ONE

30th December 2014

CHAPTER 1

Susan Sullivan was on her way to meet the one person she was most scared of.

A walk, yes, a walk would do her good. Out into the daylight, away from the suffocation of her house, away from her own tumbling thoughts. She pushed in her iPod earphones, pulled on a dark woolly hat, tightened her brown tweed coat and faced into the biting snow.

Her mind raced. Who was she kidding? She couldn't distract herself, couldn't escape the nightmare of her past; it haunted every waking minute of her day and invaded her night like a bat, black and swift, making her ill. She had tried to make contact with a detective in Ragmullin Garda Station, but had received no reply. It would have been her safety net. More than anything she wanted to learn the truth and when she had exhausted all the usual channels she decided to go it alone. Perhaps it would help exorcise the demons. She shivered. Walking faster, slipping and sliding, not caring any more; she had to know. It was time.

With her head bent low into the breeze, she trudged through the town as quickly as the frozen footpaths would allow. She looked up at the twin spires of the cathedral as she entered through the wrought iron gates and automatically blessed herself. Someone had thrown handfuls of salt on the concrete steps and it crunched beneath her boots. The snow eased and a low wintery sun glinted from behind dark clouds. She pushed open the large door, stamped her numb feet on the rubber mat and, as the echo of the closing door muted, she stepped into the silence.

Removing the earphones, she left them dangling on her shoulders. Though she had walked for half an hour, she was freezing. The east wind had cut through the layers of clothing and her scant body fat could not protect her fifty-one-year-old bones. Rubbing her face, she streaked a finger around her sunken eyes and blinked away the water streaming from them. She tried to refocus in the semi-darkness. Candles on the side altar illuminated shadows along the mosaic walls. Weak sunlight petered through the stained glass windows high above the Stations of the Cross and Susan walked slowly through the sepia haze, sniffing the aroma of incense in the air.

Bowing her head, she sidled into the front row, the wooden kneeler jolting her joints. She blessed herself again, wondering how she still had a modicum of religion after all she had done, all she'd been through. Feeling alone in the silence, she thought how ironic it was that he had suggested meeting in the cathedral. She had agreed because she believed there would be plenty of people around at that time of day. Safe. But it was empty, the weather had kept them away.

A door opened and closed, sending a whoosh of wind up the centre aisle. Susan knew it was him. Fear numbed her. She couldn't look around. Instead, she stared straight ahead at the candle above the tabernacle until it blurred.

Footsteps, slow and determined, echoed up the aisle. The seat behind her creaked as he knelt. A fog of cold air swarmed around her, and his distinctive scent vied with the incense. She raised herself from her kneeling position and sat back. His breath, short sharp puffs, the only sound she could hear. She felt him without him having touched her. At once, she knew this was a mistake. He was not here to answer her questions. He would not give her the closure she craved.

'You should have minded your own business.' His voice, a harsh whisper.

She could not answer. Her breathing quickened and her heart thumped against her ribs, reverberating in her eardrums. She clenched her fingers into fists, knuckles white underneath thin skin. She wanted to run, to get away, far away, but her energy was spent and she knew it was now her time.

Tears threatened at the corners of her eyes and his hand closed around her throat, gloved fingers tracking a line up and down her loose flesh. Her hands flew up to grab at his but he swatted her away. His fingers found the iPod cable and she felt him twisting it, curling it about her neck. She smelled his sour aftershave and she became totally aware then that she would die without ever knowing the truth.

She squirmed on the hard wooden seat and tried to pull away, her hands tearing feverishly at his gloved fingers, only succeeding in causing the cable to cut tighter into her skin. Attempting to gulp breaths, she found she couldn't. Warm liquid burned between her legs as she wet herself. He pulled tighter. Weakened, she dropped her arms. He was too strong.

As her life choked away beneath the tightness, in a strange way she welcomed the physical pain over the anguished years of mental affliction. Descending darkness extinguished the flame on the candle as his hand jerked once, then twice, and her body slackened and all fear eased from her being.

Within those last moments of torment she allowed the shadows to lead her to a place of light and comfort, to a peace she had never experienced with the living. Tiny stars pinpricked her eyes before blackness washed in a wave through her dying body.

* * *

The cathedral bells chimed twelve times. The man released the pressure and pushed her body to the ground.

Another blast of freezing air travelled up the centre aisle as he left with speed and in silence.

CHAPTER 2

'Thirteen,' said Detective Inspector Lottie Parker.

'Twelve,' said Detective Sergeant Mark Boyd.

'No, there are thirteen. See the bottle of vodka behind the Jack Daniel's? It's in the wrong place.'

She counted things. A fetish, Boyd called it. Boredom, Lottie called it. But she knew it was a throwback to her childhood. Unable to cope with a trauma in her early life, she had resorted to counting as a distraction from things and situations she couldn't understand. Though now, it had just become a habit.

'You need glasses,' said Boyd.

'Thirty-four,' said Lottie. 'Bottom shelf.'

'I give up,' said Boyd.

'Loser,' she laughed.

They were sitting at the counter in Danny's Bar among the small lunchtime crowd. She felt little warmth as the coal fire roared up the wide chimney behind them, taking most of the heat with it. The chef stood at the carvery stirring a thick skin off the top of the gravy in a tray beside his Special of the Day – wizened roast beef. Lottie had ordered chicken in ciabatta. Boyd had copied her. A slight Italian girl lounged with her back to them, watching bread brown in a small toaster.

'They must be plucking the chickens the time these sandwiches are taking,' said Boyd.

'You're putting me off my food,' said Lottie

'If you had any food to be put off,' said Boyd.

Forgotten Christmas decorations twinkled along the top of the bar. A poster, Sellotaped to the wall, advertised the weekend's band, Aftermath. Lottie had heard her sixteen-year-old daughter, Chloe, mention them. A large ornate mirror proclaimed in white chalk last night's special deal – *three shots for ten euro.*

'I'd give ten euro for just one, this minute,' said Lottie.

Before Boyd could respond, Lottie's phone vibrated on the counter. Superintendent Corrigan's name flashed on the incoming call.

'Trouble,' Lottie said.

The little Italian girl turned round with chicken ciabattas.
Lottie and Boyd were already gone.

* * *

'Who could want this woman dead?' Superintendent Myles Corrigan asked the detectives standing outside the cathedral.

Obviously someone did, Lottie thought, though she knew well enough not to utter this observation aloud. She was tired. Perpetually tired. She hated the cold weather. It made her lethargic. She needed a holiday. Impossible. She was broke. God, but she hated Christmas, and hated the gloomy aftermath even more.

She and Boyd, still hungry, had rushed to the crime scene at Ragmullin's magnificent 1930s cathedral. Superintendent Corrigan briefed them on the icy steps. The station had received a call – a body had been discovered in the cathedral. He immediately swept into action-man mode organising the crime scene cordons. If it proved to be a murder, Lottie knew she was going to have trouble extricating him from the case. As detective inspector for the town of Ragmullin, she should be in charge, not Corrigan. For now, though, she needed to put station politics aside and see what they were dealing with on the ground.

Her superintendent spouted instructions. She scrunched her shoulder-length hair into the hood of her jacket and zipped it up without enthusiasm. She eyed Mark Boyd over Corrigan's shoulder, caught him smirking and ignored him. She hoped it wasn't a murder. Probably a homeless person with hypothermia. It had been so cold recently she didn't doubt for a minute that some unfortunate had succumbed to the elements. She had noticed the cardboard boxes and rolled-up sleeping bags hugging the corners of shop door nooks.

Corrigan finished speaking, a sign for them to get to work.

Having navigated her way through the gardaí activity at the front door, Lottie strode through the secondary cordon set up in the centre aisle. She ducked under the tape and approached the body. A gaseous smell came from the tweed-coated woman wedged between the front row kneeler and the seat. She noticed an earphone cable round the neck and a mini lake of liquid pooled on the floor.

Lottie felt the urge to put a blanket over the body. For Christ's sake, this is a woman, she wanted to shout, not an object. Who is she? Why was she here? Who would miss her? She resisted leaning over and closing the staring eyes. Not her job.

Standing in the chilly cathedral, now bathed in bright lights, she ignored Corrigan and made the necessary calls to get the experts on site immediately. She secured the inner area for the Scene of Crime Officers.

'State pathologist's on her way,' said Corrigan. 'Should only take her thirty minutes or so, depending on the roads. We'll see how she calls it.'

Lottie glanced over at him. He was relishing the prospect of getting stuck into a murder case. She imagined his brain conjuring up a speech for the inevitable press conference. But this was her investigation, he shouldn't even be part of her crime scene.

Behind the altar rails, Garda Gillian O'Donoghue stood beside a priest who had his arm around the shoulders of a visibly shaking woman. Lottie made her way through the brass gates and approached them.

'Good afternoon. I'm Detective Inspector Lottie Parker. I need to ask you a few questions.'

The woman whimpered.

'Do you have to do it now?' the priest asked.

Lottie thought he might be slightly younger than her. She'd be forty-four next June and she would put him in his late thirties. He looked every inch a priest in his black trousers and his woolly sweater over a shirt with a stiff white collar.

'I won't take long,' she said. 'This is the best time for me to ask the questions, when things are fresh in your minds.'

'I understand,' he said. 'But we've had a terrible shock, so I'm not sure you'll learn anything worthwhile.'

He stood up, extending his hand. 'Father Joe Burke. And this is Mrs Gavin who cleans the cathedral.'

The firmness of his handshake surprised her. She felt the warmth of his hand in her own. He was tall. She added that to her initial appraisal. His eyes, a deep blue, sparkled with the reflection of the burning candles.

'Mrs Gavin found the body,' he said.

Lottie flipped open the notebook she'd extracted from the inside of her jacket. She usually used her phone but in this holy place it didn't seem appropriate to whip it out. The cleaner looked up and began to wail.

'Shush, shush.' Father Burke comforted her as if she was a child. He sat down and gently rubbed Mrs Gavin's shoulder. 'This nice detective only wants you to explain what happened.'

Nice? Lottie thought. That's one word she'd never use to describe herself. She eased into the seat in front of the pair and twisted round as much as her padded jacket allowed. Her jeans were eating into her waist. Jesus, she thought, I'll have to cut out the junk food.

When the cleaner looked up, Lottie surmised that she was aged about sixty. Her face was white with shock, enhancing every line and crevice.

'Mrs Gavin, can you recount everything from the moment you entered the cathedral today, please?'

Simple enough question, thought Lottie. Not for Mrs Gavin, who greeted the request with a cry.

Lottie noticed Father Burke's look of sympathy, which seemed to say – I pity you trying to get anything out of Mrs Gavin today. But as if to prove them both wrong the distraught woman began to speak, her voice low and quivering.

'I came on duty at twelve to clean up after ten o'clock Mass. Normally I start at the side,' she said, pointing to her right, 'but I thought I saw a coat on the floor at the front of the middle aisle. So, I say to myself, I better get cracking over there first. That's when I knew it wasn't just a coat. Oh Holy Mother of God . . .'

She blessed herself three times and attempted to stem her tears with a crumpled tissue. The Holy Mother of God wasn't going to help any of them now, thought Lottie.

'Did you touch the body?'

'God no. No!' said Mrs Gavin. 'Her eyes were open and that . . . that thing around her neck. I've seen corpses before but I never seen one like that. By Jesus, sorry Father, I knew it was a dead person.'

'What did you do then?'

'I screamed. Dropped my mop and bucket and ran for the sacristy. Collided head first with Father Burke here.'

'I heard the scream and rushed out to see what was going on,' he said.

'Did either of you see anyone else around?'

'Not a soul,' said Father Burke.

Fresh tears escaped down Mrs Gavin's cheeks.

'I can see you're very upset,' Lottie said. 'Garda O'Donoghue will take your details and arrange for you to get home. We'll be in touch with you later. Try to get some rest.'

'I'll look after her, Inspector,' Father Burke said.

'I need to talk to you now.'

'I live in the priest's house behind the cathedral. You can get me there any time.'

The cleaner leaned her head into his shoulder.

'I ought to go with Mrs Gavin,' he said.

'Fine,' Lottie relented, seeing the distraught woman ageing by the second. 'I'll be in touch later.'

Father Burke nodded and, supporting Mrs Gavin by the arm, he led her across the marbled floor toward a door behind the altar. O'Donoghue followed them out.

A gust of cold air breezed into the cathedral as the Scene of Crime Officers arrived. Superintendent Corrigan rushed to greet them. Jim McGlynn, head of the SOCO team, offered him a precursory handshake, ignored small talk and immediately began directing his people.

Lottie watched them working for a few minutes, then walked around the pew, as close to the body as McGlynn would allow.

'Appears to be a middle-aged woman. Wrapped up well for the weather,' Lottie said to Boyd, who was standing at her shoulder like a persistent mole. She moved back toward the altar rails, partly to view from a good vantage point, mainly to put distance between her and Boyd.

'Hypothermia's not an issue here so,' he said, stating the obvious to no one in particular.

Lottie shivered as the serenity of the cathedral was decimated by the heightened activity. She continued observing the work of the technical team.

'This cathedral is our worst nightmare,' said Jim McGlynn. 'God himself knows how many people frequent here every day, each leaving a piece of themselves behind.'

'The killer picked his location well,' Superintendent Corrigan said. No one answered him.

The sound of high heels clipping up the main aisle caused Lottie to look up. The small woman rushing toward them was dwarfed in a black Puffa jacket. She jangled car keys in her hand and then, as if remembering where she was, dropped them into the black leather handbag on her arm. She shook hands with the superintendent as he introduced himself.

'State pathologist, Jane Dore.' Her tone was sharp and professional.

'You're acquainted with Detective Inspector Lottie Parker?' Corrigan said.

'Yes. I'll be as quick as I can.' The pathologist directed her words to Lottie. 'I'm anxious to get the autopsy underway. As soon as I can declare this one way or the other, the sooner you can officially spring into action.'

Lottie was impressed with the way the woman handled Corrigan, putting him in his place before he could start a sermon. Jane Dore was no more than five foot two, and looked tiny beside Lottie, who stood without heels at five eight. Today Lottie wore a pair of comfortable Uggs, jeans tucked untidily inside them.

After donning gloves, a white Teflon boiler suit and covering her shoes, the pathologist proceeded to carry out the preliminary examination of the body. She worked her fingers under the woman's neck, examining the cable embedded in her throat, lifting her head and concentrating the examination on the eyes, mouth and head. The SOCOs turned the body on to its side and a stench rose in the air. Lottie realised the pool congealed on the floor was urine and excrement. The victim had soiled herself in the last seconds of her life.

'Any idea on time of death?' Lottie asked.

'My initial observation would indicate she died within the last two hours. Once I complete the autopsy, I'll confirm that.' Jane Dore peeled the latex gloves from her petite hands. 'Jim, when you finish up, the body can be removed to Tullamore mortuary.'

Not for the first time Lottie wished the Health Services Executive hadn't relocated the mortuary services to Tullamore Hospital, half an hour's drive away. Another nail in Ragmullin's coffin.

'As soon as you can declare the cause of death, please inform me immediately,' Corrigan said.

Lottie tried not to roll her eyes. It was obvious to everyone that the victim had been strangled. The pathologist only had to officially class the death as murder. There was no way this woman had accidently or otherwise strangled herself.

Jane Dore dumped her Teflon garments into a paper bag and, as promptly as she had arrived, she left the scene, the echo of her high heels reverberating in her wake.

'I'm heading back to the office,' Corrigan said. 'Inspector Parker, get your incident team set up immediately.' He marched down the marble floor behind the departing pathologist.

The SOCO team spent another hour around the victim before expanding their area of operation outwards. The corpse was placed into a body bag, zipped up and lifted on to a waiting gurney, with as much dignity as could be attached to a large rubber bag. The wooden door creaked as they exited. The ambulance blasted out its sirens, unnecessarily, as its patient was dead and in no hurry to go anywhere.

CHAPTER 3

Lottie pulled up the hood of her jacket and clasped it to her ears. She stood on the snow-covered cathedral steps, leaving behind the hum of activity. Every nook would be searched and every inch of marble inspected.

She breathed in the cool air and peered skywards. The first flakes of a snow flurry settled on her nose, and melted. The large midland town of Ragmullin lay still beyond the wrought iron gates now swathed with blue and white crime scene tape. Like herself, the once thriving factory town struggled to awake each day. Its inhabitants muddled through the daylight hours until darkness sheathed their windows and they could rest until the next mundane day dawned. Lottie liked the anonymity it offered, but was also aware that her town, like many others, had its share of secrets buried deep.

The life in Ragmullin appeared to have died with the economy. Young people were fleeing to Australian and Canadian shores to join those lucky enough to have escaped already. Parents bemoaned the fact of not having enough money for daily essentials, not to mention an iPhone for Christmas. Well, Christmas was over for another year, thought Lottie, and good riddance.

The drone of the ring-road traffic seemed to shake the ground, though it was two kilometres away, which denied retailers a passing trade. She looked up at the trees labouring under the weight of snow-filled branches and scanned the grounds in front of her, knowing instinctively they wouldn't find any evidence. The earth was frozen and the soft snow hardened as quickly as it fell. The morning Mass-goers' footprints were encased under another layer of snow and ice. Gardaí, clutching long-handled tongs, scoured the grounds for clues. She wished them luck.

'Fourteen,' said Boyd.

The smoke from his freshly lit cigarette clouded around Lottie as he invaded her space. Again. She stepped away. He moved into the spot she'd vacated, his sleeve brushing against hers. Boyd was tall and lean. A hungry-looking man, her mother once said, turning up her nose. His brown, hazel-flecked eyes lit up an interesting face, strong and clear skinned, with ears that stuck out a little. His short hair was greying quickly. He was forty-five and dressed in a spotless white shirt and grey suit beneath his heavy hooded jacket.

'Fourteen what?' she asked.

'Stations of the Cross,' Boyd said. 'I thought you might have counted them, so I got in before you.'

'Get a life,' Lottie said.

There was a history between them and she cringed at her drunken memory, distilled with the passage of time but still present on the periphery of her consciousness. Other things had come between them too – she got the inspector job that Boyd had sought. It didn't bother him most of the time but she knew he'd relish the chance to lead this investigation. Tough shit, Boyd. She was delighted with the promotion because it meant she didn't have to commute the sixty kilometres to Athlone each day. The years she'd been based there had been a nuisance; though she wasn't sure if being back working with Boyd in Ragmullin was more of a nuisance. But on the plus side, it meant she was no longer dependent on her interfering mother to check in on the children.

Boyd childishly blew smoke rings into the air and she turned away from the smile curving under his inquisitive nose.

'You started it,' he said. With one final pull on his cigarette he went down the steps and headed for the Garda Station across the road.

Lottie smiled despite herself and walking carefully, so as not to fall on her arse in front of half the force, she took off after the long lanky Boyd.

* * *

A few people were queuing in the reception area. As the duty sergeant tried to keep order, Lottie skipped by and hurried up the stairs to the office.

The phones were ringing loudly. Who said good news travels fast? What about bad news? Travels at the speed of light.

Sniffing the stale office air, she glanced around. Her desk was a shambles, Boyd's as neat as a TV chef's kitchen. Not an ounce of flour anywhere, well, not a file or a pen out of place. Clear signs of OCD.

'Neat freak,' Lottie muttered under her breath.

Because of the on-going renovations, she shared an office with three other detectives – Mark Boyd, Maria Lynch and Larry Kirby. Landlines, mobile phones, photocopier, clanking oil heaters and the trooping through of every guard who needed to use the toilets gave the room an air of chaos. She missed her own space where the silence allowed her to think. The sooner the work on the station was finished the better.

At least the place was buzzing, she thought as she sat down at her desk. It was as if the events in the cathedral had stripped away layers of fatigue and boredom, revealing men and women ready for action. Good.

'Find out who she is,' Lottie instructed Boyd.

'The vic?'

'No, the Pope. Yes, the victim.' She hated when he used *CSI* language.

Boyd smiled to himself. She knew he was gaining the upper hand.

'I suppose you already know who she is.' She moved files from one side of her desk to the other, looking for her keyboard.

'Susan Sullivan. Aged fifty-one. Single. Lives alone in Parkgreen. Ten-minute drive from here, depending on traffic, about a half-hour walk. Worked in the county council for the last two years. Planning department. Senior Executive Officer, whatever that means. Transferred here from Dublin.'

'How did you find out so quickly?'

'McGlynn discovered her name Tippexed on the back of her iPod.'

'So?'

'I googled her. Got information on the council website and checked the Register of Electors for her address.'

'Was she carrying a mobile phone?' Lottie continued searching her desk. She could do with a map and a compass to find things.

'No,' Boyd said.

'Send Kirby and Lynch to search her home. One of our first priorities is to find her phone and anyone who can verify her movements today.' She discovered her wifi keyboard on top of the bin at her feet.

'Right,' he said.

'Any next of kin?'

'Doesn't appear to be married. I'll have to dig further to find out if she has living parents or any other family.'

She logged on to her computer. While she felt excited, Lottie silently cursed all the activity the investigation would generate. They had plenty of work to keep them busy – court cases dragging on, a traveller feud – and New Year's Eve tomorrow would bring its usual late night trouble.

She thought of her family. Her three teenagers, home alone. Again. Maybe she should ring them to make sure they were okay. Shit, she

needed to do grocery shopping and noted it in her phone app. She was
starving. Rummaging in her overflowing drawer, she found a packet
of out-of-date biscuits and offered them to Boyd. He refused her offer.
She munched a biscuit and typed up her initial interview with Mrs
Gavin and Father Burke.

'Do you have to eat with your mouth open?' Boyd asked.

'Boyd?' Lottie said.

'What?'

'Shut up!'

She stuffed another biscuit into her mouth and chewed loudly.

'For Christ's sake,' Boyd said.

'Inspector Parker! My office.'

Lottie involuntarily jumped at the sound of Superintendent Corrigan's thunderous voice. Even Boyd looked up when the door banged,
rattling the lid on the photocopier.

'What the hell . . . ?'

Straightening her top, she pulled a sleeve over her thermal vest cuff
and banished biscuit crumbs from her jeans. She flicked a flyaway strand
of hair behind her ear and followed her boss through an obstacle course
of ladders and paint cans. Health and Safety would have a field day, but
really there was little complaint. Anything was better than the old offices.

She closed the door behind her. His office was the first to be
renovated; she smelled the newness of the furniture and the whiff of
fresh paint.

'Sit,' he commanded.

She did.

Lottie looked at fifty-something-year-old Corrigan sitting behind
his desk, stroking his whiskey nose. The paunch of his belly pressed
into the timber. She remembered a time when he was trim and fit,
bombarding everyone with healthy living ideas. That was before real life
had overtaken him. He bent to sign a form and she saw her reflection
on his domed head.

'What's going on out there?' he barked, looking up.

You're the boss, you should know, Lottie thought, wondering if the man
knew how to talk in a normal tone. Maybe loudness came with the job.

'I don't understand, sir.'

She wished she was still wearing her jacket so as to bury her chin
deep into its padding.

'I don't understand, sir,' he mimicked. 'You and bloody Boyd. Can you not be civil to each other for five minutes? This case will soon be officially a murder investigation and you two are snapping at each other like feckin' five year olds.'

You haven't heard the half of it. Lottie wondered if Corrigan would be shocked if he knew the truth.

'I thought we were being very civil to each other.'

'Bury the proverbial hatchet and get on with the job. What have we got so far?'

'We've established the victim's name, address and place of work. We're trying to find out if she has any next of kin,' Lottie said.

'And?'

'She works with the county council. Detectives Kirby and Lynch are cordoning off her house until the SOCOs get there.'

He continued to look at her.

She sighed.

'That's it, sir. When I organise the incident room, I'll head down to the council offices to try to paint a picture of the victim.'

'I don't want any feckin' painted pictures,' he roared. 'I want this solved. Quickly. I've to do an interview in an hour with Cathal feckin' Moroney, from RTE Television. And you want to paint a feckin' picture!'

Returning Corrigan's glare, Lottie masked her true emotions with an impassive glaze, an expression she'd mastered after twenty-four years in the force.

'Set up an incident room, establish your team, assign someone to the Jobs Book and email me the details. Call a team conference early tomorrow and I'll attend.'

'Six o'clock in the morning?'

He nodded. 'And when you learn anything, let me know first. Go on, Inspector, get cracking.'

She did.

An hour later Lottie was satisfied everyone knew what they had to do. The foot soldiers commenced door-to-door enquiries. Progress. Time to find out more about Susan Sullivan.

She escaped into the pelting snow.

CHAPTER 4

The county council administration offices, housed in a new state of the art building in the centre of Ragmullin, were a five-minute walk from the station. Today, it took Lottie ten minutes on the icy footpaths.

She surveyed the large glass construction. It was like a monster aquarium with a shoal of fish inside. Glancing up at the three floors, she could see people sitting at their desks and others walking up and down corridors, floating around in their glass bowl. She supposed this was what the government meant by transparency in the public sector. She entered through swing doors into the relative interior warmth.

The receptionist chattered away on a phone. Lottie didn't know who to ask for or if word had filtered in yet that Susan Sullivan was no longer in the land of the living.

The young, black-haired girl ended her conversation and smiled.

'What can I do for you?'

'I'd like to speak to Ms Susan Sullivan's supervisor, please.' Lottie returned the smile without feeling it.

'That'd be Mr James Brown. Can I say who's looking for him?'

'Detective Inspector Lottie Parker.' She produced her ID card. Obviously, it was a slow news day in the council. They appeared not to have heard about Sullivan's fate.

The girl made a call and directed Lottie to the lift.

'Third floor. Mr Brown will meet you at the door.'

* * *

James Brown did not look anything like his American soul singer namesake. One, the singer died in 2006, and two, he was black. This James Brown was very much alive, pale faced with slicked back red hair matching his red tie. His suit was an immaculate pinstripe and he was short, about five foot three by Lottie's estimate.

She introduced herself and held out her hand.

Brown thrust his small hand into hers, a strong shake. He guided her into his office and pulled out a chair from behind a round desk. They sat.

'What can I do for you, Inspector?' he asked.

Was this council speak for *Why the hell are you interrupting my busy schedule?* He had a smile plastered over a stressed face.

'I'd like to ask you some questions about Susan Sullivan.'

His only response was a raised eyebrow and a flush of red up one cheek settling beneath his eye.

'Was she due into work today?' Lottie asked.

Brown consulted an iPad on the desk.

'What is this about, Inspector?' he asked, tapping an icon.

Lottie said nothing.

'She's been on annual leave since December twenty-third,' he said, 'and not due back to work until January third. May I ask what this is in connection with?' Brown's voice seemed tinged with panic. Again, Lottie ignored his question.

'What does her job entail?' she asked.

A long-winded response revealed the deceased had managed planning applications, recommending them for approval or rejection.

'The controversial files go to the county manager,' he said.

Lottie consulted her notes. 'That would be Gerry Dunne?'

'Yes.'

'Do you know if she has any family or friends?'

'She has no family that I can recall and from what I can see Susan's best friend is Susan. She keeps to herself, doesn't mingle with the staff, eats alone in the canteen, doesn't socialise. She didn't even attend the Christmas staff party. If you don't mind me saying, she is odd. She'd be the first to admit it. However, she's excellent at her job.'

Lottie noted Brown referred to Susan in the present tense. Time to break the bad news.

'Susan Sullivan was found dead earlier today,' she said, wondering what effect, if any, her next words would have on him. 'Under suspicious circumstances.'

Until the pathologist declared it, she couldn't publicly announce a murder. Brown blanched.

'Dead? Susan? Oh, my God. That's terrible. Terrible.' Beads of sweat pulsed on his forehead. His voice increased an octave and his body trembled. Lottie hoped he wouldn't faint. She didn't want the trouble of lifting him up.

'What happened? How did she die?'

'I'm unable to comment on that, I'm afraid. But do you have any reason to believe someone might want to harm Ms Sullivan?'

'What? No! Of course not.' He twisted his hands together like stress balls.

'Can I talk to anyone here who knew Susan? Someone who could provide me with an insight into her life?'

More than you're giving me, she wanted to add. For some reason she felt he was not being totally honest with her

'This is a shock. I can't think straight. Susan is . . . was a very private person. Perhaps you should talk to her PA, Bea Walsh.'

'Perhaps I should,' said Lottie.

Some colour had returned to Brown's cheeks, his voice had lowered and the shaking ceased. He began wiping his forehead back and forth with a white cotton handkerchief.

'I'll talk to her now,' said Lottie, 'if you can arrange it. Time is important. I'm sure you understand.'

He stood. 'I'll get her for you.'

'Thank you. I'll definitely need to talk to you again. In the meantime, this is my card with my contact details, if you think of anything I should be aware of.'

'Of course, Inspector.'

'If you could direct me, please,' she said, waiting for him to lead the way.

He walked along the corridor to another office, a mirror image of his own.

'I'll get Bea. By the way, this is Susan's office.'

When he was gone, Lottie sat at the desk. She looked around the office. It was like Boyd's. Pristine. No file or paper clip out of place; just a phone and computer on the desk. A flip-over calendar showed December 23rd, with the motto, *The acts of this life are the destiny of the next.* She wondered if Susan was now reaping her destiny based on what she had or hadn't done in her life.

A birdlike woman with a tear-stained face walked in and smoothed down her navy button-through dress with quivering hands. Lottie indicated for her to sit.

'I'm Bea Walsh, Ms Sullivan's PA. I can't believe she's gone. Mr Brown told me the awful news. Ms Sullivan had so much work to do.

I was only after tidying her office and organising her files today for her return. This is awful.'

She started to cry.

Lottie assumed the woman was near retirement age, early to mid-sixties. A frail thing.

'Can you think of anyone who might want to harm Ms Sullivan?'

'I've no idea.'

'I'll need your help and the assistance of anyone you can point me to. I want to build up a profile of Ms Sullivan and her life, especially in recent times. People she met with, places she went, her hobbies, her loves, any enemies or people upset by her.'

Lottie paused. Bea looked up expectantly.

'Can you help me?' Lottie asked.

'I'll do my best, Inspector, but I'm afraid I've very little information. She was a closed book, if you ask me. A lot of what I know is hearsay.'

Lottie took some notes, though there wasn't much to write. She would have her work cut out trying to establish just who Susan Sullivan was and, more importantly, why she was killed and who did it.

* * *

James Brown rubbed his brow, wiping away sweat pooled in the shallow wrinkles on his forehead. He couldn't believe Susan was dead. Reading behind the inspector's veiled words, he knew she had been murdered.

'Oh my God,' he said.

He'd always assumed Susan would be around forever, ready to pick up the pieces every time he crumbled under the weight of their shared past.

'Susan,' he murmured to the walls.

His eyes lost focus against the magnolia blandness and he closed them. Was this, Susan's untimely death, because they'd begun to resurrect buried secrets?

He tried to clear his mind. He had to protect himself; to put in motion the plan he'd concocted if something like this happened. He had prepared for something like this, but he didn't think Susan had.

Astute enough to realise that he and Susan were dealing with conniving, dangerous people, he'd documented everything from the very start. Unlocking a drawer, he removed a thin folder. He put it in an envelope and wrote a note on the outside. Then he placed it all in a larger envelope, addressed and sealed it. He slipped it into the post basket. The recipient would know if it didn't need opening and to send it back per instructions on the note. If it did – well then, he wouldn't know much about it, would he? He stemmed his panic and took out his mobile phone.

There was nothing else he could do other than make the call.

With trembling fingers he tapped a number in his phone. He began to speak, his voice strong and forceful, belying the tormented heart bursting inside his chest. Even as he spoke the memories refused to lie down.

He said, 'We need to meet.'

* * *

1971

The Mass servers were changing back into their own clothes when the tall man with the thick black hair and angry face walked into the room. The smallest boy had the fairest skin and lightest hair. A whippet on two legs. He looked up wide-eyed, as if to say, please don't be looking at me, and pulled his threadbare jumper over a creased, once white shirt now faded grey, buttoned up to the neck.

A bony hand, veins protruding, pointed at him.

'You.'

The boy felt his eight-year-old body fold into itself. His bottom lip quivered.

'You. Come into the sacristy. I have work for you.'

'But . . . but I have to get back,' he stammered. 'Sister will be looking for me.'

The boy's eyes widened and salty tears curled at the corners of his fair lashes. Fear expanded in his heart and the man seemed to grow in size before him. Through a watery haze he saw a long finger curling, calling him. He remained rigid, one shoe on and the other underneath the bench behind him. His beige socks creased around his ankles; their elastic, melted from too much washing, protruded like little white sticks in sand. The man moved and with a single stride his shadow fell on the boy, shrouding his body in darkness.

A hand pinched his arm and dragged him through the wooden door. He silently pleaded with his eyes for the other boys to help but they gathered their remaining clothes in trembling arms and fled.

Golden angels adorned the corners of the ceiling as if they had flown up there, become trapped and were unable to come down again. White alabaster gargoyles were interspersed with the angelic cherubs, their faces tired and drained. The boy tried to hide behind a high mahogany table in the middle of the room. The dark wood seemed to him to exude a deep, penetrating air of oppression.

'What have we here, a scaredy cat? Are you a little girl, you whining good-for-nothing?' the man shouted through his pale, pink lips.

The boy knew no one would hear or come running to help. He had been here before.

A rack of black cassocks swung in a swish of air as the man passed by to sit in a corner chair. The boy shivered violently as the adult's eyes appraised him, like a farmer at market assessing a prize bull.

'Come here.'

The boy didn't move.

'Come here, I said.'

He had no option. He walked forward, his feet heel to toe like a tightrope walker, limping slightly in his one shoe.

The boy screamed as he was pulled between two bare knees, hands gripped him as robes were flung back.

'Shut up! You are going to be a goody one shoe boy and do what I want.'

'P-p-please don't hurt me,' the boy whimpered, tears streaming down his cheeks. He couldn't see, he was so close to the darkness.

His head was thrust into a gaping void and he began to gag.

Terror grappled with his breakfast of watery eggs in the bottommost pit of his belly. It rose like a tidal wave and exploded in a vomit of projectile yellow phlegm.

The man jumped up, still holding him by the hair, and hit him with a thump to his ribcage, propelling him through the rack of swinging blackness. The boy slid down the far wall, a limp piece of flesh, bewildered and terrified.

He couldn't hear the names he was being called, as the blows came hard and fast against the side of his head, thickening the rims of his ears.

He cried louder, his sobs thunderous.

Then he soiled himself.

And the angels sank deeper into the recesses of the alabaster ceiling as if they too were terrified.

CHAPTER 5

Cafferty's pub on Gaol Street was two hundred metres from the council offices. Lottie was drinking thick soup, with lumps of chicken and potato soaking in it, warming her from her toes up. Boyd was halfway through massacring a house special sandwich that would have fed two normal people. But he wasn't normal. He could eat anything, never putting on an ounce. The skinny bollocks, thought Lottie.

It was late afternoon and a few die-hards who had braved the weather sat at the bar nursing their pints of Guinness and ticking off horses on crumpled newspapers. A widescreen television on the wall, sound muted, presented the races from England. No snow there.

'Bea Walsh says Susan could've been a lesbian,' Lottie said.

'Ever tried it on with a woman, yourself?' Boyd asked, unaware of the coleslaw stuck to his upper lip, forming a makeshift moustache.

'I wish. Then, maybe, I wouldn't have this awful memory of being in your bed six months ago.'

'Ha. Very funny,' he said. He wasn't laughing.

Lottie tried to dim the image of their drunken tryst. She hated to admit it but she'd enjoyed the warmth of his body beside hers that night – what she could remember of it. They'd never talked about it since.

'Seriously though, Adam wouldn't want you to be alone,' he said.

'You've no idea what Adam would have wanted. So shut up.' Lottie knew she had raised her voice and was kicking herself for letting Boyd get to her.

He shut up and continued eating his sandwich, muttering 'bitch' jokingly under his breath.

'Heard that,' she said.

'You were meant to.'

'Anyway, Bea said it was more than likely canteen gossip, just because Susan was a loner. People love making up stories about the quiet ones.'

'What does that mean? Like a non-practising Catholic? Been there, done that, not for me any more?'

'You know I'm not a lesbian, not even a non-practising one.'

'You're not practising anything since Adam died.'

Lottie knew Boyd regretted saying it, the minute the words were out of his mouth. She said nothing, wouldn't please him with a sarcastic retort, even if she could have thought of anything smart enough to say. Either way he was off the hook. For the moment.

'Nice soup,' she said.

'Changing the subject.'

'Boyd,' Lottie said. 'I've related to you what Bea Walsh, Susan's PA, told me. As far as she knew Susan was originally from Ragmullin, spent years working in Dublin and returned here on a transfer two years ago. She also said no one could get close to her. She was a career-woman. Worked day and night, married to the job. She had to, in a man's world, to get to where she was. Bea's words, not mine.'

'But she must've had some sort of a life outside of her job,' said Boyd.

'Do you?'

'Do I what?'

'Have a life outside of the job?' asked Lottie, finishing her soup.

'Not really. Neither do you.'

'I rest my case.'

'You know what I mean.'

'Finish up your sandwich, Sherlock. We'll head to Parkgreen and see if Lynch and Kirby have found anything of interest in Sullivan's house.'

'Are you going to interview the head honcho in the council?'

'Who?' Lottie asked.

'The county manager.'

'Gerry Dunne's not available until tomorrow morning.'

'I take it you're not too impressed.'

'Take it any way you like.'

'Depends on who's giving it.'

'Would you ever grow up!' Lottie said.

But Boyd was right. She was not impressed. They split the bill and left.

* * *

They hurried up the street, leaning into each other, sheltering from the chill, their breaths rising and merging into one.

Streetlights reflected off the snow and ice, throwing yellow ochre shadows on to shop fronts. It was freezing. Bitter was the topical word of the day. Those foolish enough to venture outside scurried past, their faces snuggled into scarves and hats, shielding their skin from the stripping wind.

Rushing along the slippery pavement with Boyd, Lottie felt the polar air pierce through her clothing. At the station, Boyd started the car. Lottie sat in, rubbing her bloodless fingers together.

'Put the heater on,' she said.

'Don't start,' he said and took off, skidding dangerously close to the wall.

Just as well he has a badge, she thought, and as he drove she looked out at her town swathed in false purity, sinking into the evening darkness.

* * *

Susan Sullivan had lived in a detached three-bedroom house, situated in a secluded estate on the outskirts of the 'better end of town'. If there was such a thing any more.

The area appeared quiet as they drove up. A few children, muffled against the weather, rode their Christmas bicycles up and down the frozen road, sneaking looks from under colourful hats at the two squad cars parked outside Sullivan's gate.

A couple of uniformed gardaí stood sentry. A car in the driveway was white with a week's worth of snow. Blue and white tape, hanging loose on the front door, screamed *Keep Out*, without actually having the words written on it. These were the only outward signals that something was wrong. Lottie felt like getting back in the car and going home.

Detective Maria Lynch greeted them at the door.

'Anything for us?' Lottie asked.

She sometimes didn't know what to make of Maria Lynch, with her freckled nose, inquisitive eyes and long hair tied up childishly in a ponytail, always dressed smartly. She looked eighteen, but having served fifteen years in the force, she was closer to thirty-five. Enthusiastic without overdoing it. She was aware that Lynch was super ambitious and Lottie had no intention of falling into the female rivalry trap. But she had to admit to a slight jealousy of the domestic stability her detective possessed. Lynch was married, she assumed happily. It was said her husband cooked, hoovered, brought their two small children to school before he went to work and all that shite.

'It's an absolute tip in there. I don't know how the woman survived in such a dump,' Lynch said, wiping dust from her pressed navy trousers.

Lottie raised an eyebrow. 'That doesn't gel with the image I formed of her after seeing her office and the people she worked with.'

She stepped into the hallway with Boyd. The house felt crowded. Two SOCOs were busy and Detective Kirby's rotund rear protruded as he rifled through the kitchen garbage bin.

'Nothing in here but rubbish,' Kirby's voice gurgled, a large unlit cigar hanging from his lips, his bushy mop of hair like an antennae on top of his head.

He grinned at Lottie. She scowled. Larry Kirby was divorced and currently cavorting with a twenty-something-year-old actress in town. More luck to him, she thought. At least it might stop his flirtatious glances at her. Despite all that, Kirby was called the lovable rogue within the force.

'Put away that cigar,' she ordered.

His face reddened and he put the cigar into his breast pocket. Grunting loudly, he opened the fridge and inspected the contents.

'And make sure the neighbours are canvassed,' Lottie instructed. 'We need to determine when Sullivan was last seen.'

'Right away,' Kirby said, slamming the fridge door shut and stomping off to give the order to someone else.

Lottie could see what Lynch had been talking about. Dirty dishes piled high in the sink; a pot with potatoes, half of them peeled, on the table; an open sliced pan; a jam-pot with a knife protruding from it and white mould circling the rim. A bowl, encrusted with the remains of porridge, sat in the midst of the mess. It was difficult to determine if the woman had just had breakfast or dinner. Maybe both together. The floor was dirty, crumbs and dust everywhere.

'The sitting room is worse,' Lynch said. 'Have a look.'

Lottie turned out of the kitchen, followed her colleague's pointed finger and stood at the door.

'Holy shit,' she said.

'Good God,' Boyd said.

'Agreed,' Lynch said.

There were hundreds of newspapers stacked in every conceivable space in the room. On the floor, the armchairs, the couch and on top of the television. Some were yellowing and others appeared to have been shredded by a mouse. The room was dust-covered. Lottie picked up a paper from the nearest bundle. December 29th. Sullivan had been working her way outwards. Lottie began counting the newspapers in her head.

'Some mountain of rubbish in here,' she said. 'Must be at least a couple of years' worth.'

'This woman had serious issues,' Lynch said, from behind her.

Lottie shook her head.

'I can't marry this scene with the absolute tidiness of her office. It's like she was two different people.'

'You sure you got the right house?' Boyd queried.

Two sets of eyes glared at him.

'Only asking,' he said and slouched up the stairs, dipping his head beneath the low ceiling.

'Keep looking,' Lottie said to Lynch. 'We need to locate her phone. It'll give us her contacts and maybe information as to who wanted to kill her. I don't see any sign of a laptop or computer.'

'I'll look for them. The SOCOs are almost done here.' Detective Maria Lynch squeezed back into the crowded kitchen.

Lottie followed Boyd upstairs. He was in the bathroom.

'Pills for everything, from a pain in the arse to a pain in the elbow,' he said.

He sounded like her mother. She pushed him out of her way and peered into the medicine cabinet. Sullivan should have been on suicide watch, she thought, eyeing packets of Prozac, Xanax, Temazepam.

'Looks like she wasn't taking her medicine,' she said, quelling the urge to pocket a few blisters of Xanax. Jesus, she could function for at least three months on this lot.

'Because there's so much still here?' he asked.

'Yeah. Oxycontin too.'

'What's that?'

'Morphine,' said Lottie, remembering her own medicine cabinet, before Adam died. She checked the prescription details, recording the pharmacy name in her phone to follow up later. She looked around the bathroom. It was filthy. She edged out past Boyd and entered the bedroom.

'In here,' she called.

He joined her. 'Incredible.'

'What was going on in this woman's head, in her life?' Lottie asked.

The bedroom was sparkling clean, sterile. Nothing out of place. The bed, dressed to army standards in pure white, clean linen. A dresser, naked of any cosmetics. Wooden floor, shining. That was it.

'I can almost see myself in the floor,' she said and opened the dressing table drawer. Everything was folded with military precision. She closed it again. Someone else's job to desecrate the belongings of the dead. She wouldn't do it. Not after Adam. 'This woman was a contradiction.'

'And she lived alone,' Boyd said, checking the other bedroom.

Lottie glanced over his shoulder. It was bare. Four white walls and a wooden floor. She shook her head in confusion. Susan Sullivan was definitely an enigma.

Downstairs, she looked around again. Something didn't gel. What was she missing? She couldn't quite draw her thoughts to a conclusion.

She had to get out.

* * *

Boyd joined her outside, a cigarette between his fingers.

'Where to now?' he asked, taking a deep pull on the cigarette. Lottie gladly inhaled the smoke and yawned.

'I better go home and feed my kids.'

'They're teenagers and well able to look after themselves,' he said. 'You need to look after yourself.'

A statement that did not require a reply. It was the truth.

'I have to digest this case. I want to pull together the few facts we have, to see if I can make sense of it all. I need space.'

'And you'll get that at home?'

'Don't be smart.'

She felt his closeness, not just bodily close, but in mind. Boyd unnerved her. Conversely, she would love to feel his arm around her in a comforting hug. In the same instant, she knew she would repel it. Welcome to the world of frosty Lottie Parker. Her mood just about matched the weather.

'There's nothing else we can do this evening. I'm going to walk. I'll see you in the morning. Remember, team meeting at six a.m. Corrigan will be there, so don't be late.' Redundant words, she thought. Boyd was never late.

She trudged along the icy footpaths towards home, alone.

CHAPTER 6

The Governor's House, a nineteenth-century building adjoining the new council offices, had once been part of the old town jail. The fact that it had access to the new offices was unknown to the gardaí currently cordoning off the main building.

In the depths of the house, dungeons had been preserved and were used as meeting rooms. Few staff ventured down there. Rumour had it that those awaiting death had spent their last hours within the walls; walls which reportedly pulsed with the breaths of condemned souls.

The history of the building was not lost on the men gathered in one of the catacomb dungeons. They stood in a circle like condemned prisoners awaiting a stay of execution.

'This afternoon a member of the planning department, Susan Sullivan, was killed in suspicious circumstances,' the official said. 'It is regrettable. Terrible actually. For us, it will be a tense time. The gardaí will more than likely go through her files line by line. You need to be aware that your names may come up in the course of their investigation and it's likely you will be interviewed.'

He paused, looking at the three men in front of him.

'If our dealings become known, we could well be seen as murder suspects,' he added.

'At least her knowledge died with her,' the developer said. 'But the investigation will swing the spotlight on us.'

The banker visibly shivered. If anything, the temperatures had dropped since they arrived in the dungeon. The evening darkness outside seemed to penetrate through the walls.

'There's still James Brown to think of,' the banker said.

'Without Sullivan, it's just his word against ours,' the official said. 'However, you're right. I think we need to prepare contingency plans in light of potential garda interviews. We must maintain the appearance of working individually. They might not stumble over what we are doing.' He rubbed his hands together, trying to instil heat into his fingers.

'Don't be fooled,' said the developer. 'They are very shrewd and we'll need to be more so. If it's Detective Inspector Lottie Parker leading the investigation, I can guarantee we'll need to be careful.'

'Do you know her?' asked the banker.

'I've heard of her. She solved that traveller murder a few years ago. She was threatened and intimidated but carried on. And she got her man. She'll be like a dog with a bone once she gets her teeth into this one.'

The clergyman said nothing and the official knew this man's calculating mind was internally analysing the situation.

They huddled deeper into their wool coats, eyeing each other.

'Gentlemen, there are millions of euro involved. We have to be very vigilant. And we can't meet here again. Be careful.' The official closed the meeting and opened the dungeon door. He glanced outside. A single light illuminated the deserted private car park.

One by one, they left.

Each of them now wary of the other.

One of them could be a murderer.

CHAPTER 7

James Brown parked his black Toyota Avensis in the courtyard outside his cottage, switched off the lights, took out the keys and, as the internal beam dimmed to darkness, he sat listening to the engine cool down.

Normally he loved coming home after work, especially in springtime. Home to the serenity of the countryside, renewing his sense of wellbeing, with the sounds from the trees and glimpses of the meadows stretching untouched behind his small garden. It instilled in him a freedom he rarely felt elsewhere. Not now though. This evening he was sad and angry. Sad for Susan and angry at the rebuff he had suffered from the man on the phone. He'd contacted him to see what, if anything, he knew about Susan's death. But as he'd begun to speak, the man had hung up on him. Maybe he'd been the wrong person to call, after all.

He gripped the steering wheel with tight fists and banged his head against his hands. Susan was gone. He had to keep reminding himself. She'd rescued him from his demons all those years ago and now he had failed her.

He didn't want to leave the security of his car. He felt safe in it and he thought of the many times he and Susan had cradled each other as children, she whispering in his ear to be strong, to stand tall and proud, and he whimpering like a lost kitten in her arms. He thought of how Susan, as a child, had shown him how to make his bed to the standards dictated, how to fold his clothes and pick fluff from the floor so that it was pristine. He was convinced that she had subsequently developed a thing about clean bedrooms. Who could blame her? He thought of all they had witnessed and never spoken about, and he cried silent tears for her, for her memory and for her goodness to him. Now, he had to stand on his own two feet and be strong. For Susan if nothing else.

At last, he willed himself out of the vehicle as the temperature dissolved to ice. Lifting his briefcase from the back seat he stepped on to the snow-blanketed courtyard and locked the car with a click. The old moon was getting ready for its new phase and its light appeared dimmer than he thought it should be.

A shadow fell before him and he squinted upwards expecting to see a cloud sheathing the moon. But there was no cloud in the frosty starlit sky. A figure stood tall in front of him, a ski mask covering the face, two dark eyes visible.

Jumping back against his car, James dropped his briefcase, then remembered his phone was inside it. Too late now.

'What . . . what . . . do you want?' His tongue tightened over his words, fear dripping down his face in droplets, along his nose, dribbling like snot. What could he do? He couldn't think clearly.

'You could not stop interfering,' the man was saying, his voice a low, menacing drone.

James swung his head from side to side wondering why he hadn't noticed the car when he'd pulled up. He now glimpsed a metallic glint behind the oak tree to his right. Who was this man? How had he known he could shield his car over there?

'What? Why?' James whispered, scuffing his feet on the icy snow and staring up at the huge figure looming in front of him. The flashlight in the gloved hand blinded him.

'You and your friend made nuisances of yourselves. Not for the first time.'

'My friend?' James asked, but he knew the man meant Susan.

The man laughed, grabbed him by the elbow and propelled him along the path. James felt a suffocating ball gathering mucus in his throat and his breathing quickened as the sky clouded and snow began to fall in round thick lumps.

'What do you want?' James' fear quickly turned to terror, his brain constricting like a snail into its shell. He had to think fast. He needed to get control of the situation. He could call out for help, if only his voice wasn't lost somewhere deep in his chest. And he knew no one would hear him. There wasn't another house within two miles of his cottage.

Maybe he should make a run for it? No. His attacker was taller, broader and looked so much stronger, making James feel like an insect trapped in the jaws of a fly.

Panic swelled and strapped itself squarely inside his chest, halting him after a couple of steps. He couldn't continue. He felt like he was walking with only one shoe on. The man stopped too, pulling a length of rope from his pocket. That did it.

James leapt forward, surprising the man, who lost the grip on his elbow and fell, the flashlight lodging in a clump of snow. Skidding toward the front door, James searched with one hand in his pocket for the key. Ice crunched behind him. He had the key in the door when an arm slithered around his neck, gripped tight, and he was pulled back against a solid chest.

James fought, managing to loosen the hold on his neck, but an elbow crashed into the back of his skull. His head exploded with pain.

'You should not have done that!'

He thought he knew the voice, struggled to recognise it, but failed. He turned quickly and tried to run but felt the rope slipping around his neck, harsh nylon scraping his skin. This might be his last chance.

He drew back his arm and connected with the man's midriff but it bounced back. Pain shot through his elbow, up into his shoulder. The rope slackened and he collapsed to the ground. He turned over and scrambled to his knees. Run, he had to run. But he couldn't get his feet under him. He shouted then. As loud as he could, from his terrified throat.

'Help me. Help!' His voice sounded like someone else's echoing off the trees.

The rope tugged tighter. He tried to dig his hands into the frozen earth. He tried to halt the pull. He tried to shout once more, but the rope was taut, biting into his skin, dangerously close to cutting off his air. What could he do? Talk, he thought. I have to get him talking. He ceased his resistance but the man tightened the rope.

'Come,' the man said.

He steered James away from the cottage toward the oak tree with its branches casting demonic shapes on the whitewashed walls of the cottage. Beneath it, two wrought iron chairs, placed there for summer shade, looked out of place covered with mounds of snow.

'What are you doing?' James said, when the rope eased slightly.

The man threw one end of it into the air, looping it around a branch midway up the crusted bark. James prayed for a cloud to blot out the moon, to darken the garden into total blackness. With his eyes accustomed to the dusky light, he could see too much now and his brain filled with irrational thoughts and flashing, unframed pictures. One was an image of his mother, whom he never remembered having seen in his life. I'm going to die, he thought. He's going to kill me and

I can do nothing. His whole body convulsed in an unending trembling. He needed Susan. She always knew what to do. The man pivoted round and James looked into the masked face, stared at the eyes waltzing a wicked dance to a silent tune and he recognised them. Eyes he could never forget; eyes he would always remember.

'It was you . . . Susan . . . you . . .' he said. 'I know you. I remember . . .'

James struggled weakly, attempting to pull away, but each movement collided with a further twist of the nylon. Now he was remembering. Too late? He tried to form words to delay the man.

'The . . . night of the candles . . . the belt . . .'

'You think you are clever. You were not always the smart one, were you? Back then, you had a girl to stand up for you. Not any more.' The voice was so clear it could cut the ice into shards. The eyes ceased gyrating.

James frantically tore at the rope, pulling and jerking, scrunching his fingers under it, his stomach heaving with the strain. He couldn't breathe. He tried to wrench free. He kicked out with his legs, showering snow into the air. He had to survive. He had to get help. He had the rest of his life to live. In a desperate attempt to wrong-foot his opponent, he allowed his body to flop into a dead weight. How could the man heave him upwards then?

'Stand on the chair,' the man commanded, swiping away a mound of snow with one sweep of his hand.

James stood still as if hypnotised, the rope furrowing a ridge into his neck, the man's body heat overpowering his senses. He tasted saltiness at the back of his throat. Two arms encircled his body and lifted him on to one of the garden chairs. The furniture legs sank into the snow, wobbled, then settled. Before James could jump back down, the man hauled the rope further round the branch.

The snow fell faster and thicker. James swayed as the man stood on the other chair and knotted the rope.

'It would be a fitting destiny for you to swing from the apple tree, James, but its branches are not strong enough. This oak will do the job instead.'

The rope was secure around the thick limb, midway up the bark. The falling snow darkened the moon but its thin light still cast a yellow ray over the courtyard. The laden branches trembled with the additional weight and James pleaded, moving his lips without sound.

Before he could action further thoughts from his brain to his body, the man kicked over the chair and it settled into the snow-covered earth.

As his chest ceased to inflate, his tongue protruded from purple lips, blood leaked dots on to the whites of his eyes and James saw the moon dance along the sky through a million white lights. He thought he could smell fresh apples as his body swayed in the windless air and his bowels opened. He heard the crunch of receding footsteps, before the white lights turned red, then black.

A thick blizzard of snow tumbled earthwards. A sharp snowstorm of biblical proportions. The body paled. Merging into its white surroundings, it cooled in death.

CHAPTER 8

Rap music blared as Lottie opened her front door. Why did she let her kids listen to this trash? Because they'd listen to it somewhere else if she tried to stop them. Anyway, she couldn't monitor the hundreds of songs on their iPods and phones and online. Live and let live.

'I'm home,' she called over the din.

No reply.

The kitchen displayed the remnants of a teenage cook-in. Empty Pot Noodles, sticky forks on the table and an open, half-full bottle of Coca-Cola. More than likely there since they had their breakfast – at lunchtime. Boots, shoes and trainers were thrown inside the back door. Unopened Christmas cards stacked on the table and the few she had opened were wilting with condensation in the kitchen window. The tree was in the sitting room, out of her sight. She hadn't wanted to put it up. Sean had insisted and now he'd have the job of dismantling the raggedy assemblage of tinsel and balls. Tough.

Lottie was glad all the false décor would soon be consigned to the attic. She hated – no, despised – Christmas since Adam died. Over three years ago. Christmas was family time but now her family was decimated.

But still, she had great memories of the good Christmases. Adam and herself trying to construct a toy kitchen at three in the morning after demolishing a bottle of Baileys. Or waiting for him to come off duty from the army barracks on Christmas morning, Adam sneaking in before the children woke up and she ticking off a list to make sure nothing was left in her mother's attic. One time they'd left an Action Man there and Adam had to rush over and rouse her mother at two a.m. He'd called Lottie a coward. She smiled now at that memory. Adam wasn't afraid of her mother. Lottie wasn't either, but her mother had enough ammunition for rows without Lottie arming her with more. That's what she'd told Adam anyway. She sometimes thought that he had loved her mother more than she did. His parents had died within a year of each other when he was just eighteen, so maybe he'd appreciated all that Rose did for Lottie and the children. But Lottie knew there was an old guilt lurking in Rose's actions and, no matter how hard she tried, she could never rid herself of that feeling. Every interaction she'd had with her mother since Adam died had resulted in a disagreement. Harsh words, old accusations and banging doors. Because of their last altercation, Lottie hadn't seen her mother in months – though she knew Rose called to see the children when she wasn't around.

She tried her best for the children but it was hard keeping her heart in it. It wasn't in a lot of things. When Adam had died a part of her had died with him. Cliché or not, it was the truth. If it were not for their children . . . well, she had the three of them. Life goes on. There were other long absences in her life to cope with also – the mystery of her father's death and consequent saga surrounding her brother. She'd played the blame game all her life but her grief for Adam overshadowed the decaying memory of the others. For now.

Sean sauntered into the kitchen tipping a ball on the end of a hurley stick. The boy loved hurling, one of the most vigorous national sports, though she worried about how dangerous it was for her son. At thirteen and a half years old he was already as tall as Adam had been. His unruly fair hair masked long eyelashes. Lottie loved her son so much, sometimes it made her want to cry. With Adam gone, she had to protect him, protect all of them, and the weight of that responsibility was sometimes an unbearable burden.

'What's for dinner, Mam?' Sean asked, pocketing the ball.

'Jesus, Sean, I'm only in the door. It's seven o'clock. For once in your lives couldn't one of you have cooked dinner?' Her love quickly turned to frustration.

'I was studying.'

'You were not. You didn't even open your bag, never mind a book.'

'But we're still on holidays,' said her sulky son.

Lottie had forgotten, just for a minute. They'd been off school for the last week and would be for another long few days. What did they do all day? No, strike that, she really didn't want to know.

Unsuspecting Chloe walked into the kitchen.

'Hi, Mother, what's for dinner?'

Chloe always called her 'Mother'. Adam had called her 'Mother' in front of their children. She supposed her daughter was trying to keep him alive with these little things.

Sean escaped back up the stairs, thumping his hurley on each step. The rap music restarted, louder this time.

Chloe was dressed in tracksuit bottoms and a tiny strap top straining over her expanding (at last! according to Chloe) chest. Did she not realise it was sub-zero outside? Her long, bottle-dyed, blonde hair, scrunched on top of her head, was held in place with a butterfly bobbin. Her bright blue eyes were an exact replica of her father's. The eyes Lottie had fallen in love with lived on, immortalised in her beautiful daughter. The 'middle child', Chloe often threw at her when she felt the other two were being favoured.

'You're sixteen years of age, Chloe. You're doing Home Economics in school. Would it never enter your head to put on some dinner?'

'No, why should I? You'd come home and say I was doing it all wrong.'

Point taken.

'Where's Katie?'

'Out. As usual.' Chloe opened a cupboard, looking for anything edible.

Lottie went to the fridge. No wine. Shit. She didn't drink any more; at least not as much as she used to, she reminded herself. Times like these, she missed alcohol most. It helped relieve the stress of the day. She didn't even smoke any more. Well, maybe sometimes, when she had a drink. God, but she was a contradiction. She should've taken a few Xanax from Susan Sullivan's medicine cabinet. But she would never do that. She didn't think she would anyway. She kept a small supply in her bedside locker and had an emergency pill Sellotaped to the bottom of her drawer in the office. Just in case, she told herself. And the stash was fast disappearing.

'Put the kettle on, hon, I've had a bitch of a day,' Lottie said.

Chloe crunched a biscuit in her mouth and flicked the switch. The kettle hissed. Empty.

'For God's sake,' Lottie said.

Chloe was gone, the door swinging shut behind her.

After pouring water into the kettle, Lottie snapped on the electric fire and sat into her chair, reclining it as far as it would go. Snuggled up in her jacket, she closed her eyes and eased the buzzing in her brain by breathing deeply.

CHAPTER 9

'James Brown is dead.'

'What?' Lottie said into her phone.

Sitting with the electric fire blazing heat at her feet, she glanced at the kitchen clock. Eight thirty. She'd been asleep for over an hour; it was only the phone that had awakened her.

'James Brown is dead,' said Boyd. 'You better get back to the station. Corrigan is dancing a jig. Sky News is reported to be on the way.'

'Give me a good old-fashioned traveller feud any day,' Lottie said.

'You'll need a lift,' Boyd said. 'It's been snowing non-stop for the last few hours.'

'I'll walk. It'll wake me up.'

'Suit yourself.'

She ended the call, searched for her jacket, discovered she was still wearing it and shouted up the stairs, 'Chloe, Sean, I've to go back to work.'

No reply.

'You'll have to cook dinner yourselves.'

A chorus greeted her. 'Ah Mam!'

'Leave money for a takeaway,' shouted Chloe.

She did. Sucker.

* * *

Superintendent Corrigan was pounding up and down the corridor, ducking under ladders, swearing 'feck', head beetroot red, his permanent, stressed-out colour. He turned around. Lottie came to a halt.

'Where were you? You should've been here,' he said.

'Sir, I did a twelve-hour shift. I was at home.'

Corrigan turned around and stomped off to his office. Boyd and Lynch stood, jackets on, waiting. Kirby was nowhere in sight.

'What are you two looking at?' Lottie asked. She had fire in her belly but quelled it. 'Fill me in.'

'A call came in half an hour ago,' Maria Lynch said, curling her hair on top of her head before pulling on a knitted hat. 'James Brown was found hanging from a tree at his home. Reports from uniforms suggest it's a suicide.'

'Suicide my arse,' Lottie said. 'The same day his colleague is murdered? God almighty, when was the last time we had a murder, let alone two?'

Memory man Boyd said, 'Three years ago, when Jimmy Coyne killed Timmy Coyne in a family feud. You nailed him.'

'It was a rhetorical question,' Lottie said. 'Where's Larry Kirby?'

She glanced around. The incident room throbbed with activity. Maps of the town coloured the bare walls, reports were building up in trays and detectives were busy on the phones.

Buttoning up his jacket, Boyd said, 'No doubt Kirby's hanging out in a pub with his actress girlfriend.'

'Are you jealous, Boyd?' Lottie asked.

Lynch said, 'I'll go start up the car, it's probably frozen solid.' She escaped.

'You look like shit,' Boyd said.

Lottie said, 'And I love you too. Come on.'

* * *

Six kilometres outside Ragmullin, the forest road was lit up with the flashing blue lights of two squad cars. The roads were almost impassable and snow continued to fall heavier than it had since Christmas Eve, bulky flakes freezing as they fell.

An ambulance and fire engine, wheels chained, blocked the narrow laneway leading to Brown's cottage. Fire engine? Lottie shook her head. Lynch just shrugged.

Boyd abandoned the car and they walked the rest of the way along tracks made by the other vehicles. Their legs sank to their knees as they trudged through the depths of snow.

A gaunt, pale-faced man sat in a squad car with two uniform gardaí outside the inner crime scene tapes. Lottie was pleased with these precautions. A suspected suicide could easily be something else.

'Derek Harte,' Garda Gillian O'Donoghue said, pointing to the man in the car. 'He found the deceased. He's in a very distressed state.'

'Talk to him, Lynch. Find out exactly who he is and why he's here. If this is something other than suicide, he's our number one suspect,' Lottie said.

'There's a briefcase on the ground beside the deceased's car,' O'Donoghue said.

'SOCOs can check it out when they arrive, then get it to the station.' Lottie headed into the courtyard, Boyd beside her.

A spotlight blazed eerie shadows toward a tree. She averted her eyes for a moment to concentrate on a paramedic standing against a snow-camouflaged car.

'You didn't cut him down?' she asked.

'No. I could see he was dead and the man who found him was muttering about the victim knowing your woman murdered in the cathedral, so I thought I better call you guys. Just in case, like.'

'I suppose you watch *CSI*?' Lottie said. The man's face flushed. 'You don't have to answer that,' she added.

'I got the fire crew to put up the spotlight. Pitch black out here in the sticks.'

'Why the fire engine?'

'Haven't a clue,' the paramedic said. 'Can I smoke?'

'No,' Lottie and Boyd said together.

Turning away from the paramedic, Lottie looked up at the suspended body of James Brown highlighted by the temporary light.

'I had a feeling Brown wasn't being totally honest with me today. If I'd pressed him, I possibly could have discovered something that might have saved his life.'

'Maybe he murdered Sullivan and afterwards, full of remorse, hung himself,' Boyd said.

'*He* murdered Sullivan? Will you look at him? A skinny, five foot nothing. He couldn't kill a cold.'

'In a fit of angry passion?' ventured Boyd.

Lottie glared. 'You talk pure shite sometimes.'

Brown's body swayed slightly in the snowy breeze. His head hung sideways, twisted toward her. Eyes open wide. Staring into nothingness. Lottie turned away from the body and slogged through the snow.

'What's wrong?' Boyd asked. 'You look like you've seen a ghost.'

'Maybe I have,' she said.

She stopped and looked around the scene. A chair, lying on its side, partly submerged by the avalanche of snow; briefcase on the ground beside the car and another car parked behind it. Then she noticed a key in the front door. Garda O'Donoghue was writing down whatever the paramedic had to say. Everyone had tramped through the site. Lottie doubted SOCOs would find anything useful.

'Any suicide note?' Lottie asked.

O'Donoghue shrugged. 'I scouted round when I got here. Didn't see anything outside, though if there is a note it's buried and saturated. Jesus, I've never seen so much snow in all my life.'

'Did the Harte guy go inside?' Lottie asked, pointing to the key.

'Not that I'm aware of,' O'Donoghue said.

Lynch popped up at Lottie's shoulder.

'Harte says he is a friend of Brown and drove over to see him when he heard about Susan Sullivan's death.'

'How did he know about Susan?'

'Brown phoned him. When he arrived he saw the body straight away and called emergency. He was here, staring up at Brown, when our first car arrived. Didn't go near the house. So he says anyway.' Lynch swept away the clumps of snow, causing the ink to run on her notebook. 'He's genuinely in an awful state. Will I get a car to take him home or do you want to interview him tonight?'

'I'm too tired to formulate proper questions. We'll bring him in for questioning in the morning,' Lottie said. She spied an alarm box on the wall over the door. 'Ask him if he knows the alarm code.'

'Do you want me to call in the morning, too?' asked the paramedic, a smile burning to his ears.

'Garda O'Donoghue has your statement,' Lottie said. 'Thanks for your help.'

'Oh, I nearly forgot,' he said. 'I found this stuck in the snow by the door.'

Lottie looked at the man's gloved hand holding a small green flashlight.

'You picked it up?'

'I sure did,' he said. His eyes widened. 'Oh, sorry. Maybe I should've left it there?'

'Maybe you should have.' Lottie slipped the flashlight into a plastic evidence bag and snapped it shut. 'Was it on or off?'

'I switched it off. To save the battery.'

She felt like thumping him and turned away before she did.

'Shithead,' Boyd said under his breath as the paramedic retreated.

'Boyd, one of these days someone, besides me, is going to hear you and you'll get a broken nose. Get the SOCOs out here.'

Her phone buzzed. Corrigan.

'The boss wants to see us in fifteen minutes,' she said. 'Has that man seen the weather?'

* * *

Back in town, standing outside the station, Boyd lit a cigarette. The snow eased slightly and frosty night air hijacked the smoke. Lottie wished she could have a drag, but it would be one too many. She never stopped at one of anything. Addictive personality disorder, her mother was fond of telling her. Thanks Mam.

Stepping in to the warm reception area, she checked her phone. No messages. No missed calls. She rang home. Chloe answered.

'Hi, Mother. You coming home soon?'

'Not yet,' Lottie said. 'I'm going into a meeting with my superintendent. Don't know how long I'll be.' She rejected a pang of guilt. What could she do? She had to work and this meant unpredictable hours.

'Don't worry. We'll mind the house,' Chloe said.

'Is Katie home yet?' Lottie was worried about her eldest child.

'I think she's in her room.'

'Check to make sure.'

'Will do.'

'And tell Sean to turn off his PlayStation.'

'Of course. Chat later.' Chloe hung up.

They'd be in bed when she got home. Well able to look after themselves. They would do okay. She hoped. She wasn't so sure about herself.

Brushing snow off his shoulders, Boyd joined her.

'Come on,' he said. 'The superintendent awaits and we are late.'

* * *

'You took your time.'

Corrigan marched up and down his office, like a regimental sergeant.

'Was it suicide or what?' He didn't wait for an answer. 'Never mind anyway, it's suicide for now. One murder is enough for one day. Whatever it is, we'll get to the bottom of it. I don't want a hot-shot team from Dublin taking over, so you better get your act together. Step up the door-to-door enquiries. There's people to be interviewed, phones to be manned, press releases, media briefings.'

You're in your element, Lottie thought.

'I don't think James Brown killed himself,' she ventured.

Corrigan snorted. 'And how do you arrive at that conclusion?'

'I think . . . it feels too convenient, you know.'

'I don't know,' he said. 'Enlighten me.'

Lottie chewed her lip. How could she translate a gut feeling? Corrigan was career-minded and did things by the book. His favourite mantra regarding investigations was 'my way or no way'. Lottie had another way . . . her way. In any case, he didn't wait for her to answer.

'Inspector Parker, what you *think* is irrelevant. Look at the evidence, the circumstances. He was hanging from a feckin' tree in the middle of the feckin' countryside in a feckin' blizzard. Something fishy was going on in the council, I can smell it here. He probably killed Susan Sullivan over some work thing, found the guilt too much, so . . . he swung a rope over a tree and killed himself. Now let's plan our action.'

Lottie withheld her words and the three of them outlined the team tasks. She was too exhausted to argue with Corrigan.

When they had everything sorted as best they could, Corrigan repeated, 'I don't want Dublin sending down hot-shots. We can handle this. I want the Susan Sullivan murder solved, pronto.'

'But sir,' Boyd interjected, 'if it turns out we have two murders, won't we need the outside help?'

'Detective Sergeant Boyd! I've said what I've said. End of the matter. As of now we have one suspicious death and a suspected suicide.'

Corrigan's eyes slanted, defying them to argue. Lottie returned his gaze and pulled on her jacket.

'Get a few hours' sleep. Be back here at six a.m. sharp,' he said.

They left the superintendent's office and walked down the corridor.

'What the hell?' Boyd said, stopping abruptly.

Lottie looked at him. He'd walked into a decorator's ladder and notched a cut on his forehead. She laughed.

Boyd cursed his way out the door. 'It's not funny.'

'I know,' she said, but she couldn't stop laughing.

CHAPTER 10

Lottie smiled to herself before she opened her front door. A bundle of Sean's hurleys stood in the corner of the porch and the holly wreath was caked in frozen snow, blown there by the wind. The wooden plaque on the wall beside the bell read 'Penny Lane'. Adam had christened the house. Each of the four bedrooms, named after the Beatles. It seemed cute at the time. Now it was plain sad.

She lived in one of thirty semi-detached houses, midway along a mature, horse-shoe shaped estate. It was near enough to the greyhound stadium to hear the cheers every Tuesday and Thursday evening. But she never ventured the couple of hundred metres down the road to the track. Adam had taken the children a couple of times but they weren't enamoured by the skinny dogs and their fat handlers. Tonight the area was quiet. No racing until the ground was back in shape. Good, thought Lottie; she needed the peace and quiet.

Silence greeted her as she hung up her jacket, the rap music consigned to Sean's virtual world. Having worked eighteen hours, Lottie's body creaked but her mind was wound up.

In the kitchen, a plate with two slices of pizza was left out for her. Chloe had written a note, 'We DO love you.'

She popped the pizza into the microwave and poured a glass of water. She loved her children, but usually didn't have the time to tell them. She saw so little of Katie. The nineteen year old commuted daily to college in Dublin. But even throughout the holidays, she was never around. She'd been the apple of her daddy's eye and had been so moody since Adam died. Lottie didn't know how to handle her.

Having devoured the soggy food, she climbed the stairs to her 'John Lennon' bedroom. Chloe and Sean were in bed. She closed their doors and glanced into Katie's room. Empty. She would have to talk to that girl. Tomorrow. Maybe.

* * *

Katie Parker lay back in her boyfriend's arms.

His hair tickled her nose. She tried not to sneeze and stifled a giggle. He appeared not to notice as he inhaled deeply from the spliff clutched between his long thin fingers. When he'd filled his lungs, he passed it over. She shouldn't take it but she desperately wanted to impress Jason. At nineteen, she should have more sense. Her mother would have a fit if she could see her. Tough shit, Mam; always pontificating about the dangers of drink and drugs; maybe her mother should practise what she preached.

Katie brought the rolled taper to her lips, inhaled its acrid odour before sucking deeply. She had expected a lightness in her head, but never had she experienced this thrill.

'This is so cool,' she said.

'Take it easy.' Jason rose on to his elbow. 'I don't want you puking all over me.'

She squinted up at the ceiling and saw little stars painted there. She assumed they were painted, otherwise she was hallucinating.

'Do you have stars painted on your ceiling?'

'Yes. A throwback to my Harry Potter days.'

'I love Harry Potter,' Katie said. 'All that mystical stuff. I used to wish I could magic myself into a different world. More so, after my dad died.'

Jason laughed. She glanced sideways at him. He was gorgeous, with his designer jeans and Abercrombie hoodies. She was so lucky. Today, when he had asked her to his home, she'd nearly died. Her house would fit into his sitting room. She was glad his parents were not around, because genuinely she would not have known whether to bow or genuflect. As for his room, it was fantastic. The size of hers, Chloe's and Sean's all scrunched into one.

First year of college was a bore, but he'd picked her from all the other girls. She was floating.

'Here, give me some, you greedy thing,' he said.

She handed over the spliff and though his arm was hard beneath her head she could feel some of the softness of the pillow. She closed her eyes. Definitely floating.

Yeah, if her mam could see her, she would have a grade A fit.

'I better go home. It's after midnight,' she said, trying to sit up.

'Are you Cinderella, or what?' Jason laughed. 'Will I turn into a pumpkin if I don't get you home?'

'Be serious.' She sat up and felt around for her jacket.
'All right, spoilsport, I'll take you home,' he said.
Katie kissed him on the lips. Now she had wings.

* * *

Sean Parker watched from his bedroom window as his sister and her boyfriend curled into each other on the snowy driveway. He witnessed them kissing under the road light and saw the smile on Katie's face. When had he last seen his gloomy sister so happy?

He couldn't remember.

* * *

Lottie eased her body into bed. She reached over her hand and felt the Argos book there, weighing down the duvet, her trick to keep the bedclothes tight on Adam's side. She had tried the phone book once. But it wasn't as good as the Argos book.

She lay awake thinking of Susan Sullivan and James Brown, trying to understand what they could possibly have been involved in to warrant their deaths.

Once she heard Katie turn her key in the door, she immediately fell asleep.

CHAPTER 11

The man rubbed his skin in hard even strokes.

He had done what he had to do. Secrets had to be protected. He had to be protected. Others had to be protected too, though they didn't know it.

He lathered his body, attempting to scrub out the scent of death. Slowly and methodically he worked. From the roots of his hair to his neatly cut toenails. He stepped out of the shower and towelled his skin in precise sweeps.

Fully dried, he strolled naked to his bedroom, lay down on the white sheets and stared at the ceiling for the rest of the night.

* * *

1974

She knew what he was doing was wrong but she was too afraid to tell anyone. He had a secret place where he took her most days after school. During the school holidays, he made her call to him at least once a week and sometimes he came to her house.

Her mammy was thrilled to have a priest coming to visit. She would take down the good china and serve him tea and biscuits. When her mammy was making the tea in the scullery, he would grab her hand and thrust it down there. She felt sick when he made her do that. It was nearly worse than the other things he made her do.

Once, they were almost caught when her mammy came back to see if he would like brown bread instead of biscuits. He turned toward the front window quickly, saying he was watching his car in case young hooligans scratched it.

She did not see him for a month after that and thought it was the end but it was in fact the beginning of the nightmare in earnest. He told her mammy he had a job for her in the evenings in the priest's house, sweeping and dusting, and he would give her a few bob pocket money. Her mammy was delighted.

The little girl knew then, the horror would be daily.

Sometimes she drank her daddy's whiskey which she found in the cabinet under the television. It burned her throat but after a few minutes it warmed her insides and dimmed the reality around her. She was eating too much. Her mammy was giving out to her all the time about her weight. She wanted to tell her mammy to 'fuck off', because she had heard one of the girls in school saying it and knew it was a bad word. Sometimes the priest said bad words too when he was inside her. She hated him. She was sore and bleeding. She didn't like any of it. And she knew it was too late to stop it. Who would believe her?

The girls in school were calling her fatty. Fatty this and fatty that. When she looked at herself in the mirror, she did not recognise the person staring back at her. She looked like Mr Kinder next door with his beer belly sticking out through the buttons on his smelly shirt.

Sometimes she cried herself to sleep. Mostly she just hated herself and what she had become. What he had made her become. She vowed that some day she would make him pay. She did not know when or how, but one day his time would come and she would be ready. He had shown her no mercy, only contempt. She would be the same.

'What goes around comes around,' she told her reflection in the mirror.

DAY TWO

31st December 2014

CHAPTER 12

Lottie's car miraculously started on the second turn of the key. Someone up there must love me, she told the dark, early morning sky. She needed a clear head, so she drove the long way to work.

Driving round by the Ardvale Road, she swung left at the roundabout, passing the once bustling tobacco factory with its smokeless chimneys. She remembered the pungent smell which used to hang in the air before the plant downsized to a distribution depot. She missed that whiff; it seemed to give definition to where she lived. It was gone now, like so much else.

Stopped at the traffic lights on the Dublin Bridge, she took in the panoramic view of her snow-covered town below, nestled in a valley between two marshy midland lakes, dominated by the twin-spired cathedral to the right and the single spire of the Protestant Church on the left. Cushioned between both stood a four-storey, planning deformity apartment block, out of keeping with its low-rise surroundings.

Historically, Ragmullin was a fortress town but now its idle army barracks was a breeding ground for vandalism and rumoured to be in line to become a centre for refugees and asylum seekers. It was constructed on the highest point of the town, up beyond the canal and railway. The eleventh-century monks who'd settled here would be proud that some streets still bore names in homage to these hooded men. There wasn't much else to be proud of, Lottie thought.

Before the traffic lights changed, she scanned the horizon once again, her eyes focussing on the spires standing tall in their tree-lined surroundings. Her hands turned white as she clutched the steering wheel. She thought of the church's dominance over the lives of the townspeople in the past and the effect its long-frocked men had bestowed on her own family. The cast iron bell, snared in one spire, clanged out the sixth hour of the morning and resonated through the rolled-up windows of her car. There was no escaping it. Church and State. Two thorns in the history of Ragmullin and in her own history.

Lottie took a few deep breaths and the shattered glass of the traffic light flashed to a cracked green. She stamped down the accelerator and the car skidded, almost stealing a strip of paint from the red Micra in front of her, the only other car around. She drove over the bridge and down the icy pot-holed, deserted street with shop windows dark and shaded. She wondered how many secrets lay hidden behind them, what mysteries waited to be uncovered and if in time there would be anyone left in Ragmullin to even bother trying to unearth them.

* * *

Thirty men and women were crowded into the small incident room.

Some sat on rickety chairs while others stood shoulder to shoulder, chatting loudly, body odours mingling with diverse perfumes, aftershaves and burned coffee. Lottie looked for somewhere to sit and, not finding anywhere vacant, leaned against the wall at the back of the room. She watched Corrigan fiddling with a handful of pages, standing in front of the assembled detectives. She should be up there.

Boyd caught her eye and smiled. She grinned back. His smile could do that to her sometimes, just when she intended to scowl. Looking as neat as ever, dressed in a grey suit, his only concession to the weather was a navy sweater over his shirt. Perhaps this could be a 'be nice to Boyd day'. Maybe? Maybe not.

She gulped her black coffee, jolting energy into her tired mind. Corrigan nodded to her and she hurried to the front of the room before he changed his mind. She faced the team. Kirby's eyes were red-rimmed, probably from a bout of whiskey drinking. Maria Lynch was bright and bubbly. Was she ever any other way? Boyd dropped his smile and donned his serious face. The team were on edge to get started. So was she.

'Right,' said Superintendent Corrigan, silencing the room. 'Detective Inspector Parker will bring us up to date.'

The faces before her were full of expectation. Her team were good. They had confidence in themselves and in her. She had to deliver. And she would.

She placed her mug on the desk and, pulling down the cuffs of her long-sleeved T-shirt, a habit she couldn't break, she briefed the waiting detectives on the events of the previous day and night, and delegated tasks.

When she was finished, chairs scuffed along the floor as a heave of bodies shuffled and stretched. The noise increased from a hum to a loud chatter.

'All hands on deck,' Corrigan shouted above the din.

Lottie could have sworn she heard Boyd mutter under his breath, 'Aye, aye Captain.' She shoved him out of the room in front of her, grabbed her jacket and took a walk over to the cathedral. She had a witness to interview.

* * *

Father Joe Burke was waiting for her at the gate. The sky was still moody and dark, and Lottie craved the end of winter.

Tumbling snow obscured the cathedral, now a cordoned-off crime scene. A few early morning onlookers were braving the weather to pause, bless themselves and leave flowers. The two gardaí standing in front of the crime scene tape stamped their feet. They looked frozen. Lottie felt the same.

Lottie shook hands with Father Joe through thick gloves.

'Come on up to the house for a cup of tea,' he said warmly.

'That'd be great,' said Lottie, glancing at the priest's bright blue ski-jacket. He had a fur hat pulled down over his ears. 'You look like something out of the KGB,' she said, smiling.

He led her round the side of the cathedral, to the house.

* * *

It was warm inside the house. Old iron radiators gurgled airlocks into the silence. Tall, dark mahogany cabinets cast shadows up the walls of the tiled hallway through which Father Burke led Lottie.

'Tea or coffee?' he enquired, opening the door to a room with décor similar to the hall.

'Tea, please.' She needed to expunge the taste left in her mouth from the office coffee.

The priest spoke to a small nun who had appeared behind them. She shuffled off with a sigh, to boil a kettle somewhere in the depths of the house.

'So, Inspector Parker, what can I do for you?' he asked, sitting into a claw-footed armchair.

'I want information, Father Burke,' said Lottie, removing her jacket and taking a seat opposite him.

'Call me Joe. We don't need formality, do we?'

'Okay. Then please call me Lottie.'

She knew she shouldn't allow this familiarity. He was a suspect. Second on the scene, after Mrs Gavin, and he'd been in the cathedral at the time of the murder. Except, sometimes informality helped people drop their guard.

'I notice you have CCTV cameras inside and outside the cathedral. I need access to the discs.'

'Of course, but I don't think they'll be of any use to you. The external cameras haven't worked since the drastic fall in temperatures before Christmas and the internal ones are trained on the confessionals.'

'Why so?' asked Lottie, inwardly cursing a potential dead end.

'Bishop Connor organised it, so we priests can see who is about to enter. In case we get attacked.'

'Bit ironic, isn't it?' She looked up as the nun reappeared with crockery rattling on a silver tray.

'And the web cam wasn't working either. It usually gives a live feed from the altar via the parish website. With the holidays, we couldn't get anyone to come fix it.'

Another piece of useless information, Lottie thought.

Taking the tray to the table, Father Joe thanked the nun. She disappeared without answer. He poured the tea and Lottie poured the milk. They both sipped from delicate china cups.

'I need to ask you a few questions about yesterday,' Lottie said, hurriedly shrugging herself into work mode.

'Is this a formal interview? Do I need my solicitor present?' he asked.

She was taken aback but noticed he was smiling.

'I don't think a solicitor is necessary at this stage of the investigation, Father . . . em . . . Joe,' she stumbled over her words. 'I'm trying to establish a few facts.'

'Go ahead. I'm all yours.'

Lottie felt her cheeks redden. Was he flirting with her? Surely not.

He said, 'I did ten o'clock Mass, cleared the altar, locked the chalices and Holy Communion into the tabernacle. The cathedral was empty by then. Normally a few people stay on to pray, but I think the cold weather won out over religion. The sacristan finished up around ten forty-five and he went home. I came over here for a cuppa, then went back to the sacristy after about an hour, to write up next Sunday's sermon. Mrs Gavin arrived shortly after that and began her cleaning routine. I'd just said the Angelus when I heard her scream, so it must have been after twelve noon.' The priest paused as if praying.

'What did you do then?' Lottie asked. She made a mental note for someone to interview the sacristan. Probably another useless exercise, seeing as he had left before the murder.

'I rushed out to see what the commotion was about and ran straight into Mrs Gavin. Poor woman, she was hysterical. She grabbed me by the hand and dragged me down to the front pew. I saw the body . . . the woman . . . slumped there. I leaned over and listened for a breath but I could tell she was dead. I said an act of contrition and blessed her. Then I called the emergency services and brought Mrs Gavin up to the altar where we sat until the gardaí arrived.'

His face was pale against the black of his sweater.

'Did you touch anything around the victim? In fact, did you touch her?' she asked.

'Of course not. I thought of feeling for a pulse but I knew by looking at her she was dead.'

'Even so, you'll have to call over to the station to provide a sample for DNA analysis.' She added, 'To rule you in or out of our investigations.'

'I *am* a suspect then.' He locked his long fingers together in a steeple beneath his chin.

'Everyone is a suspect until we determine otherwise.' Lottie tried but couldn't read anything in his eyes. 'Did you know Susan Sullivan?' She watched for his reaction.

'Was she the victim?'

She nodded. His face was serene.

'No, I don't remember seeing her before.' He thought for a moment. 'There are lots of people who come to the cathedral but don't go to Mass. They might drop in to pray or light a candle. Ragmullin parish has over fifteen thousand people, you know.'

'Do you do house calls?'

'Not unless someone is sick and requests a priest. I visit the hospitals. I'm also the chaplain for the girls' secondary school. We say Mass and hear confessions, though not many go to confessions any more.' He shook his head. 'Baptisms, weddings, funerals, communions and confirmation.'

'Is that a lot of work?'

'Which part, or all of it?' His face opened up with a smile.

Lottie was silent. She recalled a priest coming to her house to administer the blessing of the sick for Adam. She'd have remembered if it was Father Joe Burke. Then again, Adam was so ill at that stage, she might not have noticed him. Unlike now.

'Can I ask what you did for the remainder of yesterday afternoon?'

'I accompanied Mrs Gavin home and waited until her husband arrived. Then I returned and read in my room for the night. I've never seen such a snowstorm in all my life.'

'So you didn't venture out in it, then?'

'No, Inspector, I didn't. Why all the questions?'

Lottie contemplated what she would say then decided on honesty. 'We have another suspicious death on our hands. It could be suicide but we're not totally sure.'

'I wasn't on duty last night and didn't attend any emergency. What happened? Should I know who it was?'

'James Brown. He worked with Susan Sullivan.'

'Don't know him. God help his poor family.' Father Joe joined his hands and bowed his head.

'We haven't been able to trace any next of kin as yet. Just like Susan. It's as if they were both plucked from thin air and dropped into Ragmullin.'

'I'll ask around. Someone must be related to them.'

'Thanks, I appreciate that.' Lottie sighed and, unable to think of anything else to delay her stay, she stood up. 'I'll send someone to collect the CCTV discs. Call over to the station today. We'll take a buccal swab and fingerprints. As the investigation progresses, I'll be back to talk to you again.'

She pulled on her jacket.

'I look forward it,' he said, helping slip her arm into the sleeve. This time she saw a definite twinkle in his eye.

Handing him her card, she said, 'In case you remember anything else, that's my mobile number.'

'It was lovely chatting with you. Pity about the circumstances.'

'Thanks for the tea.' She pulled her hood up against the swirling snow.

When he closed the door, Lottie stood for a moment, blinded by the whiteness after the dull interior, and attempted to wrap her mind around just what had gone on between her and Father Joe Burke.

CHAPTER 13

Boyd took a long drag on his cigarette and exhaled.

'We have nothing,' he said.

They were walking to the council offices. Lottie wished he would shut up. It was fine knowing they had nothing, but there was no need to remind her.

'We'll go through their files,' she said. 'There has to be a link in relation to their jobs. Both worked in the planning department and it is a highly contentious area. They don't appear to have anything else in common. For the moment, anyway.'

Boyd inhaled deeply. 'Maybe they were having an affair?'

Lottie stopped and stared at him.

Then she started walking again, shaking her head. 'So what? Both were single as far as we know.'

'It has to be something dodgy in the planning area so,' he said.

'Doh,' Lottie mimicked Homer Simpson. 'Let's see what we can find out.'

Boyd stubbed his cigarette into the snow and they entered the glass aquarium.

* * *

The building was unnaturally silent. A few staff walked around with bowed heads as they arrived for work, New Year's Eve joviality now abandoned. Detective Maria Lynch's team were conducting individual interviews with all personnel in a second-floor room. Lottie looked forward to hearing the outcome.

In Sullivan's office, a technician unlocked the computer. Lottie could have done it herself, she thought, after finding the password taped to the underside of the keyboard. Some people never learn. Seated, she scrolled through the electronic folders. Stopping the cursor on one marked private, she sensed Boyd at her shoulder.

'Why don't you start on Brown's computer,' she said.

She was being a bitch, but he was irritating her. So much for 'be nice to Boyd day'. After an hour of trawling, Lottie looked up to see him standing in the doorway shaking his head.

'There's nothing unusual here,' she said. 'Her private folders have tax returns and medical insurance. A few items could be of interest though. For example, the minutes of meetings in relation to a group called 'Residents against Ghost Estates'. There's about a year's worth.' Lottie stretched. 'Did you find anything on Brown's computer?'

'Nothing I can understand.'

'We'll need someone who knows about these things, to see if they can spot anything illegal or dubious,' Lottie said. 'I'm going to have a word with the county manager.'

'Will I tag along?'

'See about getting these files zipped, or whatever you call it, to the station. Make yourself really useful.'

She headed out without listening to Boyd's retort.

* * *

At forty-five years old, Gerry Dunne was the second youngest county manager in the country.

He managed a revenue budget of millions and a capital budget on a downward curve as the recession hit infrastructural development. During the Celtic Tiger years he had overseen multi-million-euro developments including a major motorway traversing the county. No comfort to struggling motorists, thought Lottie as she leafed through the council's annual report outside his office. People couldn't afford the diesel; they couldn't afford the cars; they couldn't afford the taxes and some couldn't afford to put decent food on their tables. Gerry Dunne continued to earn his hundred thousand plus salary annually and Lottie was sure he was one of those who changed his car every January. His biography made interesting reading for Lottie as she waited to be admitted to his office. She thought of her own dwindling bank balance and squirmed.

A secretary buzzed her in. His office was twice the size of James Brown's. A chill circulated the room. Snow had settled outside on the window ledge and mystical images imprinted themselves on the glass where the wind had blown the flakes. A networked laptop and phone were the only blemishes on the smooth wooden surface of his desk.

'I'll do anything I can to help, Inspector,' Dunne said. His striking features were lined with stress and his mouth dipped toward his chin. Short dark hair had wisps of grey shadowing his ears.

'We're all shocked at these deaths,' he said, his eyes appearing to penetrate the depths of her soul. Lottie pitied him if he could read what was written there. There was a time when these interviews wouldn't have affected her, but that was then, this was now and her life had changed. 'Two esteemed members of my staff, in one day. It doesn't bear thinking about.'

'Is there anything work-related that might lead someone to kill Susan? Or indeed James, though I should state that his death is classed as suicide for the moment.'

She interrogated his face and found little reaction.

'They both dealt with planning applications. From time to time they would've come under political and developer-led pressure. Inspector, I can vouch for my staff having the highest ethical standards.'

His voice was slow and measured. It sounded like a prepared speech.

'Any threats made against them?' she asked.

'Oh, yes. Against other staff too. During the Celtic Tiger era developers had millions of euro for land purchase. Acquiring permission to build large housing estates, shopping centres, industrial estates and the like ensured they made a profit. Those late on the scene lost everything. Others early in the game made fortunes.'

'How were these threats made?'

'Phone, letter . . .' He shrugged his shoulders and said, 'I once received a bullet in a miniature coffin.'

Lottie remembered the incident.

'And all these threats were reported?'

'Yes, of course. You should have records of them.'

'I'm sure we do. I'll double check.'

'Yes, Inspector, you do that,' Dunne said, lips tight, drawing a line under the matter.

Was he reprimanding her? Pull yourself together woman, she warned herself. He was hard to read. At least Corrigan shouted and bellowed and she knew where she stood with him.

'Their current planning files, I need to see them. I know you'll tell me they're confidential . . .'

'On the contrary,' he interrupted, 'all planning information is in the public domain. I'll ensure you have access. Will that be all?'

'Where were you around midday yesterday?'

'I returned early in the morning after a few days' holiday in Lanzarote with my wife, Hazel. I think ours was the last flight in before the airport shut down due to the weather. Once I was home, I stayed there.'

'Will Hazel verify that?'

His smile emphasised straight white teeth. His eyes never moved.

'I'm sure she will.'

Jesus, a barracuda in a pinstripe suit. God help the other fish in the aquarium. Lottie went off to find Boyd.

* * *

The smile slipped down Gerry Dunne's face as soon as the inspector left his office. He looked at the icy river below his office window.

He was not a stupid man. He knew she had conducted a character appraisal in the short time she'd been with him. She probably hadn't liked what she found. He didn't care. He didn't like himself much either.

Two members of his staff were dead, attracting attention at a time when he wanted to be so far under the radar that he was invisible.

The mask of composure, which he could wear so well, dissolved into tiny shards. He sat back at his desk and, trying to hold it all together, he cradled his head with quivering hands, wishing he was back in Lanzarote.

CHAPTER 14

Boyd struggled to keep the car upright and Lottie braced herself for impact with a ditch. He was an expert driver. Good job.

'Twenty-two,' Lottie said, rubbing cold fingers over her forehead, deepening the furrow.

'What?' asked Boyd.

'Trees on the left-hand side of the avenue.'

'And that means . . . what exactly?' Boyd asked, bringing the car to a halt.

'Observing. That's all,' Lottie said. Why was she feeling stressed? The day was yet young. She got out of the car.

A Garda Technical van, a squad car and two other cars were parked on the courtyard in front of James Brown's house. In the daylight Lottie observed the stone cottage, covered in snow-laden ivy. It dominated the enclosure. A leafless tree, a cairn of rocks circling its roots, sprouted from the centre of the frozen cobbled ground. Looks lonely, she thought. To her right the oak tree, without the body that had swayed from its branch last night, threw ominous shadows in its wake. The state pathologist had been and gone.

They pulled on protective clothing, covered their shoes and entered the cottage. From the black and white hexagon tiled hallway, they walked into the living area. Wooden beams traversed the ceiling. The walls were bare and whitewashed. A round table with four chairs stood in the centre of the floor. A cream fabric couch faced an open-hearth fireplace. Red bricks climbed up the chimney breast and extended towards the window. The entire area was stark in its brightness. Clutter free and clean. Scattered around the floor in front of the fireplace were thick white candles at various stages of melt. Lottie smelled only their wax, no vanilla or jasmine. She deduced the candles possibly served a purpose other than exuding a calm scent.

The room felt overcrowded with two SOCOs and a couple of uniforms along with herself and Boyd. Nothing looked out of place. No sign of a struggle.

'We're finished in here,' Jim McGlynn told Boyd, ignoring Lottie.

'Asshole,' she muttered, interpreting his snub as disrespect.

'Heard that,' Boyd whispered.

'Did you find anything we should know about?' Lottie asked McGlynn.

'We've taken fingerprints and samples for comparisons. That's if you find anything to compare them with. No suicide note.'

She nodded and stooped into the kitchen. Small and compact. She opened the fridge. Tubs of organic mush, she noted, lifting and probing, searching through the food. She closed it and inspected the counter. An empty sink, a breakfast bowl, mug and spoon on the drainer. No microwave. The kitchen was clean and tidy. It was obvious James Brown had no teenage children ransacking it.

At the bedroom door Boyd stood, looking in. Lottie joined him.

She sucked in a gasp. 'What the hell?'

'My sentiments exactly.'

'And I thought Brown was Mr Stuffy Boots when I spoke to him yesterday.'

Lottie explored the small bedroom. It felt oppressive, with a free-standing wooden wardrobe, chest of drawers and a four-poster bed adorned with a black silk quilt. Life-sized photographs of naked men blasting out various stages of arousal covered every inch of wall space.

'McGlynn could have warned us,' she said.

Glancing upwards, she motioned Boyd to do likewise. On the ceiling above the bed, hung a square mirror, suspended from the rafters with chains.

'Hugh Hefner is only trotting after this guy,' Boyd said.

A laptop, open on the bed, was half covered by a black silk sheet. They had his office laptop, this must be a personal one. Lottie tipped the return button with the pen from her notebook. The screen flashed to life. A pornographic site appeared. Obviously Brown was not expecting anyone but himself to return to it. The content was graphic but featured only adults, not children. She had seen worse during the course of her job.

'Would you look at the balls on that fellow.' Boyd stared at the photographs.

Uncomfortable with violating the secrets of a dead man, Lottie slammed the laptop shut and put it under her arm. The technical team could interrogate its history. Boyd began searching the drawers. She went through to a cramped bathroom.

A bottle of cologne on the shelf above the sink, a tube of toothpaste and a single toothbrush sat in a glass in the window. A feeling of sympathy for Brown grew within her. She joined Boyd.

'Anything?' she asked.

'Plenty,' he said. 'But there's nothing to point us in the direction of a murder motive, unless someone didn't like his sexual persuasion. I still think he topped himself.'

'It's all too neat.' Lottie shook her head. 'So far the only common denominator between the victims is their place of work. There must be something else connecting Susan Sullivan and James Brown.'

Boyd shrugged. They walked outside and removed their protective gear.

'Do you want to drive?' he asked, stifling a yawn.

'What do you think?' she answered, sitting into the passenger seat. 'Put the heater on, I'm freezing.'

'And I'm not?'

He started the engine and clipped the fender of one of the patrol cars as he reversed.

'What's up with you?' Lottie asked. 'Something back there excite you?'

He didn't answer.

She closed her eyes and leaned her head against the window. Maybe she should text Chloe to switch on the heating. Maybe not. If they were cold enough they'd put it on. Getting them to turn it off, that might be the problem.

Her phone rang.

'Inspector, you know we found Brown's mobile phone in his briefcase?' Kirby said.

'Yes. Go on.'

'We've extracted his recent calls.'

'Anything unusual or recurring?' She hoped they had a lead. She needed something fast.

'Being analysed as we speak. The last number he called before his untimely demise was Derek Harte's. The second last number is more interesting.'

'I'm waiting.'

'It lasted thirty-seven seconds.'

'Don't play with me, Kirby. Who did he call?'

'Tom Rickard.'

Lottie thought for a second.

'Rickard Construction? I came across that name on the ghost estate files on Susan Sullivan's computer. I remember all the hullabaloo a few years ago when he got permission to knock down the old bank on Main Street and erected his company headquarters monstrosity in its place.'

Kirby said, 'Going by your report, Inspector, James Brown made the call approximately four minutes after you concluded your interview with him.'

'Thanks, Kirby.' Lottie hung up.

'I presume our next stop is Tom Rickard,' said Boyd.

'I'm going to tackle him on my own.'

'Shouldn't I be with you?'

'I know his sort, believe me, it's better if I go it alone. I want to pick up that phone printout at the station too.'

Visibility was increasingly difficult. Boyd struggled to follow the road.

'Some way to spend New Year's Eve,' Lottie remarked, leaning over to turn up the heat. She closed her eyes as Boyd swore.

CHAPTER 15

'Mr Rickard. I hope you can spare a few minutes of your time.'

Lottie followed as Rickard brushed past her, striding to the glass lift.

'You are Tom Rickard, aren't you?' She stepped in beside him.

'Are you still here?' he asked.

She folded her arms without budging an inch.

'You need an appointment,' he said, pressing his chubby finger on the button to keep the door open.

She flashed her ID badge in his face.

Rickard glanced at it and smirked.

'I should have recognised you, Inspector, but you look different from your newspaper photos.'

'I need to ask you a few questions.'

Lottie stepped into his space.

'Joke,' he said. 'I'm very busy but as you're already here, I'll spare you two minutes.'

He pushed number three on the keypad. The doors eased closed and the lift rose quickly. His office appeared to take up most of the third floor.

Despite herself, Lottie admired the man's taste. The space was modern and sparse, with bright warm colours mirroring the sleek character before her.

Rickard removed his cashmere coat, hung it on a marble coat rack and seated himself behind his desk, indicating a chair for Lottie to sit. She didn't know anything about designer clothes but estimated his coat could cost at least a week of her wages. Perhaps two. Another world.

His grey suit had hand-stitched tucks and the double-breasted waistcoat held in a thick belly. Lottie thought he was about six foot two; mid-fifties; straight russet hair, neatly coiffured. Teeth so white, they had to be veneers. A blue shirt and dark grey tie completed his executive look. She wanted to believe he wasn't handsome but he was; his craggy jaw and bright eyes reminded her of Robert Redford.

'I'm extremely busy.' He leaned forward, two hands placed firmly on the desk. 'What can I do for you?'

'Mr Rickard,' Lottie spoke slowly. Unconcerned for his busy schedule, she would take her time. 'You are aware of the suspicious death in the cathedral yesterday?'

'I saw the news report last night. Very tragic.' He sat back in his chair, creating space between them. 'What's it got to do with me?'

'Can you account for your whereabouts, from about eleven in the morning until eight last night?'

She eyed Rickard. His expression was chameleon-like, fading from smug and pompous to enquiring and puzzled.

'Why do I have to? I didn't know the victim.'

'Are you sure?'

'Can't be a hundred per cent. I meet many people in the course of my business. I don't remember everyone.'

'I'll ask you again. Can you account for your whereabouts yesterday, in particular between eleven a.m. and eight p.m.?'

She was beginning to enjoy this encounter. Maybe she was grasping at straws in the wind, but his altering body language told her to go for it.

'I'll have to check my diary,' he said, reluctantly.

'I'm talking about yesterday, not last year. Surely you know where you were, what you did and who you did it with?'

'I travel all over the country, all over the world. I could've been on Wall Street, New York, yesterday.'

Playing for time or concocting a web to spin a story? Lottie didn't doubt that Tom Rickard wouldn't look a bit out of place on Wall Street.

'Stop wasting my time and yours,' she said. 'Dublin Airport was closed from early morning yesterday because of the snow. So spin another one.'

Opening up his iPad, he pounded an icon for his diary and index fingered the date. She peered across the desk trying to see the upside down words.

They raised their heads simultaneously, two sets of eyes, challenging each other.

'I was out and about. I had my PA cancel a meeting in Dublin – because of the bad weather. So I did a few site visits.'

She detected a hint of insolence returning to his voice.

'Can anyone vouch for you?'

'Vouch?' He laughed.

'What's funny?'

'Nothing, Inspector. Am I a suspect?'

'I'm trying to establish if you have a credible alibi.'

'Mmm . . . There was no one on any of the sites. The weather, you know. Vouch?' he repeated. 'I doubt it.'

'I'll need a list of those sites.'

He shrugged his shoulders. 'Anything else?'

'You got a phone call. Late afternoon,' Lottie said, changing the emphasis of the conversation.

Rickard shifted in his chair.

'What phone call?'

'The call James Brown made to you not long before he died.'

'He's dead?' Rickard said, his eyes widening. He appeared to gather his thoughts. 'I don't know any James Brown and I certainly didn't get any call from him.'

'Nice try.'

Lottie pulled the sheet of crumpled paper from her pocket. She unfolded it on the desk, ironing out the creases with her finger. Taking her time. She picked up his silver pen and underlined the penultimate line of digits. The rest of the page was blacked out.

Turning it towards him, she asked, 'Is that your number?'

'Looks like it.'

'It is your number. You know it's your number. What was James Brown ringing you about shortly before he apparently wrapped a rope around his neck and hung himself?'

Rickard didn't flinch.

'I won't deny I might've had dealings with Brown in the past. I'm sorry he's dead but you're not going to pin this on me, Inspector.'

'I'm not trying to pin anything on anyone. I asked a simple question.'

'He could have called me by mistake. I don't know.' He shrugged.

'The call lasted thirty-seven seconds.'

'So?'

'I'll get a warrant for your phone records.'

'Do that. We're done here. I've important work to do.'

Lottie watched as Rickard began opening and shutting drawers beneath his desk, dismissing her with his actions. She stood up.

'I'll be back, Mr Rickard.'

'I've no doubt about it,' he said. 'No doubt in the world.'

'Happy New Year,' Lottie said and walked out the door before he could reply. As she stepped into the lift, she knew she was on a collision course with Tom Rickard. That was probably not a good thing.

* * *

Tom Rickard glared at the closed door in the ensuing silence. He pulled over the piece of paper with Brown's blanked-out phone calls from the last day of his life. He stared at his own number, crudely underlined.

It was there in black and white. Date, time and call duration.

He snorted and crumpled the page into his bin.

He had too much to lose. Let them prove he spoke with Brown.

Tom Rickard would deny, deny, deny.

He tapped a speed dial number on his phone.

'We need another meeting.'

CHAPTER 16

'Brown could have been susceptible to blackmail, judging by the paraphernalia in his bedroom,' Boyd said to Lottie when she returned to the office.

She stood, too wound up to sit still.

'Having pictures of naked men on his bedroom wall? Come on, Boyd. That's nothing to be blackmailed over.' She paced up and down the small office. Corrigan's habit was catching.

She'd sent Brown's laptop to their technical guys to trawl through and assigned a detective to check out the reported planning threats. She still had to interview Derek Harte, who had found James Brown's body. She wondered who he was and what he'd been doing at Brown's house. She'd instructed Lynch to find him after he'd failed to appear for the ten a.m. appointment.

'Someone, anyone, organise a Section 10 warrant for Tom Rickard's phone records,' Lottie said. 'And check when the next District Court is on. We need to get things moving.'

'Sit down, you're making me nervous,' Boyd said.

She sat.

The desk phone rang.

'Good afternoon, Detective Inspector,' said the state pathologist. 'Are you available to come over to Tullamore? I know the weather is atrocious but there are some things I think you should see.'

'Sure.'

'I've the preliminary reports ready.'

'Can you email them?'

'There's something I want to show you.'

'I'll be there in half an hour.'

'Any news?' Boyd asked.

'Get a life,' Lottie said. He'd heard every word of the conversation. 'I wish I had my own office back.' She pulled on her jacket.

'You might as well dream here as in bed,' he said.

Jesus, he sounded more like her mother with every passing day. Lottie zipped up quickly, almost snagging her throat.

'Where are you off to?'

She didn't answer him and banged the door behind her.

'Women,' he said.

'I heard that,' she shouted back.

A minute later, she returned, having eyed the state of the road outside.

'Boyd?'

'Yes, Inspector?'

'Will you drive me to Tullamore?'

CHAPTER 17

He was heading back to his office when he saw the teenage boy heading into Danny's Bar and he had to follow. The dark interior helped him meld into the woodwork. He watched as the youngster stretched toward a girl, kiss her mouth, then remove his coat.

The man ordered a pint of Guinness, sat at the bar and angled himself on the stool so that he could see the young couple. The teenage boy shrugged his coat over his arm and linked his other arm around the girl's narrow waist. But the man wasn't interested in the girl. He loosened his tie at the collar of this shirt and continued to stare.

'Are you going to drink that or offer it up?' The barman grinned at him.

The man scowled, lifted his pint and sipped before returning his gaze to the boy's delicate features. He shoved his legs further beneath the bar, shielding the hardening muscle under the zipper of his trousers. He had plenty to be doing, but for now all he wanted to do was sit and watch and imagine what it would feel like to have that youthful flesh in his hands.

CHAPTER 18

The state pathologist, Jane Dore, greeted Lottie and Boyd. A pair of tiny spectacles were perched on her prim nose and her dark green eyes peered through the glass. A smart navy skirt suit clung to her tiny body and a blue blouse peeked out at her throat. She wore very high-heeled shoes. Lottie felt underdressed in her warm jacket, jeans and long-sleeved top with a thermal vest underneath. She'd spent the forty-kilometre drive to Tullamore in silence. Boyd sang, out of tune, to the music on the radio and she'd found it irritating but said nothing. Sometimes that was the best way to handle his moods.

'Welcome to the Dead House,' Jane Dore said, extending a petite hand to Lottie.

Lottie returned the handshake.

'Call me Lottie. The Dead House?' she enquired.

'A throwback to olden times. Come.' Jane led the way along a narrow corridor.

Lottie followed, hoping the intense disinfectant smell would help blank out the scent of death. She doubted it. Boyd slipped into step behind them.

The pathologist pushed open a swing door and entered a room with white tiles stretching from floor to ceiling. Three stainless steel tables stood in the centre. Two held bodies under stark white cotton sheeting. Susan Sullivan and James Brown, Lottie presumed. She could see reflections in the steel cabinets and recoiled from her own distorted image.

Jane Dore sat on a high stool in the corner and booted up a computer.

'This takes ages to come alive,' she said.

'Once that's all that comes alive,' Lottie said, attempting to lighten the atmosphere. Boyd raised an eyebrow, folded his arms, said nothing.

The pathologist drummed a red varnished fingernail on the bench. Lottie pulled over another stool and sat in the silence, waiting for the computer to zip into cyber world.

'Did anything unexpected crop up?' she asked as Jane keyed in her password. No Post-its stuck under the keyboard for this woman.

'Death in both cases was asphyxiation due to strangulation,' she replied. 'There is little evidence of defensive wounds on Sullivan's body. There's grazing on Brown's fingers and bruising on his neck around the ligature, as if he'd tried to dislodge the rope. I also found some blue nylon fibre under his fingernails. I've sent all fibre and hair to the forensics lab and they have the rope too. There is a slight contusion at the base of his skull. I don't know what caused it and until I have the forensic results I cannot conclusively determine that his death was self-inflicted.'

Lottie congratulated her gut instinct. She might still be proven wrong but she was almost sure Brown hadn't committed suicide. A bump on the back of the head told her someone else was around last night.

'Sullivan was in a bad way . . .' The pathologist paused mid-sentence, pushing her spectacles back up her nose.

'And she may have given birth. I'm not one hundred per cent sure until I run more tests on the tissue I've extracted.'

'Why can't you be sure?' Lottie asked.

'Her reproductive system is a mess. She was in the advanced stages of ovarian cancer. Both ovaries have tumours as large as mandarins and there's another in her uterus.'

'It had crossed my mind she might've had cancer,' Lottie said, recalling the Oxycontin in the victim's medicine cabinet.

'It's possible she confused the symptoms with menopause,' Jane said.

'She knew,' Lottie said with conviction.

'Ovarian cancer is silent. It's usually at an advanced stage when symptoms appear. Sullivan only had weeks to live, but someone got to her first.'

Lottie thought back to the day Adam received his diagnosis. Had Susan gone through the same earth-shattering scenario with her doctor? How did she react? Did she take the news in a calm, dignified manner, like Adam, or had she screamed at the doctor as she, Lottie, had?

'Are you all right?' Jane Dore raised her eyebrows, concern knitted between them.

'I'm fine. Just thinking of something else.' Lottie quickly composed herself, professionalism overriding her personal emotion. She felt like pounding her finger on the computer, it was taking so long. But her nails were bitten and uneven. Better not, she thought.

'At last,' the pathologist said, as a program pinged into life and a green hue lit up the screen.

She keyed in Susan Sullivan's name. Numerous lines of text and several icons appeared. She clicked and an image of Sullivan's body filled the screen.

'Here, you can see the ligature mark, a deep groove on the tissue. It's from a very thin plastic-type wire. This is consistent with the iPod headphones found around the victim's neck. The lab is currently running analysis to confirm it as the murder weapon. A quick jerk, tighten for fifteen to twenty seconds and the victim is dead.'

'Would the killer have to be a man?'

'Not necessarily. Using the right amount of force in the correct area, it could be either sex. There's limited bruising on the neck, so she didn't put up much of a fight.'

Lottie watched as the pathologist moved the cursor further down the image and hovered over the victim's upper thigh.

'What's that?' Lottie asked, squinting at the screen.

'I believe it's a homemade tattoo. Indian ink pounded on to the skin and jabbed repeatedly with a needle. It looks like lines in a circle. Not very clear. It's badly drawn and deep too. Incised with a knife perhaps, then daubed with ink. I'll show you,' she said. 'Put these on.'

She extracted latex gloves from a drawer at her knee and handed them to Lottie and Boyd. Jumping down off her high perch, she walked with small elegant steps to the nearest table and pulled back the sheet exposing the naked body of Susan Sullivan. A rough Y incision marked the woman's chest, crudely stitched with thick thread.

Lottie shuddered. Is this what they had done to her Adam? Dying at home had necessitated the undertaker placing his body in a steel box and bringing Adam to the hospital for a post-mortem. She'd been too distraught at the time to object. Now, she didn't want to go there, so she forced her concentration to what the pathologist was indicating.

Jane Dore moved one of the victim's legs and fingered the dead woman's inside thigh. 'See?' She pointed to the mark on the victim's inner thigh.

Lottie shifted her weight from one foot to the other, trying to shed her unease. She bent over to look. The dead woman's pubis was almost in her face.

'Yes, I see it,' she murmured. Boyd remained in her shadow.

'Now look at this.'

At the second table, Jane whipped the sheet from the body. James Brown lay there, whiter than he had ever been in life, stitches traversing his chest also. The pathologist pulled his legs apart.

Lottie stared at a mark comparable to the tattoo on Sullivan's inner thigh. Both were in similar locations. But this one was more oval-shaped, as if the hand of whoever had drawn it had slipped.

'I've sent samples of the ink to the lab for analysis. Don't hold your breath waiting for a result.'

'I'm sure it isn't a county council initiation rite,' Boyd said.

'Nothing would surprise me nowadays,' Lottie said.

'In my opinion these marks were made thirty or forty years ago. The growth of the epidermis and the fading ink would testify to that.'

Lottie opened her mouth to say something, but decided against it. It was an important link between Susan Sullivan and James Brown, besides their work.

Jane Dore printed off the tattoo images.

'Happy hunting,' she said, handing them to Boyd.

Blowing air through her nostrils, Lottie expelled the scent of decaying flesh. She peeled off the gloves, dropping them in a sterile bin beneath a bench. The pathologist scrolled down the computer screen and printed off her preliminary reports.

Once she'd finished, she gave them to Lottie and returned to the bodies to tag and bag and do whatever it was a pathologist had to do to finish autopsies. Lottie didn't want to know about that. She leafed through the pages as she strolled behind Boyd and couldn't help wondering if Susan Sullivan had a child out there somewhere.

'Find out the name of Sullivan's doctor,' she told Boyd.

Hearing the click of high heels, she turned round to find Jane Dore standing behind her. Too close. Lottie's spine tingled. She was more uncomfortable with the living than the dead. Get a grip, Parker.

'I'm going to get a bite to eat. Would you like to join me?'

'I'm sorry,' said Lottie, 'DS Boyd and I have to get back to Ragmullin. Next time?'

'I hope we don't have a next time. If you follow me.'

Lottie smiled. It was the other woman's only attempt at any kind of humour.

CHAPTER 19

The light was on, making it awkward to differentiate between day and night. Lottie assumed it was early afternoon judging by her rumbling stomach. They'd wasted no time getting back from Tullamore. She'd seen enough of the Dead House.

Derek Harte sat in the windowless, airless interview room. He had been at James Brown's house the night Brown died. He had called the emergency services and waited. Late thirties, straight brown hair cut tight above his ears and clean-shaven. His green eyes, submerged burnt-out embers, were lifeless in an ashen face. A masculine scent wafted from him and Lottie wondered if he were trying to shield his look of femininity with cologne. He wore the fragrance like it was meant for someone else. Beneath his black padded North Face jacket, the hood of a red sweatshirt nestled around his broad neck.

Cameras and microphones embedded in the walls. DVD recorder on. Formalities over, Harte began. 'James and I met last June.' He closed his eyes at the memory and a whisper of a smile creased his thin lips.

Lottie empathised with him. Fleeting memories, causing secret smiles and unbidden tears, could erupt at the most inopportune moments. She knew it too well.

'Where did you meet him?' she asked.

'This is very delicate.' He raised his eyes to meet hers.

'Anything you say will be treated with the utmost confidence,' she said, not quite believing her own words.

'I met him through the internet. I'd been on this dating site for a while and never had the courage to engage with anyone. Until I came across James. He seemed nice, non-threatening, if you know what I mean.'

Lottie nodded, not wanting to stop his flow of speech. Years of interviewing had honed her technique.

'He looked normal. No airs or graces about him. I could tell that from his photograph and bio. I decided to email him and hit send before I could change my mind. He emailed me back. Wanted to meet up. I couldn't believe he was interested in me.'

Harte looked at Lottie and continued. 'I work in a school sixty kilometres from here.'

'Where?'

'In Athlone.'

'You met there?'

'No. I felt we needed to be discreet so we met in a hotel in Tullamore.'

'What did you talk about?'

'Our jobs, mainly. How stressful they were; how we coped. We didn't approach the subject of our sexuality. Not the first few times. I suppose you could call them dates but we were just like two friends having a drink at the bar watching football. But we never watched the football.'

'How did the relationship develop?' Lottie asked, when it appeared he was not continuing.

'James invited me to his cottage. We had the most beautiful evening. He decorated the dining table with red roses and candles. I'd never experienced anything like it before. His attention to detail was exceptional. Things progressed from there.'

'Progressed how?' Lottie asked, keeping him talking.

'We became lovers. We had a future ahead of us.' Harte paused, eyes closed, then continued with an air of authority. 'James was the quietest, most inoffensive person you could meet. I can't understand why someone would do this to him. They destroyed his future. Our future.'

'Mr Harte, at the moment we are still treating his death as a suicide.'

'James had no reason to kill himself.'

'Tell me about the pictures in his bedroom,' Lottie said.

'Just posters.' He shrugged. 'Heterosexual men put up calendars of women with their tits hanging out.' He blushed. 'Sorry, but it's true. James liked his posters. There's no law against it, is there?'

'Not that I know of.'

'We were just two men in a relationship.' His shoulders slumped.

'Did you notice a tattoo on James' thigh?'

'Yes,' he said.

'Did you ask him about it?'

'He was very defensive. Told me it was none of my business. From a previous lifetime. That's what he said. A previous lifetime.'

'That's all?' Lottie asked.

'This memory, whatever it was, seemed to cause him pain so I never mentioned it again.'

Harte closed his eyes, breathing deeply.

'Are you all right? Would you like a drink? Water? Coffee?'

'I'm fine.'

'Were you with James for Christmas?' Lottie moved the interview forward.

'Yes. He drove through the snow on Christmas Eve to visit me. He was agitated, though. Annoyed that he couldn't get back for some appointment that evening but the weather was so bad he had to stay with me.'

'What appointment could he have had on Christmas Eve?'

'I've no idea. But we got to spend Christmas Day together.' Harte smiled. 'It's the happiest I've been since I stopped believing in Santa Claus.'

'When did you last see him?'

'St Stephen's Day. He went home that day. He was returning to work on December twenty-seventh.'

'Do you have a key to his cottage?'

'No. There's a place where he leaves it though.'

'Where might that be?'

'Under a stone, at the apple tree in the courtyard.'

Lottie sighed. Was everyone just like her in relation to home security?

'Could anyone else be aware of this?'

'I have no idea.'

'Was it James' key in the door last night?'

'I presume so. I didn't go near it,' he said. After a moment he continued, his voice broken. 'The minute I parked behind his car, I saw him. Hanging there.'

'Did you see anyone else around? Other cars? Anyone pass you on the avenue or the main road?'

'Nothing. I saw nothing, Inspector. Just James. Hanging there. Like . . . like . . . Oh God.' He covered his mouth with his hands, resting his elbows on the table, swallowing a sob.

Lottie wrote in her notebook, even though their conversation was being recorded. She needed to gather her thoughts.

'Do you know if he owned a small green flashlight?'

Harte shook his head. 'I don't know.'

'Why were you at his house last night?'

'We'd arranged to meet tonight . . . for New Year's Eve, but then he phoned me about Susan Sullivan's death. He sounded so upset.'

'So you decided to drive through a snowstorm?'

'Yes, Inspector, I did.'

Lottie watched him. He appeared sincere.

'Had his mood changed in recent times?' she asked.

Harte thought for a moment.

'James told me a few months ago that Susan was diagnosed with cancer. He seemed to have known her a long time but I never met her. Once I asked if he'd introduce us. He didn't.'

'Did he tell you anything else about Susan?'

'Only that she'd been through a lot in her life. He spoke as if he shared her troubles. James was like that. A sympathetic soul. Now that I think of it, he seemed obsessed with her at times.'

'Any idea why?'

'I imagine it was something to do with their work.'

'What could that be?'

'He was incensed by a vote on a council development plan. Kept saying he couldn't believe they'd rezoned something or other. I don't understand all that but I'm sure it'd be easy for you to find out. It's just a matter of knowing what to look for.'

'And therein lies the crux of the matter,' Lottie said, thinking of Kirby's bulging face, having to trawl through a morass of planning files. 'Do you have any idea when this was?'

'Not sure. Possibly June or July. I honestly don't know. It could be nothing, Inspector.'

'Leave that for me to determine,' she said. They had nothing already. What harm would another bit of nothing do?

'I have so many regrets.'

'I know the feeling,' Lottie said. She thought of all she'd buried along with Adam, feelings she couldn't cope with.

'Thank you, Mr Harte. You can go,' she said folding over her notebook, 'but I'll need to speak to you again.'

'Any time,' Harte said. He got up and walked out the door, wearing his jacket like a dead weight on his shoulders.

When he was gone, his scent remained, wrestling the air around Lottie. A bitter smell of deep loss. She recognised it and hoped Harte could mourn, putting his grief behind him. She doubted it.

And for some reason, despite all that, Lottie had a nagging doubt at his sincerity.

CHAPTER 20

'Will you sit down, Tom? You're driving me insane.'

Tom Rickard, property developer, continued pacing up and down the marble-floored kitchen, occasionally glancing at his wife Melanie. He was annoyed at his own stupidity over the call with James Brown. Even more annoyed with that detective inspector and her snooping. Melanie Rickard drained the dregs of her cabernet, went to the sink and rinsed the glass. She preferred white wine, so why had she opened his red? She was acting like a bitch because he cancelled their New Year's Eve plans without consulting her.

There was plenty of room for his pacing. Their kitchen was as large as the ground floor of a normal house. But their house was not normal. Nothing was normal where Melanie Rickard, his wife of twenty-one years, was concerned.

'What's bothering you anyway?' She dried the glass, keeping her back to him.

He didn't answer. He knew she didn't really want one. Melanie asked questions because she felt it was expected, not because she cared. She'd ceased caring about anything to do with him years ago. Of that he was sure.

The wall clock ticked the evening away, adding to the turmoil raging in his head. Melanie wanted a party. She wanted another holiday. Her wardrobe was creaking with clothes bearing designer labels and expensive price tags. She wanted everything. She got everything. He had serviced her every whim. Not any more. Everything he had was sunk in the new project. A project fast drowning in quicksand. He was sinking with it. Suffocating himself with the noose of irrecoverable debt, and now two people were dead.

He didn't know what to do. So he kept pacing. Up and down their imported Italian green marble.

When he looked up, Melanie was gone.

He needed to talk to someone. He wanted his soulmate, to feel the comfort of her arms and legs around him.

And his soulmate wasn't Melanie.

Rickard put on his coat, slipped his phone into the pocket and, wrapping a cashmere scarf about his neck, he swapped the warmth of his silent kitchen for the cold night air.

CHAPTER 21

Lottie stood outside Susan Sullivan's house. Crime scene tapes floated in the arctic breeze. She nodded at the uniformed guards sitting in the squad car. It was going to be a long cold night. She hoped they had a flask of something hot with them. She'd ordered that the house be watched for a couple of days. Just in case anyone turned up.

Darkness shrouded the house like a hooded cloak. All the surrounding homes were bathed in bright lights, some twinkling with week-old Christmas décor. She presumed the residents were chilling their champagne to ring in the new year. But the Sullivan house stood in mourning, dark windows reflecting light from the frozen snow lining the windowsills.

Before leaving the station she'd updated the incident team on the pathologist's reports and the Derek Harte interview. She left Boyd to mastermind the Jobs Book and Kirby was busy cross-referencing reports from the door-to-door enquiries. So far, nothing. No one had seen anything. Was Ragmullin the town of the deaf, blind and mute? What had happened to the valley of the squinting windows? No sign of any husband, boyfriend or even a girlfriend for Sullivan and they still hadn't located her phone or laptop.

With the team mired in paperwork, grumbling about it being New Year's Eve and the parties they were missing, she had escaped. She needed fresh air and with the cold assaulting her she had meandered along the frozen footpaths through the town, drawn to Susan's house. Experience told her there was a clue in this house. She just had to find it.

She dipped under the tape and opened the door. Flicking on the hall light, she felt the house creak and a radiator rattled somewhere upstairs, then settled. The house was warm. Heat on a timer, she concluded. As she entered the kitchen a hum from the refrigerator sounded in an otherwise silent room.

Looking around, Lottie wondered how it could be in such a state compared with the bedroom upstairs. It was as if two different people inhabited the house. Was Susan bipolar or schizophrenic or what? Could it be something to do with Susan's childhood?

When she opened the fridge, the internal light brightened up the kitchen. She pulled open the tiny freezer drawer at the top. Tubs of Ben & Jerry's ice cream stared back at her. Neatly lined up, never to be eaten.

She closed the drawer and looked through the rest of the fridge. Half a block of red cheese, hardened at the edges. Milk and the remains of a red onion. Unopened packet of sliced ham and two bars of chocolate. Behind the milk, a carton of orange juice. The tray in the bottom held green peppers and half a head of cabbage.

Before she closed the door, she opened the freezer drawer again. Removing the ice cream tubs she noticed a bag of ice. It was a plastic freezer bag, with paper inside. Pulling on a pair of latex gloves, she extracted the bag. Frozen solid. Through the frost she could see it was cash. The top note was a fifty. Jesus, if they were all fifties, there must be at least two thousand euro in it. More even. What was Susan Sullivan doing hiding money in her freezer? A holiday fund? But why would she have one of those if she was dying? Lottie wanted to count it but she'd have to wait until it defrosted.

Kirby and Lynch! How did they miss this? What else had they missed?

She looked around for something in which to carry the frozen package, then decided it'd be sensible to leave it where she found it. Forensics would need to examine it.

Returning the bag of money to the fridge, Lottie closed the door. At the window she pulled down the blinds and switched on the light. She looked in all the cupboards. Old-style teak, caked in grease. Noticing nothing else unusual, she switched off the light and closed the kitchen door.

Glancing into the sitting room at the stacks of yellowing newspapers, she quelled an urge to look through them. They would probably reveal nothing of interest to their investigation, only a collection of clutter fulfilling an obsessive mind. Beyond their columns, she surveyed the room. A television, two armchairs and a fireplace. Then it hit her, what had been at the back of her mind when she first checked out the house.

It was a blank postcard. Picture on one side, nothing on the other. A house devoid of human things. Things people collected over time, things that reflected their life. Things that told you who they were, where they had been, how they lived. No books to tell you what Susan read, no photographs of people she knew or places she had visited, no CDs to depict her taste in music, no DVDs to display her film choices, no perfumes to give you a scent of the woman. Sullivan's home was a blank canvas, no reflection of her personality, her emotions, her life. Her house was a mirror of what they knew about Susan Sullivan. Nothing.

Lottie didn't need to look upstairs again. Detectives Larry Kirby and Maria Lynch would be back. This time they'd do a thorough job. Incompetence was something she could not tolerate. Her detectives were better than this. They had to be. And Sullivan's phone was still missing; their GPS tracking system had failed to turn it up.

Pulling the front door behind her, it closed with a clunk and she headed for home.

* * *

The arctic breeze had morphed into a howling wind. Snow swirled around Lottie and she picked her steps carefully. She thought of ringing Boyd to collect her, but decided against it. It was getting late and he was more than likely celebrating the end of the old year. She took the short-cut through the dimly lit industrial estate, to avoid the revellers spilling from pubs, tripping on the snowy footpaths with their wine and cigarettes.

Tall empty industrial units echoed with the wind and electric cables swung dangerously low. Facing into the blizzard she walked rapidly, cursing the elements.

The first blow caught her in the ribs, knocking her to her knees, winding her. She tried to steady herself but the pain in her side flashed through her body. What was going on? She hadn't heard anyone approach with the wind.

The second blow to her back knocked her prostrate on the ice, hands outstretched, desperately grasping for something to hold on to. Her face banged into the ground, a weight securing her down. Her throat constricted as the cord from her jacket hood was pulled tight. She struggled for breath. She was choking. He was on top of her. An image of her children flitted through her brain and the instinct to fight back took hold and her training kicked in.

She tried to bring her arms upwards, to lean on her elbow, but the assailant was too heavy. She gagged with the metallic taste of blood pooling inside her mouth. With the pain intensifying, anger coursed through her. The attacker was pulling tight on the cord. She gritted her teeth, slid an arm beneath her and swung her other elbow backwards. The hold on her neck loosened and she gulped in the cold air.

She glimpsed lights in the distance. Car lights, she thought. The pressure returned on top of her and she was captive to the blood-stained ice. She could smell body sweat as he lowered his mouth to her ear.

'Think of your children, Detective Inspector,' he said, his voice high above the wind. He landed a sharp thump on the side of her head.

She tried to turn. He struck her again.

The lights of the approaching car flashed once, then twice and she felt her body lighten as the weight holding her down disappeared. She heard the car stop, a door opening.

'You all right, missus? I think I scared him off.'

'Take me home,' she moaned.

CHAPTER 22

'She's not answering her phone,' Chloe said.

'If I'd known she was going to work this late I could've gone to a party.' Katie sounded angry. 'Anyway, you only want her for takeaway money.'

'No, smart arse,' Chloe said. 'I want us to be a family tonight.'

'Try the station,' said Sean. 'And stop fighting or I'm going to bed.' He switched off the television.

'Hey, I'm watching that,' Katie said, raising her head.

'Will you two shut up,' Chloe said. 'Come back, Sean.'

In the hall, Lottie stared at her son. All three were at home. On New Year's Eve. Even Katie.

'Mam! What happened to you?'

Sean rushed to her. Lottie squeezed his arm and he linked her into the sitting room. She sat into the armchair beside the unlit fire. The heating appeared to be running full blast. She didn't care.

'Mother? I was just phoning your work,' Chloe said. She and Katie stood, staring.

'It's nothing to worry about. Someone jumped me in the industrial estate.' Lottie rubbed her hand across her nose. It came away with blood on her fingers.

'I'll call a doctor,' Chloe said, concern traversing her young features.

Lottie wiped blood from her face with trembling fingers.

'I'll be fine. I don't think anything's broken.' She hoped her nose wasn't; if it was, she knew the pain would be a whole lot worse.

Three worried faces, all looking at her.

'It's okay. Honestly. I just need to wash.'

She didn't want to think what might have happened had the taxi not arrived on the scene. The driver had told her he'd only seen the back of the attacker running toward the old carriages down by the disused railway track. He wanted to follow. She just wanted to get home. To see her children. To make sure they were safe. The taxi driver had duly obliged.

'I'll get you a cup of tea,' Chloe said.

'I'll help,' Katie said.

Sean sat on the arm of the chair.

She was glad to have her children around her. They were safe and so was she. For now.

'No tea,' Lottie said. 'I need to go to bed. We'll get a takeaway.'

She looked around. No handbag. The mugger had fled at the screech of the car brakes but had not got away empty handed. He wouldn't get rich on the contents of her bag. Thank God she hadn't been foolish enough to bring the cash from Susan Sullivan's freezer. Small mercies and all that, she thought.

'There might be enough change in the kitchen jar,' she said, gingerly rising from the armchair.

Slowly, she climbed the stairs to her bedroom, ignoring the clutter of clothes covering the floor and hanging on the open door of the wardrobe. After undressing tentatively she stepped into the shower, allowing the hot spray to ease her pain and cleanse her cuts.

Towelling down her warm flesh, she appraised her wounds. At worst she had a broken rib, at best bruised ribs. A deep cut lacerated the bridge of her nose. No break. Another fainter cut had settled beneath her left eye. She'd be some sight tomorrow, she figured, when the bruising erupted.

Her arms ached and her throat was raw, the skin on her neck already turning purple. He'd almost succeeded in strangling her. She consoled herself – she had fought back. Desperately. Why had Susan Sullivan not fought to save herself? Jane Dore had reported little or no defensive wounds. What kind of person has no instinct for survival? Lottie could not understand it.

She threw her clothes from the bed to the floor and eased her head on to the pillows. Needing someone to talk to, besides Boyd, she scrolled through her phone contacts for the number of her long-time, occasional friend. Lately, she hadn't seen much of Annabelle O'Shea, one of her oldest friends and the exact opposite of Lottie. Gym, yoga and whatever other fancy exercise you could think of – Annabelle engaged in it. Lottie couldn't be bothered wasting so much time on herself. Voicemail instructed her to leave a message. She didn't. Hanging up, she pulled the duvet over her aching body and wished for sleep.

She lay awake a long time, her hand on the Argos book, thinking of James Brown with his pornographic bedroom walls and Susan Sullivan with a sitting room full of newspapers, a fridge with frozen money and a house depicting nothing of her life. And her own faceless attacker. All the time, reverberating in her brain, were the words 'think of your children'. She had been targeted. Why?

For the first time in years, Lottie felt fear itching beneath her skin.

* * *

Boyd worked late, reading the pathologist's report to the sound of the cathedral bells signalling the dawn of a new year.

He opened the online planning files and began cross-referencing details against the ghost estate files. Methodical, painstaking work. Work he was good at. It kept his mind off other things. Off other people. Off one person in particular.

Succeeding in finding nothing, he went home and powered up a sweat on his turbo bike. His frustration helped pump adrenaline until his chest almost caved in.

He gave up, lit a cigarette and sat on his stationary bike, smoking. Intermittently, the room lit up from the effervescent fireworks in the night sky. And he was alone.

* * *

At four a.m. Lottie's mobile phone binged. She squinted at it on the locker. The number was unfamiliar.

A text. May the New Year bring you peace.

She texted back. Who is this?

A few seconds later, a reply popped up.

Father Joe.

She smiled and fell into a fitful sleep; dreamed of blue eyes, crosses in circles and a rope tightening round her throat until she awoke bathed in a cold sweat. She dragged herself into the shower, stood beneath hot water, then, wrapping a towel loosely about her bruised body, she lay on the bed.

Sleep did not return.

* * *

January 1st 1975

The girl woke up with a terrible pain in the bottom of her stomach.
She dragged herself out of bed and screamed as the agony increased in waves.

'Holy Mother of God. Oh, Jesus Christ,' she shouted.

Her mother ran into the room.

'What's all the commotion about?'

She stopped at the sight of blood and water pouring down her daughter's legs. All of a sudden she knew what was going on. She blessed herself then went to the girl. She put her lying on the bed.

'What have you done?'

The girl screamed. And screamed again.

Her mother looked on in horror while her daughter produced her one and only push and her grandchild entered the world.

The baby cried.

Both of them cried.

Neither of them knew what to do.

So they cried some more.

'I'll get a midwife,' her mother said. 'And the priest. He'll know what to do.'

'No!'

The girl screeched, a shrill and terrified wail of terror.

DAY THREE

1st January 2015

CHAPTER 23

'Happy New Year to me,' Lottie said as she raised the kitchen blinds.

With the darkness outside she stared at her bruised image reflected in the glass. She ran her fingers through her hair, thinking she needed to get it cut and coloured. The chestnut dye was growing out and a thin grey line was beginning to appear on the top of her head. But she had more to worry about than looking like a badger. Shit, she looked like she'd gone ten rounds with Ragmullin's Olympic boxer.

Checking her phone, she read the night-time text from Father Joe Burke. She hadn't replied. Just as well. He's a suspect, she thought.

Busying herself tidying the kitchen, she squashed up empty Coke bottles and folded the pizza box into the recycling bin. Two nights in a row her children had eaten junk food. It wasn't good enough. She had to go to the supermarket. She hoped Tesco would be open, it being New Year's Day and all that shite. She opened cupboard doors making a mental note of what she needed. Everything.

Then she remembered she had no wallet, no cards, no nothing.

Placing the last two Weetabix in a bowl, she sat at the table thinking of her attacker. Could he be the one who murdered Sullivan and Brown? Was he trying to kill her? She shook off that notion. She had to think of her children.

Her children. Chloe was under pressure at school. Katie struggled with continuous college assignments and had locked her out mentally since Adam's death. And Sean, spending all day long on his PlayStation. Lottie despaired. How could she cope with them and her job? Maybe she should ask her mother to look in on them. But their last row was still too raw.

Sighing, she poured coffee into a mug and milk on her cereal. It plopped out in thick lumps. Gagging at the sour smell, she sipped black coffee. A cigarette would be nice, she thought, as the pain in her head intensified. She searched a drawer for painkillers, found a Xanax, so she swallowed it instead. Hugging her aching sides, she wished her pain away.

Her children would probably sleep until midday. A rude awakening awaited them next week. Back to school.

For her – work.

* * *

By the time she reached the station, Lottie's mood was as cold as the icy wind whipping her face on the walk into work.

'Kirby. Lynch,' she commanded, pulling off her jacket as she entered the cramped office.

The two twisted round in their chairs, looked at each other, then back at Lottie.

'My office!' Shit, this is my office now, she thought.

Boyd was sitting at his desk, chatting on the phone. He looked up at her, then at Kirby and Lynch standing to attention. Kirby tapped his pocket for a cigar he couldn't smoke inside the building, his head looking like it was bulging with a hangover, and Lynch had pulled her hair into a sober ponytail. Lottie nodded at Boyd to disappear. He hurriedly finished his call.

'Jesus, what happened to you?' he enquired.

'Nothing.' Lottie threw her jacket on the back of her chair, avoiding his intense gaze.

'Doesn't look like nothing to me. Did you walk into a couple of ladders down the hall?'

'I'll tell you later.'

'I wouldn't like to see the other fellow.'

'Give it up, Boyd. It was just some mugger in the industrial estate, down past the old grain store. Probably one of the railway junkies looking for money. Got my handbag.'

'Are you all right? Did you report it?' he asked. 'Don't suppose you did.'

'It's nothing to get uptight about.'

'Tell me where it happened and I'll get someone to take a look for your bag.' Boyd sat on the edge of her desk.

Lottie relented. 'Last night, I went to Susan Sullivan's house to have another look around. That led to something I wish to discuss with these two. Walking home through the industrial estate, I was jumped.'

'Why didn't you report it?'

'That's what I'm doing now.'

She filled Boyd in on all the details she could recall, gave him the taxi driver's card to follow up on anything he might have seen.

'And check in with the uniforms who were guarding Susan Sullivan's house in case they noticed anyone around last night.'

'I'll be back in a minute,' Boyd said, getting his jacket.

A photocopier whined unattended, shooting out paper which was accumulating at an alarming rate. Lottie switched it off and turned her attention to Maria Lynch and Larry Kirby.

'Those cuts look bad. You sure you're okay?' Lynch asked, concern etched in her eyes.

'I'm fine.' Lottie folded her arms, standing directly in front of them. 'How well did you search Susan Sullivan's house?'

'Thoroughly,' the two detectives replied in unison.

Lottie looked from one to the other.

'Not *thoroughly* enough. Who checked the fridge freezer?'

'I did,' Kirby volunteered, a worry line furrowing a trough along his forehead. Last night's whiskey was oozing perspiration bubbles into the ridges. His breath stank. Lottie took a step back.

Lynch's shoulders dropped and her mouth creased into a straight line.

'Guess what? No, don't even try,' Lottie said, as Kirby opened his mouth. 'I found a bundle of money, quite a lot actually, frozen in a bag. In the freezer. What do you say about that?'

'Someone must have put it there after we'd searched,' said Kirby, struggling. 'All I saw was ice cream.'

'Did you look behind the ice cream? Did you take out the ice cream?'

'No, I didn't.'

Kirby traced an imaginary line on the floor with his black leather, unpolished shoe.

'I'm disappointed in you,' Lottie said. 'Both of you.'

A sharp pain wrenched her ribs, forcing her to sit down. Her mood for anger subsided. She was too sore to be annoyed any longer.

'In future I don't want anything like this to happen. You don't need me to tell you, botched searches are unacceptable.'

'Yes, Inspector,' Lynch said. She was biting her lip but her eyes were flaring anger.

Lottie knew Detective Lynch would not want this black mark against her impeccable record. It could spell trouble down the career line, but Lottie was the direct line manager and that meant reprimanding people for unacceptable work. There were more important things going on here than Maria Lynch's ambitions.

Kirby said nothing, just hung his head with a hangdog expression. Lottie understood then how a twenty-something year old might fall for him – probably felt sorry for him. She dismissed them both and they scuttled off.

Boyd returned and threw a pharmacy paper bag on her desk.

'Don't take them all at once,' he said. 'You're lucky Boots is open today.' He switched on the photocopier before sitting at his desk.

'You're a lifesaver.' She quickly swallowed three painkillers. 'Haven't you got work to be getting on with?' she asked, logging on to her computer.

'Indeed I have,' he said and began noisily banging his keyboard.

Her chin resting on her hand, Lottie sat watching Boyd and listening to the photocopier in the otherwise quiet office. Suddenly, she felt the need for someone to hug her, to hold her tight, to soothe away her aches. She almost reached out to Boyd, but didn't.

CHAPTER 24

The Ragmullin grapevine was wrapping itself into knots but Cathal Moroney, a journalist with RTE, the national television station, couldn't find anything worth reporting. He flicked through his empty notebook. He was hungry for a new angle on the murder and suspected suicide.

He'd interviewed some of the victims' colleagues but they knew nothing. He wanted the human-interest story; a story to awaken his tired audience. He wanted the scoop of a lifetime.

He kept asking himself the question everyone was asking. Were the deaths connected through planning? And was Brown murdered? If it turned out to be two murders, was there a serial killer stalking this tired midlands town? He began to sweat at the thought. Now that would be a story and a half.

Warming his hands around an early morning cup of coffee, he listened to the gossip in McDonald's. Everyone had an opinion. Everyone was talking shite.

He noticed a huddle of gardaí at a table in a corner near the toilets. Everyone knew Cathal Moroney, but this group was so engrossed in their own conversation, they didn't notice him. He slid into the dimly lit corner behind them and sipped his coffee. Listening. And he heard. Something new. It just might be the story he was waiting for. He just needed a formal comment.

He checked his phone and contacted his source.

* * *

Lottie planted her two feet on her desk and rested her head into her interlocked hands. The painkillers had eased her throbbing ribs and she'd stuck a plaster over the cut on her nose.

The preliminary technical reports did not offer much hope. DNA was found in the vicinity of Sullivan's body. Masses of skin cells and hair. All logged, ready to be cross-referenced. And probably weeks before any results, if ever.

James Brown's forensic reports were not in yet so she glanced through the preliminary autopsy reports. Maybe he did kill himself, she thought with a yawn, but what about the grazed fingers and contusion on the back of his head?

Her jaw ached and pain weakened her knees so she dragged her feet to the floor and stood up, attempting a stretch. She felt hungry. Maybe Kirby could get her a Happy Meal. She eyed the grumpy detective across the room. Maybe not.

Her phone rang.

'Inspector?'

'Yes, Don,' Lottie answered the front desk sergeant.

'Cathal Moroney from RTE is here for a statement. Superintendent Corrigan is delayed this morning but he said you're to talk to him. He's okayed it with the press office. I put Moroney in the conference room. Will you talk to him?'

No, I won't, she wanted to say.

'I'll be right there,' she sighed and headed down the stairs.

* * *

'Inspector.' Moroney flashed his megawatt TV smile. 'I'm delighted you could give me a few moments of your precious time.'

'A few minutes is all I have, Mr Moroney.'

'Call me Cathal,' he said, taking her hand in his, forcing a contact Lottie had not offered. The cameraman, standing behind Moroney, adjusted his lens and pointed it towards her.

'What can I do for you?' Lottie withdrew her hand as quickly as politeness allowed. She resisted wiping it against the leg of her jeans. Despite his disarming smile and hail-fellow-well-met act, there was something decidedly unpleasant about Moroney in the flesh, something she couldn't put her finger on, but she felt it nonetheless.

'Inspector Parker, what can you tell me about the rumours that James Brown was an active paedophile?'

Blindsided, Lottie blinked in confusion. 'I . . . what are you talking about?'

'That he was involved in some ritualistic, sadistic psycho-sexual—'

'That's enough,' Lottie snapped. 'You, turn that camera off. Now.'

'Perhaps you'd like to comment on the large amount of money found in—'

'Off. That's an order.'

'All right.' The man lowered his camera.

'I don't know what kind of game you're playing here, *Mister* Moroney,' Lottie jabbed a finger into Moroney's smug face, 'but from now on you can wait for a press office release like everyone else.'

She turned and made her way to the door.

'Oh, Inspector?'

She paused, her fingers on the door knob.

'What?'

'Your face, you got any comment on that?'

'Yes.' Lottie turned to him. 'You don't want to see it any time soon. And you better believe me on that.'

She left the room and hurried down the corridor, furious with herself, Corrigan, Moroney and everyone else. Even though Moroney's information was twisted and totally inaccurate, someone had said something they shouldn't have. A rat, she thought, great. They had a bloody rat.

CHAPTER 25

The incident room was a den of voices swearing and groaning when Lottie entered. With all leave cancelled, it looked like everyone had turned up to work.

Some detectives muttered in hushed tones on phones, while a few chatted unaware they were impinging on others' space. They all appeared to be individuals in the midst of chaos. This was her team, working with a common purpose, gathering information, searching for a clue, for anything. With such large numbers, it was inevitable idle chatter would reveal restricted information and it in turn would get contorted by the media. She presented a mini speech to the assembled troops about keeping their mouths firmly shut.

'Anything further on the cash?' she asked Kirby.

'Forensics has it now. Two and a half grand. In the fucking freezer!'

'We need Sullivan and Brown's bank records. There may be more than two and a half grand at stake here.'

'I have documents we found at both houses,' Maria Lynch said. She pulled down a file and rummaged through it. 'Here's a bank statement belonging to James Brown. Hold on a minute.' Another file, another piece of paper waved in the air. 'And one of Susan Sullivan's.' She placed both on Lottie's desk triumphantly.

'Same bank,' Lottie said, flicking through the documents. Boyd had a look.

'I'll ring Mike O'Brien in the bank. I know him a little,' Boyd said. 'He's the local area bank manager.'

'Good,' Lottie said. 'Kirby, examine James Brown's phone again. Find other instances when he called the developer, Tom Rickard. I don't like that ostentatious bastard. And where's that warrant for Rickard's phone records?'

'We need probable cause to do that.'

'Brown called him before his alleged suicide. Cause enough for me.'

'Okay,' Kirby said, doubtfully.

'Rickard's up to his neck in something,' Lottie said. 'If not murder, I guarantee he has something unsavoury cooking and I'm going to stop him before his pot boils over.'

'Swallow a cookery book?' Boyd asked.

Lottie ignored him and asked Lynch, 'The tattoos, anything on them?'

'I've scanned the images into the database and googled them. So far nothing. When the shops open tomorrow I'll try that tattoo place in town.'

'And James Brown's laptop?'

'Porn sites,' Kirby interjected. 'No evidence of any paedophilia. We're documenting his emails. Still no sign of Sullivan's laptop or phone. They could be at the bottom of the canal for all we know at this stage.'

'Keep at it,' Lottie said.

She glanced over at Boyd. 'What did the pharmacy have to say about Susan's doctor?'

'I'll follow it up now,' he said, swearing under his breath.

'And I need to know what all that cash is about.'

'We're buried under a mountain of paperwork, you know,' Boyd muttered.

'Yes, I know. I also know we have nothing,' Lottie said. 'Nothing.'

She scowled at the three detectives before storming out of the incident room. She needed to find space to dampen her temper. Damn Cathal Moroney and his gutter journalism. Maybe that was a bit unfair, but this was her own hometown and she didn't know what was going on.

She stood on the station steps, inhaling breaths of cold January air. Across the snowy road, the majestic cathedral stood tall, once open and inviting, now an enforced no-go area. Taking another deep breath, hurting her ribs in the process, Lottie returned inside, shaking the weariness from her shoulders along with flecks of snow.

She needed coffee.

* * *

Superintendent Corrigan pounded down the corridor as fast as the builders' ladders would allow. He burst into the office, mobile phone in his hand.

'Inspector Parker. Get your arse out to Bishop Connor's house.'

Projectile spit landed on his prey. Lottie steadied her mug of coffee. What now?

'Yes, sir,' she said, not feeling a bit like the lead detective on a murder case.

'How'd it go with Moroney?' he asked.

'Fine sir. Brief.'

'Good.' He peered at her. 'What the hell happened to your face?'

'Mugging, sir.'

'Do you need stitches?' he asked, eyeing the plaster askew on her nose.

'No, I'm fine.'

'You don't look fine to me.' Corrigan turned to leave.

'Sir, what am I seeing Bishop Connor about?' She struggled into her jacket.

'He will explain.'

And Corrigan was gone.

'Fine? Wait until he hears what really happened,' Boyd smirked.

'We'll cross that bridge when we come to it. Come on, I need a lift.'

'What am I now? Your chauffeur?'

'You know what, Boyd? You can fuck off.' Lottie pranced out of the office, leaving Boyd shouting after her.

'What did I say now?'

CHAPTER 26

The bishop's house, built eight years ago on the edge of Ladystown Lake, six kilometres outside Ragmullin, defied local logic. How did he get planning permission in such a scenic area?

Lottie studied what she supposed might be a genuine Picasso painting hanging over a white marble fireplace. Money oozed. Whose money?

After an impatient ten-minute wait, she followed a silent young priest along a marbled hallway to a gold-handled door. He opened it and she stepped on to a deep-pile, cream wool carpet. The priest closed the door behind her.

'Inspector Parker, is it?' Bishop Connor spoke without raising his head of short black curly hair. Sitting at his desk, he wrote on a page, a gold pen clutched between long fingers. Did he dye his hair? she wondered. She presumed he was about sixty-five years old but he looked very healthy and fit, she noticed.

'Yes.' She stood with her hands in her pockets. He continued to write.

'You may sit,' he commanded. 'Be with you in a moment.'

She sat and dug her short nails into the palm of her hand, to keep herself grounded.

He signed the page with a flourish and looked up at her from beneath piebald eyebrows.

'I know your mother. Lovely woman.' He turned over the page and placed his pen on top of it.

Lottie didn't doubt this for a minute. Everyone knew Rose Fitzpatrick.

'Unfortunate incident years ago with your father's suicide—'

'Yes, it was,' interrupted Lottie.

'Was it ever discovered why he—'

'No.'

'And your brother. Any news on that front?'

'You wanted to see me?' She ignored his inquisitive small chat. Her family's dysfunctional history was no concern of his.

'I play golf with Myles, Superintendent Corrigan. When weather permits.'

She remained silent. Was he trying to make conversation?

'Thank you for coming by so promptly,' he said.

'Superintendent Corrigan said it was urgent. How can I help you?'

'I'm afraid Father Angelotti is missing.' His face was deadpan serious.

'Who?'

'A visiting priest.'

'Visiting? From where?'

'Rome. Arrived in December.'

'And he's missing?'

'Yes, Inspector.' He leaned back, folding his arms. 'Missing.'

'Can you explain the circumstances of this disappearance, please?'

'There is not much to tell. He is not here any more and has not returned to Rome.'

'When did you realise he might be missing?' Wondering what this was all about, Lottie pulled her notebook from the depths of her jacket but couldn't find a pen.

'I have not seen him since before Christmas.'

Lottie raised an eyebrow. 'And you're only reporting it now?'

'I did not know he was missing. One of the priests here became concerned after looking everywhere for him and took it on himself to inform the gardaí. I probably would not have done so. But what is done is done.'

'You have a missing priest and weren't going to report it?'

'Father Angelotti's disappearance has been a terrible shock for me.'

'I'm not sure how much priority I can give to a missing person. We're very busy at the moment.' Logistics whirled through Lottie's brain.

'Myles will see that it gets the priority it requires,' he emphasised.

'I'll do my best.'

'I am sure you will. I appreciate this very much. Thank you, Inspector.' He nodded to the door, dismissing her.

Lottie had no intention of leaving. She picked up his pen and wrote the missing priest's name in her notebook.

'I need to ask you something,' she said.

'Go ahead.'

'Did you know Susan Sullivan?'

'Who?'

'The woman who was murdered in the cathedral.'

Bishop Connor paused, his eyes stony green marbles.

'So tragic,' he said. 'Poor woman. No, Inspector, I did not know her. I run a large diocese. Ragmullin parish, as you no doubt know, has over fifteen thousand people. I only know a handful.'

A handful? Golf buddies?

'I thought . . . maybe she played golf or something,' Lottie said.

'Really? Are you being smart with me?' he asked.

'Of course not,' she lied. 'I'm having difficulty finding people who knew her. She was killed in your cathedral and, as you now have a missing priest, it's just occurred to me, maybe there's a connection.'

'I cannot think of one reason to connect that murder with my missing priest.'

'Tell me about Father Angelotti. Why was he here?'

'He was sent over from Rome on a sabbatical. Personal problems.'

'Problems?'

'A crisis of identity or something. I was not privy to the details.'

'Had he any prior connection with Ragmullin?' She tapped the desk with the pen. With a name like Angelotti, probably not.

'I do not know, Inspector.'

'Why send him here then?'

'Maybe the Pope stuck a pin in a map?'

Lottie stared at him, dipping her chin to her chest, widening her eyes.

'I apologise,' he said. 'There was no need for that. Father Angelotti was entrusted to my care and now I cannot find him.'

'I need his personal details and I'll see what I can do.'

'He is thirty-seven years old. Of Irish extraction, based in Rome, studying a doctorate at the Irish College. Apparently, in recent months, he began questioning his vocation, his sexuality. That sort of thing. His superiors felt he needed time out and sent him here.'

Lottie wrote quickly in her own shorthand, then looked up. 'When did he arrive?'

'December fifteenth.'

'What frame of mind was he in?'

'He said little. Stayed in his room most of the time, from what I gather.'

'Can I have a look?'

'Where?'

'His room.'

'What good will that do?' The bishop's eyes were alert, his brow creased.

'Normal procedure in a missing persons case.' Lottie noticed his changing expressions.

'Do you have to do it now?'

'No time like the present,' she said.

He lifted his phone, punched one digit. The young priest entered.

'Father Eoin, show Inspector Parker to Father Angelotti's room.'

'Thank you,' Lottie said, rising from her chair.

'Can you treat this investigation with the utmost discretion?' Bishop Connor asked.

'I am always professional in my work. You've no need for concern.' Except when Cathal Moroney catches me on the hop, Lottie chided herself.

The bishop stood and shook her hand quickly. 'I will be waiting anxiously for news.'

'As soon as I know anything, I'm sure you will too,' Lottie said, with a huge dose of sarcasm.

* * *

Father Angelotti's room was sparse but functional; magnolia painted walls and a red lamp burning beneath a picture. A scowling Jesus with a burning heart.

Lottie pulled on latex gloves and scanned the room. A single bed with plain brown covers. A wardrobe and dressing table. En suite bathroom. Shaving bag, razor, toothbrush and paste, shower gel, shampoo and a hairbrush. One jacket, five black shirts, two sweaters and two trousers hung in the wardrobe. He hadn't intended to stay long, she thought. The dressing table drawers contained underwear, plain and nondescript. A faint smell of stale tobacco smoke hung in the air. A laptop was the only item on the table. Powered off.

The young priest stood at the door. She felt his eyes following her moves.

'Father Eoin?'

'Yes.'

'Did you know Father Angelotti?' she asked, bagging the hairbrush. Might be needed for DNA. With all that had happened she couldn't discount anything.

'Not really. He didn't say much. Kept to himself. Stayed in his room most of the time.'

'Did he have a mobile phone?'

'Yes.'

'It's not here. When did you last see him?'

'I'm not sure. He was excused duties. We were busy with the lead up to the Christmas ceremonies, so I hadn't many dealings with him.'

'You've no idea where he could be?' Lottie pressed.

'None whatsoever.'

'Did you report him missing?'

His face coloured slightly.

'I thought it odd,' he said. 'That's all. I mentioned it to Bishop Connor. He didn't appear concerned.'

'Why were you, then?'

'After that woman's murder, Susan Sullivan . . . I wondered where he could be,' he said, opening the door. 'Are you finished? I've things to do.'

'I think there's something you want to tell me?'

'I was anxious. Nothing else.'

Lottie picked up the laptop. 'Can I take this?'

'Sure,' he said and ushered her out the door.

CHAPTER 27

At the station, Lottie ordered a complete appraisal of the priest's laptop and logged the hairbrush for DNA analysis. Just in case of the worst.

Sitting at her desk she opened the bottom drawer and from beneath a mess of files, extracted a worn, yellowing Manila folder. Taking a deep breath, she opened it and scrutinised the faded photograph; an image which could not hide the dimpled chin, too wide eyes and spiked hair sticking up on top of his head. Whenever she looked at the picture, Lottie imagined the boy had been due a haircut. A school photograph, taken on one of the few days he had attended.

'What are you looking at?' Boyd asked, placing a mug of coffee at her elbow.

Lottie slammed the file closed and moved the mug over on top of it.

'You didn't answer my question.' He perched himself on the edge of her crowded desk.

Two pens fell to the floor. She returned the file to its resting place, banged the drawer shut and sipped her coffee.

Boyd picked up the pens and lined them neatly by her keyboard.

'It's that missing kid from the seventies, isn't it?'

'You've plenty of work to be doing without spying on me.'

'And you've enough work without resurrecting cold case files. What's your obsession with it?'

'None of your business,' Lottie said, tossing the pens across the desk. She noticed one of them belonged to the bishop.

'That file should be in a museum for restoration work; you have it thumbed to within an ass's roar of its life.'

'Get lost.' She darted him an irritated, scrunch-eyed glare.

Boyd sauntered over to his neat desk. Lottie hastily tidied her own, stacking files and throwing crumpled paper into the bin. She typed up the report of her meeting with Bishop Connor and prepared a missing person's file on Father Angelotti. She duplicated this into the Sullivan murder database. They might be linked. She could leave nothing to chance. She told Boyd about Father Angelotti.

'Do you think he had something to do with the victims?' he asked.

'We better find out,' she said. And she knew someone who might have information.

'Forgot to tell you,' Boyd said, 'Garda O'Donoghue found this.' He held up her scuffed leather slouch bag.

'Where?' Lottie grabbed the bag and rummaged through it.

'Dumped at the tunnel, down by the recycling tyre depot. Not far from where you were attacked,' he said. 'Your wallet and bank cards are still in it, though I think he stole your cash.'

'I didn't have any.'

'Why am I not surprised?'

'You know me too well.' Lottie rolled her eyes.

She grabbed her jacket and headed off without telling Boyd where she was going.

* * *

Sitting with Father Joe, in armchairs either side of a blazing coal fire, Lottie relaxed a little.

'I didn't see Father Angelotti very often. He was soft-spoken with good English. I hope he's okay. He seemed very lost in himself,' Father Joe said.

'Now he's truly lost if Bishop Connor is to be believed.'

'Why do you say that?'

'In the few minutes I was with him, I formed an opinion of your bishop. Maybe I'm wrong, but I don't think I like him.'

'In his defence, to get into high places some people have to bark their way through a dog eat dog world. It erodes their humanity.' Father Joe paused, looking directly at her. 'I don't think much of him either.'

'Isn't that paramount to blasphemy?' she laughed.

'Something akin to it. But I'm prone to speaking my mind.' He flicked a strand of hair from his forehead. 'As far as I know, Father Angelotti was dispatched to "find himself". In other words, to figure out if he wanted to remain a priest or not. I go through that every other day, so I can't understand why he'd be sent here. Unless it was for some other reason.'

'What other reason could there be?'

'I don't know.' The blue of his eyes sparkled in the firelight. 'I could try to find out.'

'Could you?' She leaned toward him.

'The Church is overprotective, so I can't promise you anything.'

'Please try,' Lottie said.

His lips curved in a conspiratorial smile. 'You don't have to tell me if you don't want to,' he said.

'Tell you what?' She blushed, flustered.

'Your face?'

'I was mugged last night. These things happen.'

'I suppose they do,' he said. 'You're a very interesting woman, Inspector Parker. I hope you don't mind me saying this, but the bruises add to your intrigue.'

An unwelcome flush crept up her injured face.

'You did tell me you speak your mind,' she said with a smile.

Her phone rang. Corrigan. The smile slipped down her face. Shit and double shit.

'I have to go,' she said.

'You're not going to answer it?'

'Believe me, I know what it's about.'

* * *

'You're an imbecile. You know that?'

Superintendent Corrigan wasn't shouting. He was talking in a soft calm voice. Worry time.

'Cathal Moroney twisted the information,' Lottie said.

'And how did he get the information to twist? Answer me that.'

'With such a large team, it's hard to secure against leaks, intentional or otherwise.'

'Lame excuse, Inspector.'

'Yes sir.'

'It's your fecking team. Who's Moroney's source?'

'I'll find out.'

'You do that.'

'Yes, sir. I take full responsibility for my team, but we are under a lot of pressure.'

'We're all under pressure, but at times like this we need to be at our best.'

'Yes, sir. You don't have to remind me. I know I might have messed up.'

'There's no "might" about it. You need to up your game. We want the media on our side. We use them, when and how we dictate.

Don't let Moroney snare you again. In future all press stuff goes through me.'

'No sir,' she said. 'I mean yes sir.' She didn't know what she was saying. Duly scolded, she felt worse than if Corrigan had roared at her. His calmness unnerved her.

And Lottie Parker did not like being unnerved.

She wondered who the snitch could be. Maria Lynch flashed into her mind. She'd bawled her out with Kirby over the botched search of Susan Sullivan's house. Lynch hadn't liked it one bit. Was she after Lottie's job?

* * *

She stopped at the incident room before heading home.

'That laptop was wiped clean,' Kirby said.

'What laptop?' Lottie asked.

'The missing priest's. A total wipeout.'

'You know that already?'

'One of the techies had a quick look. Said there was nothing on it. Not even an operating system. He said someone must have downloaded one of those new illegal applications. It has zilch, nada, nothing, empty . . .' said Kirby, wracking his brain for more words.

'I get the picture,' said Lottie.

'I wonder why it's blank?'

'Father Angelotti is missing and his laptop is blank. Maybe when we find him we'll solve the mystery.'

'Has this anything to do with Susan Sullivan and James Brown?' Kirby asked.

'I don't know.' She thought for a moment. 'But I think the only people with access to the laptop reside in the bishop's house and I don't like that implication.'

'Will I question them?'

'Leave it for now.' Lottie turned to go, then swivelled round on her heel. 'Kirby?'

'What, boss?'

'Thanks for that.'

'No problem.'

'It's after seven, I'm knackered. I'm going home. You should too.'

She left him standing there, scratching his head like he was lost. She knew how he felt.

CHAPTER 28

The party was pounding along at a thunderous pace even though it was still early in the evening. Bodies curled into each other and a weedy aroma hung in the air. Katie Parker ran her tongue along the narrow script tattoo on Jason's neck. She'd missed all the New Year's Eve parties but this one was making up for it.

I'm in love, she thought, as he pulled her head back and placed a spliff between her lips. She inhaled. He then brought it to his own mouth, dragging in on the end of the taper. She felt like they were floating in each other's arms, oblivious to the band, making their own music.

'Will you come to my house later?' Jason asked.

Katie stared through the smoky haze.

'I've to go home. My mother was attacked last night. She'll be worried about me.'

'Please?'

'Whatever,' Katie laughed. The way she felt now, her mother could go to hell.

* * *

Sitting down, at last, with a cup of tea, Lottie closed her eyes so she couldn't see the dirty dinner dishes piled up on the counter. Immediately her phone rang.

'Lottie?'

'I'm at home, Boyd. What do you want?'

'Guess what?'

'I'm tired.'

'I found out who Susan Sullivan's doctor was.'

'How? Who?'

'I called into the pharmacy named on the prescription.'

'About time.'

'You'll never guess.'

'Tell me.'

'Go on, guess.'

'I'm hanging up now, Boyd.'

'Grumpy boots.'

'Hanging up . . .'

'Doctor Annabelle O'Shea.'

Lottie put her cup on the floor. Her friend. Annabelle.

'You still there Lottie? Do you want to talk—'

'. . . to her? What do you think?'

'I'll leave it with you. Goodnight.'

'Boyd?'

'Yes?'

'Thanks.'

Finishing the call, Lottie glanced at the clock. Eight forty-five p.m. Not too late.

* * *

Doctor Annabelle O'Shea sat in a corner of the Brook Hotel bar, sipping red wine.

Her image looked effortless, making Lottie feel ancient. Unable to halt a twinge of jealousy colouring her cheeks, she pulled off her jacket, hoping her T-shirt was clean. She groaned. It was the one she'd washed with a pair of Sean's black jeans.

'What happened to you?' Annabelle asked, wide-eyed, inclining her head toward Lottie's face.

'My own stupidity. Some punk jumped me.' Lottie folded her jacket on the seat beside her. 'Thanks for meeting me.'

'Sorry I missed your call last night.' Annabelle spoke in a voice mirroring her look. Sharp and succinct. 'What're you having to drink?'

'Sparkling water. You're looking gorgeous as always.'

Annabelle signalled to the barman.

Her navy trouser suit sat snugly over a white silk shirt and an eye-catching silver pendant hung round her neck. With her legs crossed at the ankles, shod in a ridiculous pair of Jimmy Choo boots, Annabelle could be a model. Blonde hair, knotted high on top of her head, looked natural, though Lottie knew it was not.

'Wise arse,' Annabelle said. 'You look terrible.'

'Thanks. You know why I wanted to meet you?' Her water arrived and she sipped it.

'Feeling guilty for all the times you've stood me up over the last few months?' Annabelle joked.

'It's hard to fit everyone in.'

'How are the children?'

'They're fine. And the twins?' Lottie hated small talk.

'They spent the Christmas revising for their Junior Certificate.'

Lottie sighed. How did everyone else get the conscientious brainy children while hers lounged around listening to music or twiddling their thumbs on a PlayStation?

'I suppose Super-Dad is as efficient as always.' Lottie knew Cian O'Shea was the husband any woman would die for. Though she suspected Annabelle didn't share that sentiment.

'Same old Cian. God's gift,' Annabelle said with more than a hint of sarcasm.

'Lighten up. Without him working from home and running the house for you, you'd be lost.'

'That's the problem. He's always there. I never get a minute's peace. Can't even take a day off to stay at home or he's fluffing the pillows and shunting the hoover about the place. When he's not cleaning, he's working on his computer designing God knows what type of games, sound-reducing headphones clamped on and singing at the top of his voice.'

Lottie smiled wryly. She would dearly love to hear Adam's voice again, even for a minute.

'Enough about me and my lot. How are you doing?' Annabelle asked, pointedly.

'I could do with a prescription for more chill pills.'

'Lottie, it's time to start facing up to reality.'

A rush of blood surged up Lottie's face. She didn't want a lecture.

'I want to talk about Susan Sullivan.'

'Not yet,' Annabelle said, twisting round in her seat to face Lottie.

'I'm too busy for this right now,' Lottie said.

'Is your mood affecting your work?' Annabelle persisted.

'No.'

'I think the correct answer is yes.'

'Let's ask the audience,' Lottie said, but her flippancy wasn't working. 'Truthfully, I don't know,' she added.

'I told you before, you need grief counselling.'

'Feck off,' Lottie said, only half-joking.

'If you don't want to think about yourself, think of your children. You need to be in the right frame of mind to deal with their problems.'

'They're fine,' Lottie emphasised. What problems? She closed her eyes for a moment. 'No, they're not fine. I'm not fine. My house isn't fine and I fell out with my mother.'

Annabelle laughed. 'Again? Good. I always said she was a Mad Hatter without the tea-party.'

'Ah, don't be so cruel.'

'She controls you. Always did.'

'I've the upper hand now. She hasn't spoken to me in months.'

'You might have the upper hand at the moment, but for how long?'

'I don't want to talk about her.'

'And the history she buried. Your dad, your brother—'

'We're here to talk about Susan Sullivan,' Lottie interrupted. She didn't want to go down that old secret road.

'Since Adam died, you're not in a good place—'

'Mentally?'

'Emotionally,' Annabelle said and sipped her wine.

Lottie put down her glass. Picked it up again. 'So, I'm depressed?'

'Grief. It clouds your judgement of the living as well as the dead. You need time out.'

'It's been three years. Everyone thinks I'm over Adam.'

'Are you?' Annabelle raised an eyebrow. 'You'll never be fully over him. But you will learn to cope and you need to be able to give a hundred per cent to your work. Can you do that?'

'I can give a hundred and ten per cent, even if I'm knocking on the gates of hell.'

Annabelle sighed. 'Okay, I'll give you the prescription. Collect it from my office during the week. I shouldn't but it's on condition you undergo a full medical and cut down on the narcotics.'

'Add a few sleepers to the script,' Lottie chanced.

'Now you're pushing it.'

'When this case is over, I'll take a full medical.'

'And counselling?'

'I just need the pills,' Lottie said. She'd decide when she was ready for counselling. She wanted the pills, they kept her head together. One day at a time, one pill at a time. Whatever it took, to get her through the day.

'All right,' Annabelle said.

Relieved, Lottie switched the subject to the reason they were meeting. 'Tell me about Susan Sullivan.'

'God, I can't believe she was murdered. Here, in Ragmullin! Why? What's that all about?'

'That's what I'm trying to find out.'

'I don't think anything I tell you will be of help.'

'I'm trying to build up a picture of her. At this stage I've no idea what may be relevant.'

'As she's dead I presume I'm not breaking any doctor–patient confidentiality,' Annabelle said.

'When was she diagnosed with cancer?' Lottie asked, dreading the memories the C word conjured for her.

'She was my patient for the last year. Presented with abdominal pain so I sent her for a CT scan. It confirmed abnormalities on both ovaries and a biopsy tested positive for ovarian cancer. Advanced stage. I informed her of this, last June.'

'And her reaction?'

'Poor woman. She just accepted it.'

Like Adam, thought Lottie, clutching her glass tightly to stop her hand from shaking.

'I felt sorry for her, she'd such a hard life,' Annabelle said, taking a slow sip of her wine.

'Oh?'

'I advised her to see a therapist. She refused. I encouraged her to talk to me and she did, a little.'

'Tell me what she said.'

'She told me she had a baby when she was still a child herself. Her mother, a terrible woman by all accounts, made her sign it away. Susan was obsessed with finding the child. She even . . .' Annabelle looked away for a moment, biting her lip.

'What? Go on,' Lottie urged.

'Well, I suppose since Susan's dead I can say . . . She approached your mother about it.'

'My mother?' Lottie was astounded. She hadn't seen her mother in almost four months. Rose was the last person she expected to be talking about. 'Why on earth would she do that?'

'Because your mother helped deliver the baby.'

Lottie sat back, feeling a little dull-witted. Of course. Her mother, a midwife, now retired, had delivered many babies born in and around Ragmullin. She concluded Susan had grown up in Ragmullin.

'That's certainly interesting,' Lottie said. 'And do you know how she got on with her?'

'You should ask your mum yourself.'

'Maybe I'll have to,' Lottie said. 'Did Susan have any next of kin?'

'Her mother died a few years ago. I don't think she had anyone.'

Lottie sat thinking. A television channel was broadcasting a soccer match, the sound muted. Like her mind.

'Did Susan ever talk about how she got pregnant? Who the father was?'

Annabelle was silent.

'Are you going to tell me?' Lottie probed, tearing pieces off a beer mat, hoping against hope. 'It might have something to do with why she was murdered.'

'She was only a child at the time, maybe only twelve years old. All she'd tell me was that she was systematically raped from a very young age.'

'Her father? Could he have done it?'

'Lottie, I don't know who did it to her. She never told me.'

'Did you advise her to report it?'

'I did, but she wouldn't hear of it. Said it was too long ago and that she had enough to sort out in the time she'd left. I couldn't convince her otherwise.'

'I find it hard to understand how Susan coped all those years.'

'She wasn't always called Susan Sullivan,' Annabelle said.

'What?' Lottie put down her glass with a thump. 'Who . . . how?'

'I don't know what she was called before. I can only surmise that she changed her name in an attempt to obliterate her early years.' Annabelle smiled sadly. 'But changing your name cannot change the hurt. Susan carried that pain around with her, every day of her life. I think she found the cancer diagnosis something of a welcome release.'

'And then someone decided to hasten her entry to the next world,' Lottie said. She suddenly felt too warm.

'Indeed.'

'Now it's my job to find out who and why.' Lottie churned the new information over in her mind.

'And you will, Nancy Drew. Did you know I called you that behind your back, at school?'

'I knew.' Lottie wished they could talk about old times and what they remembered as good times. Memory was a strange thing, warping the past. She had learned that from experience.

'I'm sorry I can't be of more help,' Annabelle said.

'You've given me something to go on.' Lottie put down her glass and looked directly at her friend. 'What are you going to do about Cian?'

'He's driving me up the walls and back down again.'

'Honestly Annabelle! Why?'

'Fucked if I know,' Annabelle said. She rarely swore, but she could get away with it. Lottie knew Annabelle O'Shea could get away with just about anything.

'I'd say it's something to do with your mystery man.'

'Since I met . . .' Annabelle paused. 'I'm a different person since I met the man I'm now in love with.'

'You were always falling in and out of love. Who is he?'

'You're my friend but I think it best if you remain clueless.'

'I'm clueless all right. About more than your lover boy.'

CHAPTER 29

Katie draped her arms around Jason's neck and pulled him into her body.

'I'm freezing.'

'I'll keep you warm. Just wait till I get you into bed.'

'You're a creep,' she joked. He hugged her tighter and she felt a soft flutter in her stomach as he feathered her neck with his lips.

Over his shoulder she surveyed the noisy crowd behind them queuing for taxis.

'Don't look now but remember that creepy fart who was watching us in the pub the other night?'

'What about him?' he mumbled.

'He's in the queue.'

'It's a free country.' Jason turned round and leaned into the freezing air. 'Where is he?'

'I told you not to look!' Katie dragged him back. 'Now he's gone.'

'The invisible man,' Jason laughed.

'It's not funny. He's freaking me out.'

'If you see him again, tell me.'

Katie snuggled deeper into his arms and waited patiently with Jason for the elusive taxi. Somehow she didn't feel safe.

* * *

The man quickened his step once he turned the corner. That had been a close one. He was sure the girl had spotted him. He would have to be more careful in future. But it had been worth it. Just to see the boy.

* * *

Lottie couldn't sleep. Again.

Her conversation with Annabelle wrestled within her brain and confused into a knot. Her mother. The one woman who had the power to conjure up tortured memories.

Lottie closed her eyes tight. But she couldn't dim the image of Rose Fitzpatrick. Tomorrow she would have to see her.

Leaning over the side of the bed, she notched up the electric blanket, nestled deeper beneath the duvet, snuggled into the artificial warmth and drifted into an uncomfortable sleep.

Ten minutes later, she was awake. Pain cut through her ribs and her brow was on fire. She swallowed two painkillers. The pain wouldn't desist.

The events of the day were invading her night. The past, clawing its way into her present.

She needed a drink.

She really needed a drink.

She needed a real drink.

Scrunching the duvet into a ball, Lottie didn't want to revert to the unrecognisable person she'd been after Adam's death. To a time when she screwed her mouth to the neck of a wine bottle and the wine almost screwed her. Until she beat it a year ago. Still, sometimes she yearned to escape into oblivion. That desire obliterated all sense and she struggled to regain a semblance of normality. Struggling now, she fought it ferociously, twisting, turning and eventually she lost the battle.

She jumped out of the bed.

Pulling a hoodie over her pyjamas, Lottie thrust bare feet into her Uggs and tiptoed down the stairs. The kitchen clock said one thirty a.m. She took the key from the hook behind the back door and walked out on to the snow-covered garden to the shed. She wiped the white clumps from the lock. It was frozen underneath. A sign to go back to bed? She breathed on the brass. Stopped. Almost gave up. Tried again. It opened.

Flicking on the light switch, she lifted down Adam's toolbox and opened it. She eyed the bottle of vodka. Closed the lid and sat on the cold floor. One drink was never enough. She bit her thumbnail and chewed.

After a few tormented minutes staring at the toolbox, she opened it again, removed the vodka, closed the lid and, with the bottle tucked under her arm, hurried back to the house, leaving the shed door swinging in the cold night wind.

* * *

1st January 1975

She could not believe it.

He was sitting on their floral couch, in their sitting room, staring at her, while her mammy fussed with china cups and biscuits. Her daddy puffed loudly on his pipe, acrid smoke filling the void between him and the priest.

Her eyes bulged in protest. They were discussing her 'problem' like she wasn't even there. With the tea-towel in her knickers filling up with blood and goo, she held the little baby in her arms and wondered how she hadn't known it'd been growing inside her. She smiled, thinking it was a perfect baby, though the priest called it 'a fat sin with arms and legs'. How could he sit there and say such a thing?

She desperately wanted to tell them. To tell her mammy, standing there with the gold-rimmed teapot in her hand, and her daddy, sitting like a fucking eejit with his penknife chopping flakes off a tobacco bar, to tell them it was all the priest's fault.

She said nothing. Her heart was breaking into tiny pieces. She held her baby wrapped in nothing other than a towel for a nappy.

She had wanted to tell that woman, the midwife. With her smooth face and curled hair, she'd cut the cord and checked the baby's heart and whispered to her mammy to stop shouting. Almost as soon as she'd arrived, she was gone.

And now, they were talking as if she was invisible. The baby whimpered. Her tiny breast buds leaked, staining her shirt. She began to cry and they all gawked at her.

She clamped the baby to her chest. Fear, for herself and her little one, streaked through every vein in her body.

'St Angela's,' the priest said. 'That will put manners on her.'

DAY FOUR

2nd January 2015

CHAPTER 30

A man's leg was lying across her, pinning her to the bed.

Who was he? Where was she? Twisting as best she could, Lottie looked but couldn't see his face. He was lying on his stomach. Raising herself on to her elbow she winced with pain and with it came a sudden memory flash.

Shit. Shit. Shit. She'd been drinking.

She felt the tiny gum-drop tears edging out of the corners of her eyes and self-hate rose with the rotten bile lurching up from her stomach. She was going to puke.

Kicking up her legs, she dislodged his, slid out of the bed and crawled towards an open door. She reached the toilet in time to throw up.

The rancid smell of alcohol filled the bathroom as she heaved once more, before settling on to her haunches. Dressed only in her mismatched underwear, she didn't care and sat there cradling her pounding head in her hands. She only cared that she'd lost control at a time when she needed to be in total control.

A shadow fell across the doorway, then the light flicked on, blinding her.

'Would you like a cigarette?'

Boyd.

She cried in earnest then. She couldn't help herself. She hated herself.

'What have I done?' she asked, averting her eyes from his.

He eased his long body, clad only in boxer shorts, to sit beside her on the cold tiled floor.

'You were drunk and rang me to come get you, which I did. You begged me to bring you here, then you propositioned me.'

He lit two cigarettes, passed one into her quivering fingers.

'Against my baser instincts I resisted your cajoling. By that stage you weren't capable of anything other than sleep. Apart from forcibly undressing me.'

She inhaled deeply, mortification flushing her skin.

'Lottie, what's going on?' Boyd asked, blowing smoke circles in the chill air.

'I haven't a notion.'

'You need help.'

'I need to get a grip on my life.'

'You can't do this on your own.'

'Watch me,' she said.

'I am and I don't like what I'm seeing.'

'What does that mean?'

He inhaled his cigarette. Silence wrapped itself around them.

'You were crying in your sleep,' he said, eventually.

'I'll be fine,' she said.

They sat and smoked to the sound of the toilet dripping. Then he dampened the butts under the tap, threw them in a shiny bin under the sink and led her back to his bed. He tucked her in, kissed her forehead, fluttered his hand through her hair and slid in beside her. Lottie hung on to the edge of the bed, creating an imaginary line between them before falling into a soft sleep.

* * *

She awoke and sat upright. Alone. She twisted the clock to see the time: 6.38 a.m. Nestling back down into the comfort of the pillow, Lottie was thankful it was Boyd she had imposed her drunken self on and not some faceless bar pick-up. Her children! Shit. She jumped up abruptly. She had to get home before they woke.

Boyd walked in, fully dressed in black trousers with white shirt, and handed her a mug of coffee. The aroma tingled at the base of her nose. She looked into his eyes, questioning him silently.

'Don't worry. I can be discreet. Drink up. We've a long day ahead of us.'

'You're a good man,' she said. 'Thank you.'

'You've five minutes to wash and dress,' he said and walked out of the room.

'Sadist,' she said.

'It takes one to know one,' Boyd's voice echoed.

She had to smile.

She pulled on yesterday's clothes. At least she'd the sense to have changed out of her pyjamas last night. Finding a crushed Xanax in the back pocket of her jeans, she stuffed it in her mouth and washed it down with two gulps of coffee. She needed the artificial calmness to delete the night and face the day.

She picked up the pack of cigarettes and secreted them in her pocket. She only smoked when drunk. Do not go there, she warned herself and left the bedroom.

Outside, the sleet blitzed the cuts on her face before she ducked into the car.

'Drop me home first,' she said. 'I've to check in on the kids and change my clothes.'

The swishing of the wipers was the only sound in the car. Neither had much to say to each other and that which they were thinking was probably best left unsaid.

Boyd pulled up outside her house. She hoisted her long legs out of the car.

'Thanks, Boyd.'

'What'll I tell Corrigan if he looks for you?'

'Tell him I'm following up a lead.'

'What lead?'

'When I figure it out, I'll tell you.'

She closed the door with a soft thud. Time to resurrect strong Lottie. Before it was too late.

CHAPTER 31

Chloe Parker sat at the table, mascara streaking her damp cheeks. Lottie stalled at the door. Go in or run?

'I'm sorry, Chloe,' she said, entering the kitchen.

The girl ignored her, walked over to the bin, extracted the two-thirds empty vodka bottle, unscrewed the cap, emptied the remaining third down the sink, dumped the bottle back in the bin and ran up the stairs.

Lottie slumped into her chair. She'd have to talk to Chloe. Later.

She phoned her mother, knowing Rose would relish the fact that it was Lottie breaking their deadlock. She convinced herself that being in the throes of a raging hangover might help rather than hinder the forthcoming showdown.

* * *

It had taken less than ten minutes for Rose Fitzpatrick to drive across town. Now she stood at the ironing board, iron in hand, in the middle of the kitchen floor.

'Lottie Parker, you should stay at home more often. Those poor children are always starving and they haven't a stitch to wear,' she said, folding Sean's training jersey.

Lottie wanted to tell Rose that the sports top didn't need ironing but held the thought. As she'd suspected she would, her mother had taken control the minute she entered the house, without question or enquiry. Following Adam's death, Rose had tried to take his place in their lives. Interfering and controlling. Lottie suspected all this was grounded in love for her grandchildren and wrapped up in a protective streak which Rose nurtured. But everything had come to a head with their last row when Lottie had told her mother to take a hike, or words to that effect.

Standing tall, sweeping the iron over the clothes, Rose Fitzpatrick's face was a map of smoothness with just a creeper of lines at her eyes, like wilting ivy. Her hair was short, sharp and silver. At one time a monthly hair colour woman, she'd abandoned this on turning seventy, five years ago, though she still went to the salon for a weekly wash and blow-dry.

'Will I make a cup of tea?' Lottie asked, politely.

'It's your kitchen,' Rose said, running the iron along a pair of jeans, the denim like cardboard.

'Would you like a cup?' Lottie filled the kettle.

'You take a shower.' Rose folded the iron flex. 'You smell, you know. Then you can ask me whatever it is you wanted me here for.'

Lottie stormed out of the kitchen. Her mother hadn't even asked how she'd got her bruised face. She stripped off her clothes and stood under a stream of hot water until it stung her cuts. Her ribs were purple and her head ached but at least she felt clean. Pulling on a thermal vest and long-sleeved T-shirt over her jeans, she felt ready to face her.

Before going downstairs, she peered into Chloe's room. Her daughter was lying on the bed, a massive set of earphones on her head. When she spotted Lottie, the girl purposefully turned to the wall.

Glancing into Katie's room, she saw it was empty. She thought of asking Chloe where her sister was, but decided against it. Sean was in his room talking on an online PlayStation game. He'd probably been up all night.

In the kitchen, Rose was sitting at the table, holding a cup of tea. The ironing board was gone, clothes neatly piled, potatoes were hissing in a pot on the cooker, a chicken was roasting in the oven and it was not yet eight o'clock in the morning. Christmas Day. That was the last time they had a proper cooked dinner. Was this an orchestrated guilt trip by her mother? Lottie forced a smile.

'Thanks for . . .' Lottie directed her arm around the tidy kitchen.

'Isn't that what mothers are for?' Rose said. 'Cleaning up the mess their children leave behind.'

The smile died on Lottie's lips.

'So, what do you want with me?' Rose asked.

'Susan Sullivan,' Lottie said, diving straight in. She poured herself a cup of tea.

'The murdered woman? What about her?'

'I spoke with Annabelle and she told me Susan contacted you.'

'She did.'

'And you met her?'

'Yes. A few months ago. October, November maybe. I'm not sure when.'

'Go on.'

'She was trying to trace a child that was taken from her—'

'What had that to do with you?' Lottie interjected.

'Do you want to hear or not?'

'Sorry. Continue.'

'Susan's mother had refused to tell her anything about the baby. But on her deathbed, two years ago, she mentioned my name.'

'And . . .'

'She said I'd helped deliver the baby. Which wasn't true, because I'd arrived shortly after the birth. I couldn't help her back then, nor when she contacted me for information.'

Lottie twisted the spoon in her tea.

'It must be more than twenty-five years since—'

'I was a midwife? Yes, but this was way back. In the seventies. The girl was only aged about eleven or twelve. A child. Poor thing. Her name was Sally Stynes then.'

'Really? Tell me more.' Lottie stopped her idle stirring. Maybe now they could get something new with Susan's old name.

'Not much to tell.'

'What happened to the baby?'

'When she called to me, Susan stirred up old memories,' Rose said, a frown creasing a line on her brow. 'Her mother had called in a priest, the local curate. Apparently, he suggested placing the girl and her baby in St Angela's. You know the old building not far from the graveyard? Closed down now.'

Lottie nodded. St Angela's. How could she forget? They never spoke about it. But Rose was talking now.

'It was originally an orphanage run by the nuns, then it combined into a home for unmarried girls. Obviously some of the unwanted babies grew up there. The nuns also took in wayward boys.'

'A place to send wayward children,' Lottie murmured. 'That's one way of putting it, Mother.'

Rose ignored Lottie's remark.

'Of course when she met me, Susan already knew about St Angela's and the fact that the baby was probably adopted. She remembered spending time there. But she couldn't get any information from the Church about her baby. Unfortunately I had nothing new to tell her,' Rose said, with a steely resolve.

'Did you know who fathered her baby?'

'No idea. When I was in the house helping with the afterbirth, her mother was shouting at the girl, calling her a little tramp. It was very distressing, but if the girl was a tearaway, the father could've been anyone.' Rose folded her arms tightly.

Lottie recoiled from her mother's harshness and mulled over her revelations. Hopefully they would have more success finding out about Susan aka Sally Stynes. It was a coincidence that her mother had this information. Small-town people carry such secrets around with them all their lives. Coincidences were inevitable. And then again, her mother knew everyone and liked to think she knew everything. Lottie sipped her tea. A memory, deeply concealed, itched to be released.

'Do you ever wonder about Eddie?' Lottie asked, feeling brave enough to pose the question about her brother.

Rose stood up, rinsed her cup, dried it and put it in its rightful place in the cupboard.

'Eddie is gone. Don't talk about him,' she said.

Denial, thought Lottie, but she persisted. 'And Dad, can we talk about him?'

'The chicken will be cooked in another half-hour. Watch the water doesn't boil off the spuds.' Rose pulled on her coat and hat. 'You can heat everything up in the microwave for dinner this evening.'

'I suppose we can't talk about them, then,' Lottie said, wryly.

'You need a man in your life, Lottie Parker,' Rose said, hand on the door.

'What?' asked Lottie, wrong-footed.

'Boyd? Is that his name? The long, skinny one. Nice man.'

'What do you mean?'

'You know right well what I mean. And bring those kiddies to visit soon.'

Lottie wasn't keeping them away – they had made the decision themselves that they'd had enough of their meddling grandmother.

On the doorstep, Rose said, 'By the way, I saw your interview on the news.'

'And?'

'Not very impressive, madam.' She drew her hat over her ears. 'You could have masked those bruises with a touch of make-up.'

As always, her mother got in the last word.

Lottie slammed the door. She turned off the cooker, drained the potatoes and dumped them in the pedal bin. She threw out the chicken too. She was damned if she was going to eat anything prepared by her domineering mother. She would rather starve.

Her hangover was pulsating now, but she had to go to work.

CHAPTER 32

As the morning sleet eased, the temperatures rose unexpectedly.

'Listen to that,' Garda Gillian O'Donoghue said.

'To what?' asked Garda Tom Tierney.

'Snow melting.'

The sound was like a forest of humming birds, such was the intensity of the thaw. They were standing at the door of James Brown's cottage.

'Positively balmy,' Tierney said. 'A warm plus one beats minus ten on New Year's Eve.'

'I'm going for a walk around the garden. My feet are in a state of perpetual frozenness,' O'Donoghue said.

'Is that even a proper word?'

'Who cares?' she laughed and headed along the path to the back garden, enthralled by the greenery being slowly exposed through the shifting snow. The white beauty had been magical for the first few days until it became an unbearable burden. She breathed in the cool air and listened to the thaw.

As she turned, a snatch of colour under a tree caught her eye. She walked toward it, then backed away, shouting, 'Tom. Tom!'

A hand, cuffed in black, protruded from the snow.

O'Donoghue reached for the radio pinned to her chest.

* * *

By the time Lottie and Boyd arrived, the garden was a scene of organised commotion.

Lottie groaned. This was more work in three days than they'd seen in the last two years. She hadn't even had time to get her head around her mother's revelations. Boyd and Maria Lynch had met her on the station steps with the news and they'd driven to James Brown's house as quickly as the slush allowed.

She walked with Lynch around the back, both keeping their eyes peeled for any evidence that might be exposed. Boyd spoke with the uniformed officers.

Lottie spotted the SOCOs team leader, Jim McGlynn. He smirked.
'The bastard,' Lottie said.
'Who?' asked Lynch.
'McGlynn.'

He was laughing at her. Pity he wasn't under her command. She'd have him sifting pig shit for the rest of his working life, looking for invisible dioxins.

The garden was compact. A shed and a wooden table with chairs leaning against it occupied the patio area to the left of the back door. Evergreen trees bordered two sides of the enclosure, a wall at the end and snowy fields beyond. McGlynn worked the area, painstakingly removing snow and revealing the victim.

Lottie waited. Eventually the body was fully exposed. Male, face down, clothed in a black jacket and trousers. The visible hand appeared wrinkle free, with a silver ring. Pieces of glass and black plastic were scattered around and over the body. McGlynn was picking them up with tweezers and placing them in an evidence bag.

'A phone?' Lottie asked.

'Smashed to bits,' he said. 'I doubt even our best technicians will get anything from it.'

'How long has the body been here?'

'I'm waiting for the state pathologist,' McGlynn answered, sharply.

'Prick,' Lottie said, under her breath.

Jane Dore breezed on to the site suited up in her protective gear and acknowledged Lottie with a swift shake of her head.

'Someone must think I've nothing to do, they keep supplying me with bodies.'

'Agreed,' Lottie said, standing to one side while the pathologist carried out her preliminary examination.

'Appears to be strangulation,' Jane said. 'There's a ligature mark on his neck. On initial observation I can determine frozen snow under the body. It's quite possible he was killed within the last week. The arctic temperatures have preserved him in perfect condition.'

Perfect condition, except he is dead, thought Lottie. She felt like puking, her hangover unrelenting.

'Do you think this is the crime scene?' she asked and realised that if the body had been here a week, the man had been killed prior to the Sullivan and Brown deaths.

'I'll know more when I get him on my table.'

'And you'll inform me if he has a tattoo?'

'Of course,' the pathologist said and, with short, careful steps, left the scene.

Lottie's headache intensified. The body count was rising. Corrigan was boiling. The press were baying. The public were terrified and her team were no nearer any explanation for all or any of the murders. Welcome to La La Land, Inspector Parker. She scratched her head. Fucking hell.

'You okay?' Boyd was at her shoulder.

'Who is he?' she asked.

'How do I know?'

She bit back a retort and looked at Boyd. His face seemed thinner, if that were possible. 'It was a rhetorical question. The victim was more than likely killed before Sullivan and Brown.'

With the body turned over on to his back, Lottie looked at the bloated, blackened face.

'I'd estimate mid-thirties,' she said and watched patiently as the SOCOs bagged the body and removed it from the scene.

McGlynn held up a small plastic evidence bag.

'Blue fibre,' Lottie noted.

'From around the neck,' he said.

'Thanks,' Lottie said. Similar rope to that wound round James Brown's neck.

'No wallet or identification but there are two cigarette ends here,' McGlynn said, picking up one with tweezers.

'Belonging to the victim?'

'Possibly. Or his killer.' He dropped it into an evidence bag.

Lottie watched McGlynn at work for a few minutes before going into the house.

'That body isn't a million miles from the description we have of Father Angelotti,' Boyd said, trailing her inside.

'The face is unrecognisable and we've no record of distinguishing marks to check for,' Lottie said. 'We'll have to wait for a formal iden-tification. Otherwise, it's down to DNA analysis.'

'Whoever he is, someone has to be missing him.'

'There's no car,' Lottie remarked, looking out the front window. 'How did he get out here?'

'Maybe the killer drove him or he got a taxi,' Boyd said. 'Why was he here? That's another question.'

'And did Brown know him?'

'We have too many questions and not enough answers,' Boyd said. 'Find out what you can.'

'He could've been Brown's lover. He drove him here and killed him in a jealous rage,' Boyd ventured.

'I suppose now you think Brown killed this man, strangled Sullivan, then hung himself?' Lottie shook her head in annoyance.

Boyd said nothing, pulled out another cigarette and went outside to light it. Following him, Lottie stepped into the slushy yard. Her brain was a muddle.

She could do with a drink.

She settled for one of Boyd's cigarettes and told him about the conversations with Doctor Annabelle O'Shea and her mother.

CHAPTER 33

At the station they added the unknown victim and details from the scene to the incident board. Lottie supported the theory whereby visually interpreting data was more productive than information in databases which could be missed or forgotten. Not that they had much to interpret.

She assigned the task of resurrecting information on Sally Stynes aka Susan Sullivan to a detective and wondered where she could get her hands on St Angela's records. Discovering more about the institution just might reveal something about Susan Sullivan. Lottie returned her attention to the latest victim.

'If it hadn't snowed so heavily,' she said, 'the body might have been found—'

'A week ago,' Boyd interjected.

'Yes. Unless the killer was following the weather forecast, he wanted that body found.'

'And there was no attempt to cover it up.'

'Just the snow.'

'If it hadn't snowed . . .' Boyd began.

'But it did. Was it an attempt to point the finger at—'

'James Brown? When the body wasn't found, for some reason, the murderer had to kill Sullivan and Brown.' Boyd paused then continued, 'Brown could still have carried out this murder though.'

'Oh, this conjecture is pointless.' Lottie sighed with exasperation.

Looking at the board, she noticed they had no photograph of Father Angelotti. She made a quick phone call, grabbed her coat, and sidestepping Boyd, hurried out of the building.

* * *

'Hello, Sister. I'm here to see Father Burke. He's expecting me.'

The nun directed her to the room where she'd sat the first day. Lottie walked around the mahogany furniture looking at the large portraits of long-dead bishops hanging on the walls. They'd put the fear of God in you, she thought.

'Wouldn't they put the fear of God in you?' Father Joe said, walking in behind her.

'I was thinking the exact same thing.' She grinned at him. Synchronicity?

'Tea? Sister Anna will oblige.'

'No, thank you.'

'How can I help? It sounded urgent on the phone.'

'I need a photograph of Father Angelotti,' Lottie said. She didn't really need it, they had the hairbrush for DNA comparisons.

'You haven't found him yet?' He went to a computer in the corner where he printed a photograph. She could have done that herself. Wasn't it just an excuse to see him again? She shouldn't have come here. Her logic and emotion were contradictory. So was she.

Studying the photo, she wrinkled up her nose. It was possible he was the body in Brown's garden.

'Does Father Angelotti smoke?' she asked, recalling the stale tobacco smell in the priest's room and the cigarette butts at the scene.

'I don't know,' he said. 'Hold on.' He phoned someone, listened and hung up.

'According to Father Eoin, Bishop Connor's secretary, he did smoke. Why do you need to know?'

'Gathering as much information as possible.' She switched the conversation. 'What do you know about St Angela's?'

'St Angela's? Not a lot. It ceased operating as a children's home in the early eighties. I think it was a retirement place for nuns before it closed permanently. It was sold a few years ago.'

'What happened to the records?'

'I presume they were archived,' he said. 'Why the questions about St Angela's?'

'How would I go about finding out where the records are?' Lottie ignored his query.

'All very mysterious, Inspector, but leave it with me. I can do some amateur detecting for you.'

Lottie caught a glint of mischief in his eye and thought she saw the boy he once was, before the white collar of Rome shackled him to austere adulthood. She rose to leave, holding out her hand. He seemed to hold it for a second longer than necessary or was it her imagination?

'You have my number. Let me know as soon as you find anything,' she said.

'Of course I will.'

* * *

Father Joe searched the diocesan records on the local area network, using his personal password. He keyed in St Angela's.

Access denied.

Unusual.

He rang Father Eoin.

'I seem to be having difficulty finding the diocesan records database,' he said.

'Bishop Connor engaged a consultant to revamp our intranet. He wanted increased security.'

'But surely these records are available to us priests.'

'You can have my password. See if it gets you in. I'm sure Bishop Connor won't mind.'

'You're a lifesaver.'

Hanging up, he entered the new password.

He was in.

He looked at the cursor flashing on the blank screen.

There were no records relating to St Angela's.

He grabbed for his phone again.

CHAPTER 34

'You what?' Boyd exploded when Lottie told him where she'd been. 'Have you lost your mind?'

'What's *your* problem? He's sure to have avenues we don't know about.' Why was she justifying her actions to Boyd?

'You're still drunk,' he said. 'That's the only logical conclusion.'

'Lower your voice,' Lottie said, looking around to see who was listening to the interchange. Lynch and Kirby were keeping their heads studiously down.

'He's a suspect in the Sullivan murder.' Boyd paced, his long legs carrying him from wall to wall in three strides.

Her headache intensified with each step he hammered on the floor.

'I didn't tell him why I wanted the records or for that matter what records I was looking for. I need to know of their existence and current whereabouts.'

'For argument's sake, if he is the murderer, he either knows there's something you want in those records and will destroy them, if they're not already destroyed, or if he didn't know before, now he does and will destroy them anyway.'

'You're talking pure shite, Boyd.' She pulled out a chair and flopped down.

'What do you want with them anyway?' he asked, standing in front of her.

'I don't know.'

She wished she was back in her own office. At least there she could think without an audience.

'The records may have nothing to do with our case. It's just a hunch at this stage. Ticking boxes,' she said.

'Speaking of boxes, did you take my spare cigarettes this morning?' Boyd asked, throwing an empty packet in the bin.

Lottie dug the box out of her pocket and threw it at him. He caught it and marched out the door.

'Lynch?'

'Inspector?'

'I'm going out for a while.'

* * *

Lottie was convinced Ragmullin Cemetery was the coldest place in Ireland. The icy wind swirled around her and the cold sun cast a shimmering mist through the headstones. Eerie monoliths, standing in the shade of large pine trees, flung deep shadows on the graves, slowing the thaw. Crystallised snow, frosted to Christmas wreaths, added an unlikely mystical feel to the surroundings.

The wind increased momentarily and rustled the plastic wrapping on a poinsettia potted plant. The red head, blackened and wilting under the weight of snow, was a reminder that someone had visited to leave a token for those no longer alive but living on in a memory.

A tall granite cross marked the four short decades Adam had spent in this world. She hadn't visited for some time, avoided it at Christmas and now, with the solitude of the cemetery wrapping itself around her like a threadbare shawl providing little comfort, Lottie apologised to Adam.

'It's too lonely here,' she told the stone cross. 'I keep you in my heart.'

She squinted around at the other tombstones with their stories hidden deep within hewn granite. A chime tinkled in the stillness and a chill traversed her spine. Time to go. She had secrets to unearth and a killer to catch.

As she walked out through the open gates Lottie noticed the silhouette of St Angela's, across the fields about a mile in the distance, shrouded in a soft grey mist. What skeletons lay buried deep within its walls? How many lives had it damaged? She thought of Susan and her baby. She remembered another child who had disappeared a long time ago. Was he dead? Would he ever rest within the grounds of a cemetery? Was that missing boy the real reason she wanted to see the old records? She wasn't at all sure of her motives. But she knew she could never forget that child. He was missing so long, others may have forgotten about him but she hadn't. Her constant checking of his file was more than an exercise in memory, it was a means of keeping him deeply planted in her mind. The day she had joined the Garda Síochána, following in her late father's footsteps, she had promised herself she would find him. So far she had failed in delivering on that promise.

She hurried back to her car before the ghosts of the past rested heavier on her shoulders.

CHAPTER 35

Lottie sat with Boyd in front of bank manager Mike O'Brien. She'd taken an instant dislike to the man the moment he'd sat down behind his desk without as much as a hello. But Boyd knew him. They shared the same gym and coached Ragmullin's underage hurling team. Lottie wondered if he'd ever trained Sean. She knew Boyd had.

'You have the Brown and Sullivan bank statements,' O'Brien said, 'so, what else do you want from me?'

His small eyes reminded Lottie of a ferret her son had once attempted to bring home as a pet. Dark and shifty. She had the feeling that O'Brien was trying to second-guess her, puffing out his chest and desperately failing to make himself look important. Dandruff from his too-long grey hair speckled the shoulders of his black suit. Diamond cufflinks sparkled at his wrists, glittering under the fluorescent lighting. Here was a man trying to look half his age, only succeeding in looking older. Tough shit, O'Brien. But as he had led them into his office a moment ago, she had noticed his quick athletic stride. Hours in the gym paid off for some people. If you had the time, she told herself.

'Detective Sergeant Boyd analysed the victims' bank statements,' Lottie said.

'We need to know where the money was coming from,' Boyd said.

'What do you mean?' O'Brien's eyes darted between the two detectives.

'There are amounts of up to five thousand euro hitting their accounts regularly, over the last six months,' Boyd said.

'Almost thirty thousand each,' Lottie said. 'Who was giving it to them?'

'That's none of your business,' O'Brien said, a hint of arrogance sharpening his tone.

'Let me be the judge of that,' Lottie said. 'These people were murdered and this money appears to come from one account into both of theirs. I need you to tell me who paid it.'

'No,' O'Brien answered, twisting the diamonds tighter into his cuffs.

'No, what?' Lottie raised her voice.

'No, I can't tell you.' O'Brien straightened his tie. The dandruff on his shoulders seemed to intensify and a sweaty odour oozed from his armpits.

'These two people are dead,' Lottie thumped the table. 'Release the information or—'

'Or what, Inspector?' O'Brien flashed a smug smile.

'Or I'll get a warrant.' Lottie stood.

'You do that.' O'Brien pushed back his chair and stood up also. He was half a foot smaller than Lottie and maybe ten to fifteen years older than her.

'Mark my words, Mr O'Brien, we will be back,' she warned.

'You have their bank statements. I can't do anything else. Within the law.'

'Don't lecture me about the law.'

'Believe me, I wasn't trying to.'

Lottie stepped towards O'Brien and looked down at him.

'I'm beginning to think this town is full of stonewalling, obstructive *little* shits,' she hissed.

'See you at the gym later,' O'Brien said with a short wave to Boyd, snubbing Lottie.

'Maybe,' Boyd said, turning to leave.

'Sweaty little bollocks,' Lottie muttered and followed Boyd out of the office.

'Language, Inspector,' Boyd said.

'I can't believe you actually share a gym with him.'

'And he coaches Ragmullin under-twelve hurlers.'

'Thank God Sean now plays under-sixteen.'

'O'Brien's not all that bad,' Boyd laughed.

'Could've fooled me.'

With a swing of her shoulders Lottie power-walked up the street ahead of Boyd.

CHAPTER 36

As the afternoon darkened, the thaw evaporated as quickly as it had arrived and a freezing fog descended, adding greyness to the already dull atmosphere.

Boyd began compiling the warrant documents and Lottie strode down to the shop at the end of the street. She bought the newspaper and a packet of crisps.

A grainy picture of herself accompanied the headline 'Paedophile murdered?'

Moroney's interview was redrafted for all who had missed the debacle on television. She'd refused to watch it but Boyd had filled her in on her five seconds of unwanted fame. A PR disaster was how Corrigan continued to describe it, between expletives. Boyd had also related that piece of information to her. All they'd found in James Brown's house were pornographic photos and images on his laptop. Nothing to suggest paedophilia. So the most likely scenario was that Moroney had overheard idle speculation and twisted it to suit himself. Fuck him to hell, she thought.

She needed a breakthrough in the case. Something to wave as a peace offering in front of Corrigan. But what? Maybe Jane Dore had found something. She hoped so.

She got keys from the duty sergeant, took a car from the station yard and headed out into the fog.

* * *

At the Dead House, Jane Dore boiled a kettle and poured water over two camomile teabags.

'Please tell me you have something significant,' Lottie said, welcoming the tea's warmth. The forty-kilometre drive to Tullamore had eased her temper but not the thumping in her head.

'I haven't carried out the post-mortem on the body from the garden yet. However, initial tests indicate that the fibre from the scene matches the rope found around James Brown's neck.'

'Great. Evidence to link the murders. Anything else?'

'The word *Pax* is inscribed on the inside of the ring. Latin. Translates as "peace".'

'Is it a wedding ring?'

'Wrong finger, but that doesn't mean anything one way or the other.'

'A wedding ring could have the word "love" on it or even the spouse's name.' Lottie twisted her own gold band with Adam's name engraved on the inside. Her name was on his ring. In his coffin. She hadn't thought of keeping it. Another regret.

Jane said, 'I've never been married, so what do I know?' She smiled wistfully. 'Not for want of trying mind you. Never met anyone who could put up with my terrible working hours, not to mention my job.'

'He's probably our missing priest,' Lottie said, putting the cup on the desk. She took out Angelotti's photograph and showed it to the pathologist.

'Same bone structure,' Jane said and brought Lottie in to see the body. They compared the dead man's bloated face with the young vibrant one in the photograph.

'Could be him,' Lottie said, turning away from the corpse.

'I think you've found him,' the pathologist said. 'But that's just my opinion.'

'The priest's hairbrush is gone to the lab. DNA should confirm it for us,' Lottie said.

'That will take a while but I'll let you know once results are in.'

'Any estimate on time of death?'

'Going by weather reports and the preservation of the body, I estimate Christmas Eve or before. Not after, because that's when the snow and ice began in earnest.'

'It's a starting point.'

Lottie held a hand to her rumbling stomach. 'I have to get back to Ragmullin. And I need to eat.'

'The only way to cure a hangover,' the pathologist said, sipping her tea.

'Do I look that bad?'

'Yes,' Jane said with a laugh. 'I'd join you for food, but I have to start cutting. Your Superintendent Corrigan is chomping at the bit.'

'And I'm trying to avoid him,' Lottie said as she left the mortuary.

* * *

The fog had lifted and shadows swept down over the road as she drove back to Ragmullin. A silver frost glistened along the grass verges in the headlights. Once again, temperatures had plummeted below freezing.

Using her hands-free she called Bishop Connor.

'I think I've found your missing priest,' she said.

'Thank God. Is he all right?' the bishop enquired.

'He's dead,' Lottie said, crossing her fingers on the steering wheel. A little white lie might rattle his cage.

'What . . . that's awful. Where . . . how?'

'Do you have any idea why someone would want to murder Father Angelotti?'

'Murder? What are you talking about?'

'I thought you might enlighten me. Why was he really in Ireland?'

'Inspector, this is a great shock. I do not appreciate insinuations that I have been economical with the truth.'

'I didn't insinuate anything.' Lottie smiled to herself as she listened to the bishop's voice rise. Was it panic?

'Sounded like it to me,' he said. 'I will talk to your superintendent about you.'

'Join the queue,' Lottie said and disconnected the call.

* * *

Bishop Terence Connor closed his eyes and listened to the dial tone on his phone. He now had one hell of a mess to deal with.

Opening his eyes, he walked to the window and squinted into the darkness. A game of golf would be nice, but it could be weeks before the greens would be playable. Golf was his escape mechanism. To walk on the grass, hit the ball, lose himself in his strokes and putting averages. Then again, he could always drive up to the National Gallery to see the Turner exhibition. He treasured fine art. He appreciated delicate wine and gourmet food. He was a man of expensive tastes. He could afford it.

Angelotti was gone. His body had been found. That was a good thing. Wasn't it? That priest had been trouble from the day he arrived. Bishop Connor knew Rome was meddling in his affairs. So much for smokescreens about the young priest 'finding himself'. He was no fool. Angelotti was sent on a mission.

Realisation dawned on him that, after all that happened over the last few days, Angelotti's death could now give him more to worry about than dwindling parish funds and abuse compensation court cases. He could do without Inspector Lottie Parker unearthing things that didn't concern her.

He needed to talk to Superintendent Corrigan.

CHAPTER 37

The kitchen was clean when Lottie arrived home shortly after seven.

Sean sauntered in.

'You okay, Ma?' he asked. In a rare moment of tenderness, he wrapped his arms around her.

'Work pressure,' Lottie said, hugging her son.

'Chloe was like a bitch all day,' he said.

'Don't mind her,' she said. 'I've to talk to her.'

'Are you ever going to cook again? Like you used to.'

'What do you mean?' Where was her son heading with this conversation?

'You know. Proper food. Like when Dad was alive.'

Lottie's chest constricted. 'What makes you say that?'

'I loved those dinners. Actually I'm fucking starving now.'

'Don't use that language in this house.'

'You use it,' Sean said, withdrawing from his mother.

'I know I do, but I shouldn't and neither should you.'

'I'm sorry.'

'So am I.'

'I mean, I'm sorry for mentioning Dad.'

'Oh, Sean, don't ever be sorry for talking about your dad.' Lottie felt tears prick at the corners of her eyes. 'We should talk about him more often.' She swallowed the lump in her throat. 'I get it hard sometimes so I try to block out the past.'

'I know. But I think about him every day.'

'That's a good thing.'

'And I miss him.'

There were tears in her son's eyes. Lottie gave him a tight squeeze and kissed his forehead. He didn't pull away.

'You're just like him,' she whispered into his hair.

'Am I?'

She held him at arm's length. 'The fecking image of him.'

'Now look who's swearing.'

Both of them laughed.

'Okay. I'll cook something,' she said, regretting her impetuous ditching of the food her mother had cooked that morning.

'Yes!' Sean said, giving her a high five.

Lottie laughed again. He could twist her round his little finger. Just like Adam.

'Where's Katie?' she asked. 'She can give me a hand, now that Chloe's in a sulk.'

'In the sitting room. With her boyfriend.'

'Boyfriend?'

Sean escaped without answer, clambering upstairs to his PlayStation world.

Lottie headed to the sitting room. The door was firmly shut. She listened. No sound. Opened the door. Darkness. She flicked on the light.

Katie's voice roared, 'I warned you, Sean. Get out.'

'Katie Parker!'

'Oh, it's you Mam,' Katie said, untangling herself from the arms of a boy.

Lottie recognised the pungent scent in the air.

'Are you smoking weed?'

'Don't be such a prude, Mam.'

'Not in my house you won't.'

Lottie couldn't believe it. What was her daughter up to?

'And who is this? Are you going to introduce me?' She folded her arms so tight she hurt her damaged ribs.

'This is Jason,' Katie said, pulling her sweater down over her jeans. She sat up straight on the couch, wrapping her hair in a knot at her slender neck. The boy loped to a stand, his legs unsteady, Calvin Klein boxers showing at the waist of his frayed jeans. He held out his hand.

'Hello, Mrs Parker.'

He was as tall as Katie, hair to his shoulders and a black Nirvana T-shirt stretched tight over a muscled chest. A wooden stud pierced one ear and he had the general air of being unkempt.

'Katie, I need your help in the kitchen.' Lottie left the room without waiting for an objection. How was she going to handle this? Carefully, she warned herself. Very carefully.

Katie walked into the kitchen with a lazy, stoned walk.

'I don't want a lecture,' she said.

'You're old enough to know what that stuff can do to you. And, it is illegal. I could arrest you.'

Katie giggled, her dilated pupils swathed in a glaze.

'Who is he anyway?' Lottie asked, throwing potatoes into the sink under running water. The hint of vodka wafted up from the drain. She began peeling furiously.

'Jason.'

'I got that bit. Jason who?'

'You wouldn't know him.'

'Who are his parents? Maybe I know them.'

'You wouldn't know them either,' Katie said, stifling a yawn.

'Where did you get the drugs?' Lottie asked, dropping the potatoes into the pot with a splash.

'It's only a bit of weed.'

Lottie turned.

'Weed is a drug. It'll shrink your brain to the size of a pea. You'll end up in a psychiatric hospital banging your head off the wall. I'm telling you here and now, missy, you better get rid of it. And quick.'

'It's not mine. It's Jason's. I can't get rid of it.'

'Get rid of him, then,' Lottie said, knowing she was talking irrationally.

'He's my friend.'

Katie's hair fell across her eyes. Her father's eyes. All her children had his eyes. Memories of Adam had haunted Lottie all day.

'I'm concerned about you,' Lottie said.

'There's no need, Mam. I'm fine. Most of my friends smoke a bit. I'm not stupid.'

Sensing her daughter's fatigued state, Lottie decided it was not the right time to have this conversation. When would there ever be a right time? But tackling the source of this weed was definitely going on her to-do list.

'Here, chop these,' she said, taking three peppers from the cupboard.

'What are you cooking?'

'I haven't a clue,' Lottie said.

* * *

Katie left with Jason. Before the food was cooked.

'We had dinner already,' Katie said.

Lottie said, 'Where are you going?'

'Out.'

The door slammed without further discussion. Lottie sprayed air freshener throughout the sitting room, to mask the weedy scent, thinking about how quickly she was losing control of her children. One thing was sure, she would now have to monitor Katie and her friends more closely. The thought filled her with exhaustion.

She craved sleep but because of last night she was afraid to go to bed. After pouring a glass of water she sank into her kitchen armchair with her legs curled beneath her. She switched on her iPad, logged into Facebook. It had been weeks since she'd checked it.

'Holy Jesus,' she muttered when her news feed burst into life. One hundred and fourteen notifications. Probably all 'Happy Christmas' and 'Happy New Year' shit. She hadn't fourteen real friends, let alone over a hundred. There was one personal mail and one friend request red flag. She tapped the friend request first.

'What the . . .?' Lottie blinked, put her glass on the floor, kicked out her long legs and sat up straight. Susan Sullivan. The name, no photograph. Why had Susan Sullivan sent her a friend request? She glanced at the date of the request. December fifteenth. Was it even the murdered woman?

She didn't know Susan Sullivan, had never heard of her before the murder, but Susan had met with her mother. Had Rose mentioned her? Probably. But why didn't the woman contact her at the station?

She tapped 'friend accept' and accessed the woman's account. Still active.

There was nothing on the page, just like their profile of the murdered woman. She'd joined Facebook on December first. Lottie tapped in, wondering what friends Susan had.

None.

No status updates, no likes or shares either. What had possessed her to set it up? Lottie picked up her glass and sipped the water slowly, craving a shot of vodka. Maybe she could sniff the sink.

She tapped her private messages. Susan Sullivan. Again. She read the short missive from the dead woman.

Inspector, you don't know me or anything about me but I remember reading about you in the newspaper and I've spoken with your

*mother. I would like to meet you. I have some information that I
believe will interest you. I look forward to hearing from you.*

That was it.

After staring at the iPad for a few minutes, Lottie reached for her phone and called Boyd.

'I got a message from Susan Sullivan,' she said.

'Are you drunk?'

'I'm stone cold sober.'

'The dead don't speak.'

'Believe me, Boyd, this one did.'

'You are definitely drunk,' he said.

'Just come over. Now. I assure you I am sober.'

CHAPTER 38

Boyd sat in Lottie's kitchen, spooning Pot Noodles into his mouth, with one hand on her iPad.

'I wonder why she didn't follow it up?' he asked. 'Or contact you at the station.'

'It's very odd. I want to know what information she had.' Lottie leaned over Boyd's shoulder. 'Those noodles smell vile.'

'It's pure shite.' Pushing the empty carton away from him, he said, 'Did your mother say anything about this information Sullivan mentions?'

'No.'

'Maybe we should check if James Brown was also on Facebook.'

'I did.' Lottie patrolled her kitchen. 'Do you realise how many people are called James Brown?'

'Too many?'

'Exactly.'

'While you're at it, check out the others,' she said.

'Who? Father Angelotti? The missing priest?' He tapped in the name. Nothing again.

Lottie sat down next to him, took the iPad from his hand and asked, 'Are you on it?'

'For Christ's sake,' he said, 'don't you dare.'

'I bet you keep track of your beautiful ex-wife Jackie and her boyfriend.'

'He's a criminal. And she is still legally my wife.'

'You must still feel something for her if you haven't divorced her yet. Why haven't you?'

'She was a party animal. I wasn't. But I love her, I mean loved her. I suppose I just wasn't what Jackie wanted.'

'And she wanted Jamie McNally? The biggest scumbag in Ireland. Where are they now?'

'Costa del Sol, last I heard.'

'You're keeping tabs on her then.' Lottie patted his hand. He swatted her away.

'I am not.'

'It's been years, Boyd. Forget about her.'

'Don't start.'

'Okay,' Lottie said, 'I'll try Mr Ferret.'

'Mike O'Brien? Ah, stop. I know him.'

'So?' She raised an eyebrow. 'He undressed me with those sly eyes of his.'

'Bet he didn't get a view as good as I got last night.'

'Shut up.' She tapped in O'Brien's name. 'Nothing.'

'I saw him at the gym this evening. He was all chat. You know he's very fit for a man who doesn't look it.'

'You've planted an obscene image in my mind.'

'What image?'

'O'Brien in Lycra.'

'Gross,' said Boyd. 'Try Tom Rickard?'

Lottie tapped in the name. 'Too common a name. We'd be a week going through them trying to find our man.'

'Rickard Construction?'

'Yep. That's here.' She scrolled down the page. 'Mainly advertising stuff. It's his business page.'

'Who liked it?'

'Jesus, there's hundreds of likes on it. He must've had a special offer on one of his ghost houses.'

She scrolled through the names.

'I'll kill her,' Lottie said.

'Who?'

'Katie.'

'Your Katie?'

'Yes, my Katie.' Lottie pointed to a photograph. 'Jason Rickard.'

'Ugly kid, isn't he,' Boyd said. 'He must be son and heir. What's he got to do with Katie?'

'He is my beloved daughter's boyfriend! That little pup was in my sitting room earlier this evening. Smoking weed.'

'You're having me on.' Boyd raised a brow.

Lottie glared. 'I'm not joking.'

'Arrest the little fart.'

'He's not that little, and he is the son of one of our people of interest.' She struggled with the idea of Katie in a relationship with Rickard's offspring.

'You're always going on about small towns, Lottie. In the end everyone knows everyone else and they know each other's business.'

She knew it was true, but she didn't want her daughter in the middle of whatever they were in the middle of. 'Why are we always last to know?'

'Parents or the guards?'

'Both.'

'You're tired. Leave this until tomorrow.' Boyd stretched and yawned.

'I don't want to go to bed. My mind is hyper.' She glanced up at him. 'And no comment about how you can tire me out.'

'We can investigate this further tomorrow.'

'Stymied every way we turn.'

'I'm going home,' Boyd said. 'Unless you want me to stay?'

'Go,' Lottie said.

She didn't look at him. She didn't need to see the ache in his eyes.

He pulled the front door softly behind him.

She returned to Susan Sullivan's Facebook message.

'What did you want to tell me?' Lottie asked.

* * *

2nd January 1975

He watched from the window. The corridor air whispered a chill around him.

He saw the girl getting out of the car followed by a tall thin woman holding a small bundle in the crook of one arm. The girl looked pale and tired. He ducked his head as she glanced up at the white sash windows. Her eyes, veiled in a dark unseeing way, reminded him of a terrified boy he'd once seen, after suffering a beating. The girl looked just like that, walking in a stupor, pushed along by some invisible force. A man sat in the yellow Cortina, with the engine running.

Sister Immaculata hurried down the steps. She took the blanketed bundle and ushered the girl to walk beside her. Without a hug or kiss, the tall woman – he assumed she was her mother – rushed from the girl to the car and drove off quickly.

He stood there, listening to the wind, which used to frighten him before he came to realise there were more terrifying things in St Angela's than blustery corridors. He wondered about the new girl and her bundle, her baby. He knew it was a baby; her baby.

He'd witnessed many such arrivals here, but this girl's stunned eyes had unsettled him. Some remained only a short time. Not all though. Not like him. He thought he'd been here forever. He supposed that many years ago, he was like the wrapped-up bundle – a dark secret hidden deep in swaddling. Was his mother like this girl? He didn't usually allow himself such reflections but her face, painted with such uncertainty and fear, touched him. This was his home. He knew no different. Would this be her home now? What was her story and where would it end?

'Patrick, get out of that window. How many times do I have to tell you? You'll catch a cold,' Sister Teresa said, as she passed by him.

He stretched his twelve-year-old legs to the floor and welcomed the pat on his head from her old hand. He liked her. Not the other nuns. They had changed when that last priest arrived. The one with the black eyes. No, Patrick did not like him at all and the nuns were wary. Afraid? He decided he didn't really care one way or the other as he walked along the black and white mosaics to the stone carved staircase. Sister Immaculata, coming from the nursery, stood in front of him.

'Tea time, Patrick,' she said, her forehead bulging beneath the wimple of her long black veil. He shrugged.

She walked ahead of him, down the stairs in a wave of black skirts. He smelled mothballs and followed in silence.

What would she look like at the bottom, if he tripped her? This was not the first time he'd wondered that. He smiled to himself and went to wash his hands before tea.

DAY FIVE

3rd January 2015

CHAPTER 39

The townspeople of Ragmullin were wide awake and wary. News of another murder had filtered through the gossip lines. They were saying a priest was dead. Lottie frowned. The grapevine was proving very fruitful, even in the depths of winter.

Snowy icicles hanging from drainpipes dripped slowly as temperatures struggled to rise. A murky grey fog enveloped the morning. Lottie looked away from the incident room window. Extensive searches had failed to uncover the whereabouts of a phone or laptop belonging to Susan Sullivan.

'She could have used an internet cafe,' Boyd suggested.

'She could have been on Mars for all we know,' Lottie snapped.

She felt bloated, having scoffed a McDonald's breakfast on her way into work. Junk food. She binged when the urge for alcohol threatened to become something more than a desire. The investigations would drive a saint to drink altar wine. Lottie knew she was no saint but she'd endured the night without alcohol or indeed much sleep.

The technical team had searched the relevant Facebook pages and found nothing. It was like driving around a strange city without GPS or any knowledge of the local language. They were lost.

Glancing out the window again, she noticed around a dozen heavily jacketed journalists, armed with cameras and notebooks, assembled in huddles below. She turned to the sparse incident board. She felt like the murderer was an invisible man or woman. But he was out there. She turned to Boyd.

'We have to join the dots soon, and when we do the picture is going to get complicated very quickly.'

'It's complicated enough,' he said.

'We're due a break, otherwise the two of us will be working cold cases for the rest of our lives. And this one will be the coldest of all.'

'Sometimes you speak in the riddles of Egyptian gods,' Boyd said.

'Egyptian gods?' Lottie studied the prints on the incident board.

'Like hieroglyphics. You know, language of symbols,' he offered by way of explanation.

Lottie sighed. At this stage, she'd settle for any sign pointing them in the right direction. Something to fill the glaring, empty spaces. She studied the photocopies of the tattoos on Susan Sullivan and James Brown.

'I wonder if these could be ancient symbols.' She compared both the Brown and Sullivan tattoos.

'They're crosses in circles,' Boyd said.

'No, they're not crosses,' she said. 'Perhaps they're linked to a ritual or a sect. I wonder if victim number three, who is really victim number one, also has one?'

She dialled Jane Dore's private line. The pathologist answered immediately.

'I suppose it's too much to hope that our latest victim also had the tattoo?' Lottie asked.

'I did a thorough visual and haven't come across one,' Jane Dore said in her no-nonsense voice. 'I'm commencing the autopsy soon. I'll send on my preliminary report when I'm done.'

'Any word on the DNA analysis?' Lottie asked. 'I need to confirm it is actually Father Angelotti.'

'I told you it could be weeks for DNA comparisons. Don't pin your hopes on it. Get someone to ID the body.'

Another dead end. She hoped it was him otherwise she'd be in deep shit after telling the bishop it was his missing priest.

She looked at the tattoo again. Maybe Father Joe could make sense of it. Unorthodox behaviour to be eliciting help from a potential suspect, but what the heck. Just digging herself in a little deeper.

* * *

She punched the bell a second time. Eventually the crooked little nun answered the door.

'I'd like to speak to Father Joe, please,' Lottie said, finding herself bending to the nun's level.

'I'm not deaf you know,' the nun said. 'And he is called Father Burke.'

Lottie imagined the old nun in her prime, beating the life out of terrified youngsters in a classroom.

The nun kept the door closed over.

'Sorry, I should say Father Burke.' Lottie added, 'Is he here?'

'Not any more,' the veiled woman said, closing the door.

Lottie put her booted foot in the gap, hoping she wouldn't get crushed bones.

'What do you mean by any more? I spoke with him yesterday.'

'He's not here. He's gone,' the nun said with cold authority.

'Is there someone I can speak to about why he has left?' Lottie asked, dread inching up her chest. Father Joe was one of their people of interest, though she herself didn't believe he had done anything wrong.

'I can't help you. You'll have to speak to Bishop Connor.'

Lottie jumped back as the wooden slab of a door smashed against the jamb and a bolt slid into a lock. She stepped into the bitter wind and headed down the path, away from the wizened old woman.

Boyd will have a field day with this, she thought. *Done a runner*, that's what he'll say. Instinctively Lottie knew there was more to this. She tried Father Joe's mobile. Switched off. She desperately had to find him.

Blowing warm air on to her cold hands, she craved a cigarette and thought of Katie smoking weed. She needed to do something constructive. Like sorting out her daughter.

CHAPTER 40

The four men sat at a long table, cups of coffee at their hands. Each one of them was worried, suspicious of each other, troubled and afraid.

Tom Rickard spoke first. 'Well?'

'We shouldn't be meeting like this. Someone might see us,' said Mike O'Brien, nervously wiping dandruff from his shoulders. 'And I've to get back to the bank before I'm missed.'

'It's getting very near the crucial deadline. We need to be sure of what we're doing,' said Gerry Dunne. 'You wouldn't get this type of carry on at a council meeting.'

'And I need to be sure you approve that planning permission,' Rickard said, pointing a finger at Dunne. 'I want this development to go ahead, otherwise I'll be bankrupt.'

Dunne straightened himself up in his chair, smoothing the creases in his immaculate pinstripe trousers. 'I know how important this is to all of us.'

Rickard scrutinised the men and wondered, not for the first time, why he'd allowed himself to be corralled into the deal. Gerry Dunne, county manager, with the planning fate in his hands, O'Brien manoeuvring the money around banks and Bishop Connor maintaining a stake in the development after the sale.

'I heard a rumour this morning. What's this about a priest found dead? In James Brown's back garden, no less.' Rickard nodded to the bishop. 'Do you know anything about that?'

'It's of no concern to us,' Bishop Connor replied.

'For all our sakes, I hope that's true,' Rickard said. 'Two murders and now this.'

'The sooner it's all over the better,' O'Brien said.

'We're depending on you to keep your finger on the money,' Rickard said and noticed a tremble in the other man's hand.

O'Brien picked up his glass, drank quickly and started to cough. 'I need more water,' he said with a choke.

'I need another holiday,' Dunne said and knocked over his coffee.

'You all need to calm down,' Bishop Connor said as the dark liquid spread over the desk.

* * *

Lottie switched off the car engine outside the red-brick, multi-windowed mansion.

An image of her daughter, with her weed-smoking boyfriend, intruded every time she attempted to co-ordinate her thoughts into a cohesive train. Rather than let it fester throughout the day, and to avoid dealing with Father Joe's hasty departure from Ragmullin, she'd decided to talk to the Rickards about their son's illegal habit and the source of his drugs.

She stepped out of the car and rang the ornate bell before she could change her mind. As the sound echoed inside she noticed the watery sun slip round the side of the house. Trees stood tall, encircling the building like giant umbrellas. The first snowdrops sprouted through icy beds, straining against the weather. An expanse of lawn appeared in patches through the snow. Someone was going to be busy come spring. And probably not the errant son, Lottie thought.

Soft footsteps approached from behind the door. Jason Rickard opened it.

'Oh! Mrs Parker,' he said and jumped back, barefoot, on the marble tiled hallway. He was wearing yesterday's clothes.

'Are your parents home?' Her eyes were drawn to the black inscription snaking along the skin of his neck.

He stepped forward and leaned against the door frame, folding his arms over his skinny chest. 'They're not here.'

'Really? Who owns the cars outside, then?'

'We do.'

'Jesus, how many cars do you own?' Lottie blurted. Behind her, she noted four cars and a quad, neatly lined up in front of a triple garage.

'The quad and beamer are mine. The others belong to my mum and dad.' The boy guarded the entrance to his house with a hint of youthful cockiness.

A BMW? And she'd initially thought he was a bum. Wrong call, Inspector.

'I thought you said your parents are not home,' she said.

'They have other cars,' he said.

Lottie stared at him.

'What age are you, Jason?'

'Nineteen.'

'Well, if you're going to hang out with my daughter, I better not catch you in possession.'

'Possession of your daughter?'

'Listen, smart arse, I don't like you and I don't know what Katie sees in you, but take this visit as a warning. Next time I'll come with a search warrant.'

Lottie moved closer to the crack in the door. She noted Jason's eyes clouding into dark challenging arcs. Like father, like son, she concluded.

'Katie is old enough to know her own mind,' he said, closing over the door further.

'Do you know your own mind? I sincerely doubt it,' Lottie said. 'I'll be back to speak to your parents.'

The door closed.

Lottie strode away, disgruntled. Twice in one morning – a door shut in her face. Was she losing her touch? And all those cars. They needed checking out. She snapped photos on her phone camera.

Just in case the little shit was lying.

* * *

Jason sauntered from the hall to the kitchen at the back of the house and poured a glass of water. He looked out the window.

His father's white Audi, a dark blue BMW and two black Mercedes were parked in the yard. His dad had told him that the visitors were not to be disturbed. And they weren't.

He wished he could get a new car. He wished Katie didn't have such a bitch for a mother.

He turned. One of his father's friends stood in the doorway.

'I'm looking for something to wipe up a spill,' the man said, 'and a jug of water.'

'This should do it.' Jason handed him a tea-towel. He could swear that the man's fingers lingered on his own a second or two longer than necessary. Pulling his hand back, he hastily rubbed it on his jeans. He searched in the cupboard, found a jug and poured the water. The man took it and his lips curled into a slow smile, eyes flashing up and down Jason's body.

'You have grown into a fine young man,' he said and walked out, letting the door swing behind him.

Jason was rooted to the ground. It was as if someone had reached through his skin and pinched his heart.

He suddenly felt naked.

* * *

Outside the kitchen door the man took a few deep breaths, scrunched the tea-towel into a ball and tried to stop the shaking in his hand holding the jug. He closed his eyes and consigned the image of the boy's lean body to memory. He could still smell the boy's youthful scent, soft and sweet. Beautiful.

It had been years since he'd had these feelings, so why had they resurfaced over the last few months? It must relate to all the stress he was under with the project, he thought. Or was it because St Angela's was once again to the forefront of his mind? He had believed he was so far removed from the boy he once had been that nothing could resurrect the past. But now it stalked him every day. Every single day. And with it came the emotions he had suppressed. He shuddered and water splashed out of the jug. He'd forgotten he'd been holding it. Forgot for a moment where he was, who he now was.

Taking a deep breath, he dabbed at his trousers where the water had splashed and went to rejoin the meeting, the image of the boy firmly on his mind.

CHAPTER 41

In her council office Bea Walsh diligently checked through Susan Sullivan's files. With a time-driven planning process, if an application wasn't finalised within the eight-week deadline, it was deemed approved by default. All too aware of this, she scanned the database, matching files on her desk with the computer list. The screen told her she should have ten files. She had nine.

She scanned through James Brown's list. Maybe it was mixed in there. But she was efficient and knew she hadn't made a mistake. Even with the trauma of the murders she carried out her tasks professionally. The file was missing.

She rechecked the screen. Due for decision on January 6th. Realistically she knew the file could be in a number of places but all the database boxes were ticked. That meant the application contained all the requisite reports, completed and signed by the engineers and planners. Then she remembered where she'd last seen it. Susan Sullivan and James Brown, in his office, having an intense argument, and the file on the desk between them. The day before Ms Sullivan took her Christmas holidays.

Bea took off her reading glasses and rubbed her eyes.

She hadn't seen the file since.

* * *

Lottie plugged her phone into her desk computer and uploaded the photos of the cars from Rickard's house.

She keyed the registration numbers into the PULSE database.

All the cars belonged to the Rickard family. Rich bastards. Boyd looked over her shoulder at the screen.

'What did you expect to find?' he enquired.

'I don't know. Something,' she said, willing the computer to conjure up a clue.

Then she told him about Father Joe's disappearing act.

'He's done a runner,' said Boyd.

Lottie sighed. Predictable Boyd. Her phone rang.

'I need to speak with you, Inspector,' Bea Walsh's voice quivered.

Lottie was surprised to hear from Susan Sullivan's PA.

'Sure. Will I call to your office?'

'Not here. Cafferty's? After work. Would that be all right?'

'Of course.'

'I'll be there at five,' Bea said precisely and hung up.

'Wonder what that's about?' Lottie said to Boyd.

He grunted.

She looked again at the photos of Tom Rickard's cars and picked at a hole appearing on the hem of her T-shirt.

Lynch popped her head round the door. 'Derek Harte is downstairs. You wanted to speak to him again?'

'Yes, indeed,' Lottie said.

CHAPTER 42

'Did James smoke?' Lottie asked, after routine introductions for the record. Maria Lynch sat demurely, notebook at the ready. James Brown's lover, Derek Harte, sat straight in the chair opposite.

'No, but I do,' Harte said. 'Marlboro Lights. I tried to quit. Definitely won't be able to now.'

'Are you willing to provide us with a sample of DNA?'

'Why?' he asked, sitting back.

'To eliminate you from our enquiries. Standard procedure,' Lottie said, hoping they might get a match with the two cigarette butts found beside the body in the garden.

Harte nodded like he didn't have much choice. 'I suppose so.'

'You've told me previously that you and James were not at his house on Christmas Eve. Is that the truth?'

'Of course it is. The snow came down like an avalanche. No one was going anywhere that night. What are you getting at?'

'Do you think James might've been involved with anyone else?'

Harte laughed. 'Is this to do with the body you've found?'

'I'm asking the questions,' Lottie said.

Harte shrugged. 'No, Inspector, James was not involved with anyone else. He and I were committed to each other. And before you ask, I've no idea how a body came to be there.'

'Did you ever hear him speaking about a Father Angelotti?'

'No,' he said, quickly.

'You seem quite sure,' Lottie said.

'I'd remember a name like that.' Harte leaned back further into the hard chair. His attitude was beginning to grate on Lottie's nerves.

'Why would a priest be at his house?' she asked.

'No idea.'

'Did James ever say anything that might indicate his dealings with a priest?' Trying to be as diplomatic as possible, Lottie felt like she was banging against the proverbial brick wall.

'No.'

'Anything to do with Susan Sullivan?'

'No, but if I remember anything, I'll let you know.' He pushed the chair with the backs of his knees and stood up. 'Is that all, Inspector?'

'Detective Lynch will arrange your DNA swab, then you can go,' Lottie said.

As he left, she knew he'd been economical with the truth. But he was willing to give a DNA sample, so what was he hiding?

* * *

She placed a mug of coffee beside Boyd's computer.

'What's that for?' he asked.

'I think you're meant to drink it.'

Lottie went to her desk to write up the Harte interview. Every spare moment throughout the day, she had re-read all the information they had on the murders and she was no nearer a motive or killer.

Boyd lifted the mug, wiped the damp ring from beneath it, and put down a memo pad before replacing the mug.

'This Derek Harte guy comes across as genuine,' she said, stirring her coffee with the end of a pen.

'But?'

'I don't think he is.'

'His lover is dead. We found the body of a missing priest in said lover's garden. Cause enough for concern,' said Boyd.

'I want his background checked if it's not done already. And why didn't we get his DNA sample the first time he was here?'

'We had no reason to,' Lynch said. 'We were treating Brown's death as a suicide.'

'I'm sure it's murder made to look like suicide, so process the DNA as quickly as possible,' Lottie said. 'At this stage we can't leave anything to chance.'

* * *

Kirby sauntered in with an armful of newspapers.

'Any good news?' enquired Lottie.

'We're the bad guys now, according to the press,' he said. 'Not doing enough, quickly enough, the investigation has stalled and is going nowhere and there's a murderer at large.'

'Did the DNA results come in yet on the cigarettes in Brown's garden?' she asked.

'Nothing yet,' Kirby said, flicking quickly through the papers. 'You do know it could take—'

'Weeks. Yes, I know,' Lottie said, throwing up her arms. 'Someone stood there long enough to smoke two cigarettes. What were they watching or waiting for?'

'Presumably James Brown,' Kirby said.

'And he didn't turn up because he was snowbound sixty kilometres away, in Athlone,' Lottie said.

'If Derek Harte can be believed,' Boyd said.

'Any other news, Kirby?' Lottie asked.

He shoved the newspapers on to the floor and read from his screen.

'As you already know, Susan Sullivan's mother, Mrs Stynes, died two years ago in Dublin. Her husband died the year before. No other relatives, that we can find.'

Lottie sighed. 'The father dies, the mother dies, then Susan moves back to Ragmullin. She dies. Dead end.'

Were they ever going to get past the brick wall? She checked her emails. Jane Dore's preliminary post-mortem report on Father Angelotti was in.

'I love you, Jane,' Lottie shouted at the screen.

'I knew it,' Boyd said.

'Shut it Boyd.'

'So what's the excitement about?'

'Jane pulled in a massive favour. Ex-boyfriend in the forensics lab. Fast-tracked the DNA from the body,' Lottie said, reading from the screen, 'and it matches the brush hairs I took from Father Angelotti's room.'

'We've found our missing priest,' Boyd said.

'Are you sure it was his hairbrush?' Kirby asked, without raising his head. His tobacco-stained fingers thumped his keypad. The current rumour circulating had his young actress lover high-tailing it back to Dublin on the late night train out of Ragmullin, leaving Kirby in a haze of cigar smoke and whiskey fumes.

'Kirby,' Lottie said, 'what exactly are you doing?'

'Nothing,' Kirby said.

'Just as I thought.'

'Forensics can't do anything with the smashed phone.' Kirby looked up from his screen.

'Typical,' said Lottie.

She thought about Derek Harte. He'd been interviewed twice already and she couldn't help feeling she'd missed something. Was he the murderer?

'Good news at last,' Lynch piped up. 'Warrant granted to gain access to the victims' bank accounts.'

'We have their accounts,' Lottie said, 'but let's see if we can use it to put the squeeze on weasel man.'

* * *

'Diamonds are forever,' Lottie whispered to Boyd.

O'Brien's cufflink gems dazzled as he pulled up accounts on his computer.

'And a girl's best friend,' Boyd said, from behind his hand.

The banker handed over a printout.

'What's this?' Lottie asked, shaking flecks of dandruff from the paper.

The page contained a number with amounts of money. The identical figures they had seen on the Brown and Sullivan bank accounts.

'That's the account number,' he said. 'Registered to a bank in Jersey. Strict secrecy laws. So no names. Sorry.'

'I'm sure you are,' Lottie said.

'Ah, come on, Mike,' Boyd said. 'You have to give us more than this.'

O'Brien shook his head. 'That's it. You can try the Jersey bank yourselves. But as you know, it's virtually impossible to get information due to their banking laws.'

Lottie stood up, her skin bristling with rage. Another dead end. She glared down at the banker and spied a tiny indent in his ear.

'You know, Mr O'Brien, a diamond is all sparkly on the outside but inside it's just black carbon. So which are you?'

'I've no idea what you're talking about.' O'Brien rubbed his ear self-consciously. 'I think you should leave.' He stood up, his head shedding dandruff on his shoulders as he moved.

'We're going,' Boyd said, pushing Lottie through the door in front of him.

* * *

Out on the street, Boyd said, 'Why do you have to piss everyone off?'

'Comes with the badge,' Lottie said.

'Comes with you,' Boyd said.

'Jersey. Of all places.' Lottie started to walk away from him. 'I've to go to Cafferty's.'

'A bit early for drink,' Boyd said, glancing at the time on his phone. 'Can I come?'

But Lottie had turned the corner walking down Gaol Street, leaving him staring after her.

CHAPTER 43

Bea Walsh sat in the snug, inside the bar door, a hot whiskey on the table in front of her. Lottie ordered a coffee.

'Sorry, I'm a bit late,' Lottie said, checking her watch. It was quarter to six. Not too late, she thought.

'Thanks for meeting me,' Bea said.

'No problem.' Lottie sat down.

The scent of cloves and whiskey filled the air around Bea. The pub was dark and as far as Lottie could see there were only three other customers sitting at the bar. Darren Hegarty, the barman, brought over her coffee.

'Any luck with catching your murderer?' he asked.

'Working on it,' Lottie said and turned to Bea. Darren wiped down the table and returned to his lonely sentry duty behind the bar.

'Ms Sullivan cried a lot,' Bea said, wiping her nose with a crumpled tissue. 'In secret, I mean, when she thought no one was looking. I knew something was troubling her.'

Bea began to whimper.

'Are you all right?' Lottie enquired.

'Just sad.' Bea dabbed her eyes. 'About a month ago, I walked into the ladies' toilets and Ms Sullivan was there. Crying. When she noticed me, she looked embarrassed. I asked if I could do anything to help. She said she was past the stage of help. *Things are out of control.* That's what she said. *Things are out of control.*' Bea closed her eyes.

'Have you any idea what she meant?'

'I asked her but she just wiped her eyes and told me to forget about it,' Bea said and delicately sipped her drink. The smell of cloves wafted towards Lottie. 'Ms Sullivan was under tremendous pressure at work.'

'Anything in particular that I should know about?'

Bea hesitated, opened her mouth to speak, then clamped it shut.

'What?' pressured Lottie.

'Nothing.'

'Are you sure? I thought you were going to add something there.'

'No, Inspector, I've nothing to add.'

Lottie decided to let it pass. For now.

'Did Susan have a laptop?'

'No. She said she didn't need one.'

'Had she a modern phone? With internet?' Lottie wondered why she hadn't asked this question on day one.

'Yes. An iPhone, I think.'

'Would you know where it is?' Lottie crossed her fingers, hoping.

'No, sorry.'

Lottie slumped. Susan's phone remained elusive. But at this stage they should have the call logs from the service provider. Note to self: follow it up.

'I noticed documents relating to "Ghost Estates" on her computer files. What was her role with them?'

Bea drank again, her pale cheeks now flushed from the warmth of the whiskey.

'Mr Brown was more involved with those. It's a crime the way those estates were left unfinished by developers. The staff were trying to get a handle on how to get them finished, rather than leave them half built and empty.'

Lottie liked this woman; she was well spoken despite appearing timid.

Bea continued, 'What makes all this worse, Inspector, is these developers can walk away from their morgue-like developments and have the nerve to continue doing more of the same.'

'Who's responsible?' Lottie asked, wishing she had been more diligent in following current affairs.

'No one wants to take responsibility. It's said planning permission should never have been granted in the first instance. I call it greed.'

Lottie thought for a moment. 'Do you think there was any wrongdoing in relation to planning in Ragmullin?'

Bea hesitated, as if weighing up her reply. 'After what happened to Ms Sullivan and Mr Brown, I'm not sure any more. Before this, I would have said everything was above board. Now? I wonder.' Her voice trailed off like a starling escaping the winter.

'Can you point me in the direction of any files in particular? We've very few leads and anything you tell me, no matter how insignificant you think it is, might help. I'm not saying their deaths are related to their work, but at the moment it's all I have.'

At last, the little bird-like woman opened her mouth.

'That's the reason I asked to speak with you. I didn't know what to do. My job is covered by confidentiality but in these circumstances I feel I have a duty to tell you.' She paused and, teary-eyed, continued. 'There's a file missing. Ms Sullivan dealt with it and Mr Brown also. It's on the database as being processed, awaiting signature. The decision is due in a few days. The thing is, I can't find the file anywhere.' The little woman sat back, exhausted.

'Was it a contentious file?' Lottie asked.

'I think so. But my job is to check the database, make sure reports are on time and, if not, to follow up with the appropriate people. I track the files. I don't read them. But I overheard that the property was bought for a song and it was subject to development plan controversy some months back.'

'What file is it?'

'I feel I can't say it. Now that I'm here I feel foolish.'

Lottie rooted in her bag and pulled out a pen and notepad. She pushed them over to Bea. 'Will you write the details down for me?'

Bea hesitated once again.

'Please,' Lottie said.

'It may be nothing at all.' Bea began to write.

It must be something, Lottie thought, otherwise Bea Walsh wouldn't have gone out of her way to report it.

She read the woman's words. At last. Something to dig into.

She looked up at Bea, questioning her silently.

The woman nodded her head in affirmation.

The property – St Angela's. The developer – Tom Rickard.

CHAPTER 44

'You look pleased with yourself,' Boyd said.

Lottie sat at her computer and grinned.

'Go on, tell me,' he coaxed.

'Brown and Sullivan dealt with a planning application for St Angela's. Guess who is the owner?'

'Not Tom Rickard?'

'Yes Tom Rickard.' Lottie quickly logged on to her computer.

'So these murders are probably linked to current-day matters and not the past,' Boyd said.

'I don't know yet,' she said. 'Kirby, when you were checking the council planning files, did anything turn up in relation to St Angela's property?' She looked over at Kirby's desk and rolled her eyes at his mess.

He hastily stuffed a Happy Meal box down at his feet, a guilty slant on his lips.

'I hadn't time yet.' He quickly added, 'What am I looking for?'

'If I knew that I wouldn't be asking you to look, would I?'

'A hint maybe?'

'You're a detective, start detecting.'

Under his breath, Kirby cursed every woman he ever knew.

'Okay,' Lottie relented. 'Find all you can on Tom Rickard's involvement with St Angela's.'

She spent another two hours checking all their reports to date. Came up with nothing. It didn't dampen her high spirits. She sensed she might be near the kernel of the case.

She googled St Angela's. A photograph in last February's *Midland Examiner* caught her attention. Bishop Terence Connor handing over the keys to Tom Rickard, of Rickard Construction. The by-line informed her the property was to be developed as a hotel and golf course, subject to planning permission.

Jumping up, she went looking for Boyd and found him in the coffee cupboard, boiling the kettle.

'Do you fancy a drive?' she asked.

'Where to?'

'You ask too many questions. Come on.'

* * *

The day had been long and now the moon curved a shimmering light through the sky. Boyd drove. Lottie was bone weary. She directed him on to the old road out of town.

'I hope you don't expect me to visit the cemetery in the dark,' Boyd said.

'Coward. Turn left here.'

He swung up a narrow tree-lined road and stopped at a gated entrance to St Angela's.

'Intimidating-looking place,' Boyd said, switching off the engine.

Lottie exited the car. The gate was open but she wanted to walk.

The yellow neon from the road lamps provided a dim light. A four-storey building, silhouetted under the moon, stood two hundred yards at the end of the winding tree-lined avenue. Lottie looked up. A cold streak shimmied down her spine. She'd seen this place in the distance many times before. It was visible from the cemetery. But now she couldn't halt the disquiet it was causing her. Trying to calm her brain, she began counting the windows. Sixteen along the top floor.

Boyd stood beside her.

'Why are we staring at this building in the dark?'

'We now know St Angela's is the subject of a Tom Rickard planning application,' Lottie said, shielding herself behind Boyd, deflecting the sharp breeze wrestling with the branches above their heads.

'So?'

'James Brown phoned Tom Rickard on the evening he was murdered. Rickard hasn't provided us with a solid alibi.' She paused and considered what Rickard could gain from murder. 'According to Bea Walsh, Brown and Sullivan were dealing with the planning file which appears to be missing. Rickard bought St Angela's from Bishop Connor, who now has a murdered priest. And this is the place, the institution, where the young Susan, known then as Sally, was abandoned, along with her newborn baby.'

Boyd remained silent.

'Well?' Lottie asked.

'I don't like that Tom Rickard fellow,' he said, shoving his hands deep into his coat pockets.

'Is that all you have to say?'

'At the moment, yes. And I'm freezing. Come on, mad woman.' He headed to the car.

She stepped forward a few paces. A gust of wind echoed around her, causing another shiver to scuttle up her spine. She tried to shrug it away, along with the feeling of the old dark memory stirring within her. Her whole body trembled. She walked after Boyd.

'What's up?' Boyd asked, looking back over his shoulder.

'It's nothing. Go start the car.'

Once more, she stared up at the building as Boyd jumped into the car and switched on the engine. Fixing her gaze, she wondered if St Angela's had in fact anything to do with two, possibly three, murders. She noticed an alcove in the centre of the roof; a round construction housing a concrete statue. She squinted but the night was too dark to figure it out. She'd have to see it in daylight. She strolled back to the car, away from St Angela's shielding its ghosts behind shadows.

'Tomorrow, let's haul in Tom Rickard's arse,' she said, sitting in beside Boyd. 'And turn up the heater.'

CHAPTER 45

'Fancy a bite to eat?' Boyd asked, idling the engine outside the station.

'No thanks,' Lottie said.

'Come on. It's after nine o'clock and I haven't eaten since I don't know when. I'd love an Indian.' He did a U-turn and drove down Main Street. The town was deserted.

'Jesus, Boyd, if Corrigan saw what you just did.'

'Not a chance of him seeing me.'

'Why not?'

'He's at a charity dance in the Park Hotel. The Golf Ball.'

'You're joking?'

'I'm serious.'

'He has a nerve.'

'Why?'

'We're in the middle of three major investigations and he's putting himself out there at some fancy gig. The media will have a field day.'

Boyd parked the car on double yellow lines outside Sagaar's Indian Restaurant as snow started to fall.

'I should go home and feed my children or at least bring them a takeaway,' Lottie protested.

'They're not kittens. They can feed themselves. They haven't died of starvation so far,' Boyd said.

He had a point, she surmised. They got out of the car and climbed the stairs to the first-floor restaurant.

They were the only customers. Soft music, the single sound shaking the stillness. Dull wall lights muted the scarlet décor. To some it might be considered romantic, but it reminded Lottie of a room dressed for Halloween.

She selected a table by the window where she could look out over the street below while avoiding Boyd's eyes. For a moment she idly watched the snowflakes melting against the windowpane.

'I need to use the bathroom,' she said, standing up. 'You can order for me.'

She peed, washed her hands and hurriedly swiped Katie's lipstick over her pout. Katie. Tackling the source of her weed habit was still on her to-do list; a list which was growing by the day. She checked to see if her T-shirt was clean enough to remove her jacket. It would have to do.

'I ordered,' said Boyd, as she sat down again.

'I'm sorry.'

'For what?'

'You know. Ringing you when I was drunk the other night.'

'I don't mind.' He busied himself with the wine menu.

'I know you don't. That's the problem,' said Lottie.

'Wasn't a problem for me,' said Boyd. 'But . . .'

'But what?'

'I would like a call some night when you're sober.'

The waiter brought over a bottle of sparkling water and poured it into tumblers.

'Order wine for yourself,' said Lottie. 'I'll drive your car home for you.'

'You sure?'

'I wouldn't say it otherwise.'

Boyd indicated a bottle of the house red to the waiter.

'That didn't take much persuading,' Lottie said and they lapsed into another silence, both looking out the window.

Abandoning the outside view, she studied him. He was intent on the traffic below. She had to admit he was awkwardly handsome. His severe jaw line accentuated his brown eyes and, when they caught the light, they shimmered. A little piece of her yearned to delve beneath the surface of what made Mark Boyd tick, but another part of her was afraid of what she might discover about herself if she grew too close to him.

Their starter arrived.

'I hope it's not too spicy,' said Boyd.

'I could do with a little spice in my life,' said Lottie, sniffing the aroma.

'I offered.'

'I know.'

'You declined.'

'I know,' repeated Lottie, ladling mint chutney on to a chapati.

They ate in silence.

'Do you want to talk about the case or will we enjoy the silence?' Boyd asked, as the waiter cleared the plates away.

'Tom Rickard is in this up to his neck.'

'The only evidence to support that theory is one phone call from James Brown. Which, I might add, he denies having received.'

'We can prove he received it.'

'Agreed, but we'll never know what they talked about.'

'Brown could've been telling him Susan Sullivan was dead,' said Lottie. 'Rickard had to have known them from the council. He probably dealt with them over the planning application.'

'Okay,' Boyd said. 'In theory, we can infer he knew Brown and Sullivan. But why kill them?'

'I don't know, but he's a multi-millionaire. He owns at least four cars. It could've been his money popping in and out of the victims' accounts.' She looked at Boyd. 'Why, though?'

'Might not have been him. Granted, he had an application in for developing St Angela's, but he must have dozens of applications all over the country. Is this one any different? Is there something there to murder for?'

'Let's recap,' Lottie said. 'The first two victims we discovered had secrets. James Brown was having it off with a younger man and Susan Sullivan was dying of cancer and, aged eleven or twelve, she'd had a baby and was incarcerated in St Angela's. Plus she changed her name. Was she trying to exorcise her past? The property, bought by Tom Rickard from Bishop Connor, is now subject to a planning application to build a multi-million-euro hotel, golf course or whatever.' Lottie sipped her water. 'Two of the victims who worked on that file have a similar tattoo on their legs, not to mention the two grand in Susan's freezer and hundreds of newspapers stacked to high heaven in her sitting room. That's what we have so far.' Lottie took a breath. She'd been talking too fast. Boyd knew all of this.

'And the dead priest in Brown's back garden. Don't forget him,' he said.

'We have bodies, a load of questions and feck all answers,' Lottie said. She pulled at the cuff of her T-shirt, picked a stray thread and watched it unravel. 'I'm beginning to feel like the proverbial broken record.'

The waiter arrived and placed their main course in silver bowls on the table. Chicken korma aroma infused the air with coconut.

'Eat and enjoy,' Lottie said.

She relaxed as they ate. With their plates cleared away, she ordered a green tea. Boyd poured the last of his wine and looked outside.

'Drink up,' Lottie said. 'We have a six a.m. case conference with Superintendent Corrigan.'

'He'll have some head on him.'

'Pot and kettle spring to mind,' said Lottie, with a smile.

'There,' he said. 'Your face lights up when you decide to curve those fascinating lips upwards.'

She laughed, feeling light-headed.

He finished his wine.

They split the bill and left.

* * *

Lottie drove Boyd to his apartment, parked the car, handed him the keys and walked him to the door. The heavy snow had turned to light flakes.

'Thanks for the meal. I think I needed the time out,' Lottie said.

'Come in for a coffee?'

'Coffee keeps me awake all night.'

'Good,' Boyd smirked.

'I better get home.'

She lingered a moment. He caressed her cheek, tracing an imaginary line from her eye to her mouth.

'Don't,' Lottie said.

'Why not? You liked it the other night. Remember?'

'I don't like being reminded of things I don't remember doing while in a state of unremembrance.' Lottie turned her head away.

'That's not a word.'

'I don't care any more.'

'That's what you said the other night too.'

'You're a sadistic bastard, Mark Boyd.' She was laughing.

'I want you,' he said, moving his hand behind her neck, up into her hair.

'I know you do.'

His finger drew little circles at the base of her hairline. He bent his head to hers and kissed her on the lips.

She tasted wine and spices, felt a flutter in the pit of her stomach and, her hands still in her pockets, allowed herself a moment of pleasure.

Then she stopped him.

'I'm sorry,' she said, dropping her head.

'Don't be. Dear God, Lottie, don't be sorry.' He lifted her chin with a finger.

'I have to go,' she said.

'I understand.' He placed a chaste kiss on her lips. 'You should've got stitches on that nose. You'll have a scar.'

He traced one final line on her cheek, caressing the bruise beneath her eye, and she felt the softness of his sigh on her hair before he turned his key in the lock, let himself in and closed the door.

She knew he was standing in there, behind the door.

Waiting for her to put her finger on the bell.

She could easily do it. Ring the bell.

But she didn't.

She pulled her hood up and walked home, her face upturned, catching the gentle flakes.

CHAPTER 46

The town was so quiet as he drove home that he was surprised to see a woman walking alone through the snow. He almost stopped to offer a lift when she raised her head and her face was highlighted under the streetlight. Detective Inspector Lottie Parker.

He kept driving for a few minutes before pulling in at a closed garage. He hadn't had too much to drink but all the same, if a patrol car was cruising around, he was sure he was over the drink drive limit. Looking in his rear-view mirror he saw her turn up a secluded avenue. So that's where you live, he thought.

'Good to know these things. Never know when I might have to pay you a visit,' he said and then realised he was talking aloud. What was happening to him? Go home and have a proper drink, he told himself. And think about the beautiful specimen of a boy he had seen that morning.

Switching on the engine, he put the car in gear and pulled out on to the snow-covered road, wondering how long just thinking would suffice before he needed to do something.

CHAPTER 47

'Is she the one?'

Melanie Rickard was drunk. She kicked off her high heels. Tom Rickard watched them slide across the marble kitchen floor.

'What one?' he asked.

'The bitch you're fucking.'

'What are you talking about?' he asked, quietly. You did not shout when Melanie was shouting.

'Don't act innocent with me,' she mocked. 'Is she the one you fuck and then come home smelling of wild berries and jasmine? Jo . . . fucking . . . Malone . . . perfume. I'm not stupid, you prick.'

'You're drunk,' he said. Which was the wrong thing to say to a drunk and incensed Melanie.

She screamed, and banged her fists on the counter before returning to a dangerous calm.

'I'm not blind,' she said. 'Your eyes were buried down her dress, almost at her navel!'

He said nothing. He could not deny that he had ogled the beautiful blonde sitting across the table from him; wanted to reach out and run his hands along her neck, to push his lips against hers. Like he had done last night. He had cursed himself for allowing Melanie to browbeat him into attending the Golf Ball. He knew *she* was going to be there. With her mousey husband. Perhaps, subconsciously, he really did want to be there. To compare her exquisiteness to Melanie's rapidly disappearing attractiveness. But having to sit next to Superintendent Corrigan made for an awkward evening, so he'd plied him with brandy. Bunch of drunks, the lot of them, he thought, and Melanie was the worst of all. He had escaped with her, as early as he could.

'I wouldn't touch her with a barge-pole,' he said.

'So that's what was trying to break out of your trousers. Well, fuck you Tom and the horse you rode in on!' She grabbed a bottle of cabernet.

He thought she was going to throw it at him. But she uncorked it, quicker than she would have if sober, pulled a glass from the cabinet and strode in her bare feet out of the kitchen to the sitting room, where she promptly fell asleep in an oversized armchair.

He stood in the middle of the frigid room and wondered where it all had gone wrong.

He hated her.

In that instant he could strangle her.

CHAPTER 48

Facebook. Lottie logged in.

She listened to the hum of the refrigerator and the murmur of the television show Sean and Chloe were watching in the sitting room. Katie was out, again. Probably with Jason Rickard.

As she sipped a glass of water, sitting in her kitchen armchair, a friend request popped up. She idly tapped the icon. Father Joe's picture appeared. She put down the glass and uncurled her legs. Hit the accept tab. The chat box sprang up. He was online.

> — Hi.
> — Where are you?
> — Rome.
> — What are you doing there? You're a murder suspect?
> — Very funny.
> — Superintendent Corrigan will have a fit. Your bishop will have a fit.
> — I hope to be back before either misses me.
> — How do you propose to manage that?
> — I said my mother was ill and had to visit her in Wexford.
> — What are you doing in Rome, anyway?
> — Being an amateur detective.
> — You're funny. Do you know we found another body?
> — I heard it on the news.
> — Do you know who it is?
> — No. Who?
> — Father Angelotti.

There was no reply for some time. But the application showed he was active. Then he replied.

> — That's terrible. I don't understand.
> — Neither do I. Can you see if anyone in Rome knows why he was here?

— I'll ask around. Lottie?

— What?

— Remember you asked if I could find out anything about St Angela's records?

— Yes.

— I looked up our archive but there was nothing online. The records are in hard copy.

— Where?

— Normally records like this are archived by each diocese. But I cross-checked, thinking St Angela's might have been forwarded to the Dublin Archdiocese which is normal procedure.

— And?

— I talked to the archivist there. They had the records at one time. But he said that St Angela's records were transferred to Rome.

— By who? Why? That's not normal, is it?

— Not normal, no. I don't know who requested the transfer and I've never come across this before but I'm going to find out what I can.

— When were they moved?

— Don't know that either. I'll check.

— I hope you don't get in trouble.

— I won't. I hope I find something interesting.

— Thank you.

— And I'll try to find out if anyone knows anything about Father Angelotti.

— Thank you, Father Joe.

— Joe.

— Okay. Joe. Goodnight.

— Ciao, as the Italians say.

They both signed off.

Rome. Lottie wondered what was going on. Why move St Angela's records if that wasn't normal procedure? She took an A4 notepad from Sean's school bag and a pen. At the kitchen table she wrote down all she knew so far. None of it made sense. She looked at the names wondering if they were connected or if it were all a random mess.

The front door opened and shut.

'Where are you coming from at this hour of the night?' Lottie asked as Katie sauntered into the kitchen, taking off her damp jacket.

'What's that?' Katie asked, looking at the pages strewn on the table.

'Work,' Lottie said.

'I figured that. Why have you Jason's dad's name written there?'

'So, now I do know him?' Lottie studied her eldest daughter. Her eyes, though rounded with thick black eyeliner, were clear.

'Jason told me you called to his house this morning.'

'Where were you?'

'In his room. I had to stay there because there was some business meeting going on downstairs.'

The little shit Jason had lied.

'Who was at this meeting?' asked Lottie.

'How do I know? I was confined to barracks, as Dad used to say when he sent me to my room.' Katie opened the fridge door and scanned its meagre contents. 'Why were you there anyway?'

'Because I want to get to the bottom of this weed thing. It's serious, Katie.'

'Mother! I'm not a child.'

'You're my child and I'm not going to have you dying in some doorway with a needle in your arm. And I can guarantee Jason Rickard will run a million miles from you when he loses interest.'

'Whatever! I'm going to bed,' she said, pulling the wrapper off a cheese string.

'Did you eat today?'

Katie waved the cheese from the fridge at her and hurried out of the room before Lottie could further admonish her.

Sitting at the table, she mulled over Tom Rickard and who else might have been at the meeting. Why did he have to conduct business at his house? He had a perfectly grand office in the centre of town. Was something underhand being discussed?

Gathering up the pages, she put them in her bag and sat on her armchair with her legs curled up. Closing her eyes, she fell into a fitful sleep and dreamt about black crows circling a bleeding statue of a woman with a blue nylon rope tight around her neck. One of the crows swooped low, stabbed its feathery body into a cot, before flying away with a squealing baby wedged in its beak.

Lottie awoke suddenly, a cold sweat sending rivulets between her breasts.

* * *

2nd January 1975

Sally saw the boy sitting in the window as she followed the nun up the steps and through the door to the sound of the car leaving her behind.

The hallway was cold and the floor threw up a wax-polish smell. Panic threatened to overwhelm her as the nun disappeared down a corridor. With her baby. A door banged and she followed the echo.

A baby cried and she wondered if she would be able to recognise the sound of her own child and wasn't at all sure that she could. She inched along, stepping on the wooden patterns until the floor changed to multi-coloured mosaics. She paused outside a door before turning the handle. Her knickers were sopping, the blood trickling down her legs staining her white knee-socks red. Her tiny breasts were sore and leaking. She wanted to curl up in her own bed and die.

She twisted the handle and opened the door.

Three rows of iron-barred cribs, five to a line and a baby in each. The nun stood in the centre of the room and turned, casting her arms wide. Sally wondered which cot held her baby. They looked like dolls. Little dolls in cages.

'These are the devil's work, children of sin, spawn of Satan,' the nun snarled.

Sally felt her knees buckle and blood ooze between her legs.

The black robes swished towards her, smelling like the drawer in her dead granny's wardrobe. Most of the nuns in her school wore shorter skirts and some even ventured to show a lock of hair. This one, shrouded in old-style robes with a stained white cotton apron tied at the waist, was tall and her transparent skin wore a washed-out threatening face.

'Where is my baby?' Sally asked, anxiously looking along a row of cots, straining to see behind the nun. All the babies were now quiet, some asleep, others awake – their little eyes pleading towards the cracked ceiling.

'It is not yours any more,' the nun said. 'They all belong to the devil.'

Sally gathered her strength and with fear fuelling her momentum, she pushed past the nun, ran to the end of the room and back. Tears blinded her. Frantically, she searched for her baby. But which one was hers?

'Where's my baby?' she cried. 'Tell me.'

The room began to swirl. The stink of dirty nappies and sour milk clogged her nose. Babies began to wail, disturbed by her scream.

As she hit the floor, she saw the blue and white statue at the end of the room. The Virgin Mary, a serpent wrapped around her swollen belly choking the life from the infant before it was even born.

DAY SIX

4th January 2015

CHAPTER 49

The six a.m. conference was seriously in need of 'the hair of the dog'.

Superintendent Corrigan had a hangover. Boyd had a hangover. Kirby had a hangover. Lottie and Maria Lynch were caught in the crossfire.

Once she had dragged herself from the kitchen armchair to bed, Lottie's night had been filled with more nightmares. She'd woken up at five, drenched in sweat. She was glad of the early morning briefing, needing something to concentrate on, to banish the night terrors.

Outlining the progress they'd made, she wished that today might see more success. And pigs might fly. She looked at Corrigan, dubiously.

'I'm going to have a chat with Tom Rickard today,' she said.

'A chat?' Corrigan bellowed, then winced and lowered his voice. 'What kind of chat?'

'I want to see what information I can discover about his development of St Angela's. It's all we have to go on. It might be a blind alley but we have to pursue it.'

'Don't go charging down any feckin' alleys, like the proverbial bull in a china shop. He's an acquaintance of mine. Talked with him last night, I did. Grand man. I don't want him on the phone again, yelling about you harassing him. Especially not today.' He stroked his bald head, increasing its sheen.

'Of course.' Lottie was in no mood for arguments either.

The duty sergeant thrust his head around the door.

'We hauled in a drunk last night. He's awake now, shouting the place down. I think you need to hear him, Inspector.'

'I'm in the middle of a case conference.'

'He says he knew Susan Sullivan.'

'Right,' said Lottie, gathering up her papers. 'Put him in an interview room and I'll be there straight away.'

'He's a bit worse for wear,' the sergeant warned.

'Aren't we all,' said Kirby.

Every pair of eyes in the room turned to him. Kirby dropped his head.

'I'm on my way,' said Lottie.

* * *

The air reeked of soft rotting onions.

Lottie's stomach heaved and she attempted to stem the rise of bile. Boyd sat beside her and she knew he was itching to light a cigarette. She looked across the table at the drunk and checked his name on the charge sheet.

Patrick O'Malley was a mess; his face was a map of pulsing pimples and he continuously licked, with a swollen tongue, cold sores on cracked lips. His quaking hands, sprouting long crooked nails stuffed with the remnants of whatever he'd eaten last, were sheathed in fingerless gloves. An old woollen coat, reminding Lottie of one her father had worn, hung over at least two faded hoodies. Here is a man, she thought, who wears his journey through life, not only on his clothes, but in his eyes.

'Mr O'Malley,' she said, 'I appreciate you talking to us. You know your rights and we are recording this interview.'

He averted his eyes, glanced longingly at the door, then lowered his head.

'Would you like a cup of tea?' she asked.

He looked up slowly from under sticky eyelids and she realised his trembles were not only fuelled by alcohol – he was terrified of authority.

'No, ma'am, Inspector,' O'Malley said at last, his voice low and cracked. 'I'll be grand.'

'If you're sure?'

'Yeah.'

'You had a bit of a rough night?'

'Yeah, I did,' he said, furtively looking around the small room.

'Had a few of them myself, recently,' Lottie said.

O'Malley laughed hoarsely.

Lottie decided he was now reasonably relaxed for her to find out what he'd been roaring about in the holding cell.

'You mentioned to my colleagues that you knew Susan Sullivan. Is there something you want to tell me?'

'You could say that,' he said. 'Then again, you might not.'

Lottie swallowed a sigh, hoping this wasn't going to be one of those cryptic interviews, resulting from the ramblings of a drunken mind. She might puke all over him before they finished. She wondered how Boyd was coping, but dared not look at him.

'Wasn't I only lying in the doorway of Carey's Electrical Shop, trying to keep warm, mind. It's hard in this weather with only this old coat and a few bits of cardboard. But I suppose you wouldn't have to think about that, Inspector, would you?'

Lottie shook her head.

'Didn't think so. Fine woman like yourself. I'm sure you have a man to keep you warm at night.' O'Malley chuckled, immediately curling up in a coughing fit. Yellow phlegm coated his lips.

'Are you all right?' Lottie looked around for tissues, found a box behind her and offered it to him. He pulled out a bunch and stuffed them deep into his pocket, without cleaning his mouth.

'I'll get you water,' Boyd said and escaped to fetch it.

'I've this cold, you see. Can't get rid of it.' He paused while his lungs rattled loudly in his chest.

Boyd returned with two plastic cups and handed one to O'Malley. He drank it in one thirsty gulp.

'Here, have mine,' Boyd said, sliding it over.

'Thank you, sir,' O'Malley said and lowered his head.

'Go ahead, Mr O'Malley,' Lottie said. 'You have something to tell me.'

'What was I saying?'

He looked from Lottie to Boyd as if he were trying to remember where he was. Not only where he was in the conversation, but where he actually was in reality. Lottie fought to control her impatience.

'You were outside Carey's,' she coaxed.

'Having a drop of wine, before your lot hauled me in here. Minding me own business, I was. I wasn't always a drunk or homeless, you know, like. Then again, maybe I was.' He puckered up his face.

Jesus, he's going to cry. Lottie stole a glance at Boyd, but he was staring at a point on the wall above the man's head.

'You must be very busy with all these murders, Inspector. Don't want to be wasting your time.' He paused, allowing another fit of coughing to pass.

I'll choke him myself, thought Lottie, but she smiled warmly, easing the way for him to speak up.

'I saw the news on the television in the shop window. The other night, you know, like. Couldn't hear it, only saw the pictures. Her photograph was on it.'

'Whose photograph?' Lottie prompted.

'I knew her.'

'Who?'

'Sally used to bring the soup round at night, to all of us sleeping rough. She was one of the few people who was nice to me.'

He stopped talking, closed his eyes and lowered his head, his chin resting on his chest.

Sally? Did he mean Susan? If so, delivering soup to the homeless was new information. Lottie wrote it down.

'This soup kitchen? Tell me about it.'

O'Malley choked up with a cough. After a moment, he said, 'That's all there's to tell. She came with the old woman. Every night.' Tears glistened at the corners of his yellowing eyes.

'Who was this old woman?'

O'Malley shrugged without a word.

'So this Sally you're talking about was Susan Sullivan,' Lottie said.

'Used to be called Sally, before she was Susan,' O'Malley said. 'I remembered her from back then, you see. The first night she brought me the soup, I looked up into her eyes. I saw that look in them.' He scratched at the table with a dirty nail. 'The fear. We all had it. When we were kids, not more than twelve years old. In St Angela's.'

Lottie locked eyes with Boyd. St Angela's!

* * *

2nd January 1975

That evening he saw the girl at tea.

The refectory was loud and smelly. She was sitting at a table with Sister Immaculata and two other boys. Patrick wanted to find out more about her so he bounded down between two rows of chairs and slid to a stop behind them.

'Sit, Patrick. You make me nervous,' said Sister Immaculata.

He sat in noisily beside them.

'This is Sally. She is staying here with us for a while. I want you to make her feel at home.'

'I hate fucking home,' Sally said, tears streaked dry on her cheeks.

'Dear God in heaven, we do not allow such profanity. You will be punished. But first you must eat,' said Sister Immaculata, picking up her fork with a bony hand.

Patrick looked at his plate of scrambled eggs and the slice of bread with a hard, two-inch crust. Grabbing for his glass, he knocked it and the milk spilled out across his plate. It saturated the bread and watered the eggs into a runny soup.

Sister Immaculata drew back her arm and hit him hard across the top of his head.

Sally jumped.

'You can have mine,' she said. 'I don't like eggs.' She pushed her plate towards him.

'You stupid boy,' the nun screamed.

He smirked, insolence plastered on his face, his eyes twinkling devilment. He turned and smiled at Sally. She stared at him wide-eyed, open-mouthed.

The nun hit him again.

Sister Teresa hurried down between the tables. She took Patrick by the hand and dragged him away from Sister Immaculata's tyranny.

He kept looking behind him on the hurried trek from the crowded room, his eyes locked on Sally's the whole way.

* * *

'No one ever showed me much kindness before Sally arrived,' O'Malley said. 'She didn't mix with the others, so me and her became friends. And then, all these years later, when she was giving out the soup, she used to have little chats with me.' He tightened his cracked lips into a line. 'I should say nothing.'

'You can tell me,' Lottie urged. 'Please go on.'

'I suppose I can. It won't make much difference now the two of them are dead.'

'What two? Who are you talking about?'

'She told me she worked with James Brown. And now he's dead too.'

'Did you know him?'

'Yeah. He used to be in St Angela's with us.'

Lottie stared at him, then turned to Boyd, who had quickly straightened up. This was good. The link between Susan and James that she'd been hankering after.

'James Brown was in St Angela's?' she asked, incredulously.

'Isn't that what I'm after telling you.'

'I didn't know that.' Lottie felt her jaw drop. She thought of the tattoo on the victims' legs. 'James and Susan had similar marks on the inside of their legs. Like a crude tattoo. Do you know anything about that?'

O'Malley said nothing.

'Was it something to do with St Angela's?'

'You could say that,' he said, eventually.

'What does it mean?' Lottie pressed.

'I don't know.' His face closed up.

'Did they get the tattoos when they were in St Angela's?'

'Yeah.'

Lottie thought for a moment. 'Do you have one?'

O'Malley stared at her, as if he was deciding whether to tell her or not. He said, 'I do, Inspector. I do.'

'So what is it all about?'

He licked his lips and shook his head. 'Can't remember.'

He was lying but Lottie didn't press it, afraid he might clam up totally. She wanted to hear more about St Angela's.

'Tell me about Susan and James.'

'We tagged along together, the three of us. In St Angela's.' He smiled. 'We were friends with another lad too. I can't remember his name. Do you know, a lot of them changed their names when they got out? I couldn't be bothered. James neither, I suppose.'

'How long was Susan in there?' she asked.

He looked confused.

'In St Angela's,' she added.

'I don't know. It could've been a year, it could've been more or less. To tell you the truth, I don't even know how long I was there.'

'What did you do all day in St Angela's?' asked Lottie, scribbling notes.

'We went to school in the mornings after Mass. In autumn we picked apples.'

'Apples?' Lottie dipped her chin and raised her eyes.

'The nuns made apple jelly.'

'To eat?'

'To sell,' said O'Malley. 'There was an orchard there. We used to pick the fallen apples off the ground. If you got punished for something, you had to pluck the maggots and flies out of the mushy ones. Bad luck if you were afraid of maggots,' O'Malley said with a short laugh, but Lottie noted his eyes were deathly serious.

'Apple jelly,' mused Lottie, remembering the glass jars, cloth lids held in place with rubber bands, on the breakfast table in front of her mother.

'Yes, Inspector,' said O'Malley. 'I remember the year Sally arrived. That was a bumper year for apples. Not a good one for us though.'

* * *

August 1975

'Sort through that basket of apples, Master Brown,' the tall priest said, pointing to a bruised pile of fruit.

'Please Father, I don't like worms. Don't make me do it,' said James.

The priest stretched to his full height. The boy cowered, as if expecting a slap.

'Leave him alone,' said Sally.

Patrick stood beside Sally and another boy called Brian. She had an apple in her hand. It was bruised and black. Patrick thought she might throw it at the priest. A bastard, that's what Father Con was. They all knew it. They were all afraid of him.

Patrick watched warily as Father Con stepped towards James and extended his hand into the basket. He plucked an apple, scrutinised it and threw it back. He took out another. This one was almost in mush, a maggot sucking on the flesh. He thrust the fruit towards the boy. James kept his trembling arms wedged to his sides.

'Eat it,' the priest shouted, shoving the apple under the boy's nose. 'Eat.'

'Don't make him do it,' Sally cried.

'You shut your mouth,' the priest said.

Patrick gripped Sally's arm. There was no point in them all getting punished.

'I said eat!'

James held out his hand but was barely able to hold the apple. His fingers were white to his wrists. He dropped it, turned and ran.

'This is your fault,' said the priest, grabbing Sally's hair.

She screamed. Patrick froze in his shoes. James reached the end of the orchard and shrunk into the brick wall.

The priest grabbed Brian by the arm. 'You will take Brown's punishment.'

Then he pulled Sally towards him.

'Girl, get that apple and make Brian eat every last morsel.' His voice was a sinister whisper. 'I'll be watching.'

Whatever was in his eyes, Patrick saw it terrify Sally into silence. She held the apple to Brian's mouth. The boy shrieked.

'Please,' Sally said, pleading with Brian, tears flowing down her face.

'No,' Brian screamed.

She shoved the apple into his open mouth.

The priest pulled tighter on her hair. James ran back up towards them. Patrick stood motionless.

'Again,' Father Con said. 'Again!'

Sally pushed the apple into the boy's mouth and a black worm wriggled at the corner of his teeth. Her eyes widened in horror. She dropped her hand and the fruit lodged in the boy's mouth, stifling his screams.

Patrick stood still as Sally turned to him.

Pleading.

But he couldn't move.

* * *

O'Malley's eyes were closed, deep in his reminiscences.

'That's horrific,' Lottie said. Her skin crawled from the images he'd painted and she clenched her fist. 'Who was this Father Con?' She looked at the name she'd written.

'A bollocks, that's who,' O'Malley said, rage flaring his eyes wide open. 'A scourge, a fucking plague.' He paused. 'Sorry for the language, Inspector.'

'Do you know his full name?'

'Only knew him as Father Con.'

'Was this Brian the friend you mentioned?'

O'Malley laughed. 'Brian was no friend of ours, Inspector.'

'And you don't know his full name either?'

'No, ma'am.' He sat in silence for a moment. When he spoke, his voice was a painful creaking sound. Dear God, thought Lottie, had he more to tell?

'Sally and James,' O'Malley said. 'They weren't the first to be killed, mind.'

Lottie locked eyes with him, while he dredged up another memory from the depths of his being.

* * *

August 1975

Patrick heard Sister Teresa screaming. Then he heard the commotion. Nuns running up and down the corridors. Children rushing out of their rooms. Everyone wondering what was going on. A baby was missing from the nursery. Whose baby?

Patrick felt a terrible fear tie his chest into a knot. He hoped it wasn't Sally's eight-month-old tot. Not that Sally was ever allowed into the nursery to visit. The nuns saw to that.

Everyone searched for hours, adults and children, until they found the baby nestled in a basket, underneath an apple tree, surrounded by fresh, smooth-skinned apples. The cord from a boy's pyjama bottoms was wrapped tight around the tiny neck.

The children stood huddled together as a weeping Sister Teresa clutched the chalk-white, doll-like body to her chest. She swept slowly through the hushed crowd, which spread apart like the Red Sea for Moses.

As they watched the nun walk up the steps, Patrick held one of Sally's hands and James held the other.

'Jeepers creepers,' said James.

'Crap,' said Patrick.

'Is it my baby?' asked Sally.

No one let her see the body. No one told Sally anything.

Patrick squeezed her hand. She squeezed his back and the two boys led her inside.

* * *

'Were the gardaí called in?' Lottie asked O'Malley.

'Are you mad or what?' he said, his tongue flicking in and out of his mouth as if searching for his cold sores. 'Herded into the hall like animals, we were. Told us it was a tragic accident, so they did. Liars. And we were frightened enough to keep our mouths shut.'

'What happened after that?' Lottie asked, a little too loudly, unable to mask her disbelief.

'They buried the kid. Under one of them apple trees.'

'And Sally?'

'She convinced herself her baby had already been adopted. But no one would confirm or deny that was the case. Thinking it was already gone kept her from going mad in that place.'

'Had you any idea who did this, back then?'

'Sure how would I know, Inspector,' O'Malley said. 'Maybe the priest. Or that Brian fella. After all, it was Sally who shoved the apple into his mouth. Anyway, I don't know. The terrible thing is, they blamed it on another boy. A red-headed whippet tearaway. Younger than us, he was.'

'Who was he?'

'Can't remember. My head is a bit addled with the drink, you know.'

He pointed to a patch of skin just below his eye.

'But I do remember him sticking a fork in my face one time. Could've blinded me, but for some reason, we became something like friends. Not real friends. Respect for each other maybe. Hard to explain.' O'Malley stared at a point on the wall above Lottie's head. 'Poor bastard.'

Lottie's brain was swimming with all this new information.

'They killed him too.' O'Malley's voice was soft in the silence.

'What do you mean? Who killed who? When?' Lottie asked, confusion constricting her thought process.

'Ah, it was months later. Winter time. Fierce cold it was. Beaten to a pulp he was. Buried him beside the baby in the orchard.' O'Malley's head sank into his chest.

Lottie wondered for a moment if he was making it all up. But she concluded the man was too distraught to do that. What had gone on in that place? Who murdered the baby and who murdered this nameless boy? Who was the baby? Was it Susan's? A flood of questions crackled at the tip of her tongue without being spoken.

She watched O'Malley, his eyes boring a hole through the wall, and she knew he had said all he had to say. He moved his head and looked at her and she felt his deep brown eyes peer into the back of her skull.

'We used to call it the night of the black moon,' he said.

'The black moon,' said Boyd. 'I think I heard of that.'

'I can tell you, we might have been afraid before that boy was killed, but it was nothing to the fear we carried around with us after that.'

'And you don't know who he was?' Lottie asked again.

He shook his head. 'Must've blocked it out.'

'If it comes back to you, let me know.' Conundrum time. She glanced at Boyd. He looked as stymied as she felt.

O'Malley gave her a tired nod.

She glanced down at the name she'd scribbled on her pad.

'Do you know where this Father Con is now?'

'I hope he's dead.'

'And Brian, do you know what happened to him?'

'I never liked him and I always had my suspicions about him and the dead baby. So I hope he's dead too.'

* * *

Lottie stood beside Boyd outside the station door watching the hunched O'Malley shuffle through the snow on his way down the street.

Boyd lit a cigarette. Lottie took it from him. She inhaled and he sparked up another for himself.

'That was some hell-hole,' she said.

'St Angela's?'

'Yeah. Jesus, how many lives did it wreck?'

'You only have to look at Patrick O'Malley. The poor shite.'

'And how many more are out there, like him?' Lottie asked. 'I think Susan Sullivan was haunted all her life by her experiences, and probably Brown too. But at last I'm convinced there's more to this case than planning permission.'

'You're sure their past is a factor?' asked Boyd.

'Of course it is.' Lottie was adamant. She knew Boyd wasn't convinced.

He said, 'Two apparent murders, almost forty years ago. I can't see how they can be linked to the murders we have now.'

'I can't either. Not at the moment.' Lottie stamped out her cigarette.

'I wonder who this Father Con is and where he is,' Boyd said.

'In jail, if he's lucky.'

'I'll run his name through PULSE and see what turns up,' said Boyd. 'But without a full name, I don't hold much hope.'

'Find out what you can about that soup kitchen too,' Lottie said.

'Is this O'Malley a suspect?'

'God help him, but he has to be in the frame. Somewhere. He's linked to Brown and Sullivan through their shared past. We better keep an eye on him.'

'I don't think he could be sober long enough to kill anyone.' Boyd attempted to blow smoke rings but they died in the air.

'And he'd leave a trail of skin behind him to fill every forensic lab in the country.' Lottie glanced toward the cathedral and jumped as the bells rang out ten chimes.

'I'm going to visit our developer friend, Tom Rickard,' she said.

'Shake his tree and see what falls out,' said Boyd, dousing his cigarette in the snow.

'And I'll have to find out how Bishop Connor fits into all this.'

'Ask your priest when you find him.'

'Who?'

'Don't act all innocent with me, Lottie Parker. I think you've taken a shine to Father Joe.'

'Your imagination is so vivid, Boyd, it's blinding me.'

Lottie zipped her jacket and hurried down the street before Boyd could see the flush on her cheeks.

CHAPTER 50

Tom Rickard was letting her know he was busy, rattling desk drawers, stacking files in front of him and tapping his keyboard. Simultaneously.

His eyes appeared closer together, scrunched in a scowl.

'I can do without your interruptions,' he said, shuffling out of his suit jacket. He rolled his shirt sleeves, slowly and methodically, up to his elbows.

Ready for battle, Lottie surmised, wondering how he had ever spawned a son. Then again, he was a rich bastard. Sometimes money could compensate.

'Why did you buy St Angela's?' she asked, without any preamble.

She had caught him on his way into work, hoping he might have a hangover like almost everyone else she'd encountered this morning. He wasn't impressed with being doorstepped. Reluctantly he had allowed her a few minutes of his precious time.

'That's none of your business.' Rickard ceased fidgeting.

'I have two murder victims, both of whom worked on the planning application for the property you bought from Bishop Connor. I also have a dead priest. And you tell me it's not my business?'

'It's simple,' he said. 'I bought St Angela's because I happen to believe it's a prime site for development. I've sunk a lot of money into this project and I stand to make profits from it in the future. I don't appreciate you getting involved in my business affairs.' He gave the drawer one last thump and folded his arms.

'It is my business, if it helps me find a murderer.' Lottie paused for effect. 'Tell me, why did James Brown contact you after Susan Sullivan was murdered?'

'Are you deaf? I've already told you I didn't speak with him.'

'The call lasted thirty-seven seconds,' Lottie persisted. 'You can say a lot in thirty-seven seconds.'

'I did not speak with the man,' Rickard said, his voice slow and determined, his veneers flashing.

'Maybe it went to your voicemail. Did you check?'

'I did not speak with him,' he said, a snarl curving his mouth upwards.

'How much did St Angela's cost you?' Lottie changed tack.

'That's definitely none of your business,' Rickard said, unfolding his arms and thumping his desk.

Lottie smiled. Shaking the tree was working.

'Mr Rickard, I've discovered you purchased St Angela's for no more than half its market value.' Bea Walsh had supplied Lottie with this news. 'That information might interest the financial gurus in the Vatican. I hear they're hard up for funds. What do you think?'

'I think you're out of your depth, Inspector. It's of no concern to anyone how much I paid for that property.' His nostrils flared like an enraged bull. 'I don't see how this has anything to do with your investigations.' His face was getting redder by the second.

'I beg to differ,' Lottie said, calmly. 'With the burden of expense this parish is carrying, I think the media will be very interested in your little deal.'

'You better discuss it with Bishop Connor then.'

'I intend to.'

Lottie felt like she was in a schoolyard sparring match. Rickard was adept at wheeling and dealing, and playing his cards close to his chest. She preferred to go straight to the suit of hearts.

'I think you bought St Angela's with strings attached,' she said.

'Think what you like.'

'So who was at that meeting at your house yesterday morning?'

'I've absolutely no idea what you're talking about.'

'Do you deny there was a meeting?'

'I don't have to confirm or deny any such thing.' He opened and banged a drawer once again.

'Were you ever in St Angela's?'

'I own the damn place. Of course I've been in it.'

'I mean as a child, a young lad. Were you ever in it back, oh I don't know . . . in the seventies?'

'What?' Rickard puffed out his cheeks, heightening the colour from red to purple sweeping up his jaws, and threw his hands upwards.

'Were you?' Lottie noticed damp patches seeping from his armpits. The room was beginning to hum with the smell of his sweat.

'No. I never set foot inside St Angela's until I became interested in acquiring the property.'

'Mmm.' Lottie wasn't convinced. But she'd no way of proving it, not at the moment anyway.

'You can *mmm* all you like,' he mimicked.

Lottie smiled her sweetest smile and asked, 'On another matter, do you know your son is dabbling in drugs?' She wasn't about to let him away scot-free.

'What Jason does or doesn't do has nothing to do with you.'

'On the contrary it has everything to do with me, because Mr Rickard, much as it galls me, he happens to be in a relationship with my daughter.'

She watched Rickard intently. His mouth opened to fire a reply, but he stopped as if realising what she had said. The first sign of uncertainty crept into the lines around his tired eyes and his lips slackened. He got up and walked to the window. She had wrong-footed him, at last.

'*Your* daughter?'

'Yes. *My* daughter Katie.'

Rickard turned round to face her, the wintery sun behind him silhouetting his rounded belly now slack without his waistcoat to hold it in. Distant traffic sounds reverberated from the street below.

'What my son gets up to or gets up his nose has no bearing on anything. And hear this loud and clear, Inspector Parker, I had nothing to do with those murders. If you continue to harass me I will report you.'

You and everyone else, Lottie thought. She had heard enough from Tom Rickard. She stood up too.

'I hope you're not challenging my professionalism. Because, I can assure you, Mr Rickard, I will get to the bottom of this in an honest and transparent way. I don't operate the way you run your business.'

'And you are implying . . . what exactly?'

'You know exactly what I'm implying. Brown envelopes, backhanders, whispered promises in council corridors. Think what you like about me, but I warn you, do not underestimate me.'

Lottie turned on her heel, snatched up her jacket from the back of the chair and left him staring out the window of his modern office, listening to the mid-morning traffic far beneath his feet.

She almost skipped to the lift. She felt good. No, not good. Great.

* * *

Rushing through the crowded reception back at the station, she bumped into Boyd. He took her arm, turned and steered her back out the door.

'What's up?' Lottie asked, trying to maintain her balance.

'Corrigan. He's had a call from Tom Rickard. Something to do with you threatening his family.'

'That's a load of bollocks,' she said, wrestling her arm free. She spun Boyd round to face her. 'Total bullshit.'

'Maybe. But a little time out of Corrigan's line of fire mightn't be a bad thing right now.'

He gripped her arm. She relented and walked with him to the car.

'Where are we going?' she asked, fastening her seat belt.

'The soup kitchen.'

'Is that a new restaurant?' she asked, dryly.

Boyd reversed the car. 'You know right well it's where Susan Sullivan did her charity work.'

Lottie calmed down and Boyd switched on the radio. Some rapper blared and she thought of Sean.

'Am I a bad mother?'

'No, you're not. Why?'

'Since Adam died, I can't manage my home life. I've thrown myself into my job. I abandon my kids to their own devices. God knows what Chloe and Sean get up to all day. And Katie's going out with a millionaire's junkie son. I think I'm losing control, Boyd.'

'It could be worse,' he said.

'How so?'

'Katie could be going out with a junkie without the millions.'

CHAPTER 51

Mellow Grove, a local authority estate of two hundred and ten grim houses, was a short drive through town.

Boyd parked the car outside number 202, an end, pebble-dashed affair, with a small flat-roofed extension to the side. A young boy, no more than five years old, with dirty blond hair sticking out from under a peaked Manchester United cap, walked up to the front bumper and eyed the two detectives.

'Who you looking for, Mister?' he asked.

'Mind your own business,' said Boyd, pushing open the rusted gate.

'Fuck off, you long lank of misery,' the boy shouted.

Lottie and Boyd turned, looked at him, then at each other and laughed.

A lime-green, 1992 Fiat Punto, was parked outside the wall. Two black cats and a German shepherd sat guard on the step.

The woman who opened the door, her body framing its width, had a head of grey hair curled tight to plump pink cheeks. An unevenly buttoned, knitted cardigan hung over a black polyester midi-dress. Swollen legs in elastic stockings led down to well-worn tartan slippers.

'Mrs Joan Murtagh?' Lottie enquired. 'We rang you a few minutes ago.'

'Did you?' The woman checked their ID and guided them past her, into her home. 'My memory lets me down at times.' She shooed the dog down the path. He stretched and walked away, his warm paws trailing footprints in the snow behind him.

Lottie sniffed the scent of fresh baking inside. Entering the kitchen, she spied brown bread resting on a wire rack.

'Would you like some?' Mrs Murtagh asked, noticing Lottie's line of sight.

Without waiting for a reply, she sliced up half the loaf, placed it on a plate and took the lid off a butter dish. A wooden walking stick hung, unused, from the table edge. She moved surprisingly quickly and Lottie thought she was probably around her mother's age.

'Eat up,' Mrs Murtagh said. She poured boiling water from the kettle into a teapot. 'You both look like you could do with a decent feed.'

'Thank you.' Lottie buttered the bread and took a bite. 'Delicious. Try some,' she told Boyd.

'I'm on a diet,' he said, taking out his notebook and pen.

Mrs Murtagh broke into a robust laugh.

'Diet me hole,' she said. She looked over to Lottie. 'Dangerous job for a woman, being in the guards.' She placed the teapot on the table and sat down.

Lottie fingered her damaged nose. 'I like my job.'

'I bet you're good at it too,' Mrs Murtagh said, pouring black tea into three mugs.

'When did you first meet Susan Sullivan?' Boyd asked, looking around for milk.

'You'll have to bear with me. I'm liable to forget important stuff. Early Alzheimer's, my doctor thinks. So let me think. It must be five or six months ago.' Mrs Murtagh munched the bread. Crumbs stuck to facial hairs at the corner of her lips. 'Susan heard about my charity work with the homeless. I was fundraising for a shelter, wanted to convert the extension at the side of my house into a type of hostel. Did you notice it on the way in? Poor Ned, my late husband, built that himself, God love him. A heap of crap it was.'

Lottie nodded.

Mrs Murtagh continued. 'The council stopped me. Said it wouldn't be in keeping with the general area. I know the neighbours complained. Got a campaign up and running to oppose me, they did. Didn't really matter in the end. I hadn't enough money at the time.'

'What did Susan do?' Lottie asked.

'She called to see me. Wanted to help. Gave me ten thousand euro straight up. Cash. No questions asked. You don't look a gift horse in the mouth, do you? I got the extension renovated and installed a restaurant-style cooker. Kitted it out top notch, I did. And we started our own soup kitchen.' Mrs Murtagh sipped her tea, her face alight with pride. 'Did I show you?'

'Maybe later,' Lottie said. 'How did you operate it?'

When Mrs Murtagh raised an eyebrow, Lottie said, 'The soup kitchen.'

'Oh. We cooked up the broth, poured it into flasks and drove around town delivering it to the poor unfortunates. A few of them live on the streets and there's another crowd down by the industrial estate. You know, along the canal, behind the train station.'

Lottie knew. Her ribs still ached from the mugging.

'Did Susan give you any idea why she was doing this?' Lottie buttered a second slice of bread. If Boyd wasn't going to eat, it was his loss.

'She wanted to help those who couldn't help themselves. Concerned with children sleeping rough, she was. It's a national disgrace, what's going on in this country, so it is. All those houses boarded up and the poor have nowhere to sleep.'

Mrs Murtagh banged her fist on the table, eyes flaring. Her passion surprised Lottie. Pity there weren't more like her, she thought.

'Susan ranted on about developers building all those ghost houses. Said it was criminal the way the council allowed them to carry on,' Mrs Murtagh said.

Lottie looked at Boyd. He returned a knowing look.

'But she worked for the council,' Lottie said.

'I know. But she never had the final say. That's what she told me.'

'Did she ever mention Tom Rickard? He's a developer.'

'I'm not stupid, just forgetful. I know who he is. With his snooty wife and junkie kid, looking down their noses at us mere mortals. I tell you, I've more wealth in my heart than Tom Rickard will ever have in his bank account, Detective Dottie.' She slammed the lid back on the butter dish.

'Did you have a run-in with him?' asked Boyd.

Lottie caught his smirk at Mrs Murtagh's inaccurate mention of her name. She ignored him.

'Not personally, but I know his kind,' Mrs Murtagh said. 'Susan didn't have much time for him anyway.'

'Why not?' asked Lottie.

'Something to do with him owning St Angela's. That's the big empty orphanage place out the road. She mentioned one time about him buying his way through the development plan. I don't know what that means but I can make a fairly good guess.'

Lottie drained the remnants of her tea. Mrs Murtagh started to refill the mugs.

'How many people are involved in the soup kitchen?' asked Boyd, declining the tea.

'Just me, now Susan's gone. I don't know how long I can keep it going, with no money coming in.'

Lottie had a feeling that Mrs Murtagh would keep her soup kitchen going until the day she died, money or no money.

'Have you any idea why someone would want to kill Susan?' Boyd asked.

'I don't know.' The woman shook her head, sadly. 'She was a decent soul. Only wanted to do good for people. It's a mystery to me.' She wiped tears from her eyes. 'A lot of things are a mystery to me nowadays.'

'She must have spoken to you about her life. Had she any worries or concerns?'

'She told me she was dying. I've never met anyone who accepted a death sentence like she did. Resigned to her fate, she was.'

'Did she ever tell you where the cash came from?'

'Cash?' Mrs Murtagh was silent, thinking for a moment. 'Yes, she said it was owed to her, from a long time ago. "Everyone pays in the end." Susan said that. Funny how I can remember these things and not others. You know, I have a feeling there's something else I need to be telling you. But I can't remember for the life of me.'

Lottie digested the information.

'Did anyone have a grudge against her?' asked Boyd, tapping his notebook impatiently.

'Susan was a quiet soul, just wanting to help people. I don't know why anyone would want to harm her.'

'Did she have a boyfriend or partner?' Lottie asked.

'Not that I knew of.'

'Did you know she had been in St Angela's as a child?'

The older woman was silent for a time, nodding away to herself.

'She told me it was a terrible place. No child should be abandoned by a mother the way she was. Said she was one of the lucky ones, if you could call being scarred all your life lucky. The Catholic Church has a lot to answer for in this country.' She shook her head wearily.

'What did she tell you about the search for her child?' asked Lottie.

'Broke her heart it did, them taking away her chisler. She was never sure what actually happened to her baby.'

'So, she'd no luck tracing it?'

'She went through every avenue available and got nowhere. The biggest obstacle was the Church. She even met with the bishop. Fat lot of good that did her.' Anger flashed in the old woman's eyes once again.

'She met Bishop Connor?' Lottie nudged Boyd on the elbow. The bishop had denied knowing Susan and now it appeared he'd actually met with her.

'Yes, she did. Let me think for a minute.' Mrs Murtagh closed her eyes, then said, 'When she came back here afterwards, she was very upset. So I couldn't understand why she returned a second time.'

'A second time? When? Why?' asked Lottie, itching now to have another go at Bishop Connor.

'I don't know. I told her not to go back, but she was adamant he had information.' Mrs Murtagh dropped her eyes. 'Poor soul. That man told her she was nothing only a slut and said that's why she must've been put in St Angela's. He's a bastard. God forgive me.' Mrs Murtagh blessed herself again.

Lottie digested this information. Why had Bishop Connor lied?

'When was this second meeting, Mrs Murtagh?'

'Christmas! Yes, it was before Christmas.'

'Any idea when, exactly?'

'Susan was on annual leave from the council. Christmas Eve. That's it! We had three pots boiling on the big cooker. Did I show you the cooker? Of course I didn't. Remind me before you go. Normally one or two pots would be the maximum. Funny how I can remember that when there's so much I can't. It was snowing like the dickens and the weatherman said it was going to be minus twelve or something ridiculous like that. So yes, I'm fairly sure it was Christmas Eve.'

Boyd made a note.

'How did she get on at the second meeting?' Lottie asked, taking another bite of bread. She hadn't realised how hungry she was.

'I don't think I even asked her. When she came back we filled the flasks, loaded my car and off with us, through the blizzard.'

'Had her mood changed?'

'How do you mean?'

'After her visit with the bishop. Was she troubled or upset?'

'I imagine she was the same Susan as always. Troubled, very troubled.'

Lottie thought about Bishop Connor and felt an increasing sympathy for Susan Sullivan. She had been wronged throughout her life and the more she learned about her, the more determined she became to afford Susan some sort of justice, albeit too late.

'When did you last see Susan?' Boyd asked.

'The night before her murder.' Mrs Murtagh wiped another tear from the corner of her eye. 'We did our soup runs every night over the Christmas.'

'She was off work,' Lottie said, 'so what did she do during the days?'

'I don't know. Susan kept to herself.'

'She lived at the opposite end of town. But her car looks like it hasn't been moved in weeks. Did she walk everywhere?'

'She liked her exercise. Always had that music thing in her ears. What do you call it?'

'An iPod.'

'Loved her music, she did,' Mrs Murtagh said wistfully.

'Anything else you can tell us?' Lottie asked.

'Two cups of wholemeal flour, teaspoon of yeast, tablespoon of butter, a pinch of salt and twenty minutes in the oven.'

'I'm afraid I don't bake,' said Lottie. 'And even if I did, I don't think I could ever make bread as delicious as this.'

She wondered if the old woman was changing the subject. She dreaded the thought of her mother ever getting Alzheimer's. Or maybe it might be a good thing. Hard to know with Rose Fitzpatrick.

'You're trying to flatter me. I'll get some tin foil and you can bring the rest of the loaf home with you.'

Lottie began to protest, but decided it was too good an offer to refuse.

Wrapping the bread, Mrs Murtagh said, 'And you, young man, you could do with a slice or two.'

Boyd smiled and remained silent.

Lottie returned to the conversation.

'I'm led to believe St Angela's was a brutal place. What did Susan tell you about it?'

'She told me something one time. Said she'd never told a living soul. A baby was murdered there and a young lad was beaten to death.' Mrs Murtagh made the sign of the cross, forehead, chest and shoulders, slowly and deliberately. 'She called it the baby jail; all them little mites in cots with iron bars. And she wasn't sure if it was her baby that was murdered but she convinced herself it wasn't.' She paused, tears damp on her cheeks. 'Not knowing, that was the worst.

The poor tormented soul. Do you know, she bought the newspaper every day to look at the photographs? Thought she might recognise her child, all grown up now.'

'We saw the newspapers in her house,' said Boyd.

'Obsessed she was. As if she could recognise someone she only saw as a baby. I tried talking to her. But she said if she saw a picture, she would know.'

Dismissing the futility of Susan's newspaper quest, Lottie said, 'Patrick O'Malley. Did you ever hear of him?'

'Of course. A demented man. One of our soup clients,' Mrs Murtagh said. 'Susan was very kind to him but never spoke to me about him. Detective, I only knew Susan for the last six months of her life but it felt like I knew her forever. It's so sad. Why do these things happen to the good people and the bad bastards walk around scot-free?'

Lottie and Boyd said nothing. There wasn't much they could add to that.

The woman rose, gathered the three mugs, placed them in the sink, turned on the tap and rinsed them under the flowing water. Leaving them to dry on the draining board, she picked up her walking stick and pointed to the side door.

'Come on. I'll show you our soup kitchen. We were so proud of it.'

Lottie hadn't the heart to refuse.

* * *

All four wheels intact and the foul-mouthed little boy was nowhere in sight.

'That's some set up,' said Boyd, starting up the car.

'Wherever Susan got the money from, it seems she put it into the soup kitchen.' Lottie placed the bread at her feet. 'I hope whatever Mrs Murtagh can't remember to tell us is nothing too important.'

'We need to go through Susan's phone records again.'

'For sure.'

'Where to next?' asked Boyd. 'Or can I guess?'

'Bishop Terence Connor,' said Lottie. 'He has some explaining to do.'

CHAPTER 52

'I see you have brought the cavalry with you, Inspector.'

Bishop Connor indicated two chairs in front of his desk. Lottie and Boyd sat.

'When are you going to release Father Angelotti's body?' he asked.

'That's up to the pathologist,' Lottie said. 'Is there anything you can add to our investigation regarding his murder?'

'I am devastated,' he said. 'To think he was only here a few weeks, then this abomination happens.'

'Why was he at James Brown's home?'

'I have no idea.'

'Did he ever mention James Brown or Susan Sullivan to you?' Lottie pressured.

'He never mentioned anything, Inspector. He barely communicated with me.'

'Did he have access to a car?'

'I am sure he could have got one if he needed it.'

'But there was no car at Brown's house. How did he get there?'

Connor hesitated. Imperceptible eye movement, but Lottie caught it.

'A taxi?' he said. 'I'm sure you can check with the local companies.'

'Doing it as we speak,' Lottie said, making a mental note to follow this up.

'You told me you'd no knowledge of Susan Sullivan. Is that correct?' she asked, flicking through her notebook, for effect rather than substance. The intense green eyes that had tried to intimidate her on her first visit were now eyeing her with suspicion.

'I believe that to be correct,' he said, emulating Lottie's words.

'You need to think very carefully,' she emphasised. 'I have proof you met with Ms Sullivan on at least two occasions.' Hearsay, but he didn't know that.

'And what proof might that be?' The bishop's eyes flared.

Lottie gave Boyd the floor. He was better at fudging the truth.

'We have phone records, proving Susan Sullivan rang you. And her computer diary, detailing a scheduled meeting with you,' Boyd said, bluffing with confidence.

'I thought you could not find her phone.' Bishop Connor sat back and smiled.

'And how would you know whether we did or not?' asked Lottie.

'My sources are very good.'

'Your sources are incorrect and you lied to me,' Lottie said.

'I did not know Susan Sullivan. I will admit, however, that I did meet with her. There is a difference between knowing someone and meeting with them.' He caressed his fingers over his smooth chin.

'You're being evasive. I could arrest you for obstruction.' Arsehole, thought Lottie.

'I do not believe I have any information that could help you,' said the bishop.

'Let me be the judge of that. What were the meetings about?' She was fed up with the pussy-footing.

'Private matters. I do not have to tell you anything further.'

'Bishop Connor, you were acquainted with two of our three murder victims. One of whom, Susan Sullivan, I know met with you, the other, Father Angelotti, was in your care. And you say you don't have to tell us anything.' Lottie kept her voice strong and challenging. 'The longer you play this game, the more I think you're guilty of something. And believe me, if I get a sniff that you're giving us the run-around, you might begin to experience what hell on earth is like.' She leaned forward, breathing rapidly.

'Are you threatening me, Inspector?' The bishop returned her glare.

Boyd broke the confrontation.

'We're not threatening you, Bishop Connor. We're telling it like it is and we'd like to know why you denied having met with Susan Sullivan. You must admit it all looks very suspicious.'

Bishop Connor took a breath and reclined into the comfort of his chair. Lottie remained forward, coiled so tight she could spring across the desk any minute. Boyd put a hand on her arm. She refused to move. Damned if she would let Connor away this time.

'And don't invoke the superintendent threat,' she said. 'I don't give a flying fuck how many golf balls you and Superintendent Corrigan have hit together. Or how many whiskeys you've downed on the nineteenth hole or how many birdies, eagles or albatrosses you can claim. It doesn't wash with me. I want answers. If I've to haul your unholy arse down to the station, so be it. But one way or another, you will talk to me.'

Bishop Connor smiled, incensing Lottie further.

Boyd said, 'Allow me to outline our position. Father Angelotti arrived here from Rome on December first. On Christmas Eve, you met with Susan Sullivan following a meeting earlier in the year. Our best estimate is that Father Angelotti was murdered on Christmas Eve. I think it's time you started talking.'

'And I think it is time for you to leave,' Bishop Connor said.

'What are you hiding?' asked Lottie, keeping her eyes locked on the bishop's darting emeralds.

'I have nothing to hide,' he said, a pink shadow creeping up his cheekbones.

'But you won't talk to us,' Boyd said.

'I am busy . . . if you would be so kind . . .' He pointed to the door, his phone already in his hand.

'You're wasting your time talking to Superintendent Corrigan,' Lottie said, stomping out the door.

'And you are wasting your time talking to me.'

He shut the door behind them.

* * *

Settling into the car, Lottie said, 'If I was so inclined, I could murder that bastard, myself.'

'Me too,' said Boyd. 'And how do you know so much about golf?'

'Sean went through a Rory McIlroy phase with his PlayStation games.'

Boyd nodded as if he understood.

'Connor's hiding something,' Lottie said.

'I need a drink,' Boyd said.

Lottie looked out over the lake as they drove away, the water rippling silver under the moon's reflections. 'It's almost seven. I should check in at home.'

Boyd concentrated on the road.

'On second thoughts, why not?' she said, reclining the seat. She planted her feet on the dashboard and closed her eyes.

He remained quiet.

She was glad of his silence. Rickard and Connor were giving her the run-around and, after today, she was convinced they were hiding something. But what? She was almost certain it related to St Angela's. She didn't know if it had to do with the past or the present. One thing was sure though, she was determined to find out. She owed it to the victims.

CHAPTER 53

The man left his office saying he'd be back in an hour. He needed fresh air, even if it was full of tumbling snow.

As he strolled through the half-deserted town, a teenage couple laughing and leaning into each other rushed past him. A blast of wind lifted the scarf from the boy's neck and the girl tugged it around her own. The black tattoo stood out against the white flakes falling from the sky. The man idled at a shop window as the girl pulled the boy toward her and the two kissed. He could see her pale hands rub along the youth's thighs then move upwards until they were caressing his neck.

He tried to control his breathing; it was so loud he thought they would hear it. The neck. The tattoo. That beautiful boy.

The young couple resumed their walk and headed into Danny's Bar.

He needed to touch that skin.

Soon.

CHAPTER 54

Detectives Larry Kirby and Maria Lynch were already in Danny's Bar, sitting in front of the fire, when Lottie and Boyd arrived.

Two pints of Guinness held centre stage on the round table beside Kirby, his hair wilder than usual. Lynch was drinking a hot whiskey. A hum of chatter filled the air and a group of teenagers, piercings and tattoos highlighting their pale skin, sat in a semi-circle in a dim corner. A pot of tea with a multitude of cups and saucers cluttered their table. Tea time in the zoo, thought Lottie, easing in between her two detectives. She passed no more heed on the youngsters. Boyd went to order the drinks.

'You drinking for two, Kirby?' Lottie asked.

'I'm sitting here thinking about the second one,' he said, taking off his jacket, ready for a session. A wad of paper and three chewed Biros stuck out of his shirt pocket.

'And the first one?'

'It'll go down so quick I won't even remember drinking it.'

He took the pint, raised it to the two women either side of him and downed the drink in three swallows. He wiped his mouth with the back of his rough hand and put the empty glass back on the table.

'Needed that,' he said.

Lottie smiled across at Lynch. Boyd arrived with a glass of red wine for himself and a white for Lottie.

'I thought you didn't drink any more,' Kirby said, white frothy Guinness lingering on his upper lip.

'This isn't any more,' said Lottie. 'This is now. I need it as much as you needed that first pint.'

'Totally agree with you,' said Kirby, taking a large gulp, following it with a loud belch, without any trace of embarrassment.

The four detectives drank their alcohol and the blazing fire restored heat to their bodies.

'Don't look now, Inspector,' Lynch said, nodding behind Lottie with a swish of her ponytail, 'but your daughter is sitting in the corner.'

Lottie turned immediately. Katie! She was lounging with her head on Jason Rickard's shoulder. Her eyes were tired slits, while a smirk curled at the corners of her pouting red lips. Her face, artificially pale from intense white foundation, challenged Lottie.

'Stay where you are,' advised Boyd.

'I've no intention of moving. I've had enough confrontation for one day.'

Sipping the illicit wine, Lottie really wanted to slaughter it, like Kirby had with his pint. She didn't have his gut though and needed to be able to walk home. Katie could wait. But she was annoyed that Maria Lynch was a witness to her family strife. She turned to her colleagues and told them about the progress she and Boyd had made.

'Give me five minutes with that bishop and he'll talk,' said Kirby, licking his lips.

'How was your day?' Lottie asked, studiously ignoring the teenagers behind her.

'I had a bit of a bingo moment,' said Kirby. 'I reviewed Brown's phone records and discovered some of the calls he made were to a mobile number belonging to none other than Father Angelotti.'

'James Brown knew Father Angelotti!' Lottie finished her wine with a gulp. 'So we now have a conclusive link between James Brown and the dead priest.' She placed the empty glass on the table. 'When was this? What date?'

'Dates,' Kirby corrected her. 'There were a few calls. Mid-November was the first one. Hold on.'

He extracted the sheaf of papers from his shirt pocket and unfurled them. Yellow highlighter illuminated the pages, circling a myriad of numbers.

'Here it is,' Kirby said, pointing with a stubby finger. 'November twenty-third at six fifteen p.m. And two others, December second and December twenty-fourth.'

'What time on December twenty-fourth?' asked Lottie, feeling a surge of excitement.

'Ten thirty a.m. and seven thirty p.m.,' said Kirby, taking one of his pens and drawing yet another circle around the digits.

'And according to our pathologist's best guess, Father Angelotti was murdered on Christmas Eve,' said Lottie.

'And Susan Sullivan met with the bishop on Christmas Eve. Even though the pretentious bastard refuses to tell us what it was about,' said Boyd.

'What ties all this together?' Lynch asked.

'St Angela's and the developer Tom Rickard.' Lottie threw a glance over her shoulder at Rickard's son. He was nuzzling her daughter's neck. She turned away, wrinkling her nose in disgust.

'How does Father Angelotti fit in?' Boyd asked.

'I don't know yet but we could presume Brown rings him at ten thirty a.m. to arrange to meet and called later to say he couldn't make it back in time,' Lottie said. 'That's the appointment his lover Derek Harte referred to.'

'But Father Angelotti was already there,' Boyd said. 'And someone else, also.'

'Apparently,' said Lottie. 'Who?'

A barman came between them to tip a bucket of coal on to the fire. The flames dampened momentarily and then leapt up the chimney. Sparks settled on the hearth in front of the detectives. Kirby ordered another round. The four of them settled into silence. A burst of laughter amongst the chatter behind them ruptured the air.

Lottie tried to concentrate on Kirby's information. At the same time she wanted to know what her daughter was up to. She looked down at her empty glass, willing the barman to return with the refills. She noticed the frayed edges on her T-shirt sleeves. If Adam was still alive, she'd have more money. Was it the Rickard kid's wealth that attracted Katie?

The drinks arrived. Boyd passed them round. Kirby paid. Lottie heard laughter behind her again. She twisted around.

Katie was looking straight through her. The girl's open mouth displayed a tongue piercing reflecting the firelight. When did she get that? Jason had his arm around Katie's shoulder, fingering her collarbone. When she felt Boyd tugging her arm, Lottie realised she'd stood up.

'Leave her be,' he said. 'She's just a kid having fun.'

'What would you know about it?' Lottie snapped, brushing Boyd's hand away.

'Not much, I agree. But I do know this, making a scene with your daughter in front of her friends is the wrong move. Sit down.'

She did. Boyd was right of course. She sighed and allowed the wine to layer a thin numbness on to her brain.

'I hate to say this, but your other daughter, Chloe isn't it? She's just walked in,' Lynch said.

'Sweet Jesus.' Lottie swung around in her chair. Chloe waved and walked over.

'Hello, Mother,' said Chloe. She nodded at the other detectives. 'So this is your busy schedule.'

'Sarcasm doesn't suit you,' said Lottie. 'Where's Sean?'

'Well, he's not with me.'

'Obviously,' retorted Lottie, quoting one of Chloe's favourite words.

'He's at home. We had Pot Noodles for lunch,' said Chloe, lingering behind her mother's chair.

'Yuk,' said Boyd, turning up his nose.

'What are you doing here?' asked Lottie, feeling the guilt trip her daughter was sending her on. 'You're underage.'

'Stating the obvious, Mother,' said Chloe, pulling at the string of a pink hoodie underneath her white puff jacket. She looked twelve, not sixteen. 'I'm looking for Katie and now I've found her.'

'I think you should go home,' said Lottie, aware they were now the focus of hushed attention. 'Wait for me outside. I'll catch up with you in a minute.'

Chloe turned, her blonde hair bobbing on top of her head, and she marched out of the pub.

'Don't fret about them,' said Lynch. 'Things will get better.'

'When?' asked Lottie. 'That's what I'd like to know. It goes from bad to worse.' Was that a smirk she noticed on Lynch's lips? She needed to keep a closer eye on Lynch. She didn't think she could trust her at all.

Ignoring her unfinished wine, she pulled on her jacket. 'I'll see you all at six in the morning. Thanks for the drinks. I owe you.'

'Need a lift?' asked Boyd. He remained seated.

'We'll walk. I want to clear my head. Thanks anyway.'

'Watch out for muggers,' said Kirby.

Lottie stopped for a moment in front of Katie and her friends, said nothing, kept going.

Boyd, Kirby and Lynch said nothing either. They sipped their drinks, listening to the fire crackling.

Outside the pub, pulling up her hood against the blizzard, Lottie thought it was sometimes easier to battle against the weather than the tumultuous storm raging within her. Chloe linked her hand through her arm and at last, Lottie felt warm.

* * *

The man stayed in the dark nook, obscured from the general crowd, until the detectives finally left the bar following another round of drinks. He was sure they hadn't noticed him. But it was getting to the stage where he didn't really care one way or the other. When the youth with the neck tattoo went to the bar, he joined him.

'Buy you a pint?' he asked, ordering one for himself.

'No thanks. I'm with a crowd.'

'You sure?' He waved a fifty.

'Would you ever piss off?'

The man stared into the dark eyes for a moment before paying for his pint and pocketing the change. And as he moved away, making it appear as accidental as he could, he brushed his hand down the young lad's spine, feeling the vertebrae beneath the cotton T-shirt.

'Oh, sorry,' he said. 'Bit crowded here tonight.'

'Fuck off, you pervert.'

The man returned to the nook, his fingers tingling and his body hardening. The anticipation was too much to bear. He would have to do something about it.

CHAPTER 55

Tom Rickard sat on the edge of the bed tying his shoelaces.

'Have I told you how beautiful you are?' he said.

'Only every five seconds in the last hour,' the woman said, her long hair framing her face. 'Tom, I don't know how much longer I can do this.'

He sighed as she pulled the sheet up to her neck, her damp body seductively outlined beneath it and a silver chain hanging down one glistening shoulder.

'Don't say that.' He turned and, leaning over, kissed her roughly on the lips.

She struggled to a sitting position, the sheet falling away to expose her flesh, warm and inviting. He wanted her again. Had he time?

'It's getting too difficult making up excuses,' she said. 'And some day someone is going to see us coming and going from here.' She paused. 'Tom, are you listening to me? Look at this place. How long can we keep this up? I hate it.'

He didn't trust himself to speak. He picked up his jacket from the narrow wooden chair and slipped it over his creased purple shirt. He scanned the room, seeing it for what it was. An inadequate two-bar electric heater in a corner, peeling paint dripping from the damp ceiling and cracked floorboards which had, more than once, resulted in cut feet for both of them. His lust had conjured the room into a lovers' paradise. The beautiful creature on the creaking bed deserved more than an ancient dormitory. But they were too well known to have their trysts in hotels. Definitely not now, with Melanie sniffing around him.

'Can we discuss this another time?' He sat back on the edge of the bed.

'There's no need to talk to me like I'm one of your junior employees. You can't just schedule me in your appointments diary for a quickie and then bugger off to Mrs Versace Rickard. We shouldn't even be in here, regardless of what we're doing when we're here.' She slumped on to the damp pillow and closed her eyes.

'Give me a while longer. I'm working things out. Honestly. We'll make it work. Together.'

'And how do you propose to do that? Get real, Tom. You are pathetic.'

'You want out?' he asked, horrified she might actually agree.

'No. Yes. I don't know. This isn't right.' She squeezed her eyes shut.

'Soon, very soon. I'm nearly there. Don't do anything rash. Not yet. Give me time.'

Her eyes flashed open and he shivered under the intensity of her gaze. Then she appeared to relent.

'Give me a kiss and I'll get dressed. We can leave together. This place turns my blood cold.'

He leaned over, ran his tongue along her shoulder, sucking on the chain in the curve, locked his mouth on hers and assaulted her with a violent kiss. A sharp scream escaped from her lips and he realised he had drawn blood from her mouth.

'Why did you do that?' she cried, pushing him away. She jumped out of the bed, pulled on her underwear. The smell of sex clung to her skin, musky, like yesterday's perfume. 'Sometimes I wonder about you,' she spat, disgust lacing every word.

'I'm sorry,' he said. The frustration of not being able to touch her last night at the ball bulged like a tumour inside him. He couldn't get enough of her. 'I'm sorry,' he repeated.

'So am I. I'm sorry I got involved in this sordid mess.' She zipped up her dress. 'I'm not so sure I want to be with you any longer.'

'Don't say that. I love you. We are meant for each other,' he pleaded.

'You see. That's what I mean.' She buttoned her cardigan, then her coat. 'You can be so immature. I've been through this before. I've watched men crumble under the weight of affairs. And you're turning out exactly like the rest.'

He watched her fasten the belt on her coat. When she laughed at him, it cut right through him. He stood with his mouth open.

'Oh, come on now. You honestly don't think this is my first time in this kind of situation. Grow up.' She laughed once more, picked up her handbag and pulled it on to her shoulder. 'You need to find another place for your regular shag. I'm never setting foot in here again.'

She banged the door. The windows rattled and he felt his heart shrink. Sitting down on the stained sheets, Tom Rickard shook his head. First Melanie losing it, now his lover. Add to the mix the financial mess he would be in if the St Angela's project failed, plus Detective Inspector Lottie Parker with her bloodhound nose, and he wondered how things could possibly get any worse.

Then he started to laugh.

He had faced worse and had come out the other side. This time would be no different. He was a fixer and he would fix this.

CHAPTER 56

It was snowing hard as they walked home and the cold air helped dilute the wine in Lottie's bloodstream. She trudged along with her daughter in silence; it was too miserable to talk, constantly looking over her shoulder to ensure she wasn't being followed. She didn't want to be paranoid, but still she worried the mugger might strike again.

At home she hung her jacket on the banister of the stairs and Chloe went into the sitting room. Sean was lying on the couch flicking through indiscriminate television channels. Chloe flounced on to the chair opposite him, arms folded. The room was warm, the atmosphere cold.

'I'm sorry,' said Lottie. 'I should've come straight home after work. But it was a long day and I needed to unwind first.' She leaned against the door watching her children. Why did she have to explain herself? Guilt?

Chloe lunged out of the chair and skipped over to her.

'No, I'm sorry,' she said, wrapping her arms around Lottie, hugging her. 'I was worried you might be on a binge. That's the real reason I went to the pub.'

Lottie welcomed her daughter's concern.

'You don't need to fret over me,' she said. 'I only had a couple. I won't be making it a regular occurrence.'

'You needn't think I'm going to hug you,' said Sean, smiling at them over his shoulder. 'I need a new PlayStation.'

'It's only two years old. What's wrong with it?' asked Lottie, freeing herself from Chloe.

'It keeps freezing. Niall looked at it and said it's almost at the red light of death. It can't be fixed,' said Sean. 'And I've had it four years, not two. I got it way before Dad died.'

'And Niall is an expert, is he?'

Lottie knew Sean's best friend was a master at taking things apart and building them up again. She hoped he was wrong. Red light of death? What the hell was that? Her budget wouldn't stretch to a new PlayStation.

'He *is* an expert. When can I get a new one?' Sean beseeched, the little boy in him overriding the teenager. 'I have some money in the bank.'

'You can't touch your money. You know it's held in a trust fund until you reach twenty-one.' She had invested Adam's small life insurance money in special accounts for the children.

'I know that. But I have a few hundred in my own account,' Sean sulked.

'I'll see what I can do. You're back to school in a few days so you'll be studying,' she said, hopefully. 'No time for PlayStation then.'

'I'll die without FIFA and GTA. There's nothing on the telly.'

Lottie sighed. Maybe she should cancel her Sky subscription.

'Come on, Chloe, let's see if there's anything besides Pot Noodles in the kitchen.'

Sean returned to his channel hopping, settling on a re-run of *Breaking Bad*.

Lottie wasn't sure if it was suitable for a thirteen year old, but hadn't the energy to protest.

CHAPTER 57

Mike O'Brien had left the bank in a foul mood, after he had dispatched Rickard's loans account to Head Office. He knew there could be repercussions. One day. Not yet, though. He had massaged the figures as best he could. Now, he had to wait and hope the account might get lost in cyber world. The diversion on his way home had done little to assuage his temper.

He sat with his orange-striped cat on his knee, as he did most nights. Classical music filled the air from the music system speakers. It usually served to relax him. Not tonight.

Chewing his nails, he stroked the purring creature. Most of his life was spent alone. He liked it that way. Loneliness and aloneness went hand in hand with him. He'd never been one for forming friendships, let alone relationships. He had a few acquaintances at the gym, Boyd the detective included. But they were not friends. His sexual inadequacies warped his sense of belonging. He had learned to live with it. Found ways to supplement it. Not always tastefully, but he survived. And another couple of months before the hurling season resumed. He missed training the young lads. The activity helped fill the spring evenings.

The doorbell sounded, screeching into his reverie.

Flinging the cat to the ground, O'Brien looked around wildly. Had Head Office sent the crime squad already? Could they be on to his fraudulent activity with the Rickard loans so quickly? That was insane. Not at nine o'clock at night.

He switched off the music, flicked back the curtain and peered into darkness. Living on the outskirts of town had its disadvantages, particularly since his home was in the middle of a Rickard ghost estate. Twenty-five houses, enclosed behind high walls, was the original plan, but only half were completed and the erection of intercom gates had not transpired. The remainder struggled against rusted scaffolding and wind howled through windowless concrete. The sound resonated through O'Brien's skull.

Pulling back from the window, his reflection in the glass was all that remained. He let the curtain fall and smoothed down its creases.

The doorbell rang a second time.

He cursed and went to answer it.

* * *

Bishop Connor had an anxious scowl scrawled on his face.

'Let me in, before someone sees me,' he said, pushing past O'Brien.

'What's wrong?' asked O'Brien, his smile faltering. He closed the door, having first checked no one else was outside.

'I hate cats.' Bishop Connor walked straight into the living room, eyeing the ginger cowering beneath a Queen Anne chair.

O'Brien clenched his hands into tight fists. This was his home.

'I'll take your coat,' he said, rescuing it from the back of the couch where Connor had dropped it. A cat hair clung to the shoulder. O'Brien plucked it away and hung the coat in the hall.

He returned to find Connor holding a fragile Lladro ornament of a young boy.

'Your décor could do with a facelift,' Connor said, returning the ceramic piece to the mantle.

'It serves me well. I don't see any reason to waste money unnecessarily.'

'Ah, yes. Ever the banker.'

'Drink?' asked O'Brien.

He poured generous fingers of whiskey into two crystal tumblers and handed one to Connor. They clinked glasses, remained standing and sipped the alcohol.

'That interfering Inspector Lottie Parker is poking her nose around,' said Connor.

'She has a job to do.'

'She knows I met that Sullivan woman and she's snooping about Father Angelotti.'

'That had nothing to do with you,' O'Brien said. 'Did it?'

'I do not need her joining any more dots.'

'What about your friend, Superintendent Corrigan? Won't he help?'

'I think I have exhausted that line of friendship.'

'Sit?' O'Brien indicated a chair. The cat sulked beneath it.

'I will stand,' said Connor, taking up centre position in the room.

O'Brien's legs felt weak, he needed to sit, but remained standing. 'What do you want me to do?'

'Get her off my back. We need to transfer her focus somewhere else.'

'And what do you propose?' O'Brien asked, a sense of helplessness swamping him. His throat constricted so he swallowed another draught of whiskey. Lottie Parker had ridiculed him in his own office yesterday. He'd love to make her pay for that, but what could he do?

'What about Tom Rickard? What does he have to say?'

'I am talking to you, not Rickard,' said Connor, his voice a shaft of steel.

The room seemed smaller with the bishop in it. O'Brien perspired uncontrollably and the glass slipped slightly in his hand. He placed it on the mantelpiece behind him.

'You and I know how important it is that nothing is uncovered.' With one step, Connor moved into O'Brien's personal space. He flicked a flake of dandruff from the banker's shoulder. 'Secrets have to remain just that. Secrets.'

O'Brien stepped back. His ankle collided with the fireguard. He had nowhere to go. Both men stood eye to eye. The sour whiskey odour turned his stomach. Connor's neck was naked of any religious collar and his carotid artery throbbed visibly in his pulsing throat. He watched it expand and contract, hypnotised, imagining it pumping blood into the bishop's heart, if he had one. He held his breath.

'What do you mean?' O'Brien asked, eventually.

'Do I have to spell it out for you?'

'No . . . no, I don't think so.'

Connor's eyes darkened. He put his glass beside the Lladro boy and planted his two hands on O'Brien's shoulders.

'Good. I cannot afford to lose out on this deal,' said Connor. 'You are the money man. You see to it that my finances and . . . everything else, remain untraceable.'

Each word reverberated throughout the room. He gave O'Brien a shake, removed his hands, picked up his whiskey glass, drained it and replaced it on the mantle. He turned away. Only then did O'Brien exhale.

'I hate cats,' Connor said again on his way out to the hall.

O'Brien didn't speak. He couldn't. The odour from the bishop's breath almost suffocated him. He rested against the fireplace for support.

Connor put on his coat.

'No need to see me out,' he said.

When the cat appeared from beneath the chair and rubbed against his leg, only then did O'Brien move.

* * *

To reach the position of a local authority county manager required a lot of hard work, brains and a good business acumen. It also helped that your father had once been a county manager. Gerry Dunne was no fool, he knew his father had worked behind the scenes to ensure his success. Now he regretted it. The job brought him too many problems for which he had the final decision. He hated making tough decisions, especially when he would be held responsible.

He had left work earlier but returned to check the file once more and silently cursed his interfering father. He flicked through St Angela's planning application file, thankful that James Brown had handed it over to him for final consideration, just before his untimely death. Consigned it to his desk drawer. Locked it. The project wasn't as contentious as it should be since they'd succeeded in contravening the development plan. But Tom Rickard wanted to be doubly sure, so he was willing to pay over more cash. Dunne wasn't about to decline the offer. Soon he hoped he could forget about it and get on with his life, without Rickard's claws scratching all over him. He looked out at the falling snow and wondered where the hell he was going to procure salt from, to last the rest of the week.

He picked up his coat, switched off the light and headed for home. Never before in his life had he felt this much pressure.

* * *

Switching the shower to full power, Mike O'Brien allowed the hot water to pinch his skin. He stood in the cubicle feeling very small.

Demons crawled along the inside of his scarred epidermis, choking out gasps of panic. He willed them away. He didn't like being reminded of the past. It was buried. For good. No one was going to resurrect it. No one. He scrubbed harder, his nails drawing red streaks along his arms and torso. He tried to drown the escalating rage that threatened to suffuse him.

He needed to escape the mental torment that was quickly overtaking his brain. Switching off the water, he allowed the bathroom air to cool his naked body.

There was only one way to calm his inner torment.

He dressed, fed his cat and went out into the night.

* * *

Bishop Terence Connor drove around for a while, then parked and sat for a long time. Going over and over his encounter with O'Brien.

He worried that he might have pushed too hard. Desperation was getting the better of him. Too many worms were escaping the can and he urgently needed to put a lid on it and nail it down tight. He didn't need another loose cannon, plus he had to make sure Tom Rickard kept his part of the bargain. They were all in this together. Drastic times called for extreme measures. He wondered if they were all up for it.

He sat there for a long time looking through the sleet, out over the frozen lake, visualising a sunny day, playing golf on the new St Angela's development. Yes, he thought, there were good days on the horizon.

CHAPTER 58

'I've had a visit from our friend, the bishop,' O'Brien said, settling into an armchair.

'What's that ugly bastard after now?' Rickard asked, offering O'Brien a drink.

O'Brien shook his head.

'I'm driving and I've had a couple already.'

'Suit yourself.' Rickard poured his own. 'You look nervous.'

'Yes, well, he has a way of scaring the shit out of me.'

Tom Rickard laughed loudly. 'Oh come on, don't be such a wanker. What'd he want?'

'He doesn't like the gardaí, especially Inspector Parker, snooping around our business.'

'Too late for that. Two of the victims have a link with our project, tenuous though it is. But we have nothing to hide.' Rickard scrutinised O'Brien. 'Have we?'

'No . . . no. I don't think so.'

'You don't think so?' Rickard towered over O'Brien. 'You better know so.'

'It's just . . . all those loans. I'll be in deep shit if you don't repay them soon.'

'That has nothing to do with our mutual friend.'

'Your loans support the deal.'

'I know my own business.' Rickard walked around his white leather couch. 'It'd answer Bishop Connor better if he minded his own business.'

'There are other things . . .'

'What are you talking about?'

'I . . . I can't say. But if they come out . . .'

'Jesus Christ man! Spit it out.'

'You don't need to know.'

'I'll tell you now, if the gardaí find something that I don't know about, this deal is off the table. Do you hear me? Off . . . the . . . table.' Rickard slammed down his glass, splashing whiskey on the arm of the couch. This night was going from bad to worse.

'You're not serious?' O'Brien said, widening his eyes in dismay.

'Oh, but I am. If you and Connor have concocted something behind my back, I will pull out.' Rickard folded his arms over his wide girth. 'Where will that leave the two of you then?'

'I . . . I . . . I . . .' O'Brien stood up, waving his hands in the air.

'I don't like you, O'Brien. But you know what? I don't have to like you.'

'Why not?'

'You know me, I call a spade a spade and you are the shite waiting to be scooped up. So you make sure the money is safe and keep out of my face.' Rickard turned to the door and opened it. 'Get out of my house.'

'I . . . I'm going.'

'You know what, O'Brien?'

'What?'

'You dress up all fancy, with your diamond cufflinks and designer suits, but that persona doesn't hide the fact that you are a sham without your costumes.'

'You're insulting me,' O'Brien said. Hadn't Lottie Parker reached the same conclusion? What right had either of them to do this to him? He hung his head.

'Get out,' Rickard shouted. 'Insults are nothing to what I'll do if you don't go now.'

O'Brien scuttled out the door.

Rickard poured another drink and went to the window.

'The little shite,' he said.

He flicked the curtain open, saw O'Brien's tail lights disappear down the drive, then he closed it over again, swallowed his whiskey and headed to his drinks table. He didn't like being kept in the dark and O'Brien had hinted there was something he should know about. That creep was too afraid of the bishop. What hold did Connor have over O'Brien? The banker was right about one thing, Rickard concluded. They could do without Inspector Lottie Parker messing up their project. Things were getting a little bit out of control.

He poured two more fingers of whiskey and drank greedily. The door opened and Jason sauntered into the room, hand in hand with Katie Parker. Melanie was behind them. Rickard stared at the young girl, seeing only her mother.

'I think you should go home, missy,' he said, pointing with his tumbler.

'Why?' asked Jason, his arm encircling Katie.

'Because her mother is a fucking detective inspector, that's why.'

'That's not a good enough reason,' said Jason. 'You're drunk.'

'Don't you dare question me,' Rickard roared, stepping closer to the pair.

'Well, you don't question me,' Jason said, pulling Katie tighter to his side.

Tom Rickard clenched his fist, reached out and struck his son on the cheek. The glass tumbled from his other hand to the ground and smashed. He hit the boy a second time, full on the jaw. Jason fell to the floor.

Katie screamed, turned and fled.

CHAPTER 59

Lottie stacked the dinner plates into the dishwasher, swept the floor and put the second load of the night into the washing machine. Clothes were drying on all the downstairs radiators and she turned up the boiler thermostat. The house was hot and the fresh scent of fabric conditioner floated around in the heat.

Stifling a yawn, she stretched her arms and thought about what else she had to do at this hour of the night. Looking around the kitchen, she felt comfortable in her own house. It wasn't a palace but it was her haven; a home for her and her children. She wished she could be here all the time. Not an option. Maybe she should ask her mother to do a few hours' housework? Then again, maybe not, she thought grimly. But she knew, in reality, she would have to make up with Rose soon. After all, she was her mother and she did love her, despite all Rose had done in the past. If only she could get to the truth of the matter. Another item for her to-do list. She replayed the conversation she'd had with Rose about Susan Sullivan. Maybe the murders had something to do with Susan's search for her child?

The front door opened, banged shut and footsteps thumped up the stairs.

'Katie?' Lottie called.

No answer. She went after her daughter and found her sobbing into her pillow. Sitting on the edge of the mattress, Lottie put her hand on Katie's shoulder.

'You're sopping wet. Did you walk home?' She wiped flecks of snow from her daughter's hair.

'It's your fault,' Katie sniffed. 'You and that job of yours. You've ruined everything for me. As usual.'

'What are you talking about?'

Lottie knew the girl was quite possibly half-stoned earlier in Danny's Bar, but her eyes were now wide with anger. Streaks of mascara blackened her chalk-white cheeks and the child Lottie had once nurtured was nowhere to be seen. She had no idea how to cope with Katie's dope smoking, though she was damn good at advising junkies' mothers she met through her job. She needed to address the issue. She would have to talk to that Rickard kid and get him, and his drugs, far away from her daughter. Boyd would help.

'Missus *Detective Inspector*,' Katie spat. 'You think you're so important, sitting in the pub with your three stooges. All grand and powerful. You know what? You're only a drunk. That's what you are. A drunk! You've ruined my life.' She buried her face into the pillow, smothering her cries.

Lottie jumped up, the words causing her skin to sting like an allergic reaction. She couldn't speak. She wrung her hands, biting back humiliation. She counted the posters on the wall. She counted the cubes of eye shadow on the dressing table. She counted the shoes lined up beside the bed. She looked around the room wildly. Panic and hurt pushed tears to the corners of her eyes. She wanted to reassure and comfort her daughter, but she didn't know how.

Katie raised her head from the pillow.

'Jason's dad hit him tonight,' she whimpered, once again the little girl Lottie knew and loved. 'I eventually got a taxi, after walking for miles. In the snow. In the dark. I was so scared.'

'Oh my God. You should've called me. Here, I'll help you out of those wet clothes and then you go to sleep.'

'Why would he hit him?' Katie sat up and struggled out of her damp jacket.

'I don't know why people do these things,' said Lottie. 'I honestly don't know.'

All she could think of was her wild daughter walking along the lake road on a dark winter's night. And three murder victims lying in Jane Dore's Dead House.

Had she taught her kids nothing?

CHAPTER 60

After Jason stormed out of the house, Tom Rickard watched Melanie turn away from him, a mixture of fear and disgust contorting her face.

His hand trembled as he poured another whiskey. Never in his life had he hit his son. What had possessed him to do it now? No matter what was going on in his business dealings, it was no justification for striking the boy.

Maybe he should just have another drink.

He loosened his tie and gulped the amber liquid.

Answers were like snowflakes on the window, disappearing before he could grasp them.

* * *

He hated his father.

In the instant the punch had connected with his jaw, Jason detested him more than anything or anyone in the world.

He'd run out of the house, rushed past his car, shoved his hands into his jeans pockets and marched off down the avenue. He'd turned on to the main road without knowing where he was going. He just needed to get away. He hoped Katie was all right. Shit, he'd let her walk home alone. In the dark. He stopped walking. He should ring her. Oh my God! He'd left his mobile at home on the hall table, with his keys.

And he'd left without his jacket. The snow was soaking through his T-shirt, into his body, clinging like a second skin. He was still stoned, but he couldn't go anywhere without his phone.

Turning to go back home, car lights lit up the road behind him. Realising he was walking on the wrong side, Jason stepped into the ditch to allow the car to pass. It slowed to a stop and the window rolled down.

'Need a lift, son?' the man asked, leaning across the passenger seat.

Jason thought he recognised him. A friend of his father's? The man from the bar? He couldn't be sure with the haze swarming around in his head. But he wasn't about to refuse a lift.

'Thanks. I don't know where I'm going, though.'

'No bother,' said the man. 'Neither do I.'

Jason opened the door and sat into the warmth. The man smiled, shifted the gears and drove. The wipers swished back and forth and the man clicked on the radio, drowning out the repetitive hum.

They drove through the night with the clear tone of Andrea Bocelli filling the silence. As snow fluttered and died, a sharp frost descended and a bright moon rose from behind the clouds. Jason shivered to the haunting strains of the blind man singing and he knew how it felt.

CHAPTER 61

Mrs Murtagh parked her Fiat Punto and hoisted her rucksack up on her back. She struggled with the large flask and plastic cups stuck out at an angle from the top of the bag. She hobbled on her walking stick, thinking how strenuous it all was, without Susan to help.

She missed Susan. Why was she killed? Hopefully it was nothing to do with any of their unfortunate clients. Poor desperate people. Concealed during the day from the eyes of the unseeing and uncaring people of Ragmullin, they blended into the bricks and mortar of the town. At night, they were the streetscape.

The air temperature quickly dropped to minus figures. Her breath hung in the air, preceding her as she shuffled along the icy footpath toward Carey's Electrical Shop. She set her flask on the ground. Patrick O'Malley was usually here, whether he was drunk or asleep.

Looking around, she saw no sign of him. Checked her watch. Same time as every other night. Keeping a regular timetable had been Susan's idea. Give these people at least one thing they could depend on, she'd said.

Mrs Murtagh sighed deeply. She picked up the flask and walked further down the street to her next wretched customer. With any luck, Patrick wasn't lying frozen to death somewhere.

More than likely, she thought, he was dead drunk.

CHAPTER 62

The building was dark, its windows sunken, hollow holes in the concrete.

'What're we doing here?' asked Jason, blinking his eyes open. Shit, he'd fallen asleep.

'Somewhere for you to kip for the night,' the man said, idling the engine.

'No way. Bring me home. I need my phone. I've to check my girlfriend's okay.'

'I'm sure she is fine. Who is she anyway?'

'Katie. Her mother is a detective.'

'Really?' The man was silent for a moment. 'How interesting.'

'I should go home,' said Jason, his body trembling with the cold.

'I thought all you youngsters loved adventure. I want to show you around. Give you a history lesson.'

'It's late and I hate history,' said Jason. He sat up straight as the man manoeuvred the car, headlights dimmed. He couldn't get a good look at him but he seemed familiar somehow.

'Ah, but this will be an interesting lesson,' the man insisted. He switched off the engine.

'It's very dark,' Jason said, trying not to sound like a little boy.

'Come on,' said the man, getting out of the car.

Jason got out and hitched his damp jeans to his waist.

The man turned on his phone's flashlight and walked up the steps towards the large solid door. Jason stood on the bottom step, undecided. Not wanting to be left outside alone in the dark, he followed.

The door creaked as the man pushed it open with his shoulder. He hurried inside. Sweeping the light around the marbled hallway, he shouted, 'Honey, I'm home.'

He laughed. The sound, loud and ugly, echoed around the walls. And he walked toward the staircase. The wooden banisters seemed to evoke some memory in him; he stroked the timber with his fingers and laid his cheek down, as if feeling the smoothness underneath.

Jason toyed with running back down the steps, out the gate and home. But his father had been a total jerk. His jaw still throbbed from the impact of the fist. He craved a joint. Hell, if Katie was with him, they'd have some laugh at this shithead kissing the staircase.

'Up here,' the man said, walking up the stairs, leaving Jason in a wake of darkness.

A loud shriek echoed high above their heads.

'What's that?' Jason ducked.

The man sniggered.

'Only the wind whistling along these old corridors,' he said. 'Or birds. Never know which. Come, I want to show you something.'

Jason, cold and wet, itched to see what was up the stairs. Anger at his father fuelled his resolve. He stomped up the stairs.

What harm could it do?

CHAPTER 63

Lottie's phone rang at quarter to midnight.

She was going over her case notes, cursing the fact that she'd left Mrs Murtagh's brown bread in Boyd's car. Superintendent Corrigan's name flashed on the screen. She ignored it. Too late to listen to a tirade. The phone stopped. Instantly, it rang again. Knowing Corrigan wouldn't give up, she answered without looking at the caller ID.

'Yes, sir?'

'That's a very official-sounding greeting.'

Lottie smiled and folded up her notes.

'Father Joe. Good to hear from you.'

'How's the investigation going?'

'Slow is an understatement.'

'Come visit me in Rome. The weather is beautiful. Cold with blue skies.'

'Sounds nice. But—'

'You're wondering what I'm doing ringing you at this hour, right?'

'Mind reader.'

He laughed. 'How're you keeping?'

'I'm okay,' Lottie lied.

She wasn't okay at all. She'd cradled Katie to sleep before returning to the kitchen with her daughter's words reverberating in her brain. A drunk? Was the girl correct? Wasn't that what she'd become since Adam died? She controlled it most of the time but not totally and she was becoming more dependent on her pills. Great role model for her teenage children. She sighed.

'You're not okay. I can hear it in your voice,' he said. 'Come to Rome. I've sourced interesting information. You need to look at it, first hand.'

'Have you uncovered another Da Vinci code?' joked Lottie.

'Not quite. I found St Angela's records. They're in a secure location, all hard copy. It would be impossible to photograph them to fax or email. It would take forever. And if I was caught I'd be excommunicated. In all seriousness, you need to look at them yourself. Could you swing it with your superintendent?'

'Not a chance,' Lottie said. 'I've been stepping clumsily on your bishop's toes. I think he's reported me again.'

'You're only doing your job.'

'He is Superintendent Corrigan's golf buddy.'

'If I were you I'd stand very hard on said bishop's toes. Believe it or not, he's not the goody two shoes he makes himself out to be.'

'Do you honestly think what you've found will help?'

'I don't know. But it will provide you with background information. Fill in a few gaps, maybe.'

'Bishop Connor is definitely being economical with the truth,' Lottie said.

'I'm not surprised, after the documents I've seen.'

'You have me interested now. Anything relating to Father Angelotti?'

'I met a friend of his. He thinks maybe Father Angelotti was sent over there to keep an eye on Bishop Connor; not the other way around, as we were led to believe.'

'Then Father Angelotti goes and gets himself murdered.'

Father Joe had piqued her interest and now she wanted to see what he had found. She wanted to see him.

'Lottie, the stuff I've seen here tells me there might also be another reason why Father Angelotti was in Ragmullin.'

'Tell me.'

'I'm not comfortable discussing this on the phone,' Father Joe whispered.

'Are you in bed?' Lottie asked.

'Now who's the mind reader?' He laughed. 'I've to go. I hear my roommate coming up the stairs.'

'Not got your own room?'

'I don't intend being here long enough to warrant having my own place,' he said. 'Just bunking in the Irish College for a couple of nights. Lottie, see what Superintendent Corrigan says, okay?'

'Right. Will I get you on this number?' She looked at the line of digits on the screen.

'Leave a message if I don't answer. I could be saying Mass.'

Lottie imagined his smile.

'Good night, Lottie.'

She said goodnight and disconnected the call.

She tidied up the last of her notes and went upstairs to check on Katie. Fast asleep. She feathered a kiss on her hair and went to switch off the lamp. A photograph on the locker, framed with seashells, caught her attention. She lifted it up to have a better look. The five of them. Lanzarote. Four years ago. The last time they'd had a holiday together. She ran her finger over the dusty glass. All smiling. Happy. Taken as they began a jeep trip up Timanfaya volcano.

She slumped down on the bed and Katie sighed in her sleep.

The photograph had stirred a vision of a time when things were so different. Routine, secure and loving. Conflict raged inside her. She was torn between her stable past and uncertain future. Three years and she couldn't let Adam go. But contemplating flying to Rome to meet up with a priest she'd only met a week ago made her think that maybe the wheels on her wagon were well and truly coming off.

* * *

30th January 1976

Sally cried in her sleep and awoke.

She half-expected to see her mother standing at her bed. It was Patrick.

He put his finger to his lips and made a shushing sound. She sat up, inquisitive as to why he was in the girls' dorm. She scanned the room through the darkness, hearing only the soft murmur of sleep.

'Come with me,' Patrick whispered, yanking off her blanket. 'I need to show you something.'

She crept out of bed, pulling her flowery flannelette nightdress tight to her chest. He didn't give her time to fetch her dressing gown.

'Where are we going?' she asked.

'Ssh,' he said and grabbed her hand.

Outside the dorm, a muted light escaped from beneath a dusty lamp-shade hanging over the staircase. The duty nun's room was at the opposite end of the corridor and Patrick led Sally down to the second floor. They crept to the end of the hall and through a door. She had not been here before. They scurried in the darkness and he opened another door heralding a short passageway. Moonlight shone through the three windows, lighting up their faces like corpses. An archway lay before her.

She stopped.

'I'm afraid, Patrick.'

He turned and, still holding her hand, said, 'This is serious, Sally. Please. You have to see it.'

She sighed and allowed herself to be led through the archway, down the narrow, stone staircase. Her feet were cold. She had forgotten to put on her slippers. On the bottom step, Patrick paused. They were in the chapel. She turned to look at him. He shook his head, a warning to be silent. This was the first time she'd come this way.

She noticed the altar lit up with burning candles and she smelled their grease. Then she saw Father Con. She gripped Patrick's hand tighter. The priest was kneeling on the steps of the altar, wrapped in a heavy cream and gold cape, the one he wore for benediction. His hands, outstretched toward the mosaic of the Virgin Mary holding the baby Jesus, in an alcove in front of him. His long leather belt was sitting on top of his neatly folded clothes, on the step.

Sally sidled up to Patrick, leaning into him. Though the air was cold, he wore thin pyjamas and she could feel heat rising from his body.

'Patrick, what's going on?' she whispered.

He shook his head, shrugged his shoulders and led her to the right, along the last row of kneelers. He pulled her into the corner behind a wooden confessional. Someone else was there. Two people. She almost screamed. Patrick looked at her, anger flaring in his eyes. She held her breath, hoping the scream would die somewhere in her belly.

As her eyes became accustomed to the shadows cast by the candles, she recognised the boys in the corner. James and Fitzy. Patrick shoved her in beside them and they huddled together. She wanted to ask a thousand questions but kept her silence. Patrick continued to hold her hand. She was glad.

A low hum rose to a crescendo then fell again. She widened her eyes and bit her tongue between her teeth, willing herself to be silent.

The priest bowed, up and down, chanting. A curtain, at the side of the altar, opened. Brian stood there, naked, his body crisscrossed in deep, red welts. She looked away, then back again and tightened her hold on Patrick's hand in case he might leave her there. The priest stood up and beckoned Brian to him. The naked boy shuffled forward, arms tight against his sides. He must be freezing, Sally thought.

The boy was pushed to his knees and the priest enclosed him in the gold cape. She couldn't bear it and this time she did scream.

Patrick clamped a hand over her mouth. Father Con swung round, his nakedness emblazoned by the candle light. His eyes were black. This frightened Sally more than the fact that they were all in deep trouble.

'*Run,*' *Patrick shouted, dragging Sally behind him.*

She ran, Fitzy clipping her bare heels. James brought up the rear. As they raced up the stairs, the image of Brian imprinted itself on her brain. Naked body. Open mouth. Dead eyes.

In the room with two doors they stopped to catch their breath. Sally began to cry. Fitzy put his arm around her shoulder. James stood beside Patrick, uttering over and over, 'Jeepers creepers. Jeepers creepers.'

'*What was he doing to Brian?*' *Sally asked, but she knew. Father Con had forced her to do the same thing numerous times. She couldn't quell the image of the boy with his mouth open and the white stuff stuck to his lips.*

'*He's a big shite, that's what he is,*' *Patrick said.*

'*I'll burn the bastard with one of them frigging candles. Burn him in the goolies,*' *Fitzy said. His voice echoed off the walls.*

Sally heard the fear crawling around in their breathing, smelled it oozing from their skin. It manifested itself so painfully clear, she believed she could see it, touch it even. She listened at the door, hoping the priest hadn't followed them. She didn't like the dark.

'*We have to do something,*' *she whispered.*

'*Yeah,*' *Patrick said, 'like what?'*

'*I mean it. Honestly. What can we do?*' *Sally sobbed, gulping down her tears.*

The slap of bare feet thumped up the stairs. She swirled round and saw the whites of the boys' eyes shining in the moonlight. Terror had struck them immobile.

'*Lads, what are we going to do?*' *she cried.*

James began to sob.

DAY SEVEN

5th January 2015

CHAPTER 64

Detective Sergeant Larry Kirby was tacking computer-printed photographs to the board in the incident room when Lottie arrived just after five thirty a.m. She hadn't slept well and a bitch of bad humour was itching to escape.

'You're up early,' she said, placing her lukewarm coffee on the windowsill and pulled off her jacket.

She'd left her car at the station the night before but the walk into work had done nothing to brighten her mood. She stood beside Kirby. Cigar smoke clung to his clothes, like dirty socks in the bottom of her laundry basket. She was glad she'd cleared all the laundry last night. One less chore to worry about.

'Didn't go to bed, so I didn't have to get up,' he said, clumsily pushing thumbtacks into the photographs. His tobacco-stained fingers were too large for the small steel pins. One fell on the floor, joining a multitude already gathered there.

'What are you doing?'

'Decided to reorganise the incident board. It's a week since all this started.'

'Don't remind me. Do you want me to do that for you?'

Kirby shook his head.

Lottie shrugged, picked up her coffee and sat down behind him.

'Tell me what I'm looking at.' Maybe she should have brought a coffee for him. He looked like he could fall asleep any minute.

'Photos of the main players in our drama,' he said.

She scanned the board. So far, he had Patrick O'Malley, Derek Harte, Tom Rickard and Gerry Dunne hanging crookedly side by side. He held the bishop's photo in one hand, a tack in the other.

'I wouldn't do that if I were you,' she advised.

He looked at her, his grey-haired belly showing through an open button halfway down his creased, off-white shirt, a spotty tie poking out of his jacket pocket.

'And why not? After your episode with him yesterday, I think he's the star of the show.'

'Superintendent Corrigan might have something to say about that,' said Lottie. 'After all, they are golfing friends.'

She hadn't returned his call last night. She'd be in for a bollocking soon. Hopefully Mrs Corrigan had sent her husband out with a smile and a full stomach this morning.

'To hell with him,' said Kirby, sticking a thumbtack squarely in the bishop's neck, as if he couldn't be arsed jamming in three more pins. He stepped back and admired his handiwork. A tired grin crawled up his face toward bloodshot eyes, like a creamy head forming on a pint of Guinness.

'They're not really suspects,' said Lottie.

'They're the next best thing.'

He slumped into a chair. They sat in the silence of the morning. She handed him her coffee. He took it, raised it in a mock toast and drank.

'We've a very narrow spectrum of candidates,' he said, looking up at the lopsided display.

'We could add Mrs Murtagh, Bea Walsh, and Mike O'Brien the bank manager,' she said, 'then we have the sum total of all the people we know about who knew the victims. Christ, it's like Brown and Sullivan lived in an enclosed order of nuns.'

'Shit, where did I put O'Brien?' Kirby rooted around a pile of papers on the chair, found what he was looking for and pinned another photograph on the board.

'What about Father Joe Burke?' asked Boyd as he walked in, his cropped hair glinting under the fluorescents, fresh from his morning shower.

'What about him?' asked Lottie, her defences bumping tiny goosepimples up on her skin.

'He was first on the Sullivan crime scene after Mrs Gavin, the cleaner,' said Boyd, sitting down beside Kirby. He had a mug of coffee in his hand. Lottie took it from him and drank.

'We better get a photograph of Mrs Gavin too,' she said, unable to disguise her sarcasm.

'Let's be serious here for a minute,' said Kirby.

Lottie knew Kirby didn't like anyone denigrating his work into a sideshow. He was over-tired.

Kirby pointed at Derek Harte's photo.

'Lover boy could have killed the priest, Father Angelotti, in a jealous rage,' he said. 'Then killed Brown when he found out.'

'But why kill Sullivan?' asked Boyd.

Kirby glared at him. 'I don't know . . .'

'Yet,' Lottie added.

'Next, we have Tom Rickard. Property developer extraordinaire,' said Kirby. 'Acquired St Angela's for a song. Got a Material Contravention of the development plan pushed through the council, probably with a bribe, so he can build anything he likes on the site. Once his friend, Gerry Dunne, grants planning permission.' He pointed over at the victims' photographs. 'The two council employees could've been trying to stop him or maybe were running a blackmail caper. Hence, the large sums of money transferred into their bank accounts, some of which resided in Sullivan's freezer box. Brown called Tom Rickard, before he met his maker. With both Sullivan and Brown out of the way, he can give everyone the finger behind their backs.' Kirby jabbed his thick forefinger at the photo of Rickard.

'For a minute, let's assume you're right, where does Father Angelotti fit in?' asked Boyd.

'I haven't the foggiest,' said Kirby, scratching his head of wiry hair. 'But he might've been following the money.'

'Continue,' said Lottie, getting more interested in Kirby's little drama.

'Speaking of money . . . Mike O'Brien.' Kirby studied the photograph for a second. 'He knows who transacted the monies into the victims' accounts. Is he a middleman? I don't know. Maybe we should look at him more closely. And then we have our mutual friend, Bishop Connor.'

He paused for effect, then continued. 'He sold St Angela's below its market value. Who is to say he didn't get a fat brown envelope bursting with euros, straight from Rickard's paw? We should check his freezer too.' He laughed at his own joke, then smothered it with a cough. 'Back to Father Angelotti. Why was he here? I don't buy this "finding himself" shite. He came here for a reason.'

Lottie said nothing. She was thinking of her late night conversation with Father Joe. She looked out at the sleet, beating against the window, eating up the frost. A day in sunny Rome might be a good idea.

'I still think Father Joe Burke's photo should be up there,' said Boyd, the bone securely between his teeth.

'Put it up then,' Lottie said, prickly as a thorn bush.

'Touchy this morning, Inspector,' said Boyd.

'Don't you two start,' said Kirby, his eyes drooping with exhaustion.

'Did I miss anything?' asked Maria Lynch, entering the room, her ponytail bobbing from side to side. She had a bag of croissants in her hand.

Three sets of eyes turned to her.

'No,' came the synchronised reply.

Superintendent Corrigan followed Lynch, spraying spittle over the seated detectives before words even reached his mouth.

'Detective Inspector Parker!'

He stood, hands on hips, legs apart, his face as flushed as Kirby's. So, he hadn't been sent to work with a fry.

'Sir?' Lottie queried.

'My office.'

Corrigan turned on his heel and headed down the corridor.

Handing Boyd the coffee, Lottie mentally formulated responses to the inevitable questions. Prepared for the fight, she followed Corrigan into his office.

'Before you say anything, sir—' she began.

'No, Inspector Parker,' he interrupted, raising his hands. He sat down on his leather chair, air hissing out under his weight.

'Before *you* say anything, don't feckin' feed me excuses. I don't want to hear them. Are we clear?'

Lottie nodded, not trusting the words that might find their way to the tip of her tongue.

'You better have a good reason for upsetting Bishop Connor. Again.'

'Was that a question, sir?' So much for keeping her mouth shut.

Corrigan's spectacles slipped down his sweaty nose, his eyes bulging over them, the top of his head like a boiled egg about to be cracked with a hot spoon.

'Explain yourself. Before I get the chief superintendent to suspend you.'

'Suspend me?' This was serious. Shit. 'What for?'

'I'll think of something,' he said, his voice reducing the size of the room.

She held her breath before blurting out, 'I want to go to Rome.' Might as well go for the full monty, she thought.

'Ro . . . Rome?' Corrigan stammered. 'Do you want to insult the feckin' Pope now?' He pushed his spectacles back into place.

Lottie kept her mouth firmly shut.

'And sit down. Sit down, for God's sake. Standing there like a giraffe lost in the feckin' zoo.'

Lottie sat.

'Are you stupid?' Corrigan raised his hands despairingly. 'What's got into you?'

'I need to go to Rome,' Lottie chanced again. 'I think Father Angelotti is the link to the Sullivan and Brown murders. And the answer to that link is in Rome.' She hoped she sounded convincing, because she didn't know what Father Joe had uncovered. She continued before Corrigan could interrupt. 'I need to see St Angela's records. Two children were murdered there, almost forty years ago, and two of our victims were resident there at that time. I believe those records may help establish a motive. They should be archived in the Dublin Archdiocese but for some unknown reason they've been transferred to Rome. So I need to go to Rome.'

'You're either drunk or mad,' Corrigan said. 'And I can't smell alcohol so it must be the latter.'

'That's a no, is it?'

'Most definitely.'

'Can I explain where I'm coming from?' Lottie asked.

'You can't even explain where you're going to,' Corrigan thundered. 'But I'll explain something to you, Inspector Parker.' He stood up and paced around her. 'We are a week into these investigations and so far you've come up with sweet Fanny Adams. I'm giving daily press conferences, talking a load of shite, because you, Boyd, Kirby, Lynch and the other clowns in your circus out there are too busy playing stick the feckin' tail on the feckin' donkey photos to give me any answers. The people of Ragmullin are scared shitless. The murderer is out there laughing at us and what do you want to do? To go arsing around feckin' Rome. Hah!'

He ceased his tour round her and sat down, more air escaping. Lottie wondered if it was from the chair or his arse.

'There's a logical explanation and I've a gut feeling—' She stopped mid-sentence as Corrigan's cheeks flamed purple.

'I don't want any bullshit about women's intuition or gut feelings, do you hear me?'

'Yes sir.'

'And stop harassing Bishop Connor. If I see his name appear on my phone again, I'll have you suspended before I answer the call. Are we on the same page, Inspector?'

'Yes sir,' Lottie said, biting back that Connor might be ringing for a round of golf.

'And stay away from Tom Rickard too.'

'Yes sir.'

'Now get out and do constructive work, if you still know what that means.'

Superintendent Corrigan took off his spectacles, rubbed his eyes, and when he replaced them, Lottie was halfway out the door. She heard his words as she retreated.

'Rome me feckin' arse.'

CHAPTER 65

Tom Rickard chewed his breakfast. Vigorously.

'Jason never came home last night,' Melanie said.

'I know.' Rickard stuffed a sausage into his mouth.

'I'm worried,' she said, refilling his mug from a red Le Creuset teapot. 'He often stays out, but after what went on last night, you know . . .' Her voice cut as sharp as the knife he was holding.

Rickard raised his head, picked a piece of egg from between his teeth and swallowed it.

'He'll be home soon enough.'

'You never hit him before, even when he was little. Not so much as a slap. What got into you? And in front of his girlfriend. You are despicable.'

Running his tongue around his teeth, Rickard lifted the fork and finished his breakfast. He stirred three spoons of sugar into his tea and gulped it loudly.

He said, 'He's hanging out with the wrong sort. I'm going to put a stop to it this very day.'

'You do realise there's a murderer out there and our son has disappeared.'

'Don't be stupid,' he said. 'He probably spent the night wrapped around that young one.'

'Like you? Where did you take off to late last night?'

'Don't go there, Melanie.' Rickard watched her through the tines of his fork.

'You hit our son, then you do your disappearing act,' Melanie sneered. 'Were you with your perfume blonde?' She sniffed the air as if he carried around the other woman's scent.

Rickard refilled his cup. He wondered how many pieces the teapot would shatter into if he threw it at the wall. Or maybe at her head.

A phone rang in the hall. Rickard got up to answer it, thinking it had just saved him from an act of madness.

* * *

Katie Parker awoke with a headache banging behind her eyes. She pulled her phone from under her pillow. No missed calls. No texts.

She tapped Jason's number. Why had his father been so angry?

Voicemail. His voice laughed through the message. 'Hey bud, I'm obviously not able to take your call, don't bother to leave a message. Ha. Ha.'

Katie smiled.

'Hi hon. Hope you're okay. Ring me when you wake up. Love ya.' She hung up, then sent him a text with two lines of happy emojis.

She nuzzled into her pillow and groaned as more memories of last night hit home.

She'd called her mother a drunk.

She buried her head under her duvet and moaned.

* * *

Tom Rickard stared at the phone in his hand. His son's mobile; it quickly registered with him that Jason had left last night without it. It stopped ringing. He saw the name 'Katie' on the screen and the voicemail icon flashed.

He listened to the girl's words, realising Jason had not spent the night with her. He looked at the boy's phone in his hand. Jason went nowhere without it. So where was he?

Going back to finish his breakfast, Rickard figured he hadn't hit the little prick half hard enough.

* * *

Jason Rickard woke to scratching sounds above his head. Tried to sit up. Couldn't. His hands and feet were tied with a rope, wound up his torso and around his neck. Tremors convulsed his body. Fuck, fuck, double fuck. What happened? He tried to remember but his mind was blank.

He moved his neck a little, trying to see around him. Nothing. Dark. Black. He turned his head. The rope tightened at his throat. Pain throbbed as if a beetle had burrowed through his ear and lodged in his brain. He realised he was trussed up like a Christmas turkey.

This was no prank.

This was serious shit.

Relaxing his body on to the cold floorboards he tried to call out, but instead succumbed to loud sobs.

He wanted his mother.
He wanted Katie.
He wanted to kill his bastard of a father.

CHAPTER 66

Lottie followed Boyd into the cupboard canteen. He boiled the kettle.

'Who does Corrigan think he is?' she hissed. Clenching her teeth, she thumped the makeshift counter.

'He's the boss, that's who,' Boyd said. He found two clean mugs and spooned in coffee.

Leaning against the wall, with her arms folded as if they might keep her anger under wraps, she said, 'I even put on my subordinate act. He didn't buy it. Wouldn't even listen to me.'

'I wouldn't listen to you either,' he said. 'Look at it from his viewpoint. We haven't turned up a solid piece of evidence in any of the murders. Now that it's out about Sullivan working in the soup kitchen, she's on the front pages again. Corrigan has to answer to his hierarchy and to the public. The locals think we're doing feck all to find this killer.'

'Jesus, you sound just like him,' Lottie spat back. She took a couple of deep breaths. 'I might have a solid lead in Rome but he didn't want to know.'

'What are you talking about?'

She told him about her talk with Father Joe. Boyd's face remained passive. She wished he'd show some emotion, anger even.

'Be sensible, Lottie,' he said. 'With modern technology I'm sure *your* priest can figure out some way of sending on this information.' The kettle boiled and he poured the water into the mugs. 'There's no milk.'

'I don't want milk. I want answers. One possible lead and I get stonewalled.' She took the mug, sipped the coffee and allowed the silence to restore stillness to her mind. 'Maybe you're right,' she said eventually.

'About what?'

'Maybe I should contact Father Joe again. See if he can find some way to send me whatever he found.'

'That's a start anyway,' Boyd said.

Her phone rang. She looked at the screen.

'It's Katie. Another problem I have to sort out.'

'Can't help you there. Sure what would I know?'

Boyd eased past her, his body brushing against hers. He dipped his head in apology and kept walking.

She pretended not to notice his fleeting touch but it warmed her.

'Katie, are you okay?'

'. . . and I haven't heard a word from him,' Katie was saying.

'Start again. I was distracted,' Lottie said.

'Jeesuus Mam! It's Jason. I don't know where he is. His mother rang me from his phone. He didn't come home last night.'

Lottie glanced at the time.

'It's only just gone seven. He's probably kipped down in a friend's house somewhere.'

'Mam! He goes nowhere without his phone. Mrs Rickard said he left shortly after me. After his dad hit him. I'm worried.'

'Well, there's nothing to worry about. Trust me. He's probably nursing his bruised ego. His father was wrong to hit him but Jason has to sort it out himself. When he figures how to do that, he'll be home. He's nineteen, not nine.'

'I hope you're right,' Katie said. 'And I'm sorry.'

'For what?'

'Calling you a drunk. I didn't mean it. Honest. You're the best mother anyone could have.' Katie's voice filled with tears.

'Thank you,' Lottie said, a surge of relief shaking the mug in her hand. 'Look, I've to go. I'll talk to you later. I'm on a warning from war-horse Corrigan. Eat some breakfast and let me know as soon as you hear from Jason.'

Lottie went back to the incident room. Glancing at the board, she noticed Kirby had stuck up Father Joe Burke's photograph.

CHAPTER 67

Mike O'Brien was working hard at pretending to work.

His PA, Mary Kelly, wiggled her bottom as she leaned over her desk outside his office. For a moment he studied her figure through the open door. But he wasn't interested. Too many thoughts clouded his brain. Bishop Connor had rattled him last night. Tom Rickard had angered him. Between the whole lot of them he was teetering on the edge.

His fingers shook as he tried to type in figures. It was gobbledegook. Air. He needed air. Nice cold wintery air. He logged off and pulled on his coat.

'Mary, I've to go out. Take messages if anyone is looking for me. I won't be long.'

He buttoned his coat.

'If Head Office ring about the figures you sent yesterday, what will I tell them?'

'Tell them to go and shite,' O'Brien said and kept walking.

* * *

Bishop Connor unlocked his car and sat into the cream leather seat. Should he have been so hard on O'Brien last night? Maybe he shouldn't have gone on about putting off the inspector. That might in fact make her more suspicious. God knows what O'Brien would do and, if he cracked, he was liable to do anything. He was the weak card in the deck. But you always need a money man, he thought.

What was done was done. He was not one for doubling back on his convictions. At least Father Angelotti was out of the way. That was good. There were enough meddlers in his affairs to last him until his deathbed. The project would go ahead. A new hotel and golf course. Membership for life, with all the time in the world to enjoy it.

Things were going well. At last.

He turned up the radio and cruised along the road, humming to the music.

* * *

The traffic was crawling on the icy road.

Gerry Dunne wanted to be at work early. Not looking likely now. He needed to go over the file one last time. His phone rang. Bea Walsh. He ignored it. She was an interfering busybody. Only yesterday she had tried to tell him that the file for St Angela's was missing. He had politely told her it was in hand. In hand? One more day, then it would be out of his hands and he'd be off the hook, with a fat envelope of euros. He wondered if his wife Hazel would like another week in the sun.

As the car idled at the traffic lights on the junction of Main Street and Gaol Street, in his rear-view mirror he saw Mike O'Brien pull out of a parking space, scream down the street and drive straight through the red light. Who put ants in his knickers? Dunne couldn't wait for all this to be over.

Another week in the sun? It was looking more attractive by the minute.

CHAPTER 68

'What are you doing?' Boyd asked, peering over Lottie's shoulder.

'I'm checking flights to Rome,' she said, cursing Ryanair and what seemed like a million boxes she must tick.

'Are you totally mad? Who's paying?'

'Me.'

'Well, that's a first. I've never in my life heard of a detective paying their own way for anything to do with work.'

He wheeled over his chair and sat beside her.

'Don't look at what I'm doing and you won't have to tell any lies,' she said, tapping the keyboard.

'Did you hear anything I said to you earlier? This is crazy.'

'You said that already. Stop repeating yourself.'

'I want nothing to do with it.' Boyd stood up.

'Who asked you?'

Kirby glanced up at them, shaking his head.

'Why don't you go and do something useful?' Lottie muttered.

'Like what?' Boyd asked.

'Talk to Brown's lover Derek Harte again. See if you can get anything else out of him. He's holding something back. Follow up with that young priest in the bishop's house, Father Eoin. Is that his name? Talk to Patrick O'Malley. Find the elusive Father Con. Will I write you a list?' They'd had no luck finding Father Con, whoever he was, and she realised there was a lot of things they still hadn't got a handle on.

Boyd kicked back the chair, clattering it into a radiator, grabbed his coat and banged the door on his way out.

A flight was leaving at one thirty. She glanced at the clock. Enough time to get to the airport. If she hurried. Seventy-nine euro including taxes. Not too bad. She couldn't really afford it. Could she? The powers-that-be wouldn't reimburse her unless she had prior approval and she hadn't time for that. It was going to be at her own cost. But she needed to do this. Clicked it.

'For feck's sake,' she said.

'What's up?' Kirby glanced over his screen.

'Nothing.'

She looked in her drawer for a pill to calm her nerves. Couldn't find one. As she slid it shut she noticed the old file. Alone in the midst of the chaos. Sitting. Waiting. For an answer? Could the old records now in Rome give her answers after all this time? If so, it would be worth the expense.

'Seventy-nine euro one way; return flight in the morning, another fifty-five,' she said. Kirby pretended he wasn't listening.

Definitely can't afford it. She searched her wallet for her credit card. The bill was due. She bit her bottom lip thinking; churning everything over in her head. Had Father Joe really found something useful? What if she was wrong about him? What if he was the one who murdered Sullivan and Brown, even Father Angelotti? What was the truth? But she realised, whatever she might owe on her Visa bill, she owed this to the victims.

She reached into the drawer and removed the old file on the missing boy. It haunted her like a tenacious ghost. Placing it beside her keyboard, she opened it and looked at the boy's photograph. Ran her finger over his freckles. Made her decision. If Corrigan wants to suspend me, might as well give him a good reason. Entered her card details. Transaction complete. Boarding card printed. Before she could change her mind.

'Shit.' She ran both hands through her hair, scrunching it tight.

'What now?' asked Kirby.

'I've to get someone to mind my kids.'

Kirby shook his head and went back to what he was doing. 'That's definitely not on my CV.'

Lottie dug her nails into her head. Swallowing her pride, she called her mother.

CHAPTER 69

He must have fallen back asleep because when he opened his eyes he could see a thin stream of light.

The man. Standing in the doorway. Jason blinked. He couldn't see properly.

'What do you want with me?' he croaked.

'I am not sure. Not sure at all. I picked you up on a whim. Never done that before. It felt quite exciting having such young flesh sitting beside me.'

'You're a pervert.'

'Silly boy, calling me names. You might be sorry.'

'What did you do to me? If you touched me, I swear to God, my father will kill you.'

'Going by what you told me last night, I would not count on him.'

'Did you . . .?' Jason's voice quivered.

'Did I what?'

Jason knew he was being mocked.

'Did I touch you? No. Not yet anyway. Thinking about it. Long and hard.' He laughed and rubbed his hand along his groin.

Jason's body convulsed.

'Did you drug me?'

'A pill sent you to dreamland. I could not risk you fighting back. That would defeat the purpose of the exercise.'

'What exercise?'

'As I say, I have not quite figured that out, yet. Are you hungry?'

'I'm thirsty. Please untie me.'

A gusty sound filled the room as the man snorted.

'Maybe some food and water. Next time.'

He turned to leave.

'Please let me out of here. I want to go home,' Jason said, breathing a white fog into the cold air.

'You will do exactly what I tell you.' The voice rose, then faded, trailing unspoken menace in its wake.

The door clunked shut and a key turned in the lock.

Jason waited. Listened. Scratching in the ceiling above him and a bird cawing somewhere in the distance.

That's all he heard, otherwise it was deathly silent.

CHAPTER 70

After numerous protestations, Boyd agreed to cover for her.

'It's only until tomorrow,' Lottie said.

'I shouldn't—'

'Thanks Boyd. I knew I could count on you.' She squeezed his arm. 'If asked, I'm searching the victims' homes again. Following up clues. Talking to suspects.'

'What suspects? What clues?'

'Is there an echo in here?' Lottie cupped her ear. 'You'll think of something.'

If Father Joe had found something worthwhile, she was in the clear, but Corrigan would probably suspend her anyway once he found out she had disobeyed his orders. Then again, he hadn't categorically said no. Had he? Feck him.

Back at home, Lottie emptied Sean's school rucksack, stacked his books on top of the drier and ran upstairs to find clean clothes. Dragging shirts and sweaters from hangers, she watched the pile grow into a leaning tower on the bed.

'What are you doing?' Chloe asked, standing in the doorway, still in her pyjamas.

'I'm going to Rome. Work stuff. I rang your grandmother to stay the night.'

'What? Ah no.'

'I know, I know,' Lottie said. 'But I need to be sure you're all safe.' She held a red satin blouse up to her chest, looking for approval.

The sixteen year old scrunched up her nose and shook her head.

'Let me have a look,' she said. 'What do you need?'

'Something nice and clean.'

From the heap, Chloe extracted a cream silk blouse with tiny buttons, a strap top and a pair of dark brown jeans.

'What do you think?' Chloe asked. 'They'll go with your Uggs.'

'Perfect,' said Lottie. 'Will you fold them into the bag? You know what I'm like.'

She searched through her clothes, found a navy long-sleeved T-shirt and changed into it. Checked her jeans were presentable and decided they'd have to do.

'Some day, I'm going to burn those T-shirts,' Chloe said.

'They're comfortable. I'm not so sure about that blouse though.'

'It's stunning. You should try harder. You might catch a nice man,' Chloe said.

Lottie stared at her daughter, eyebrows raised.

'Where did that come from?'

'You need to go out to nice places and meet people. You're too young to be single for the rest of your life. I know Dad would want you to be with someone.' Chloe picked up a small tub of moisturiser from the dressing table. 'I'll get a clear freezer bag for this. For security, at the airport.'

Lottie watched her daughter leave the room. It had never occurred to her that her children might want her to meet someone new. After all they'd gone through with Adam's illness, they continued to surprise her.

Sitting on the bed, she contemplated her desecrated wardrobe. Noticing a thick knitted sweater on the top shelf, she leapt up and tugged it down. Adam's fishing sweater. Holding it to her nose, she craved a trace of him but she knew it'd been obliterated by the wash. His unique smell, clinging to his clothes, had been the only physical thing remaining before Rose Fitzpatrick had thrown everything into the washing machine last summer, complaining about moths. The rift that had been festering boiled over that day. Lottie had lost it with her mother, banished her from the house and cried into the basket of damp clothes. It wasn't her mother's fault, deep down she knew that, but she had felt violated. All she had been left with was an overwhelming sense of loss.

She clutched her little piece of Adam's memory tightly to her chest before folding it and stuffing it back on the shelf. She would have to make up with her mother. Soon.

Chloe returned with a clear plastic bag, threw in the jar of moisturiser and placed it at the top of the rucksack.

'Have you packed a change of underwear?' Chloe asked.

Lottie rummaged in a drawer, pulled out a bra and knickers, shoved them into the bag.

'What would I do without you, Chloe Parker?'

'I really don't know, Mother,' Chloe said, shaking her head with a laugh.

'Granny will be here soon.'

'I suppose we can suffer her for one night.'

'Just one thing. Keep an eye on Katie. She was upset last night. And, no fighting.'

Chloe rolled her eyes.

'It's always about Katie. What about me and Sean?'

'I know I can count on you. Please?'

'Sure,' the girl said. 'I promise not to kill Katie, at least not until you get back. You watch out for those Italian stallions.'

Lottie gave Chloe a tight squeeze and a kiss on the forehead and went to say goodbye to her other two children.

'Any word from Jason?' she asked Katie.

'No,' she said. 'I'm going round our friends' houses in a while, to see if I can find out anything.'

'Don't be fretting,' Lottie said. 'He probably smoked too much weed and conked out.'

'Mam!'

'And when I get back we're going to talk horticulture,' Lottie said.

'What?'

'How to get rid of weeds.'

Katie smiled. Lottie hugged her.

Sean was standing at the door.

'When can I get that new PlayStation?'

* * *

Lottie closed her front door just after eleven a.m. Boyd was leaning against his car. He took the bag from her shoulder.

'I'll drive,' he said, getting into his own car.

'I don't want any sermons,' Lottie said, sitting in beside him.

'And I don't understand what's got into you,' he said, reversing the car. 'Okay. I'll say nothing about it. Have you eaten?'

She shook her head. He leaned over, took a bar of chocolate from the glove compartment and threw it on her lap.

Boyd concentrated on driving on the icy roads and they travelled in silence, reaching the airport in fifty minutes despite the weather. He parked in a set-down bay outside Departures. She hustled the rucksack to her knee.

'If I'm wrong about this, so be it. But I owe it to the victims to find out anything I can.'

'It's career suicide, you know that. You shouldn't go,' he said.

'Watch me,' she said.

As straight as she could, Lottie walked through the glass doors, her stride carrying her with a sense of vague purpose – probably because she hadn't a clue what she was doing.

* * *

Boyd drove back to Ragmullin without dispelling his anger. He sat down at Lottie's desk wondering how she was going to get herself out of this mess. However much of a maverick she was, this was crossing the line.

The office seemed hollow without her. Like his heart. He picked up her coffee mug. Untidy Lottie. As he got up, he touched the old file on her desk. She guarded it like a state secret. He'd never been bothered with it before. Now, though, his interest piqued, he opened the cover.

The boy in the photograph had an impish twist to his lips, as if he was contemplating what mischief he could get up to next. Boyd read quickly. Incarcerated in St Angela's. Reported missing by his mother when the authorities at the institution informed her that he had absconded. He looked at the boy's name again. Immediately he knew why the file and the missing boy were so important to Lottie. Why hadn't she trusted him enough to tell him? Did their friendship count for nothing?

He continued to read and, when he had finished, Boyd wondered if he really knew anything at all about Lottie Parker.

CHAPTER 71

Alighting from the airport express train at Rome Termini, Lottie's skin tingled with anticipation. It was a mild evening under a light sprinkling of rain. She put her watch ahead to reflect the one-hour time difference.

Stepping on to a cobble-stoned street, she crossed the road. She'd never been in Rome before but had studied the map on the train, memorising the directions to her hotel. Straight ahead, then left and she should be beside it. And she was.

She stood in a small piazza facing the Basilica di Santa Maria Maggiore. Its magnificence halted her. Bells rang out the sixth hour and the square came to life, as pigeons flew from picking damp crumbs on the cobbles to soar into the grey sky.

Entering the hotel foyer, she was immediately blinded by the incredible marble floors and walls. The male receptionist greeted her.

'*Buongiorno, Signora.*'

Lottie loved his accent and wished she could converse in Italian. Confirming her reservation, he presented her with a key.

'It is our deluxe room, *Signora.* Elevator to the fourth floor.'

'*Grazie,*' Lottie said. At least she knew one word in Italian.

At the end of a white marbled corridor she found her room. Compact, clean and welcoming. Silently, she thanked Father Joe for finding this place at short notice when she'd texted him from Dublin Airport. And, he insisted on paying for it. Out of diocesan funds, he said. She didn't argue.

She opened the window and the sounds of Rome swirled around outside, then settled into the room. The scent of aromatic coffee rose up from the espresso bar below. The view across the rooftops filled her with excitement. She'd love to see the sights. Not this time though.

The shower was a struggling stream of tepid water. She persevered and emerged energised. Dressed in her brown jeans and long-sleeved cream silk shirt. In front of the mirror, she opened the top two buttons and let the collar hang loose. That's better, she thought, before buttoning them up again. She checked her watch. Father Joe would be waiting for her.

* * *

The narrow winding streets carried her deep into the heart of old Rome. Cars honked, mopeds sped by and sirens wailed. As the drizzle cleared, she eventually exited the maze of cobbles to see St Peter's Basilica across the Tiber, shimmering in the glow of streetlights. She crossed over a bridge and made her way into Vatican City. Checking the streets against the directions on the text message, she turned a corner and saw him.

'Inspector Parker, welcome to Rome.'

'Great to see you,' she said and held out her hand, surprised she'd found him so quickly.

He grabbed her in a bear hug. She felt a hot flush race up her cheeks. He released her and held her at arm's length.

'You've lost weight since I saw you last. Working too hard. And those bruises look worse.'

Lottie grinned. 'Don't be daft, you saw me a couple of days ago.'

'I'm glad you came,' he said. 'I want to show you all of Rome. You'll love it.'

'I'm here to work,' she warned. 'I've only a few hours.'

'Enjoy it while you're here,' he said. 'A quick tour of the basilica, before it closes?'

She knew she should get down to business straight away, but she also wanted to see the building.

'Okay, but let's not delay.'

As she walked by his side, he pointed out exterior architectural features before guiding her up the steps and through the security check.

'Wow,' she said, catching her breath.

Inside was as splendid as the outside; incense filled the atmosphere. They swept up and down the impressive aisles. Lottie was drawn to Michelangelo's *Pietà*, its polished stone gleaming under spotlights, behind protective glass. The Virgin, her face sorrowful yet resigned, as she held her dead son in her arms. Lottie thought of Adam and how she'd embraced his body as he cooled in death. She hoped she'd never have to hold her son thus. A gasp escaped her mouth and Father Joe put his hand on her shoulder.

'It's beautiful,' she whispered.

'Magnificent,' he said.

They left the basilica and walked along narrow laneways, stopping after ten minutes in front of a fifteen-foot-high wooden door. Father Joe refused to answer her questions along the way, telling her he was bringing her to the source of his find. He pushed an intercom button. A grainy voice answered in Italian and the door creaked open.

A narrow vestibule lay before them with a fountain commanding the centre, surrounded by prancing stone cherubs. Numerous stairways meandered up to apartments. It reminded Lottie of Gregory Peck's abode in the film *Roman Holiday*. She half-expected Audrey Hepburn to pop her head over one of the staircases.

A door opened two floors above them and a rotund, five-foot man, dressed in a flowing black robe, took flight down the stairs, a string of Italian emanating from him in a melodic tune.

'Joseph, Joseph!' he said, wrapping his arms around Father Joe.

'Father Umberto. This is Detective Inspector Lottie Parker,' Father Joe said, extracting himself from the embrace. 'The Irish detective I mentioned to you.'

The small man leaned up on his toes and brushed his cheek to hers.

'Umberto,' he said. 'Call me Umberto.'

'You can call me Lottie.'

She followed, as Father Umberto led Father Joe by the hand up the stairs, like a mother bringing a child home from school. A door stood wide open at the top. Squeezing into the room, Lottie was astonished at the number of books scattered everywhere. The small priest attempted to tidy up, hands flapping in a fluster.

'Excuse me, I no time to tidy,' he said in broken English. His spectacles appeared glued to his nose, as if he had grown too fat for them. Lottie sat at a mahogany bureau overflowing with paperwork.

The two priests chatted in Italian. Lottie caught Father Joe's eye.

'Perhaps we should converse in English,' he said.

'*Sì*,' the Italian said.

'Umberto, please tell Inspector . . . Lottie why Father Angelotti went to Ireland,' Father Joe said.

Umberto was suddenly reticent. His ebullience disappearing.

'He is dead. It is . . . how you say . . . terrible.' He blessed himself and bowed his head. When his mumbled intercessions ended, his eyes darted round the room. 'I know it be bad. I know.'

'What do you mean?' Lottie asked. A church bell rang out and she flinched. It might well have been in the room with them.

'I think . . . he try to cover up. Cover up mistakes.' Umberto suddenly sat down on the floor. There was nowhere else to sit.

'Father Umberto is curator of Irish pastoral records,' Father Joe explained. 'That is, any files or correspondence sent to the Pope from the bishops, he is responsible for cataloguing and filing them. In recent times some Irish diocesan records have been housed here. His immediate superior was Father Angelotti.'

Umberto pried off his spectacles and his earlier passionate fervour transformed into intense weeping. Lottie stared out through the tiny window to avoid looking at him. Emotional men were not her forte.

'I sorry. So upset. Angelotti, he my friend.'

Father Joe asked, 'Can I get you some water?'

'No, I okay. I cannot believe my dear friend will not come home. It break my heart.' His shoulders rose and fell as more sobs tore from him.

Lottie questioned Father Joe with her eyes. He turned his head, avoiding her gaze.

'Can you help us? ' she implored Father Umberto.

'I help, *sì*.' He rose to his feet, squeezing his spectacles on his nose. 'No one can hurt me. *Sì?*' He wiped away his tears, attempting to restore a modicum of calm.

'Why did Father Angelotti go to Ireland?' Lottie asked, hoping the priest would tell them something worthwhile soon. Time was slipping by quickly and the prospect of losing her job seemed more realistic with each passing second.

'He get correspondence . . . that is why he go.'

'Do you have a copy of this correspondence?' she asked.

'No. A message. On his phone.'

'But you must know something,' she persisted.

The priest sighed, glanced at Father Joe, then turned his attention to Lottie. 'I no remember when. Summer maybe? He receive phone call from a man. James Brown. He ask for investigation. Into St Angela's. He say, it sell for small money. He say, Father Angelotti must also look for adopted baby. You understand? My English not good.'

Lottie said, 'I understand.'

'Father Angelotti, he spend many hours with the ledgers after that. I know there was more correspondence with this James. December, Father

Angelotti, he tell me he must go. He say he make big mistake. He say he must talk to people. To make things right.'

'What mistake?' Lottie asked.

'He say he mix up numbers. That is all he say. He tell me not to ask questions. So I no ask.'

'Can I show Inspector Parker the ledgers?' Father Joe asked.

The priest nodded.

'My dear friend he is dead.' He paused, then said, 'I go for a *passeggiata* . . . a walk. Then I tell no lies when I do not see.' He pulled on a coat and without another word went out into the night, leaving them alone.

Father Joe stood up.

'Bishop Connor ordered all the old St Angela's ledgers to be moved from Ireland to here. It was about two years ago. I've no idea why. They're now stored in the basement. Come,' he said and opened a door which Lottie thought was a bathroom. It revealed a winding staircase.

'Surely they should be in a more secure location?' Lottie asked.

'This is secure. There's a multitude of offices like this one scattered all over Rome. Very few people know about them.'

They reached the bottom of three flights of stairs.

A thick wooden door lay open, an iron key in its lock. Lottie looked at Father Joe, and entered the room.

CHAPTER 72

'This place is unbelievable,' Lottie said.

Shelf after shelf of leather-bound ledgers. History consigned to the back streets of Rome.

Father Joe opened a ledger on the desk. 'St Angela's,' he said.

Lottie breathed deeply, realising she'd been holding her breath. He carefully turned the faded pages until he reached the year he was looking for: 1975. She glanced at him before perusing what had been written, decades before.

Lists. Names, ages, dates, sex. All female.

'What are we looking at?' she asked, though she had already guessed.

'These pages refer to girls placed in St Angela's in 1975,' he said. 'I've gone through it but I can't find a Susan Sullivan anywhere.'

Lottie sat down, turned the leaves, reading through the lists.

'Here she is,' she said. 'Sally Stynes. She changed her name.' She traced her finger along the row.

'That's why I couldn't find her,' he said.

'These are reference numbers,' she declared. 'This one, beside Sally's name, AA113. What does it mean?'

'It refers to another ledger somewhere here,' he said. 'I haven't found it yet. But look at this.' He handed her another smaller book.

'Sweet Jesus,' she whispered. 'I don't believe it. Dates of birth. Dates of death. Joe, they were only babies and little children.' Lottie scanned the pages, horror choking her.

'I know,' he said, quietly.

'Cause of death – Measles, Cholic, Unknown,' she read. 'My God. Where did they bury them?'

'I've no idea.'

'It all seems so methodical, impersonal,' she said. 'These were people's children.'

'I'm not sure it has anything to do with your investigations. The reference number you pointed out, I can't see it here,' he said, leaning over her shoulder.

Lottie tried to control her trembling body. Shocking media headlines of dead babies in septic tanks came back to her. It was international news a few years ago. Now her hands held evidence of something similar. Was that why the books had been relocated? She went back to the first ledger he'd shown her.

'This ledger,' she said, 'only lists female admissions. There were boys in St Angela's.' She remembered the missing boy's file, buried in her drawer. Another mystery associated with St Angela's. She hoped this place might throw some light on it.

'They'll be in another ledger. I'll keep looking. There were so many children in that school over the years,' he said, pointing to the rows of black spines on the shelves.

'Don't call it a school,' she said, thumping the table, unable to suppress her anger any longer. 'It was an institution. One that slipped under the radar.'

'Until now.' His voice was flat. Resigned.

'Who is this Father Cornelius who signed each page?' Lottie asked, diverting her eyes from the tragedy scripted before her. Could he be the Father Con that O'Malley referred to? He must be, she thought.

Father Joe pulled down another ledger from the shelf.

'You have to see this first,' he said, opening a page he'd already marked. 'This set of records is like a tracking device,' he explained. 'It lists priests and where they served.'

Lottie took the small ledger and placed it on top of the others with trembling hands. The name headlined the page in neat ink script – Father Cornelius Mohan. The rows beneath it confirmed movement between parishes and dioceses. No reason given for such transfers.

'Most priests might serve three, maybe four parishes in a lifetime,' Father Joe said.

'But there must be twenty, thirty here.' She ran her finger down the page, counting. Then she turned to the next one. More parishes. She kept on counting.

'He served in forty-two different parishes throughout the country,' she said, shaking her head.

'Tells a story doesn't it,' he said. A statement, not a question. He paced the confined space.

'He moved around because of abuse?' she asked.

'Doesn't state it, but priests are not normally shifted from parish to parish in that fashion. I'm sure there are bulging files of allegations on him. Somewhere.'

'Jesus Christ, his last address is Ballinacloy. That's not far from Ragmullin,' Lottie said. 'Do you know if he's still alive?'

'I'm sure I would have heard if he had died, even if he is retired,' Father Joe said, nodding his head, his shoulders slumped. 'He must be in his eighties.'

'Do you know him? Have you met him?'

'I don't know him. I was shocked when I discovered this.'

'Someone manually updated these ledgers?'

'None of this goes on a computer. Would you want this traced? Not the Catholic Church. It would want this hushed up, hidden and covered up.'

'Can I make copies?'

'That's not allowed.'

Lottie observed him for a moment and his eyes told her what she needed to know. She fingered the phone in her pocket.

'Didn't you say you have to use the bathroom?' she asked.

'Don't tear out any pages,' he said. He knew what she was planning.

'Thank you.'

'I'm trusting you.'

Listening to Father Joe slowly climb the staircase, Lottie thought his footsteps sounded heavy with the weight of the sins of his church.

She felt physically ill studying the script, couldn't read any more, so she quickly photographed the pages with her phone camera. She tried to record as much of the large book as she could. Calculating a grid in her head, she photographed in chronological order; she would piece them together on her own computer. This will not remain hidden, she vowed silently. The names inked on the pages seemed so impersonal, devoid of humanity; she wanted to read each one in her own time. They referenced a life story, a heartbeat and a heartbreak. And she was confident they related to the current murders in Ragmullin. James Brown and Susan Sullivan had spent time together in St Angela's. And she was sure the connection to their murders was buried somewhere in this dungeon of ledgers.

When she'd finished photographing, she turned her attention to the shelves and scanned the dates inscribed on the dusty spines. Early 1900s up to the 1980s. She doubled back and plucked out a thin, 1970s ledger with references A100 to AA500. She located what she thought to be the relevant pages, hurriedly photographed without reading and returned it to the shelf. She searched for the boys' ledgers. She discovered them on a bottom shelf, found 1975, photographed each page and returned the ledger to its dusty resting place. She did the same for the first half of 1976. She couldn't bring herself to read it all now. And she wondered why Father Joe hadn't just photographed the pages and emailed them to her?

The door opened. Father Joe stood with his hands thrust deep in his pockets.

'You inferred last night,' Lottie said, 'that all this had something to do with Bishop Connor, but I don't see any evidence here.'

'Look at the signature at the end of each row of the priest's movements,' he instructed.

She did. A spindly scrawl, but there was no doubt whose name it was. Terence Connor.

'I need to ring Boyd,' she said.

'Why?'

'I want him to talk to this Father Cornelius Mohan. He served in Ragmullin parish and was assigned to St Angela's for three years.' She looked at her phone. No signal.

'Let's get some air,' she said.

Nausea threatened to overcome her, after what she'd just read. Brushing past Father Joe, taking two steps at a time, she hurried as if the dead had risen from the dusty pages and were following in her footsteps.

Outside, she walked in small circles under a streetlight. The tall buildings, leaning inwards, appeared to be grasping the shadows and throwing them around her like gravel in a sandpit.

'Will you continue to search the other ledgers for me?' she asked. 'See what you can find? I'm sure everything connects to St Angela's.'

'Yes, of course,' Father Joe said. 'But how can you be sure?'

'It has to be a cover-up and the mistake Father Angelotti made must have something to do with the reference numbers.' Lottie tapped her phone. 'Things are beginning to make some sense.'

She checked the signal and called Boyd.

CHAPTER 73

It was closing time at the gym. The thump-thump music was consigned to the depths of nowhere and someone was flicking the lights on and off. Boyd completed his warm-down, switched off the treadmill and hurried to the locker room.

Mike O'Brien was buttoning his shirt at the neck, twisting in his cufflinks, his face red, bulging from exertion. He had turned his back and was pulling on his jacket when Boyd's phone rang.

Boyd checked the caller ID, swore and answered.

'Boyd,' he said and listened as Lottie spoke.

'Father Cornelius Mohan,' he repeated, searching his gym bag. 'I can't find a pen, hold on.'

O'Brien held out a ballpoint, extracted from his breast pocket. Boyd took it, nodding a thank you.

'Go ahead. Yes, I have that. Ballinacloy. Very good. Yeah, straight away.'

He wanted to ask Lottie a whole lot more, but she had hung up on him.

'And I love you too,' he said sarcastically to the phone in his hand.

He handed the pen back to O'Brien, lifted his bag and left the gym without any small talk.

* * *

Ballinacloy, a village of almost two hundred souls or sinners – whichever way you wanted to look at it – was situated fifteen kilometres outside Ragmullin, on the old Athlone Road.

Out in the yard, Father Cornelius Mohan packed turf into a basket. A cigarette hung from his chapped lips. Proud of his agility at his age, he was frustrated with how the snow had debilitated him. He feared falling and fracturing a hip.

As he turned to go back inside, the light dimmed. Someone had walked in front of the door, blocking the glow of the bulb. The old priest raised his white head and looked directly into a set of dark eyes. He felt pain grasp his heart and his breathing laboured. The turf basket crashed to the ground and the cigarette fell from his mouth on to the snow, sizzling for a moment before the red butt blackened and extinguished.

'Remember me?' The voice echoed, distorted by a gust of wind.

The old priest looked at the face, partially shielded by a black hood. Though the face was older, the eyes held the same coldness from long ago; an emotionless being he himself had helped nurture. And he knew a day like this would come.

Turning away, he kicked the basket and tried to run. His old legs refused to move quickly.

'Go away,' he shouted. 'Leave me be.'

'So you do remember me.'

A hand grabbed his shoulder. The priest shrugged it off and hobbled to the corner of the house before he stumbled on an iron grill over a drain. As he fell backwards his assailant jumped on top of him, pinning him to the ground.

'What do you want from me?' the old priest croaked.

'You stole from me.' The tone was menacing.

'I never stole anything in my life.'

'You stole my life.'

'Your life was already nothing,' he spat. 'You should thank me for saving you from evil.'

'You introduced me to evil, you mad old bastard. All my life I've waited for this moment and now at last I can send you on your way to the eternal fires.'

'Go to hell.'

Father Cornelius was already struggling for air when the cord tightened around his throat. He thought he heard the ringing of bells, before his world went black.

* * *

Boyd kept his finger pressed on the doorbell. It was bright inside and he could see the backyard light was on.

No answer.

'Come on,' he told Lynch and walked around the side of the house.

The yard was lit by a solitary bulb, too low a wattage to cast light any distance. The moon, though low in the sky, cast the trees in a soft silhouette.

Lynch tiptoed behind him. He was glad he'd called her. He needed the company.

At the rear of the house, a figure lay motionless on the ground. Boyd struck out his arm, stopping Lynch in her tracks.

'What?' she asked, bumping into him.

Boyd looked back at her, put a finger to his lips and listened.

'Wait here,' he whispered and inched towards the figure, careful not to walk on anything that might be evidence.

He crouched over the white-haired priest and held two fingers to his throat. He knew his action was fruitless when he saw the cord tight around the neck. The face was blue under the dim light, the tongue protruding and the unseeing eyes appeared to be staring straight through him. The rancid stench of defecation in death wafted up, obliterating all other smells. Boyd rose up and scanned his surroundings as far as the weak bulb allowed.

'Lynch?'

'What?'

'The bushes . . . over there. I thought I saw something.'

'I don't see anything.'

'There! Do you see it?' Boyd ran through the garden in the dark.

'Wait,' Lynch shouted. 'Where do you think you're going?'

He vaulted the hedge and pressed on his phone light. It began to ring. He ignored the tone, concentrated on the dark figure running ahead of him, along the narrow lane.

'Boyd, you eejit,' Lynch yelled. 'Wait!'

He ran fast, slipping and sliding, trying to keep the target in sight. Branches smashed into his face, wet leaves flew back and violently slapped into him. A thorn bush tore up his nostril and a branch scratched his head. He needed to catch his prey. It was the killer. He was sure. Adrenaline fuelled his legs and he subconsciously thanked the hours he'd spent sweating in the gym.

The moonlight was strong but it was difficult running on the slippery paving stones. His breathing rattled, fast and hollow. A wheelie-bin crashed across his path and the shadow sped up the alley. At the end, a wall. Boyd climbed over it in one movement and followed the spectre into the night.

Ahead of him, a field stretched into obscurity. He stopped, catching his breath. Which direction did he go? Boyd couldn't see a thing. Frustration welled up and he swore.

Without hearing a sound, he felt something encircle his neck. He flung up his hands, grasping at nothingness, cursing his idiocy. He was strong but caught unawares he was at a disadvantage. Lottie would have something to say about this, he thought wildly. He elbowed the man behind him. The grip remained steadfast.

He kicked back. His foot crashed against bone. Good. The noose tightened. Bad. Blackness descended while the cold air waited in a dark chill around him. He felt powerless and hysterical, simultaneously. His throat constricted, his hands flailed, the cable tightened. He desperately fought the compression. But his knees weakened and snow seeped into his bones.

He couldn't see anything but he sensed the man leaning over him. A knife sliced through his clothes, into his flesh. A sharp pain in his side. He gurgled a cry. His phone rang in a distant sphere. Lottie would be totally pissed off with him for dying on her. A knee bore into his spine. He gagged and the moon lit up the shadows for one second, before complete darkness plunged like a black veil over a widow's face.

Darkness.

CHAPTER 74

Lottie felt Father Joe's arm slide through hers, steering her along the walled city through Borgo Pio and across the river.

'I hope the ledgers help you,' he said. 'How is the overall investigation going?'

'Don't ask.'

'You don't want to talk about it?'

'Not with you, Joe. You're still a suspect.' An uneasy tinge crept into her voice.

He laughed. 'Ah, there's gratitude for you. I told you I could be excommunicated for what I've just shown you.'

'I'm sorry. Thank you.'

'You're welcome.'

'I still can't understand why Father Angelotti travelled to Ragmullin,' she said. 'It seems implausible that he went on the basis of correspondence with James Brown.'

'I don't know,' he said, leaning in closer to her as they walked.

'You don't know what?'

'Why he travelled to Ragmullin.'

They looked back across the Tiber at St Peter's Basilica. Father Joe scratched his head. 'Lottie, there are niggly things crawling around in my brain. And I don't like that feeling.'

'Go on,' she said.

'There's always been scandal associated with the Catholic Church through the centuries. In recent decades there's the rumours of inappropriate financial dealings and the disgraceful child sex abuse cases.' He closed his eyes for a moment. 'I think maybe Father Angelotti was on a mission to cover up something that was threatening to explode. I'll try to find out who might've sent him. But it is possible he acted on his own initiative.'

'There've been a multitude of abuse cases. The Tuam babies, the Magdalene Laundries. Why now? Why kill him? It doesn't make sense.'

Lottie raised her hands, then lowered them. He gripped her arm, turning her toward him.

'None of it does, Lottie. But there has to be a plausible motive or scenario. And when you study the copies of the ledgers I'm sure you will find something.'

'This case is like a spaghetti junction,' she said, feeling his fingers through her jacket. 'Going everywhere and nowhere. No leads, no nothing. And moving those records to Rome, it's very unorthodox.'

'Not unorthodox, just the Catholic Church doing what it does best. Covering up.' He began walking again. 'I'll go back to Umberto in the morning and look through the other ledgers.'

'I appreciate all you're doing, you know that.'

'But I'm still a suspect?' he asked.

Lottie said nothing. They strolled the rest of the way in silence.

Standing on the pavement outside her hotel, Lottie asked, 'Where are you going now?'

'I don't know, to be honest.'

She felt soft raindrops on her head.

'Do you want to come in for a coffee?' She didn't want to be alone with the images conjured up by the old ledgers and she felt Joe could be her friend.

'Perhaps I will,' he answered and followed her into the warm lobby.

'Shit,' she said.

'What's wrong?'

'The bar is closed.'

'Perhaps I should have booked a more upmarket hotel for you,' he joked.

Lottie thought for a moment. 'This is not very appropriate but do you want to come up to my room? There's a kettle and cups there.'

'Inspector Parker, that is a totally inappropriate suggestion,' he said, a smile brightening his face. 'One which I accept.'

In the elevator, Lottie put space between them, gripped her bag to her chest and sighed. What was she after doing now? She liked Father Joe. But was it like a brother or was it something more? She wasn't at all sure.

The room was as she had left it. Curtains fluttered in the breeze and the scent of fresh rain rested on the windowsill. When she turned he was standing directly behind her. The room was suddenly too small.

'Excuse me,' she said, sliding past him to grab the kettle.

She filled it with water from the bathroom. When she returned, he was sitting on the narrow wooden chair at the desk, his coat thrown over the end of the bed. He hadn't uttered a word since they'd left the lobby. She flicked on the switch, busied herself tearing open the miserable coffee sachets and poured the small grains into cups.

A wave of exhaustion seeped through her sinews. She rubbed the back of her neck. He was out of the chair and standing behind her.

'Ssh,' he said, massaging the spot where her fingers had been.

Tremors travelled like lightning down to her toes. Holy God, she thought, I'm like a cliché. He's a priest. It's okay. He's only rubbing my tired neck.

She felt the sleeve of his sweater, rough against the silk of her blouse. She smelled his soft soap. She stood still, entombed by his touch, and wondered if she was craving this contact so that he might absolve her of all the horrors of the last few hours, the last few days, the last few years and of the horrors yet to be revealed.

'That's enough now, Joe,' she laughed nervously and wriggled away from him. She began busying herself with the kettle. 'Let's have that coffee.'

'Of course,' he said, sitting down on the chair.

Handing him a cup, she said, 'I hope I haven't given off wrong signals. I like you as a friend. Nothing more. My life is complicated enough.'

He laughed then and the tension in the room seemed to slip out the window with the billowing curtain.

'Dear God, I hope I wasn't being improper. I was only trying to release the pressure from your neck. It's been a tough day for you.'

She felt a blush sweep up her cheeks. Shit, she had made a fool of herself. She put down the cup and turned away.

He stood up and placed his hands on her shoulders, forced her to look at him.

'You are a good woman, Lottie Parker. I want you to know that I will be your friend and I'll do my best to help you solve the murders.' He held out his hand. 'Friends?'

'Yes,' Lottie said and shook his hand. He clasped her hand, holding it in his own.

He left then, without saying anything further.

Leaning against the door, she listened to his steps disappearing down the marble corridor. She waited for her breathing to return to normal. She waited for the chiming of the Maggiore bells.

When at last she could move, Lottie tried phoning Boyd. She just wanted to hear a familiar voice.

No answer.

She looked out over the city and counted the silhouetted spires. She counted the car horns and the sirens. As her body relaxed she flipped open her laptop. She needed to go home. Tonight. Finding a flight leaving in two hours, she booked it and hurriedly stuffed everything into her rucksack, left the hotel and ran to catch the shuttle-train.

She called Boyd again.

No answer.

CHAPTER 75

A bell tinkled and a light flickered above his head. Jason opened his eyes and turned his head slowly, focussing through the shadows.

'Time for a little ceremony, server boy.'

The voice chanted a hum of incantations. A light dimmed and flickered.

'What do you want?' Jason croaked.

'Whatever you have to offer me will never be enough.'

'My father—'

'This is partly his fault. So you can blame him.'

'What . . . what do you mean?'

'You don't need to concern yourself with it.'

Jason squeezed his eyes shut to keep tears from escaping. Hands unshackled him, hauled him to his feet. A finger trailed down his spine. The man exhaled a loud sigh and pushed him out the door, along a corridor, and down steps.

He was in a small chapel. The man carried a bell, clanging it in time to some unknown beat within his body.

The wooden pews offered Jason no comfort; he was forced to stand, hypnotised by the scene before him.

Dressed in a flowing white robe, buttoned from hem to neck, the man sang his mad tune, his voice rising and falling, almost in time to the candles blowing soft and slow in a captured breeze.

'I killed a man tonight,' said the singsong voice.

Jason grew cold, though his skin radiated sweat. Combined with whatever drugs he'd been fed, the flickering candles and incessant chanting, he felt dizzy.

'Actually I might have killed two.' The hysterical laugh resonated throughout the stone vestibule.

A crow circled high in the rafters and flew into a stained glass window, a feather floating through the air in its wake. A mist descended over Jason's eyes as the marble welcomed his fall. He hit the floor and lay unconscious beside the black feather.

CHAPTER 76

Lottie leaned against the oval airplane window. Closing her eyes, she thought of the few hours she had spent in Rome, her mind consumed by the old ledgers. Numbers scrolled through her mind. Susan Sullivan was a number. Her child was a number. Suddenly, she sat bolt upright in the seat, waking the woman beside her.

'I'm sorry,' Lottie said. 'I think we've another hour to go.'

The woman scrunched her chin into her chest and went back to sleep.

Lottie stared at the seat in front of her. What was within her grasp? A clue. Something she'd already seen but hadn't yet registered. It would come. She knew it would. The photographic evidence was on her phone. Once it was uploaded, she was sure she could tie it all together.

Jealous of the woman with the soft snores, she couldn't rest easy. She needed to talk to someone. She needed Boyd. She needed to get back to work. She needed to sleep.

Her heart sank deeper as the plane rose higher above the dark clouds and she struggled with the sins she'd committed and the ones to which she'd practically succumbed.

Would she ever be able to sleep again?

CHAPTER 77

The boy looked like an unfinished sculpture, the man thought. Just like he himself. Weak. Fragmented. Incomplete. Here in St Angela's – his nemesis.

He'd spent his miserable childhood within this enclosure and he'd grown, like ivy inhabiting a cracked concrete wall, wild and untethered. His soul darkened day by day, as he became enshrined in his own world. Abuse and deceit engulfed him but as the years passed he learned to bury embryonic evil beneath a daily facade of normality.

And now St Angela's had once again resurrected the devil, exhumed the darkness, bringing him on this final journey.

Back to where he had started.

And he knew it would finish here.

He kicked the boy lying on the ground and when he moaned, he dragged him to his feet, pushed him up the steps and back to the room. He thrust him down on the mildewed floorboards, banged the door shut and locked it. Leaning against the worn timber he breathed heavily.

He had spared the boy.

Kept the demons at bay.

But for how long?

* * *

30th January 1976

The four of them huddled together when they should have been running. The door swung open. Brian stood there, a white robe covering his body. His thin arm edged up the wall, his narrow fingers flicked on the light. Sally shielded her eyes against the brightness.

'Are you all right?' she asked.

'No,' Brian said. 'I'm not all right. Neither are you. You're all to come down to the chapel. Father Con orders ye to come.'

'Are you mad or what?' Patrick asked, stepping in front of Sally. She wanted to tell him she was brave enough to stand up for herself but didn't. Because she wasn't.

'I asked you a frigging question,' Patrick said.

'You've all to come with me,' Brian said, his voice deadpan like his eyes.

To Sally he seemed a lot older, standing there in the doorway. She put her hand on his arm and felt bone beneath skin. He jumped as if she had pinched him. He grasped her hand and pulled her out the door. She screamed and Fitzy snapped out of whatever stupor he had been in and dragged her back into the room with Brian still holding on to her.

Sally fell and curled into a small heap at the boys' bare feet. Her body jerked with shivers.

'Please, Brian,' she pleaded. 'Let's all go back to bed and forget about this.'

'You better come with me. He's waiting,' Brian said, before he was pushed into the room.

From behind him, Father Con, eyes as black as the night, reached in and yanked Sally to her feet. A scream tore from her throat as he dragged her out and down the stairs. She heard the shuffle of the boys as they followed.

At the altar, he glared down at her and she up at him. She knew every line on his face, every hair in his eyebrows, every whisker on his jaw, every tooth in his mouth and she hated every inch of him.

'Bad girl,' he said, his mouth snarling, teeth biting his bottom lip, fingers cutting into her arm.

'You're the one who turned me into a bad girl,' Sally said.

The hint of bravado was a lie. At least the boys were there, standing like a band of warriors though they hadn't a weapon between them.

One of them shouted, 'You tell him, Sally.' Probably Patrick, she thought.

The priest reached out his hand and seized the boy nearest to him. Fitzy, with his red hair gleaming in the candle light. She could count the big flat freckles bridging his nose. And she saw fire burning flames in his eyes.

'I'm not scared, you bully,' Fitzy said, squaring his shoulders. Sally wished he would keep his mouth shut. He was too young to be this brave, or was he plain silly?

The priest surveyed him as if he was a prize fish.

Sally whirled her head around in a frenzy. They had to get out of here. Get help. But from whom? Not the nuns. Sure everyone was afraid of Father Con. He was the boss man. She didn't know what to do. She looked at Patrick. He appeared as hopeless as she was. Then, secluded in the flickering shadows behind the altar, she spotted the young priest with the ugly eyes. Standing there, in the dark alcove, doing nothing. Staring, rubbing his hands through his *thick black hair, as if he did not know what to do either. His silent, passive presence was as terrifying as the maniac holding Fitzy. What were they to do?*

A scream from Fitzy drew her eyes back to Father Con. He was twisting the boy's arm up his back.

'I will teach you to respect your elders. You were bad news from the day you entered these walls. And you will be bad news until the day you leave it,' he said.

'You're nothing,' Fitzy said bravely. He looked very small.

The priest tightened his hold with one hand and with the other plucked a candle from the altar. He held it to Fitzy's face. The flame flickered and danced, singeing his red hair black. Sally gagged at the smell.

'Say you are sorry. You're nothing only a bad bastard and your mother is a prostitute.' Fitzy squirmed and wriggled. He couldn't break free of the stranglehold.

Sally watched his helpless body convulsing and wished they could do something. Anything. They were as powerless as the stupid statues on the walls. Why didn't the other priest do something? She glanced over. He was still standing there. Immobile.

Father Con threw the candle to the floor, kicked over his folded clothes and picked up his long leather belt.

'Brian, use the cord from your robe and tie this murdering brat's hands behind his back.'

Sally saw a film of sweat on Brian's brow. She looked from Patrick to James, her eyes questioning. What's going on? They shook their heads vigorously.

Fitzy kicked, lashed out and bit. The priest held fast. Brian did as he was commanded. Once bound, Fitzy was pushed, by Father Con, to his knees before the altar.

'You murdered that baby, didn't you?' the priest shouted. 'The one we found under the apple tree.'

Fitzy spat out a full mouth of phlegm. 'I didn't, you lying bastard.'

Tightening the belt round his hand, the priest drew out his arm and slashed the leather into Fitzy's face. The brass buckle cut into his cheek and blood poured from the wound. The priest repeated his action, again and again. Sally scrunched her eyes behind her hands, then squinted through splayed fingers. When she couldn't bear it any longer she screamed and, mustering up as much courage as she could, she ran at Father Con. He turned, lashing at her with the leather. Patrick pulled her away and dragged her down the aisle. She thought of dashing back, but it was hopeless. She caught James by the hand and the three of them scrambled up the stairs, shouting for help.

Over her shoulder, Sally witnessed Brian holding Fitzy by the shoulders, while the lunatic brought the leather up and down, again and again and again. As long as she lived, she would never forget the sound of leather tearing flesh and the boy's helpless screams. And the ugly young priest with the thick black hair, standing in the corner, watching, doing nothing.

As they fled toward the corridor, Sally heard a voice, loud and clear behind them.

'Stop!'

The three of them turned in unison, coming face to face with the young priest, a halo of light from the crypt below, encircling him like a satanic fire.

He walked up to them. Sally leaned into the boys' bodies. They were three, dissolved into one shadow.

'Be quiet. We do not want to wake everyone up, do we?' The priest flashed a sly smile, his face colder than ice, eyes blacker than coal, voice sharper than a cut-throat razor.

'You do not need concern yourselves with what you saw. I will deal with it. Do not utter this incident to anyone. Anyone! Do you hear?' His voice a slow, severe whisper.

The three nodded their heads like wooden puppets with an unseen force holding the strings.

'If I ever hear of this again . . . well, you have seen what happened to that boy. I will not warn you a second time. Now return to your beds.'

He melted back down the stairs. Sally and the boys looked at each other, eyes wide, brimming with tears.

'What about Fitzy?' Sally whispered.

'You heard what he said. We'll have to forget about him,' Patrick said.

'He's one unlucky fecker,' James said. He slid to the floor and fell against an iron radiator, his arms around his knees, shivering and sobbing.

Sally sat down beside James. Patrick joined them. And the three of them cried together for Fitzy.

DAY EIGHT

6th January 2015

CHAPTER 78

Five a.m. and Lottie stood outside the Arrivals door at Dublin Airport cursing that she had no car. She switched on her phone.

Five missed calls from Kirby. Nothing from Boyd. She tried him first. No answer. Then she rang Kirby.

'Jaysus boss, I've been trying to get hold of you for hours,' he panted.

'What's wrong? My kids! Are they all right?'

'They're fine.'

'Thank God. Boyd's not answering his phone. And I need a lift home.'

'He's in hospital.'

'What? What happened? Is he okay? Tell me he's okay, Kirby.'

'No, he's not. Stabbed, strangled. He's in surgery. You better get back here.'

'What the hell happened?'

'That priest you sent him to talk to is dead. Murdered. Boyd took after the killer and almost got himself killed in the process.'

'Oh my God. Is he going to be okay?'

'I've no idea.'

'I'll be there in less than an hour.'

'And boss?'

'What?'

'Superintendent Corrigan is looking for you.'

Lottie hung up, ran to the taxi rank and jumped into the first car. Sinking into the seat, she looked out at the grey dawn rising on the horizon with only one person on her mind.

Boyd.

* * *

The narrow hospital corridor, lined with empty beds and lockers, had staff in green scrubs, unrecognisable as doctors or nurses, flitting along, heads down, scanning patient files. In and out of the ICU swinging doors, whooshing wind over the stifling air, they hurried. Lottie was tempted to push open the door to see for herself how serious Boyd was, but rationale ruled. Two plastic chairs facing the ICU lockdown were free beside a dozing Detective Lynch. Detective Kirby was lounging beside her.

'How long since he returned from surgery?' Lottie asked.

'Half an hour,' Kirby said, standing up straight. 'No word yet.'

Lottie paced, then sat.

'Let's get a coffee,' Lynch said, stretching.

'Let's not,' Lottie snapped.

'Calm down,' Kirby said.

'Tell me exactly what happened.'

Lynch filled her in.

'And Father Cornelius . . . I'm assuming it's the same MO as the other murders.'

'Yes. Strangled. The lads are searching the database to see if he had any connection to the other victims,' Lynch said.

'I found a connection in Rome. That's why I rang Boyd to go talk to the priest,' Lottie said.

'What did you find?' Lynch asked.

'In his interview Patrick O'Malley mentioned a Father Con. I found out that Father Cornelius Mohan was a priest in St Angela's when Sullivan and Brown were there. After that he was moved around institutions and parishes more times than a carousel. He had to have been a serial child abuser.'

'But what's the motive for the murders?' Kirby asked. 'And how does a paedophile priest fit in?'

'He does. Somehow.'

Lottie nursed her head, attempting to keep a headache under wraps.

'Boyd better make it,' she said and they lapsed into silence.

A doctor rushed out of ICU. Lottie sprang from the chair and marched over to him.

'I'm Detective Inspector Parker. I need to see Detective Sergeant Boyd.'

'I don't care who you are, no one goes in there until he's stable.'

'How long might that be?'

'As long as it takes.'

'Doctor? Please.'

'I've managed to save his ruptured spleen. He's a very lucky man. No other internal damage that I could see. He'll be in ICU for the rest of the day. I suggest you all go home for now and call back later.'

Lottie swayed in the draught from the swinging door as the doctor brushed past.

'Come on,' she said. 'We can do more for Boyd by finding the murdering bastard who did this to him. This just got personal.'

CHAPTER 79

Kirby dropped Lottie home to pick up her car. Her mother was busy mopping the kitchen floor.

'Did you ever hear of a Father Cornelius Mohan?' Lottie asked, after thanking Rose for looking after the children.

'I did. He lives out in Ballinacloy. Retired this long time.'

Jesus, her mother really did know everyone. 'And?'

'He was a local curate in Ragmullin, back in the seventies.'

'Do you know anything else about him?' Lottie watched her mother's face.

Rose Fitzpatrick stared back.

'What's this about?' she asked, squeezing out the mop.

'Background information.'

'As far as I can recall he was one of the chaplains in St Angela's for a time.'

'Really?' Lottie knew her mother was being evasive.

'Come on, Lottie. I've answered your questions about my conversation with Susan Sullivan and I know you're itching to ask me something else.'

'Was there ever a hint of scandal surrounding him, especially in St Angela's?'

Rose turned, put the mop and bucket into the utility room, grabbed and buttoned her coat. She pulled her hat down over her ears and paused at the door.

'I know full well, Lottie Parker, you already know the answer.'

'And you know full well that's where you dumped Eddie after Dad died.' Lottie stated grimly. This was the first time she'd ever accused her mother.

Rose's hand dropped from the door handle. She took a step toward Lottie. There were tears in her eyes.

'You know as well as I do that your precious father killed himself. He didn't just die.' A sob broke from her throat. 'And I didn't dump anyone anywhere.'

'I'm sorry.' Lottie hunched her shoulders, reached out and placed a hand on her mother's shoulder. She waited for Rose to shake it off. She didn't.

'No. I'm sorry. You were too young to understand it all. I could never talk about it and I've always grieved for their loss. You know about grief; how hard it is to carry on without a husband by your side. I did everything I could to make things right for you. Everything.'

Lottie did know, but she had lived with the gaping hole in her existence every second of the day. Now she wanted answers.

'I want to know what happened and why it happened. You owe me that much, at least.'

Rose pulled away from Lottie's hand and lowered her voice.

'After all I've done for you and your children, I don't think I owe you anything.'

'But why did Dad kill himself?' Lottie persisted.

'I don't know.'

'Okay, I will accept that. For now. But Eddie? My little brother? You put him in that place, left him to rot there. I cannot accept that.'

'You don't know what it was like back then. The stigma attached to suicide. I was a widow with two young children. And Eddie, he . . . he was impossible. I had no choice.'

'There's always a choice, Mother. You just made the wrong one.'

'Don't judge me, Lottie.'

'Then tell me why you placed Eddie in there.'

'It was the only place that could handle him.'

Lottie laughed wryly. 'Only they couldn't, could they? He ran away, didn't he? What must it have been like for him?' She shook herself as images of the horrors of 1970s institutions invaded her senses.

Rose shuffled into her coat and walked to the door. 'I live with what I did, every day of my life. And now I'm going. I didn't come here to be interrogated and accused. Goodbye.'

Lottie stood bristling for a long time after her mother left. Wrenching her fingers into her hands, she counted the cobwebs woven over the top of the cupboards. Took deep breaths. Tried to ground herself. How did Rose manage to turn every question into an accusation? She was the one person who could leave her truly shaken.

* * *

After checking in on Katie, Chloe and Sean, and still in a stupor, stung by her mother's unwillingness to give her the answers she had so long coveted, Lottie changed her clothes, dodged a shower and drove to the station. Her lack of sleep was replaced with adrenaline.

She set Kirby and Lynch to work. They needed to keep their minds off Boyd's critical state and find some concrete evidence to advance the murder inquiries. She was convinced the deaths of the two priests, Cornelius and Angelotti, were connected to Susan Sullivan and James Brown, and the common thread was St Angela's.

Uploading the ledger photos from her phone to the computer, Lottie squinted with gritty eyes as the entries appeared on the screen. Each held an untold story, every name was someone's heartache. And that pain had been suffered in the halls, rooms and grounds of St Angela's. She needed access to the building, to get a feel for the place, to discover if it held the answers she wanted.

'Print these photos and stick them together chronologically,' Lottie told Lynch before heading to the makeshift canteen. She boiled the half-empty kettle. Mug in hand, she turned to find Corrigan framing the doorway. Not now, she thought.

'Morning, sir.' Lottie sipped her coffee as nonchalantly as she could.

'You look like shit, Parker.' He folded his arms.

No escape, he wasn't going anywhere. She straightened her weary body, raised herself to her full height and mustered up a lame attempt at bravado.

'Thank you,' she said, forcing a smile.

'I'm not stupid,' Corrigan said, calmly. Too calm. She braced herself for the onslaught.

'I know,' she said. What else could she say?

'Don't be smart with me,' he said, unfolding his arms. He leaned in behind her. She flinched and ducked, then noticed he was only switching on the kettle while keeping the exit blocked.

'You travelled to Rome,' he growled.

'Yessir.' No point in denying it.

'You disobeyed my direct order. I could suspend you, fire you, have your balls on a plate, if you had any.'

'Yessir.' Lottie pulled at the sleeve of her shirt, not about to argue with anything he said.

'I hope it was worth the trouble you've created, for yourself and everyone else,' he said, pouring the dribble of water.

'I think it was.' Lottie handed him a carton, her nose twitching with the smell of milk ready to turn.

'I'm listening,' he said, arms folded again, mug on the counter of boxes.

'Okay sir. The way I see it, the murders relate back to incidents which occurred in St Angela's in the seventies. Possibly a murder, if not two. And yes, I admit I went to Rome. I was following a lead.'

'What lead might that be?'

'Father Burke found ledgers with information. He asked me to go take a look. There was no way he could send the information to me.'

'Go on.'

'I saw these ledgers detailing children's admissions to St Angela's. Dates, names, adoptions, deaths. I've yet to analyse the information and I've no idea of the importance of it, but the signature on some of the pages is significant.'

'I'm listening.'

'Father Cornelius Mohan.'

'The Ballinacloy victim from last night?' Corrigan asked, unfolding his arms, taking his coffee, spilling it on his shirtsleeve.

'Yes,' she said. 'And in another ledger there're details of his movements, including his stint in St Angela's. He moved to over forty different parishes. Tells its own story, don't you think?'

'And there he was, living fifteen kilometres outside Ragmullin, next door to a primary school. Madness.'

'All approved by Bishop Connor. Who, incidentally, arranged for the ledgers to be moved to Rome.' Lottie watched Corrigan's face as he digested it all. She added, 'I contacted Boyd last night, asked him to go to Ballinacloy and interview Cornelius Mohan. I believed he might have information about the victims.'

Corrigan's lips hovered over the rim of his mug. 'I don't believe in coincidences,' he said, 'so how did the killer get to Mohan before Boyd? Was he tipped off?'

'Not sure, but it's all too convenient,' Lottie said. 'I need to find out who knew we were after the priest. He had to know something that warranted his murder.'

Puffing out his cheeks, Corrigan said, 'I'm giving you a stay of execution. I can't afford to be down another detective with Boyd out. But when this is all over, you may well end up on indiscipline charges in front of the chief superintendent. For now, get back to work. And Parker,' he said, drawing his face level with hers.

'Yes sir?'

'I'll be watching your every move.'

His gaze bore tiny holes into the backs of her eyes, almost hollowing them out of their sockets, before he walked off, shaking his head.

Lottie sighed. The threat of disciplinary action was now swinging over her head. But she still had her job. For now. One positive in a mire of negativity.

CHAPTER 80

Detective Maria Lynch dropped the copies on the desk. Lottie picked them up. Names swarmed in front of her as a thought struck her. Father Joe had allowed her to take the photographs. And he'd been there when she had called Boyd. Her heart plunged a full two inches down her chest. He was the only one who knew what she'd told Boyd. No. Could he have sent someone after the old priest? He couldn't have. Could he? She was burning up. Why did he bring her to Rome, show her all the records, then double cross her? He was her friend. Wasn't he? It didn't make sense. On the other hand, what other explanation could there be? Nothing made sense. She sprang up, as if scalded.

'Kirby?' she shouted.

He glanced over. 'You all right, boss?'

'Any news from the hospital?'

'Not yet.'

'Did we run a check on Father Joe Burke?' She forced her voice to appear normal.

'First murder, second person on the scene, Joe Burke?'

'I'm not in the mood, Kirby.'

'I'll print it off for you.'

His fingers echoed loudly as he stumped up the name on his computer. Clickity click, clickity click.

Running her hand along the back of her neck, she didn't know whether she was tracking the memory of Father Joe's fingers or stemming the rise of bile.

As Kirby banged away, Lottie heard Tom Rickard before she saw him, the developer's voice thundering abuse at the end of the corridor. The sound, like galvanised sheets loose on a shed roof in a force ten gale, preceded his entry to the office. Superintendent Corrigan hung behind him.

Lottie swivelled to meet Rickard's dark raging eyes. The storm just might be upgraded to a hurricane.

He crossed the floor to her desk. 'Inspector.'

'Good morning, Mr Rickard,' she said in her sweetest voice.

She wheeled over Boyd's chair. Rickard sat, his buttocks precariously balanced on the edge. Nodding to Corrigan that she had everything under control, he scuttled out the door.

'Are you here about St Angela's?' Lottie found a notebook and picked up a pen.

'St Angela's has nothing to do with anything,' Rickard said, a white handkerchief appearing in his hand. He wiped his pulsing forehead. 'It's my son, Jason. He's missing.'

Lottie scribbled without raising her head. Katie had said she couldn't get hold of Jason yesterday. She should have listened more carefully. She tried to stem the beginnings of alarm. Surely Jason would at least have contacted Katie? Something wasn't right.

'Missing? According to Katie, you and Jason had something of an altercation. When was that?'

Rickard looked as if he was going to object but said, 'That's right. Night before last. He stormed out of the house and hasn't been home since.'

'Did you check with his friends? His usual haunts?'

'Yes. And scoured the town, the lakeshore,' he said. 'We had a fight. He fecked off.' His feet were planted firmly on the ground but his head shifted from side to side.

'I understand how worried you are, but Jason is over eighteen and an adult. Do you think his disappearance could have anything to do with your St Angela's dealings?' she asked, emphasising the name of the institution.

Rickard shot up from the chair. Lottie recoiled instinctively.

'You're one callous bitch,' he said.

'Sit down, Mr Rickard,' she said, writing more notes on a page, allowing him time to regain composure. 'Any ransom calls?'

'What?' Rickard clenched his fists on the desk. 'That's absurd.'

'No ransom requests then.' She wrote a note then raised her head. 'Mr Rickard, I have to ask awkward questions. You're a wealthy business-man. Kidnapping is one option. Suicide or running away are some of the others. If you want us to investigate, you have to co-operate.' This was bullshit, but she wasn't letting go. It might be her only chance to get information from him.

'How can my business affairs have anything to do with Jason?'

'Probably nothing, but the way I see it, you hit your son, he ran off in a huff and now he's cooling his heels somewhere until he figures out how he's going to tackle you about it.'

'Why isn't he holed up with your daughter then? Why hasn't he contacted anyone? His phone is at home, but all his friends have mobiles, Facebook and Twitter stuff. Wouldn't he at least contact his girlfriend? What did she tell you?'

'Katie was very frightened when she came home and she told me you hit your son. She hasn't heard from him since but Jason is an adult, Mr Rickard. In normal circumstances, I'd advise you to go home, hold your wife's hand and wait while we make enquiries.'

Blood flushed the veins in his cheeks. He remained silent.

'However, as you know,' Lottie continued, 'things are not normal in Ragmullin at the moment. People have been murdered so you have cause for concern.' She was genuinely concerned for Jason, but she couldn't help being bitchy. She needed to know what Rickard knew.

He remained immobile except for his bottom lip twitching as if he wanted to say something but was unable to get the words out.

'It's not normal procedure as he is not a minor, and we should really wait a bit longer, but I'll process a missing person's report and put out a bulletin,' she said.

'That's it? A missing person's report?'

'I'm even bending the rules at that.'

'Rules my arse. Where's Corrigan?' Rickard stood up.

'Tell me about St Angela's,' Lottie said, without raising her head.

'St Angela's has nothing to do with Jason.' He sat down again.

Chewing her pen, Lottie tapped her computer awake and pressed a few keys. She clicked Susan Sullivan's pathologist report, scrolled down to the photos, zoomed in on the victim's throat and turned the screen toward Rickard. She had nothing to lose.

'What're you playing at?' he asked, the handkerchief appearing again.

'This is our first victim.'

She was a total shit doing this to him, but being at a low ebb he might volunteer some useful information.

'Please . . . Inspector, don't,' he said. 'Do you honestly think I'd something to do with this . . . this monstrosity?' He puffed out his chest, shaking his head.

Lottie closed the document and opened another.

'James Brown.' She eyed Rickard. 'He phoned you a little while before he died. So tell me. What was going on?'

Rickard chewed the inside of his cheek.

She imagined his brain forming a response. Before he could answer, she said, 'Think of your son. Do you want me sitting here in a few days' time scrolling his post-mortem photos for your wife?'

He swallowed noisily and leaned in towards her. She waited.

'None of this has anything to do with St Angela's,' he said through gritted teeth. 'I'm a businessman, I formulate plans, conclude deals, make money, develop property, realise profits. Sometimes I lose, but more often than not, I win. St Angela's was a site ripe for development, a way of clawing back what I'd lost with the ghost estates. I had a vision for it, a master plan. I wanted to develop it into a beautiful hotel, build a magnificent golf course, bring business, jobs to the town.' He straightened his back. 'And it has nothing to do with the disappearance of my son.'

'Just humour me,' Lottie said.

'You don't give up, do you?'

'Never.'

She knew Rickard was considering her, forming a reply he thought she might want to hear. She sat rigid, displaying no emotion. He looked around the room, then back at her and seemed to come to a decision.

'First off, I want you to be clear that I did not murder those people or arrange for them to be murdered. I had nothing whatsoever to do with those crimes. I might be a lot of things, Inspector, but I am not a murderer.'

'Go on,' Lottie said.

'Should I have my solicitor present?'

'Depends on whether you've done anything that warrants you needing one.'

Rickard exhaled. 'James Brown did ring me, that evening, before he was killed.'

'Go on,' Lottie repeated. Nothing new there. They had the evidence.

'I knew both Brown and Susan Sullivan through their work on the planning application. He told me Susan Sullivan was dead, that she might've been murdered. Said he wanted to meet me. That was the sum total of the conversation.'

'Why did he contact you?' Lottie asked.

'I don't know. He said he wanted to tell me something, urgently.'

'Did you meet with him?'

'No. Told him I was busy. Hung up. Then he was killed a few hours later.'

'Someone met him and then possibly killed him. Who did you contact after James' phone call to you?'

'No one.'

'Come on, Mr Rickard. We can access your phone record.'

'I rang my partners to inform them of Sullivan's death and Brown's phone call.'

'Your partners?'

'No need for you to know them, is there?'

She would get it out of him later. 'Had any of them reason to kill Sullivan and Brown?'

'How would I know?'

'You must have some idea. What were the victims up to?'

Rickard inhaled a couple of deep breaths.

'Brown and Sullivan. A right pair when they got going,' he said. 'They knew I'd wrangled the alteration to the county development plan to progress my plans for St Angela's. Had it in for me, the two of them did. Tried to blackmail me. Said they wanted reparation for past sins or some such shite. I hadn't a clue what they were talking about. When Brown first contacted me with their . . . their scam, back in July, I told him to go fuck himself.'

Lottie thought of the money in the victims' bank accounts and the cash in Susan Sullivan's fridge.

'But you gave in.'

'I did not.' He banged the desk. 'I rise above such challenges, Inspector. I don't give in.'

'So what did you do? They'd threatened you with blackmail.'

'I convened a meeting with my partners. I told them about the blackmail threats and we decided to ride it out. Brown and Sullivan were not a danger to our plans. They'd no concrete proof of any wrongdoings. In all honesty there weren't any wrongdoings – just speeding up the planning process.'

'And how was that done?'

'A few quid in a few back pockets of councillors. But that's not the issue, is it?'

Lottie decided to ignore his admission of planning manipulation. She had enough going on. She decided to change direction. 'Were you ever a resident in St Angela's, Mr Rickard? As a child?'

'No, I was not and I don't know what that has to do with anything.'

Lottie wasn't sure if this was the truth but she needed him to confirm it.

'Who else is involved in this project?' she asked. If he was telling the truth, and she suspected he was, who sent the money to the victims' bank accounts?

'I don't see what you knowing who my partners are has to do with my son's disappearance.'

'You don't know that. I want to know who they are.'

'Will you find my son?'

'I'll do my best,' Lottie said.

'Alive?' Rickard asked. His bulk appeared to have shrunk since he had entered the room.

She didn't answer. That was a promise she couldn't make, however confident she was that the boy had skived off to get away from his overpowering father. She hoped that was the case, thinking of her last missing person. Father Angelotti.

He told her the names. Gerry Dunne, Mike O'Brien and Bishop Terence Connor.

'You need to tell me the whole story,' she said, her fatigue from lack of sleep evaporating.

'There is no story, Inspector. Just a few men pulling a couple of strokes to make a quick buck. Bishop Connor sold me the property below market value in exchange for lifetime membership to the new golf club. Mike O'Brien massaged a few figures so that I could finance the deal and Gerry Dunne is to ensure the project gets full planning approval.

'That's it. We're not involved in anything dark enough to warrant murder. I suggest you start looking elsewhere. Otherwise you're wasting valuable time when you could be looking for Jason.' Rickard searched his pocket for something.

'As you appear to have a fascination with St Angela's, here, take these,' he said, slapping a ring of keys on the desk. 'Go, see for yourself. It's just an old building in need of renovation. Bricks and mortar. Satisfy your curiosity. And then, for God's sake, find my son.'

Lottie placed her hand over the keys and pulled them towards her before he changed his mind.

'Thanks,' she said. 'Go home to your wife. Let me know the second you hear anything from Jason. I'll do likewise.'

She indicated their interview was over.

Rickard stood and, without a word or a backward glance, walked flatfooted out of the office, his tailored suit as wrinkled as his craggy face.

Opening the bottom drawer, Lottie extracted the yellowing Manila folder and gazed at the young boy in the photograph. She knew exactly what it was like to have someone missing. She hoped against hope that Jason Rickard was only nursing a sore ego. Anything more sinister than that, and they were in a completely new sphere.

CHAPTER 81

Sean Parker listened to Katie sniffling in her bedroom next door. It reminded him of his mother's night-time crying after his dad had died. The difference was his mam got up each morning red-eyed but in denial, going about her work as if nothing was wrong. He'd wanted to shout at her, remind her of the crying keeping him awake at night. But he remained silent, his young heart breaking for her, for his sisters and himself.

Katie's sobs were different and he felt sorry for her. He'd been in awe of Jason since he'd let him have a pull on a spliff. He'd managed a few drags before the sitting room swam in a myriad of shapes and colours. Then he'd vomited for twenty minutes. He hadn't told Jason that.

He pressed his camouflage controller and stilled a soldier's action on the screen. He wished his mam was home more. But she had her job and was busy with the murder investigations. Everyone told him he was the man of the house, now his dad was gone. So what would the man of the house do?

He tried to switch off the PlayStation but it froze. Wouldn't go on or off.

He needed a new console. Badly, like right now.

He had some savings. Searching his locker for his bank card, his fingers touched cold steel and curled around the Swiss army knife his dad had bought him years ago. He liked to flick open the different shaped blades pretending he was a character from Grand Theft Auto. In all the years he'd had the knife, he'd never taken it out of the house. Today he would. After all, there was a murderer around. You never knew when you might need a Swiss army knife. His dad had told him that. He checked the time on his phone. Just gone half past eleven. He'd be there and back before lunchtime.

He put his bank card in his pocket along with the knife and, pulling on two hoodies, left the house to the sound of Chloe calling Katie a drama queen.

CHAPTER 82

Kicking off her boots, Lottie massaged her foot with one hand while clutching the keys to St Angela's with the other. She caught Kirby eyeing her over the top of his monitor.

'What?' she asked.

'Nothing.' He returned his gaze to the computer.

'Kirby, for once in your life will you say what you're thinking?'

Pocketing the keys, she stamped her foot to the floor and shuffled her aching feet back into her boots. Trailing a hand through her limp hair, she took her phone off silent. No messages. No missed calls. No nothing. She hoped Boyd was doing all right. She looked up to find Kirby standing beside her with a page in his hand. He squeezed her shoulder.

'You wanted something on Father Burke,' he said and went back to his desk.

Lottie looked at the passport-sized photo of Father Joe with his boyish fringe and blue eyes, an open and inviting smile. She skimmed the report until her eyes landed on a local newspaper article from Wexford.

'Did you read this?' she asked.

'I did,' said Kirby. 'He appears to be something of a ladies' man.'

The words on the page merged into each other. Lack of caffeine or sleep deprivation? She felt like throwing up; tried to focus but her mind refused to register what she was looking at. A small article quoting a local woman in Wexford Town. She had claimed Father Joe Burke had pursued her, wanting a relationship. She'd ignored his advances and when he'd persisted she'd reported him but the guards wouldn't do anything about it. Lottie couldn't believe this had actually been printed. Then she thought of the journalist Cathal Moroney and his secret source. She still had to find out who was behind that leak.

She raised her head to Kirby.

'Chasing after female parishioners,' he said, 'is only a crime in the Catholic Church. Vow of celibacy and all that. If you ask me—'

'I didn't,' she said, tuning him out.

She'd been taken in by Father Joe's good looks and sweet charm. Had he been trying to seduce her when she only wanted friendship? Was that why he insisted she go to Rome when really he could have photographed and emailed the relevant ledger pages?

She shoved back her chair, grabbed her phone and, with one arm inside her jacket, was out the door without hearing another word from Kirby.

* * *

She fully intended to go have a look around St Angela's but as she left the office she bumped into Maria Lynch at the car pool.

'I'm heading back out to Ballinacloy,' Lynch said. 'You coming?'

'Sure. I'll drive,' Lottie said, making up her mind on the spot. St Angela's could wait. Maybe she might find something at the old priest's abode.

Father Cornelius Mohan had lived in a bungalow to the left of a small church. Four cottages, early twentieth century, lined the road to the right, a hedged laneway snaking behind. Between the small houses and the church stood a five-class primary school, *Thomas the Tank Engine* painted on the oil tank. A playground curled around the school. And, for the last ten years, a paedophile priest had lived next door. All this had been facilitated by none other than Bishop Connor. Lottie shook her head in bewilderment.

The garda, standing at the gate, lifted the crime scene tape, allowing them through. With Lynch talking to the SOCOs in the yard out the back, Lottie pulled on latex gloves and opened the front door. She surveyed the dark rambling hallway and entered the kitchen with its high ceiling. Everything was murky brown and the air stank of smoke – turf and cigarettes. A clogged ashtray sat on the table beside a chipped mug half-full of stagnant tea. The stove door was open, its ashes as cold as the dead priest.

She pushed open another door. A narrow streak of mid-morning glow seeped through at the bottom of thin curtains. As she drew back the cotton, a shaft of brightness illuminating a crest of dust floating in the air threw light on an unmade single bed, a locker, chest of drawers and a two-door stand-alone wardrobe.

Lifting up a plain blue blanket, Lottie eased gloved fingers under the pillow, felt around and extracted a bulging wallet. It was full of fifty and one hundred euro notes. One five hundred euro note folded in the back behind a laminated card of St Anthony holding the child Jesus. In all, she counted one thousand, six hundred and twenty euro. Robbery was definitely not Cornelius' murderer's motive. It was evident that the old priest was the only person to have entered this room, in a very long time.

She opened drawers, then the wardrobe. Both held a minimal amount of clothing, all of it black, smelling of mothballs and staleness. Kneeling, she looked under the bed. Two pairs of black shoes were lined up with a brown leather suitcase behind them. She dragged out the case, covered with a layer of grime, and unclasped the locks. Yellowed newspaper clippings, folders and notebooks.

Lifting up one of the hard-backed notebooks, she opened it. Short pencil strokes neatly aligned on page after page. Figures, totted up in columns. Household accounts, she guessed, and picked up another notebook. The same. Come on Mohan, she willed, give me something.

Kneeling on the dusty wooden floor, she flicked through six notebooks, all containing figures. She lined them up beside her and took out the next one. Similar navy hardback. She opened it. No figures. Handwriting. She held her breath. The now familiar pencil, in well-schooled handwriting, a methodical, even structured, script.

Words merged and fluttered as she read. A history of abuse, documented in fading pencil, fell from the pages, letter by letter, word by word, floating around her, an incomprehensible pall of sentences. It wasn't enough, she thought, that he'd perpetrated such acts on the innocent, he'd also recorded it. A chronicle of secrets, inscribed with fading pencil, in a navy, hard-backed notebook, incarcerated in the brown leather suitcase of a murdered, child-abusing priest. It assaulted her very soul. She felt her heart break and harden at the same time.

Unable to finish reading, she placed the notebook in a plastic evidence bag and shoved it into her inside jacket pocket. It didn't matter where she placed it, she knew she'd never be able to expunge the horror inscribed by the hand of a demon. He must not have thought about what would happen to these notebooks when he died. Otherwise he would have got rid of them. Unless he had used them to revisit his crimes. What kind of sadistic animal had he been?

She called for Lynch, okayed it with the SOCO team and carried the suitcase to the car. She fled the house, unable to shake off the sound of soft footsteps belonging to little abused children trailing behind her.

The bell in the small country church chimed and the village resonated with the hollow midday toll.

CHAPTER 83

The queue outside the bank ATM seemed to go on forever.

Sean stamped his feet in the snow and decided to take his chances inside. At least it was warmer there. He waited in line for a machine to become available.

The woman in front of him, struggling with a toddler and a screaming baby in a buggy, eventually got her money. He keyed in his PIN number and extracted two hundred euro. That should be enough, he thought, knowing he hadn't much left now. He could trade in his old PlayStation for the balance.

He wondered where Jason could be. He decided he would ask his own friends if any of them had seen him. Not that his friends mixed with the likes of Jason Rickard. But you never know until you ask. He stuffed the money into his trouser pocket and headed for the door.

* * *

The man watched the boy.

Running his hands up and down his suited trousers, he glanced around to ensure no one noticed him.

He recognised the young teenager. Detective Inspector Parker's only son. He stepped behind a rack of leaflets. The stirring in his trousers was so intense, he stuffed his hands in his pockets to quell the rising hardness.

It was too risky. He already had one boy. But if he truly wanted to re-enact the old experience he needed two, didn't he?

As the boy pushed the green button on the internal security door, the man moved quickly to get in line behind him. When the door opened, he entered the small enclosure and smiled. The boy grinned back.

CHAPTER 84

The noon sky was dark, more like late afternoon, and it was snowing once again.

Leaving the village of Ballinacloy, Lottie checked to see if there was any word from the hospital. Nothing. At the station she accompanied Lynch inside with the suitcase. They registered the contents and Lottie flicked through the old notebook once more. She recoiled from the written horrors and bagged the book for evidence.

'I'll be back in a while,' she said.

Badly in need of a shower, she picked up her own car. She also wanted to visit Boyd. But first stop, now that she had the keys, would be St Angela's.

* * *

A sore throat was itching to take root. Lottie coughed and it ached even more. Standing at her car looking up at the old building, she needed to ease the stress constricting her brain. She counted the windows once, then twice. Careful not to slip on the fresh sheen of snow, she walked up the steps.

At the door, key in hand, she had an uncharacteristic surge of dread. She was fearful for herself, her past, her decisions, her attitude, her grief and what she was becoming. In an instant, she wished Boyd was with her, jibing her. She missed him.

Slipping latex gloves over numb fingers, she turned the key in the old lock and pushed open the door, surprised it extended inwards with comparative ease.

The entrance hall was smaller than she expected. An icy chill took her breath away. Colder inside than out. She half-expected to see water running down the walls from burst pipes. Before her stood a large staircase. The mahogany banister twisted upwards, enclosing wide concrete steps, leading to a crossroad of dark corridors. She didn't bother with the light switch, it might not work and she didn't want to find out. Sometimes you were better off not knowing, rather than finding yourself literally in the dark. She comforted herself with that thought.

She listened. Stillness inside, while the wind outside hurled snow against the windowpanes, rattling their frames. A draught rustled dead leaves at her feet. She closed the front door and kicked the remnants of snow from her boots. She decided to check out the upper floors.

At the top of the first flight of stairs, she moved along a corridor lined on one side with doors and windows on the other. Subconsciously, she counted the windows – couldn't help it – and mentally filed the numbers away. Doubling back, she headed along the other corridor, counting these windows; their frames creaked, then settled. She repeated the exercise on the other floor. Counting. It didn't add up.

She ran down the stairs. Counted again. Only thirteen windows. Sixteen on the outside. Both ends of the corridor were bookended by concrete. She traced her hand along the wall and knocked intermittently, wondering if they were hollow. They appeared solid. Perhaps Tom Rickard could provide the answer. She was curious about the inaccuracy but had no idea what significance it might have, if any.

A bird shrieked above her head, its wings crashing against the wooden rafters, and disappeared. She would have screamed if her throat wasn't already raw. She leaned against the wall and felt the vibes of the past. O'Malley's story reverberated in her brain. The clamour of children running along corridors, nuns screaming behind them, hair pulling, squealing, jaws clattering with the backs of wizened hands. The image was so vivid, if she reached out, Lottie thought she might touch it. The anguish, the loneliness of abandoned children. There was no sense of dreams or expectation, it was all despair and loss.

Once again her thoughts were invaded by the image of the yellowing file in her bottom desk drawer. The missing. The dead. The young red-headed boy – had he been murdered or had O'Malley's drink-addled brain conjured up a myth? She recalled the words scripted in the navy hard-backed notebook, and the ledgers, full of truths and lies. The overwhelming emotion charging through her being was devastating helplessness.

The blackbird quietened down, nestled in the eaves of the roof and Lottie retraced her steps, counting the faded brown doors along the corridor, with tarnished brass knobs, paint peeling beneath from years of hands, young and old, twisting and turning. Since it had been abandoned to itself, the building had died.

Doors needed to be opened. Doors to a forgotten past. Maybe Susan and James had tried to unlock them, in the metaphorical sense. Look what had happened to them. Her gut was telling her this building held the key to the overall puzzle. She opened and closed a few doors to empty desolate spaces and she assumed the rooms had once been small dormitories. She turned the handle on the next and stepped inside.

It was similar to the others, though here black plastic bags covered the windows, smothering the room in darkness. She felt along the wall and flicked a switch. A low wattage bulb, suspended on a dust-covered wire, spread a modicum of light over the space. Lottie looked around.

An iron-framed bed, against a wall, dressed in white sheets. Stepping further into the room on bare, uneven floorboards, Lottie twitched her nose. A faint hint of washing powder lingered on the cotton. She turned the pillow and raised the mattress. Nothing.

A clinking sound caused her to pause, sheet in hand. Silence. Ears alert, all she heard was the wind brushing snow against the window and the refuse bag rustling in a breeze through a gap in the sashes. She studied the room. A bed, a small gas heater in one corner and a wooden chair in the other. Nothing else, except paint peeling from the ceiling and shadows deepening in yellow tremors from the slightly swaying light-bulb.

Turning to leave, she caught a glimpse of a sliver of metal at the leg of the bed. She swept her fingers through the dust and touched the object. She slid it toward her, cradled it between her cold fingers and lifted it to the light. The silver pendant shimmered against her latex swathed hand. She knew exactly who the pendant belonged to.

* * *

Jason twisted his head, sure he'd heard knocking against the wall. The binds, on his arms and legs, constrained him to the floor. The gag in his mouth prevented him from shouting.

Someone was looking for him! Exhilaration rushed through him and he strained his body against the ropes. But he was securely bound.

Despair overtook him and he slumped against the floor. If they were in the main part of the building, would they search further into this section? Would they know it even existed? He hoped they wouldn't give up too easily. He was getting weaker. He strained his ears once again, listening, seeking a sound, however small.

His moment of hope shattered, doom settling into the pit of his stomach where it churned and lurched. To the echo of birds crowing high in the rafters of the roof he vomited over himself.

CHAPTER 85

'Hello there. Sean Parker, is that right?'

Outside the game shop, Sean turned round.

'What's it to you?' He leaned against the shop window.

'I recognised you, that is all.'

'So. What d'you want?' Sean asked and waved at one of his friends, across the street.

'I know your sister and Jason very well. Do you know he is missing?'

Sean inched back further but there was nowhere else to go.

'Yes, I know.'

'This may seem odd, but he is not missing. I actually know where he is.'

'Why don't you go to the gardaí then?'

'Jason does not want them involved. There's a family dispute or something.'

'Okay, but it's nothing to do with me.' Sean edged closer to the door of the shop.

The man shook his head and took a step back.

'That's fine. Sorry to bother you.' He turned to walk away.

Sean bit his lip, sized the man up and down. He looked respectable, well dressed, clean, even though he had no overcoat in the freezing cold snow. Odd. He looked familiar. Had he seen him somewhere recently? He couldn't remember. He didn't appear to be a threat. Just some old guy who knew his sister.

Sean asked, 'Where is he?'

The man faced him. 'I cannot break any confidences, but I can show you where he is. That way you can say . . . you can say that you stumbled over his hiding place.'

'Sure.'

'Come with me.'

CHAPTER 86

Lottie banged the steering wheel. The car wouldn't start. Snow lay thick on the ground. Not freezing. Not yet.

She continued to turn the key, getting an empty click in reply. With the pendant in a plastic bag in her pocket, she sat thinking. She knew who owned it and thought she knew how it got there. And she had to talk to Rickard about the windows. The anomaly was bugging her, crawling under her skin.

Jane Dore's number flashed on her phone.

'Hello, Jane.'

'I've completed Father Mohan's post-mortem.'

'You are busy, and quick,' Lottie said. 'Same as the others?'

'Not the same, no,' the pathologist said. 'Less force was used by the perpetrator, but then he was an old man.'

'Do you think it might have been a copycat killing?'

'I doubt it. Cornelius Mohan has the same tattoo as Susan Sullivan and James Brown.'

Lottie held her breath for a moment. An old priest with a tattoo? What next?

'It's like the others, old but more defined. I scanned the image and enlarged it,' Jane said. 'The tattoos on the other victims were faded and looked like lines in a circle, but with this one I can actually make out the drawing.'

'Go on,' Lottie said, hoping it was something definite.

'It looks like the Madonna and Child icon, often depicted as a sculpted statue in churches. So Wikipedia tells me.'

Lottie glanced up at the top of the building in front of her. The statue she'd struggled to see through the darkness at St Angela's the other night with Boyd was the Virgin Mary with the infant Jesus in her arms.

'You could be right,' she said. 'But I still don't understand why Susan and James had it.' And Patrick O'Malley, she recalled.

'If it means something, you better find out. Before any more bodies end up here.'

Listening to the dial tone, Lottie knew she had to speak to O'Malley again. He was looking increasingly very important. As a witness to a murder perpetrated decades earlier or was he involved back then, involved now, even? No matter what, he potentially held vital information. She'd have to get him to remember. Her phone interrupted her thoughts.

'Inspector, this is Bea Walsh . . . from the council.'

'Hello, Bea. How're you?'

'I just wanted to let you know the planning permission for St Angela's was approved today.'

'I suppose it's easy to blame the dead for that,' Lottie said. 'So, Rickard can go ahead with his hotel plans?'

'Not exactly. There's a waiting period for the public appeal process, though I don't think there'll be too many objections. This development will create jobs.'

'Thanks for letting me know.'

'And, Inspector, the file wasn't missing at all. Gerry Dunne, the county manager, had it.'

Lottie mulled over the two phone calls. Attempting to assemble the information in her head, she failed. Intruding on her brooding was the fact that her car wouldn't start and the cost of getting it fixed.

Longing for a cigarette or anything else on which to concentrate, she scanned the expanse of grounds blanketed with snow. Her eyes rested on a walled enclave sweeping to the rear of St Angela's. A crescent of snow-covered trees inched above the stone walls. The orchard. An image zoomed through her mind. Young Susan and James, with O'Malley and Brian, whoever or wherever he was, being terrorised by Father Con.

At least three of them were now dead.

CHAPTER 87

'Do you really know where Jason is?' Sean asked the man, as he sat into the car.

'Yes, I do.'

'That's some coincidence, isn't it?'

'What coincidence?'

'You knowing me and also knowing Jason,' Sean said. 'Can you put the heater on?'

'Of course I can.' The man pulled out of the car park into the line of traffic and turned up the heat. 'It won't take a minute to warm you up, young man.'

Sean asked, 'How do you know who I am?'

'I know your mother too, see, and you are the image of her. I would recognise you out of her, a mile away.'

'Everyone tells me I'm the spitting image of my dad.'

'I do not know your dad,' the man said, waiting for the lights to turn green.

'He's dead.'

'Sorry for your loss.'

'So how do you know my sister and Jason?'

'I am a friend of Jason's father. You could say we are in business together.'

Sean lapsed into silence as the man drove the car carefully through town. Swirling snow slowed their progress. Once Jason was home, Katie would be happy. She'd owe him, like forever. Sean smirked, proud of himself.

'What are you smiling at?' the man asked.

'Oh nothing,' Sean said, still grinning.

* * *

'Where to?' Kirby asked, chewing his unlit cigar.

'This car stinks,' Lottie said, pulling on her seat belt.

Stale tobacco smoke crawled off the seats into her clothes. She'd had to leave her car until they got jump leads. Kirby didn't have any.

'I want to talk to Tom Rickard but first I need to see Boyd.'

'You won't get near him,' Kirby said.

'I don't give a shit,' she said. 'Mind the icy road.' She gripped the dashboard as Kirby swerved, narrowly avoiding an oncoming car. 'Smoke your cigar if you want.'

'Your wish is my command.' He lit the cigar with one flick from a lighter.

'I found this in St Angela's.' Lottie held up a small plastic evidence bag containing the silver pendant.

Kirby eyed it sideways. 'Nice. Why would it be in that old place?'

'That's what I'm going to find out.'

'So you know who owns it?'

'I do,' Lottie said. 'Will it cost much to fix the car?'

Kirby said, 'The price of a pint.'

'I can afford to buy you one pint. My budget won't stretch to two.'

'That bad, huh?' Kirby grunted.

Lottie nodded. 'You don't by any chance know how to fix a PlaySta-tion?'

* * *

'Moron,' the man said, righting his car.

He exited the main road and drove up the side road and through the rear entrance gate into St Angela's.

'Where're we going?' Sean asked.

'You ask a lot of questions,' the man said, through gritted teeth.

'Just wondering.'

The man edged his sleek vehicle in behind the small chapel and switched the engine off.

Sean slipped his hand around the cold metal in his pocket, glad he had this talisman with him. Something suddenly told him he should run like mad, to get as far away as he could. Before he could react, the man gripped his elbow tight, propelling him towards the arched wooden door with a shiny new padlock.

Though he was not yet fourteen, he was tall, but in the time it took the man to open the padlocked door, Sean felt tiny. He didn't know if it was because of the man's eyebrows tightening into a scowl or the secure hold on his arm. One thing for certain, he was glad he had his knife with him.

The door closed and the man slid a bolt in place.

'Why'd you do that?'

'Security. This way.'

Sean stood his ground.

'If the door was locked from the outside,' he began, 'how can Jason be in here of his own free will?'

The man's jaw tightened. Sean backed against the door.

'I told you I would bring you to Jason. Be a good lad and do as I say.'

'He's not here at all,' Sean screeched. 'Who are you?'

He held on to the knife in his pocket, hoping the man wouldn't notice. How stupid, to let himself be dragged here. What was the best thing to do? Hope Jason was here and go along with the man to find out or fight back and escape now? If he used the knife, he could get out the door. What if he was leaving Jason behind? What would his mother do? He had to think fast, or he was going to be in a shit load of trouble.

'Stop asking questions. Come.'

Sean made his decision and allowed himself to be led down the dull, narrow corridor, his hand clenched firmly around his knife.

CHAPTER 88

Standing outside the nurses' station, Kirby said, 'At least he's out of ICU.'

Lottie rolled her eyes. He was annoying the shit out of her. Never shut his mouth, always had to be saying something. She took a deep breath, trying to instil a calmness she could feel.

'How did you get on in Rome?' he asked.

'Did you just wink at me?' Lottie walked up to him, locking eyes. He stepped back.

'I didn't mean to. It sort of happened.' Kirby pulled at his unshaven jaw.

'Don't try to be like Boyd. It doesn't suit you.'

'You can see the patient for five minutes. No longer. He's weak, but conscious.' A young, blue-uniformed, blue-eyed nurse held the door open.

'Only one of you,' she said, the upturned palm of her hand stopping them.

'You go.' Kirby allowed Lottie to pass.

* * *

Boyd lay propped up on the bed, a multitude of wires meandering from various areas of his body to monitors standing like robots around him. The nurse pressed a tube, peered at the liquid passing through. Satisfied, she turned to Lottie.

'Five minutes.' She left Lottie alone with Boyd.

Pulling over a chair, Lottie sat close to Boyd's head. His eyes blinked recognition, their hazel hue dulled. He tried an unsuccessful smile.

'I'm sorry,' she whispered. 'I shouldn't have traipsed off to Rome leaving you to get into trouble without me.'

She smiled as Boyd attempted a weak grin.

'I know you're not supposed to talk but can you remember anything about your assailant?'

'No small talk?' A crusty croak from Boyd.

'When Kirby told me what happened, I was terrified,' Lottie said. 'I thought you were going to die but I tried not to think about that. You know me – buried myself in work all morning.'

She clasped his hand, feeling the length of his fingers in her own, bent her head and kissed the scratched skin of his forehead.

'Don't cry,' Boyd whispered.

'Chance would be a fine thing,' Lottie said.

'I saw the killer's back . . . familiar . . . not sure. I'm no help.'

'Could it have been O'Malley?'

'Don't know.'

Lottie found tissues on the locker and wiped spittle from the corner of his mouth.

'It doesn't matter. I'll get him. He'll be one sorry bastard when I'm done with him.'

'Be careful,' Boyd said, his voice gathering strength. 'No point in ending up here too. Or maybe they've a double bed.'

'Wise arse,' Lottie said. 'I'm baffled why the killer struck when you were on your way to see the priest. Did you tell anyone besides Lynch?'

'No . . . no one.'

She mulled over this for a moment. Confident that Lynch had nothing to do with it and, if Boyd had told no one else, then the only other person who knew was Father Joe. She noticed how weary Boyd looked. This wasn't the time to tell him of her suspicions. His eyelids closed.

'Get better quick. I'm lost without you.' She fluttered her lips on his brow as the nurse returned.

With a backward glance at the now sleeping Boyd, she left the room, determined to put an end to the killer's quest.

CHAPTER 89

'I've no further information regarding your son, Mrs Rickard, but I need to talk to your husband.'

Lottie leaned against the doorjamb of the Rickard residence. Melanie walked inside. She followed. Tom Rickard rose from his armchair in anticipation. She shook her head. His face slumped.

'As I told your wife, I've nothing new on your son's whereabouts. We've issued a press statement. It's on social media and we'll get television coverage.'

'Inspector, I'm fierce worried,' Rickard said.

'We're doing all we can.'

Lottie sat opposite him in the chair he indicated. Sitting in his crumpled suit, Rickard's eyes were red-rimmed. A log fire blazed. The room was warm.

'Tea? Coffee?' Melanie Rickard asked.

'Tea, thank you,' Lottie said. She felt something in the atmosphere between Melanie and Tom Rickard. Ice? Melanie escaped to the kitchen.

'About St Angela's . . .' she began.

'I'm more concerned with my son's welfare at the moment,' he said.

'Who else has keys to the building?'

Rickard shrugged. 'My partners. You have my set.'

'Why do they have them?'

'I provided them with keys ages ago, in case they needed to check out the place. I never asked for them back. I've no idea if they used them or not,' Rickard said. 'What has this got to do with anything?'

'I don't know, is the honest answer,' Lottie said. She held up the bag with the pendant. 'Do you recognise this?'

Rickard glanced away. 'No. Should I?'

'I thought you might. Are you sure?'

'Goddammit woman, what are you doing to find my son?'

She rose to leave. The fire was too comforting to sit any longer. 'Another thing, do you have St Angela's original floor plans? I need to see the layout.'

Rickard shrugged, sighed and hauled his bulk from the armchair, a bear waking from winter's hibernation. He extracted a rolled-up document from a desk in the corner and handed it to her.

'Keep it. I've lost all interest in the project,' he said and returned to stand beside his chair.

'Even though you've got your planning permission?'

'My son is more important to me now. When you've finished with those you can burn them. Just find Jason. Make it your priority. I'm begging you.'

Rickard turned towards the fire, staring at the orange flames leaping over the burning timber.

Lottie rose to leave. Melanie arrived with a tray. She put it on the table and placed a hand on her arm, lips silent, eyes pleading.

Lottie nodded, feeling the other woman's anxiety.

She left the couple to their lonely despair.

CHAPTER 90

'Look at this, Kirby,' Lottie said, pointing to the plans laid out on a desk in the incident room. 'I was right.'

'About what?'

She rolled her sleeves to her elbows and drew a circle on the page with a yellow highlighter.

'The plans show the corridor with sixteen windows on the second floor. I counted thirteen inside, but sixteen on the outside.'

'Which means what, exactly?' Kirby asked, searching his pocket.

She tapped the drawing with the marker.

'It means there are three windows behind a wall, which also means there's an extra room or rooms blocked off.'

'So what?' he ventured.

'So why?' Lottie asked. 'Why do that? Who did it? When? That's what I want to know. What does it mean?'

'What has it to do with the murders?'

'I don't know, but we have nothing else and I need to find out. Do we have an address for O'Malley?'

'He lives on the streets.'

'Go look for him.'

She glanced around the room, noticed Lynch studying the incident board.

'Something doesn't add up,' Lynch said.

'What do you mean?'

'Derek Harte. Brown's lover. I've reviewed his statements and I think something's not right. He either lied to us or was economical with the truth. I can't find him registered as a teacher in any school.'

'Follow it up ASAP.'

Lottie hadn't time for this now. She was on a mission. 'I think Mrs Murtagh, the woman who runs the soup kitchen, might know where Patrick O'Malley's hanging out. Give me the car keys, Kirby.'

* * *

'I haven't seen him,' Mrs Murtagh said, leading Lottie inside, shooing the dog out.

The kettle was boiling and warm bread rested on a plate in front of Lottie.

'Where are his usual haunts?' Lottie asked.

'Patrick O'Malley could be anywhere, Inspector. At night, he usually beds down on Main Street. Sometimes you'd come across him behind the train station; in the carriages or in one of those houses, you know, the old terrace with the roofs caved in. But I haven't seen him anywhere, these last few nights.'

Lottie sighed, 'I'll get someone to look for him.'

Mrs Murtagh poured the tea and they drank from mugs.

'Where is your skinny partner today, Detective Dottie?'

'The name is Lottie and DS Boyd was injured last night. He's in hospital.'

'That's awful. I'll say a prayer for him. What happened?'

'Nothing for you to worry about.' Lottie checked the time on her phone. 'I ought to be getting on. Thanks for the tea.'

'That reminds me of what I was trying to think of the last time you were here.'

'What does?'

Mrs Murtagh fidgeted with the crumbs on her plate. 'The phone.'

'What about it?'

'Not your phone.' The old woman hesitated, said, 'I have Susan Sullivan's mobile phone.'

'You what?' Lottie abandoned her smile and clenched her hands. 'Where is it? It could be vital to our investigations. Why didn't you give it to me before?'

'I forgot I had it and now I'm not sure I even want to give it to you,' Mrs Murtagh said, folding her arms rigidly.

'I could charge you with impeding a murder investigation. We might've been able to prevent another murder. There could be vital information on that phone.'

Lottie knew she was being irrational. They'd got all the information from the service provider. Seeing the look of confusion on Mrs Murtagh's face, she tried to soften her voice.

'It is okay. Don't worry. As long as you hand it over now it will all be fine.'

'It mightn't even work.'

'That's beside the point.' Lottie dug her nails into the palm of her hand and gritted her teeth. 'How come you have it?'

'I've just remembered it all now. Susan let it fall into the soup. Ruined one batch completely. We had to make more. Such a hullaballoo.'

'When was this?'

'The evening before her murder. I put it in a bowl of rice in the hot-press. That's what Susan said you're supposed to do.'

'Why didn't she take it with her?'

'We were busy, forgot all about the phone when we came back from our soup run. Then the poor soul was killed.'

'And you kept the phone?'

'She was murdered the next day,' Mrs Murtagh explained, tears in her eyes.

'You should've given it to me.'

'I forgot I had it.' She raised the teapot questioningly.

Lottie put her hand over her mug, refusing the gesture.

'Susan is dead. Her secrets could help solve her murder. Can you get me the phone now, please.'

Mrs Murtagh rose slowly and went out to the hall. Lottie heard a cupboard opening and closing.

'It's hard to know what could be on it after the soaking it got.' The woman returned and handed the phone to Lottie.

Not much, thought Lottie, putting it into a plastic bag before sliding it into her handbag.

'There's something else too . . .' Mrs Murtagh began, rubbing her forehead.

'Go ahead.'

'St Angela's. Susan mentioned there were two priests there.'

'Go on.'

'After she met Bishop Connor, she was in an awful state. She'd arranged to meet him to see if he could release records to help in her search for her baby. I thought she'd seen a ghost. Did I tell you that? She told me she recognised the bishop as a priest from her early days in Ragmullin.'

'What?'

'I'm telling you what she told me.'

Lottie struggled to get her head around the implications of what she'd been told. Of course Susan had been back in Ragmullin only a couple of years. She'd have had no reason to see the bishop before her arranged meeting with him. Did it also mean Bishop Connor knew two of the victims from their time in St Angela's? He hadn't mentioned it. Then again, it might not have been him at all. Something else for Kirby to pin on the incident board.

'Susan and James looked out for each other over the years. You need to look out for them, now that they're gone,' Mrs Murtagh said.

Lottie stood up, desperately trying to batten down her anger.

The old woman wrapped the brown bread in tin foil. 'I'm sorry,' she said, handing over the bread.

'So am I,' Lottie replied, placing the bread on the table. 'And if you see Patrick O'Malley, contact me immediately.' Before you forget, she thought. 'I need to speak to him.'

Mrs Murtagh suddenly looked older than her age. Grasping the crooked handle of her stick, she walked Lottie to the door.

Lottie didn't even say goodbye as she sat into Kirby's cigar-stinking car.

CHAPTER 91

Sean opened his eyes. His head throbbed.

Attempting to sit up from the ice-cold floor, he found he was bound with a rope around his neck, his arms and legs similarly constrained. He struggled to remember where he was. What had happened? He lay still and listened. No sound. He thought hard. Memory flashed and dimmed. The man pushing him through the door, knocking him to the ground and . . . and that was it.

He twisted around, trying to see something, anything. Enveloped in darkness, he focussed his eyes but it was blacker than anywhere he'd ever been. His stomach bubbled with fear and terror crawled under his skin.

His phone vibrated in his pocket. No way of getting his hand to it, and he realised the bastard hadn't taken it, so maybe he'd missed the knife. Couldn't tell. Tears flitted unshed at the corners of his eyes. It didn't matter. There was nothing he could do now. Suddenly he was a little boy, all bravado disintegrating with the realisation of the hopelessness of his situation.

And he began to cry, like the boy he was at heart.

CHAPTER 92

Lottie paced the cramped office, after dispatching Susan's phone to the technical geeks.

She informed Kirby what Mrs Murtagh had said about Susan recognising Bishop Connor.

'I told you to let me kick the shite out of the lying bastard,' Kirby said.

'Quick word?' Lynch touched Lottie's elbow.

'Just a minute, I need to call home.'

She phoned Chloe. 'How are things there?'

'Fine. Sean went into town earlier on.'

Lottie said, 'Why'd he go to town?'

'He hasn't stopped complaining about his PlayStation so maybe he wanted to check out a new one?'

'Put him on.'

'He's not back yet. Probably gone to Niall's house. I texted him to see what he wanted for lunch. He didn't text back.'

'Probably no credit.'

'Typical,' laughed Chloe.

'Message him on Facebook.'

'Why didn't I think of that, Mother?' Chloe said with mock sarcasm. 'How's Katie?'

'Thick. As usual. Any sign of Jason?'

'I'm working on it,' Lottie said. 'Let me know when Sean gets home.'

'Will do.'

She hung up and turned to Lynch, 'You wanted to ask me something?'

'I want to talk to you about Derek Harte. Is now okay?'

'I need something to distract me. Go ahead.'

Lynch folded her arms, a file clasped to her chest. 'I reviewed all the paperwork, examined his statement again, then I ran a check on him.'

'Tell me.'

'I think we've fucked up, Inspector. Big time.'

'Oh shit.'

Lottie pulled two chairs over to a hissing radiator and they sat beside the heat. Lynch flipped through the file on her knee.

'Harte told us he works in a school in Athlone. We assumed he was a teacher.'

'But he's not?' Lottie stared at Lynch. 'For God's sake!'

'He's not registered as a teacher anywhere. But he does odd jobs. The last known place was St Simon's Secondary School in Athlone. He gave false information on his application and an address in Dublin. I searched PULSE. Found him.'

'Convicted of something?'

'Served five years of an eight-year sentence for the abduction and sexual assault of a minor. Released from Arbour Hill prison eleven months ago.'

Lottie mentally weighed up the enormity of Lynch's revelation. Whose fault was this mess? Her own, everything was her responsibility as senior investigating officer. She would definitely be hauled in front of the chief superintendent, if not the garda commissioner. Corrigan would explode. And Lynch would escape without blame. Shit! As for the school, they mustn't have checked him out at all. What about Garda Clearance certification? What a mess.

'Christ almighty,' she shouted. 'Why wasn't this discovered days ago? I can't tolerate incompetence. And to think I empathised with the little prick in his fake grief. I'll kill him myself when we catch up with him.'

'I've checked out the address he gave us. He rents a bedsit.'

Lynch handed Lottie a photograph of the convicted Derek Harte. He looked totally different from the grief-stricken man who had found the body of James Brown. Shaggy beard, long hair. Dark, dead eyes. The bastard. He had now soared to number one on her suspect list.

'Give me the good news,' Lottie said, throwing down the photo and pulling at her worn sleeves, feeling a tightness in her chest. She began to cough.

'Are you all right?' Lynch asked.

Lottie tried to answer, but couldn't. Lynch fetched a paper cup, poured water from the dispenser.

'What's wrong?' She handed the cup to Lottie.

Lottie sipped and felt the wave ebb.

'You're exhausted,' Lynch said.

She didn't want Lynch's sympathy.

'It's only a cold. Find Harte. You and Kirby chase him down. Before Superintendent Corrigan gets wind of this latest fuck-up.'

'Straight away.'

'Print off his history. I need to know what we're dealing with.'

Lynch scooted through the door, ponytail slapping against her shoulders.

Lottie glanced out the window, over the road at the cathedral, standing majestic in the afternoon sepia fog. The streetlights were warming up. The scene appeared surreal. Just when she thought she had everything connected, she was thrown another curve ball.

And she had things to discuss with her doctor, other than a cold. She opened her drawer, picked up the silver pendant she'd found at St Angela's, pocketed it, banged the drawer shut.

CHAPTER 93

Annabelle O'Shea looked as extraordinary as usual. An impeccable navy skirt suit, a white shirt with the hint of a red bra visible through the sheer silk. Making a statement, Lottie thought. After her five-minute walk on icy footpaths to the doctor's Hill Point surgery, she was soaked in sweat.

'I didn't have time to make an appointment.'

'You look dreadful. Sit down.' Annabelle offered a chair to Lottie before perching on her leather-topped desk. 'I have your prescription.'

'I haven't time to go to the pharmacy. Can't you give me a few pills? Just for now.'

'What's the matter?' Annabelle enquired. She leaned back to a cabinet behind her, extracted a couple of boxes, read the labels and handed one over.

Satisfied it contained benzodiazepine, Lottie pocketed it and took the small plastic bag from her pocket and placed it on the desk.

'This is yours,' she said, pointing to the silver pendant in the bag. 'Explain how I came to find it under a bed in St Angela's.'

Annabelle glanced at the pendant, face inscrutable. Lottie imagined her friend's brain whirring, formulating what she thought might be a satisfactory answer.

'This is not mine,' Annabelle said, pushing it away from her.

Lottie's laugh broke up with a cough.

'Others might believe you, Annabelle O'Shea, but I don't.'

The doctor picked it up again. 'I'm sure lots of people have a similar pendant.'

'I haven't time for games and I'm definitely not in the mood,' Lottie said.

Annabelle threw the jewellery down on the desk, stood up and walked to the door. Short, sharp, steps. 'You got what you came for. Please leave.'

Lottie remained seated, turning the small plastic bag round in her hand.

'Tell me, Annabelle. I want to know.'

'If it is mine, what does it matter to you?'

'Because St Angela's is part of my investigation into the murders in this town.'

'Nothing to do with me.'

'For Christ's sake, Annabelle. Tell me.'

'Okay. Calm down.'

Annabelle sat. Lottie did too.

'I go there, now and again. With my lover,' Annabelle said.

'Who's this lover?' asked Lottie, blowing her nose, too loud in the confined space.

'You don't need to know that.'

'I do.'

After a pause Annabelle said, 'Tom Rickard.'

'What?'

'He said he'd leave his wife,' Annabelle said. 'When we had enough money to set up together. He's always involved in some scheme or other.' She paused, closed her eyes and then opened them wide. 'To tell you the truth, I'm getting weary of him.'

Lottie snorted her disgust. 'Same as always. Wanting what you can't have. Never stopped you, though.'

'Not everyone can have the marriage you had.'

'But what about Cian . . . your children?'

'But what, Lottie, what? You think it's just me.' She laughed bitterly. 'You do, don't you? You think I'm the only one fucking around in their marriage?'

'You're a bitch,' Lottie said, leaning over the desk.

'You know me. I take what I want, and I wanted Tom Rickard.'

'Were you with him the day of the Sullivan and Brown murders?'

'Probably. When was that again?'

'You know right well it was December thirtieth.'

'Mmm . . . let me see.' She checked her computer diary. 'Yes, I believe we were together then. Some meeting of his was cancelled and I wasn't working, so we met up.'

And a few more puzzle pieces slid into place for Lottie. 'That's why he couldn't provide a definitive alibi. He didn't want to betray you.'

'Didn't want his wife to find out.'

'You should've told me this when I spoke to you about Susan Sullivan.'

'You never asked.'

'Clever answer,' Lottie said. She'd had enough of Annabelle, her secrets and lies. She rose and went to the door. 'Sometimes you can be too clever for your own good.'

Annabelle was silent.

'When did you last meet him?' Lottie asked.

'Two days ago.' She shrugged her shoulders. 'I think.'

'At St Angela's?'

'Of course.'

'I pity you, Annabelle. You have brains, money, a good family and here you are acting like the spoiled brat I always knew you were. Goodbye.'

* * *

Outside the doctor's surgery, Lottie leaned against the wall until her breathing returned to normal. Tom Rickard could have saved her a lot of trouble if he'd been truthful with his alibi from day one. She started walking back to the office.

Sirens were blaring down by the train station as she crossed the canal bridge. The water was frozen, a sheet of snow glistening on it under weak lamps. Blue lights flashed beyond the old carriages. She hurried down the hill and through the town, oblivious to the still twinkling Christmas lights forlornly inviting non-existent customers to venture through shop doors. Cold chewed into her bones but she was too numb in her heart to feel it on her skin.

On the steps of the Garda Station, a black crow stood on the snowflakes, his beak, hard and grey, claws long enough to pluck an eye out of its socket. Flapped his wings once, but didn't move. Lottie felt him staring as she walked up the steps. An icy shiver travelled the length of her spine and she knew what people meant when they spoke of foreboding.

The chattering in the incident room dropped a decibel when she entered.

'What's up?' she asked. Oh God, she thought, gripping her sides with her folded arms. 'Boyd?'

'No,' Kirby said, twisting in his chair.

'Well, are you going to tell me?'

'We found another body,' he said.

'Jason?' Lottie sat down quickly.

'No. A body was found beyond the old railway carriages, in one of the dilapidated terraced houses.'

'I hope it's not O'Malley.' She got up and walked around the desks. 'He was looking like one of our most likely suspects.'

Lynch said, 'The body was probably there for a few days. The face, gnawed by vermin. One arm missing and two fingers gone from the other hand. The toes too. A bag of bones and rags.' She spoke in the abstract, not referring to the body as a human being. It helped distance the horror.

'It better not be O'Malley,' Lottie snapped. 'According to Mrs Murtagh, that area was one of his haunts.' She banged the desk in frustration. 'Is there any indication yet if it's murder?'

'Possibly hypothermia,' Lynch said. 'The state pathologist is at the scene. Will we head down there?' She grabbed her coat. A soft murmur of activity resumed as detectives returned to their work.

'You go. I'll stay here.' Lottie gripped the back of her chair, hoping they hadn't another murder on their hands. If O'Malley was dead, who was left to answer her questions? Would St Angela's' evil remain secret forever? She hoped not.

'Did you track down Derek Harte?' she asked.

'He's not at either of his addresses and his phone is dead,' Lynch said at the door.

'Find him.' Lottie went to find solace at her desk.

'And get me the journalist, Cathal Moroney.'

CHAPTER 94

It must be getting dark outside, Sean thought, because he was much colder now. He hoped his mother was out looking for him. Would she even know he was missing? He hoped so.

He heard footsteps, strained his ears. The door opened and a shaft of muted light silhouetted the man framed in the opening.

'How is my young man?' The voice was hoarse and gruff.

'What . . . what do you want? Where's Jason?' Sean asked.

'Ah, no patience, the youth of today.' The man tut-tutted and entered the room.

Sean felt the ropes and chain loosening. Dragged to his feet, he stumbled, then straightened up. But his knees buckled once more. The man's arm crested under Sean's, leading him from the room. Let the bastard think he was weaker than he actually was.

The man halted outside another door and opened it. Sean felt a push in his ribs and staggered inside. The stench of vomit filled the air. Squinting, he tried to see in the darkness. On the concrete floor, Jason was lying in a foetal position, his hands covering his head. His chest and feet were bare and his jeans open at the waist.

'You wanted to see Jason. There he is,' the man said, trudging over to the boy on the ground.

Jason didn't move a muscle and Sean wondered if he were asleep or even dead. What was going on? Should he run? In the time it'd take him to find his way out, Jason could be dead. Instinctively, he knew the bastard was going to kill both of them.

Urging up a well of energy, Sean quickly ran back into the hallway, pulled the door and turned the key in the lock. Maybe he was consigning Jason to his death, but if he had this chance to escape, he was taking it.

He breathed a sigh of relief leaning against the door, then turned to find his way out of the building. And stopped. The man was standing in front of him, a rope in his hands.

'How . . . how . . .?' Sean stammered, his feet grounded to the floor.

The man grabbed his arm and twisted the rope in a knot around Sean's wrist and around his hands. Sean kicked out, catching the man's knee. He'd aimed for the groin. Missed. Turning, he pulled on the rope, trying to get away, all his energy concentrated on escape.

'Stop it,' the man wheezed, catching Sean and doubling the rope around his waist, restraining his movement instantaneously. Now disabled, Sean collapsed against the man.

'Where did you come from? How did you—?'

'Did you ever hear of a room with two doors?'

The key turned and the door opened once more. Sean was pushed inside.

'Have a nice chat,' the man said. 'I'll be back.'

There was no sound from Jason. Arms still bound, Sean crawled over to him.

'You okay, bud?'

Jason groaned, sounding like an animal caught in a trap. Sean had heard a sound like that once before, the only time his dad had taken him hunting. What would a hunter do, if he were trapped? Thoughts twisted around in his head and he switched his mind to his PlayStation games. Maybe he would find an answer in the virtual world – he always won in that domain. Closing his eyes, he gently laid his bound hands on Jason's shoulder.

'We'll get out. Don't worry,' he whispered. But he wasn't so sure.

CHAPTER 95

'Did our tech guys find anything on Susan's phone?' Lottie asked.

'They're working on it,' Kirby said. 'But I doubt there's anything different to what we got from the service provider. The only calls were to and from work. She didn't appear to be into texting. Oh, and Tom Rickard is ringing here every five minutes.'

'We'll get Jason's disappearance on the six o'clock news. You have a photograph?'

'Got this off the lad's Facebook page,' Kirby said, waving a photo at Lottie. 'Not a bad-looking kid. Ugly tattoo though. Is your Katie going out with him?'

'I suppose she is,' Lottie said, tired of small talk. At least Boyd had a knack of lightening a banal situation. She missed him. She took up her phone to ring the hospital.

Corrigan put his head around the door.

'Cathal Moroney is at the desk asking for you,' he said, pointing an accusatory finger at Lottie.

'It's okay. I want to see him. About Tom Rickard's son,' Lottie said, putting away her phone.

Cathal Moroney edged by Corrigan into the office.

'How did you get up here?' Lottie stood up.

'I smiled at the lovely young one at the desk,' Moroney said.

Corrigan backed out of the office. Kirby gathered a couple of files and shuffled off after him. Moroney sat himself at Boyd's desk without being asked. Lottie was about to object but decided she needed Moroney on her side.

'What's this about another body?' Moroney switched on his phone recorder. 'Can I get my camera crew to the scene?'

'In a minute. First I need your help,' Lottie said, trying to be polite. 'And turn that off.'

Moroney made a dramatic display of holding up his phone and putting it in his inside jacket pocket. 'How can I be of service?'

She showed him the photo of Jason Rickard.

'Is he dead?' Moroney asked.

'I hope not. He's the son of the developer, Tom Rickard, Rickard Construction. He's missing and we need help in locating him. Can you run a story on the evening news?' She passed over the details.

'Is this connected to the murders?'

'Not that we're aware of.'

'Is it on Facebook and Twitter?'

'Yes. We're monitoring social media for any response. I'd appreciate some television coverage.' It was galling her to be nice to Mr Mega Watt.

She handed him another photograph. 'We're also looking for this man.'

'I recognise him.' Moroney tapped the picture. 'Can't put a name to the face though. Did he used to have a beard?'

'Derek Harte,' Lottie said.

'The bollocks who abused that kid up in Dublin six or seven years ago? Isn't he behind bars?'

'Not any more.'

'A convicted sex abuser and a missing teenager. Come on Inspector, I didn't come down in the last shower. Enlighten me. Why do you want his mug-shot on the news?' Moroney leaned over the desk, a spark of interest glinting in his eye.

Lottie had to be careful with her words. Realistically she couldn't say he was a suspect, she might be sued. Better to keep the reporter in the dark on that issue.

'We are concerned for Jason Rickard's safety. We need to locate Derek Harte. Can you help us?' she smiled, sweetly.

'Certainly,' Moroney said. 'Your face is healing up nicely, Inspector.'

'Just concern yourself with the faces in those two photographs, Mr Moroney.'

* * *

After eventually getting rid of Moroney, Lottie found Chloe and Katie standing outside her office.

Chloe held a pizza box and a two-litre bottle of Coke.

'We thought you could do with an energy boost. Bet you haven't eaten all day,' she said.

'You're just like your granny,' Lottie said, 'and of course you're right. I haven't eaten.'

She led the girls into the office. 'Where's Sean?' she asked.

'Haven't seen him,' Chloe said. 'Must be at Niall's.'

Katie sat herself at Boyd's desk. 'Mam, where could Jason be?'

'We're looking for him. Don't you be worrying.'

Chloe perched on the edge of Lottie's desk. 'He's probably having a weed party somewhere. You're just jealous.'

'Girls, please. I'm tired. Don't start.' Lottie placed the box on her desk and dished out slices of warm pizza. She was hungry but in no form for eating. She ate it, anyway.

The girls were silent, eyes downcast. Guilt welled up inside Lottie. She wished she could spend more time at home. She thought of the mothers who had abandoned their children to St Angela's. Her own mother had abandoned Eddie. Was she as bad? Did it run in her genes?

'Wish Sean was here,' Chloe said.

'Sean is fine,' Lottie said. 'I'll ring him now.'

'Leave a voicemail if he doesn't answer,' Chloe said.

'Sean, you better ring me back or, if you've no credit, message the girls on Facebook. I'm giving you five minutes.'

Chloe said, 'You are so intimidating when you're mad, Mother.'

'No I'm not.' Lottie smiled.

'First Jason, now Sean,' Katie said.

'Shut up,' Chloe said, slamming the pizza box shut.

'Don't be crazy Katie, it's only five o'clock.' Lottie wiped her hands on her jeans and called a taxi to take her daughters home. Should she be worried?

'Do you think . . . Is Sean all right, Mam?' Katie asked. 'I'm so freaked out over Jason.'

'They are fine. Now go home and wait. I'll get my mother to call round.'

'No!' Chloe said. 'We'll be fine without Granny. You'll be home soon, won't you?'

'Things are a bit hectic at the moment but I promise, as soon as I can escape, I'll be home.'

'First Jason, now Sean,' Katie repeated, walking down the corridor with Chloe.

Lottie rubbed her hands up and down her arms trying to ease the rising goosebumps. Sean better be home when the girls got there. Her phone rang. Father Joe's name flashed up on the caller ID.

'I hope this is important,' Lottie said, curtly.

'Just checking in to make sure you got home safely,' he said.

'I'm busy. I have to go.' Lottie hung up. She didn't need further complications in what was already a minefield of a day.

The phone rang again. Father Joe's ID. She sent the call to voicemail.

'Are you not getting that?' Kirby asked, hauling his bulk through the door.

'Mind your own business,' Lottie said.

'I've the printout from Susan Sullivan's phone. Same info we got from the service provider.'

'So, no leads there.'

'But we've accessed her photographs.'

'Really? I suppose you're going to tell me there's nothing of interest in them either.'

'There's just the one.' Kirby handed Lottie a print.

There wasn't a photograph in Susan Sullivan's house but she had one on her phone. Curious woman, Lottie remarked to herself.

A shady colour photograph of a tiny baby. Light hair and thin cheeks, eyes closed. Was this all Susan was left with? The only image the poor woman had of the child she'd given birth to? And where did she get the photo from?

Holding the picture, Lottie felt sadness for the murdered woman and her fruitless quest for her child. She hoped she could at least bring Susan's killer to justice.

'Any word on the body at the railway?' Lottie asked.

'It's been removed from the scene,' Kirby said.

Her mobile rang.

Boyd.

'I remembered something.' His voice was low and brittle.

'You should be resting.'

'I'm tied to this bed with tubes and wires. I'm going nowhere.'

'Good. You need to get better. Soon.' Lottie couldn't dwell on the image of an incapacitated Boyd. 'What do you remember?'

'Not much, but I sensed there was something familiar about my assailant. I still can't pinpoint what exactly. He was fit and strong. I got a good kick at him and I think my fist connected with his jaw. So whoever it is, he could have a bad limp or a bruised face.'

'I've got a bruised face,' Lottie said, feeling a weight lifting for the first time that day.

'I imagine yours is prettier than his.'

'Thank you, Boyd. You're a tonic.'

'I could do with one.'

'I'll keep a look out for fit guys with bruises and limps.'

Boyd laughed weakly.

Lottie saw the missed call flashing on her phone with Father Joe's name. 'Boyd, can you remember who else might have known you were going to visit Father Con?'

'I took your call when I was at the gym.'

'The gym? Could anyone have overheard you?'

'Sure. There were lots of people around. Mike O'Brien even gave me his pen to write with.'

'Mike O'Brien?'

'Yes, Lottie, and a whole bunch of other people. Don't jump to conclusions just because you don't like him because of his dandruff.'

Lottie's stomach stirred. Maybe it was the pizza or maybe, just maybe, Father Joe was in the clear. Where did that leave Mike O'Brien?

'I'll have to find out where O'Brien went after the gym,' she said.

'Wish I was there to help you.'

'Me too,' Lottie said and hung up.

* * *

Maria Lynch came up behind her.

'Here's the information on Derek Harte.'

Lottie began to read. She noticed his date of birth: 1975. Something clicked in her brain.

'I need to see the copies of the Rome ledger records.'

She sucked in her lips, looking at the picture of Derek Harte, his personal details printed underneath.

Lynch spread out the pages. Lottie hadn't had time to analyse them since getting back from Rome and now she ran her finger down the entries and stopped at one. The reference number. She raised her head.

'What is it?' Lynch asked.

'I'm not sure.' Lottie checked the date of birth on the file again.

'Does that mean what I think it means?' asked Lynch, looking over Lottie's shoulder.

'I don't know what it means,' Lottie said and closed her eyes.

CHAPTER 96

Looking up, Lottie was surprised to see Jane Dore standing in the office.

'Hi, Jane, anything wrong?' Lottie frowned. Why was the state pathologist visiting the station?

'I've finished at the railway. I thought you might like to know.'

'Thanks,' Lottie said, still not understanding why Jane was here.

'I did a quick preliminary examination of the body at the scene. There's no tattoo on the inside thigh that I could see. The body is in a bad state so I'll know for sure when I do the autopsy.'

'What?' Lottie sat up straight. She wracked her brain trying to recall if O'Malley told her he had the tattoo. She was sure he did. 'I thought it might've been Patrick O'Malley.'

'Whoever it is, my guess is he succumbed to hypothermia,' Jane said. 'Though, I don't normally do guesses.'

Lottie laughed tiredly.

Jane smiled and handed Lottie her phone.

'What's that?' Lottie asked, squinting at the dark image. It was a photograph.

'This was in the vicinity of the body.'

'I can't make it out.'

'Wait a minute. I'll email it to you,' Jane said and sent the photo from her phone. 'The body was in an area used by a number of vagrants. Sleeping bags, crates, cardboard, plastic bottles, you name it. SOCOs found this inside a sleeping bag. I thought it might be important enough for you to see it straight away.'

Lottie clicked her email, bringing up the attachment. Handwriting. She read the words and they bolted through her.

'Is it relevant to the recent murders?' Jane asked, placing a hand on Lottie's shoulder.

'I'm not sure. It might concern an old crime,' Lottie said. In an effort to prevent further questions and to shake off Jane's hand, she asked, 'Would you like a coffee?'

'I better get back to the Dead House. It's filling up faster than Tesco on Christmas Eve.'

Lottie tried a smile. It didn't work.

'You're exhausted,' Jane said.

'Long day.'

Lottie printed the picture. When she looked up, Jane was gone.

* * *

Kirby and Lynch were watching her.

'What does it say?' Lynch asked.

Lottie picked up the page from the printer and read.

'*Dear Inspector, the red-haired boy killed with the belt was called Fitzy. You need to find Brian . . .*' The words trailed off as if the nib had broken or the author no longer had the will to write. The page, smudged and crimpled, pencil strokes shaky.

Removing the old file from her drawer, Lottie slid the note under the photograph of the boy. He'd been missing for almost forty years but was still smiling in his school shirt. She ran her finger over the freckled nose, then closed the folder. Was he Fitzy, the boy murdered in St Angela's? Dear God, she hoped not, because then it would be too personal.

She wondered if Sean was home yet. Tried his number again. No answer. 'I'm so going to kill you, Sean Parker,' Lottie said to the phone in her hand. And still nothing on Jason Rickard's whereabouts either.

She had to find Patrick O'Malley.

They found Derek Harte first.

CHAPTER 97

Uniformed gardaí brought Harte to the station, an hour and a half after the six o'clock news aired. Moroney's television news report had stirred the public and a stream of phone calls resulted in locating Harte, almost by accident.

Lottie and Kirby sat in the warm, sticky, interview room. Harte had agreed to the recordings and waived his right to a solicitor.

'Mr Harte, at 19.13 this evening, sixth of January, you were apprehended attempting to gain access to a property belonging to the late James Brown. Can you inform us as to your reasons and intentions in doing so?'

Lottie sat across the table, eyeing Harte. It was difficult to conceal her loathing, as she recalled the heinous crime for which he had spent five years behind bars. Abduction and abuse of a minor. His smug face added a hint of insult. He rubbed his hands incessantly. She wanted to slap him, to make him stop. Instead she fingered a pill out of the pack in her jeans pocket and slipped it into her mouth. She needed to maintain control of her emotions. And locate Jason Rickard, and find out what her son was up to. She shifted uneasily. She should have asked Lynch to carry out the interview with Kirby. Too late now.

Harte remained silent, breathing through flared nostrils, short, sharp bursts, a sly sneer flushing his cheeks.

'I haven't time for this,' Lottie said, crashing her chair back against the wall. She leaned across the table, grabbed him by his shirt, pulled him towards her. Kirby jumped up, ready to intervene. Harte's mouth curled into an ugly snarl.

She saw then the reality of his personality as his facade faded, revealing a cruel and sadistic pervert. The real Derek Harte. Tightening her hold, she shoved her knuckles against his throat until his face reddened. She didn't care that it was being recorded. He was scum.

'This is brutality,' Harte spluttered, his first words since he was apprehended. 'Maybe I might get that solicitor.'

Lottie drove her hand deeper against his Adam's apple, wanting to do damage, to leave her mark. If Boyd was here, he'd have pulled

her back already and they'd have a laugh over it later. Giving Harte
one last shake, she thrust him back into his chair. She'd have paced
if there'd been enough room. Kirby was in the way. No option but
to pick up her chair and sit down.

'Where is the boy?' she asked, through gritted teeth. The urge to
choke him was overwhelming. Concentrate.

'Boy? I don't know what you're talking about,' he sneered.

'You like young boys, teenagers.' Lottie slid Jason Rickard's photographs across the table.

He glanced down, then quickly looked up at Lottie. 'I don't know him.'

'Why do I not believe you?' Lottie took back the photograph. 'The
posters in James Brown's house, did you put them up?'

'No comment.'

'Why did you wrangle your way into his life?'

'None of your business.'

'It is my business. I could arrest you for murder.'

'Arrest away. You've no evidence.' Harte tapped his index finger on
the table, gritting his teeth. 'Because I didn't do it.'

'Brown was a deviation from your normal prey, wasn't he? Not a ripe
young child. Why did you go for an older man? Had he something you
wanted? Money? Information?'

'You're talking pure shite. I haven't a clue what you're on about.'
Harte folded his arms.

'Why the charade about being a teacher?'

'I never said that.'

Lottie thought back to her earlier interviews with him. He could be
right. She had misinterpreted what he initially told them.

'Tell me then, why were you attempting to break into Brown's house
tonight?' Lottie asked, changing the subject rapidly.

'I wasn't breaking in. I was going in. I knew where the key was.
Only it wasn't there. I tried the back door and window. I forgot you
lot would've taken the key and switched on the alarm.'

Lottie studied him. He looked so different from the man who'd
feigned grief. She was furious with herself for falling for his ruse. She'd
thought he was genuine. So much for her intuition and gut instinct.
Losing your touch, Parker, she chided herself.

'Now you've an opportunity to put the record straight,' she said.

'If you don't mind, Inspector, I'm saying nothing until I get a solicitor.'

'Mr Harte, the least I can charge you with is obstructing our enquiries. And I will. This is your last chance.'

Lottie read a range of emotions crossing Harte's face, like rolling isobars on a weather chart. His body sank into the chair as he appeared to reach a decision.

'Okay. What's in it for me?'

'Talk to me and I'll know what I'm dealing with.'

'Can I have a coffee first?'

Lottie wanted to say no, but the truth was, she needed to get away from the self-righteous Harte. If only for a few moments.

'Right,' she said, 'Interview suspended.' She switched off the recording equipment. He'd got under her skin and it itched worse than a mosquito bite. She sought air.

* * *

Pulling the cellophane from the pack, Lottie extracted a cigarette with numb fingers. Leaning against the newsagent's window, she flicked a lighter and inhaled. Harte's words swirled around her brain.

The awning over the shop sagged in the middle with accumulated snow. Traffic crawled up and down the street and she idly counted the red ones. Snow fell in thick clumps. A group of boys, hoodies shrouding their faces, lounged at the corner of a laneway across the road, drinking from cans. An occasional 'yahoo' emanated from their huddle and Lottie thought of Sean. She looked at her phone: still no contact. She rang Chloe.

'No, he's not home,' Chloe said. 'Katie is driving me mad.'

'Don't mind her. Try Niall again and Sean's other friends.'

'What other friends?'

'Just do it, Chloe.'

This was unlike Sean. A knot of fear gathered in the pit of Lottie's gut but she felt somehow detached. How could she be this calm when her own son might be missing? The pill she'd just taken or because she wanted to believe he was all right? Of course he was.

Shaking herself out of her musings, Lottie knew there was something rotten in her town; there had been for a long time. St Angela's, with its walled-in secrets, was at the core of it. The tattoos, the records, Father Con, Patrick O'Malley, Susan and James, even Derek Harte. St Angela's was *the* den of iniquity.

Pulling up her hood, she caught a glimpse of her face in a shop window. A ghost-like apparition peered back at her. As quickly as she could, she headed to the station. Harte was her next target. She was ready for him.

* * *

Pacing, one step one way, then the other. Lottie had to be doing something or she would hit him.

'So, Mr Harte, what have you to tell us?'

'Right so,' he said. 'You better not charge me with anything. I don't want to go back to jail.'

She waited without replying. She wasn't going to promise the bastard anything.

'I suppose I better tell you what I know,' he said.

Lottie nodded at Kirby to be sure everything was being recorded.

'I got a call from a priest in Rome. Father Angelotti.'

She hadn't been expecting that. She sat.

'He said he had information for me. Talking all about me being adopted and my birth mother wanting to meet me.' His eyes flitted around the room.

'Go on,' she said.

'I knew I was adopted but I hadn't given it much thought. So when he contacted me, I was curious.' His eyes never stopped moving.

'You were in St Angela's as a baby,' Lottie stated. Earlier she'd seen his name on the Rome ledger. 'You want me to believe you are Susan Sullivan's son?'

'Hard to believe, I know. I hardly believed it myself. That priest sounded convincing on the phone. Said he was coming to Ireland later in the year, with the proof.'

'How did he find you?'

'He told me he'd had enquiries about a woman trying to find her child. From the date she gave him, he discovered the adoption records or something. That's what he said, anyway.'

'Sounds fanciful to me,' Lottie said, but she was thinking of the ledger copies on her desk. She stood up and paced again.

'I'm telling you what I know. I was in prison for five years; my name's been in the news, so it was probably easy enough to find a jailbird in this country.' He smirked.

Lottie cringed. Father Angelotti had been a better detective than she was. How had the school where Harte worked not checked him out? Someone would be in deep shit over that.

'And he told me her name. He was all apologies then. Said he shouldn't have said it.'

'Did you meet with the priest?'

'No, I didn't,' Harte said, raising his head. The dancing eyes looked hollow. 'He told me he was coming to Ireland. Asked me if I was willing to meet with my birth mother. He wanted to know if I'd agree, before he spoke to her. I didn't care one way or the other.'

'So you met Father Angelotti?'

'No. I never met him.'

'Yet we found his body in James Brown's garden. Odd that, don't you think?'

'I didn't meet the priest. Ever. I didn't kill him. So I can't explain it.'

'Odd too, you shacking up with James Brown.'

'Coincidence.'

'I don't believe in such a thing,' Lottie said.

She considered Harte. He appeared to be weighing up his strategy.

'Okay,' he said. 'When the priest first contacted me he told me the enquiries were made by a James Brown on behalf of this woman. I did some research of my own. I found out this woman he mentioned, Susan Sullivan, worked in the council here in Ragmullin. I went online; saw where she worked, who she worked with. I googled a few of them and stumbled across James Brown on this dating site. That bit was true and we really did like each other. I was sorry when I heard he was murdered.'

'I don't believe that for a minute,' Lottie said. 'So, why did you murder your lover?'

He laughed. 'I am many things, Inspector, but I am not a murderer.'

'Did you try to contact Susan?'

'No. I left that up to the priest.'

Lottie paced in front of him, fitting in two steps, fatigue eating into her joints. She eyed Kirby. This was getting them nowhere.

'Coincidences, all coincidences. I don't believe you,' Kirby said, breaking his silence.

'I know I was in St Angela's. I'm sure you can verify it and I had no reason to kill anyone.'

The first part of his statement was true, Lottie knew. 'Why were you attempting to get into Brown's house this evening?'

Harte sucked in his jaws. Debating with himself? It better be the truth this time, Lottie thought.

'James kept money in his house and Susan Sullivan kept money in her house.'

Lottie sat. 'What money?'

'They were blackmailing someone. Don't ask me who, because James never told me. He let slip one night that they got cash in hand as well as money into their accounts. Said no more but told me not to be asking questions about it.'

'Pull the other one,' Lottie said. 'So where's this phantom cash?'

'Not sure. In the house somewhere.'

Lottie eyeballed him.

'Okay then,' he relented. 'The suspended mirror over the bed . . . that's where the money is hidden.'

Lottie looked at Kirby. They'd missed it.

'What about Susan Sullivan's cash? You know where that is?'

'You got it, didn't you?'

Lottie looked at him and wondered if he were the cause of her mugging. He dipped his eyes, avoiding her bruised face.

'Did you . . . ?' Lottie reached across the table towards him. Harte squeezed back against the wall, his chair screeching on the tiled floor.

'Easy, Inspector. I couldn't get in. A guard was sitting in the squad car in front of the house. I saw you coming out. Followed you. Thought you might have the money.'

Lottie shot out of her chair. Harte jumped back against the wall. She jabbed her finger into his chest.

'You bastard—' she said. Kirby grabbed her by the elbow.

'Didn't mean to hurt you as bad. But sure you're okay.'

'How did you know about my children?'

'Guessed,' he said. 'Wanted to scare you, get you thinking the mugger might be the murderer.'

'Guess what I'm thinking right this minute?' Lottie shouted, pounding his chest.

'I didn't kill you and I didn't kill anyone.'

Lottie sat down. And when Harte resumed his seat she reached out and grabbed his hand, twisting it round until he groaned.

'You're a little prick,' she said.

'Whatever you say, Inspector,' he said, his arrogance restored. He eyed the camera in the corner of the ceiling. Lottie dropped his hand.

Kirby fidgeted and she knew he was itching to kick the shit out of Harte too. But if he was telling the truth, that left someone else out there who was the murderer. But why should she believe him?

'Jason Rickard,' Lottie said. 'Where is he?'

'I don't know any Jason Rickard,' he insisted.

Lottie sighed heavily and, leaving Harte alone with his conceited eyes, she switched off the recorder and followed Kirby out.

CHAPTER 98

In the incident room, Lottie, Kirby and Lynch looked at the photographs on the board.

'Arrest him for breaking and entering. For mugging and robbery. Anything else we can charge him with? Come on guys, help me out here.'

'We've no evidence Harte killed anyone, so if it's not him, who's the murderer?' Kirby said.

'And where is Jason Rickard? Was he abducted? If so, why?' And where is Sean? she wondered. He better be home by now. Ignoring the icicles freezing her spine, Lottie walked away from the board and rummaged through the ledger copies, scanned down through the names and dates without really seeing them. Tried to recall O'Malley's story. Could he be their prime suspect?

'There was a murder in St Angela's years ago,' she added, 'and my theory is someone is killing the witnesses. That's the only conclusion I can come to. But what has Jason Rickard got to do with it? And Father Angelotti. Where does he fit in?'

'Just got uniforms' report here. They talked to all the taxi drivers. Not one of them has a record of going to Brown's house on Christmas Eve,' Kirby said.

'He couldn't walk that far,' Lottie said. 'Not in that weather, so someone drove him there.'

'The killer?' Kirby suggested.

'Possibly. More than likely,' Lottie said.

Lynch peered over her shoulder. 'Why is all this happening now?'

'We need to talk to Bishop Connor again. Another lying bastard.' Lottie picked up her bag. 'And we've to see Mike O'Brien. Boyd said he was in the gym when he took my call about Father Con.'

'Conspiracy theories, now?' Kirby asked.

'And I need jump leads for my car.'

'I'll look after it.'

'First, I want to see where this latest body was found.' She put the old Manila folder in her bag.

'Any word from Sean?' Lynch asked.

Lottie stopped at the door. 'What time is it?'

'Eight forty-twoish.'

She tried not to panic. 'Kirby, this is Sean's phone number. Can you get our tech guys to see if they can locate where he is via the GPS?'

'Sure, Inspector. Straight away.'

'I'm trying hard not to worry,' Lottie said, 'but this is totally out of character for Sean. I better go look for him now.'

'Don't fret,' Lynch said. 'I'll get the traffic corps to keep watch out for him. We'll find him. Do you have a list of his friends?'

Lottie said, 'Chloe already tried them but contact them again. Chloe will have numbers.' She fought back tears of anxiety. 'We need to track down where Mike O'Brien might be at this hour of the night.'

Her phone rang.

Father Joe.

'Not now,' she said and hung up abruptly. 'Maybe I should stay here, in case Sean comes looking for me.'

'If he does, I'll contact you immediately,' Lynch said.

'Okay,' Lottie relented. 'I'll keep myself busy.'

But where was her son? Her chest constricted with fear, and exhaustion threatened to overwhelm her. She searched her bag for a pill and remembered she had taken one a little while ago. She saw the silver pendant in her bag, plucked it out and flung it on the desk.

'What's that?' Kirby asked.

'Tom Rickard's alibi,' Lottie said. 'Hurry up, Kirby. We've things to do.'

CHAPTER 99

Jim McGlynn and his SOCO team were still at the scene in one of the roofless terraced houses by the train station.

Lottie scanned the area under the glare of the temporary lights. No sign of any other life except the SOCOs working like ants, quickly and efficiently. She left them at it and entered one of the old carriages to her left and switched on her flashlight.

'He has to be somewhere,' she said, upturning empty sleeping bags, a stench rising with the material in her hands.

'He's not here,' Kirby said, standing well away from Lottie's frenzied search.

Lottie heard a shout.

'Are you looking for me?'

She turned, dropping the matted strip of cloth that had come away from a damp cardboard box. Patrick O'Malley. Standing outside the crime scene tape, his hands deep in his pockets. He looked a lot cleaner than when she'd last seen him.

'Where've you been?' she demanded, walking toward him. She couldn't visualise him as a murderer but evidence was suggesting otherwise.

'Trying to knit my unravelled life back together,' he said.

Ducking under the tape, Lottie grasped him by the elbow and steered him up the hill to the car. She was anxious to get away from the oppressive air of deprivation emanating from the old wooden railway carriages. It clawed at the back of her throat. A small black hump of movement caught the corner of her eye and she hurried her steps, thinking of the vermin who had feasted on the faceless man who'd sought nothing more than shelter.

O'Malley leaned against the car door.

'Sit in out of the cold,' Lottie said and followed him into the back seat.

Kirby sat up front, chewing his cigar and watching in the rear-view mirror. O'Malley was clean-shaven, his clothes fresh. Gone was the scent of sickly unkemptness.

'Where have you been?' she asked again.

'The hostel on Patrick Street,' he said. 'They took me in.'

'Why did you not go to them before now?' She twisted round to look at him.

'I never bothered. Just drifted along. But . . . after Susan and James . . . I felt different.' He paused. 'Inspector, I owe it to them to pick up the pieces of my life and begin again.'

'Mr O'Malley, I ought to bring you to the station for questioning.'

'Grand so. I've nothing to hide.'

Lottie considered him. His face seemed naked of any fear or guilt.

'The note,' she began, 'found in a sleeping bag. You wrote it?'

'Ah yes. You could say that,' he said. 'I started it. Didn't finish it. I decided to get myself together. Never came back for my stuff. Not that there was anything worth getting.'

'So why are you here now?'

'I heard earlier this evening that a body was found. I only came up to see what the commotion was all about. I think it's old Trevor over there. Frozen to death, poor eejit.'

'Tell me what you were writing,' she insisted.

'Things started coming back to me. After we talked at the station, like. Thought I was going to be next. I didn't want to die, so I picked myself up, brushed myself down and told myself I wasn't going without a fight. Just like young Fitzy.'

Lottie took the old file from her bag and showed him the photograph of the missing boy.

'Might this be Fitzy?'

O'Malley tore at his chin, scratching. 'I'm not sure, Inspector. It was a long time ago.'

'But you think it could be?'

He studied the boy's face for a few more seconds. 'Like I said, I'm not sure.'

'The murder you described, can you think when it took place? What year?'

'I can't remember much. Too many bottles of wine since then. But like I told you before, we called it the night of the Black Moon. '75 or maybe '76. It was after Christmas so it might've been January.'

'Black Moon,' Lottie said.

'When there's two new moons in the month,' Kirby piped up from the front seat.

'When evil stalks the earth,' O'Malley said.

Lottie felt an icicle slither along her spine.

'Mr O'Malley, you baffle me. Did you kill Susan and James? Father Con even?'

'I'm shocked . . . totally shocked that you . . . you could even think such a thing of me. But then again, who am I? I'm only a nobody to you.'

'That's not an answer,' Kirby said.

Lottie shrugged. 'It's obvious to me that everything connects to St Angela's. You too. You knew Susan and James, and Father Con back then. Now they're dead and you're the last man standing.'

'Don't forget Brian . . .'

'What about him? We've tried to find out about him but it's possible he changed his name. He might even be dead. Can you tell me anything about him?'

'I haven't seen him from that day to this.'

Lottie recalled Mrs Murtagh's recent revelations. 'Mr O'Malley . . . Patrick, have you ever met Bishop Connor?'

His laugh broke up in a fit of coughing.

'What's funny?' Lottie asked.

'Me? Me! You think I'd know a bishop. I'm a down and out, a homeless nobody. What would I be doing with a bishop?'

'I take it that's a no.'

'For sure,' he said, 'and . . .'

'And what, Mr O'Malley?' Lottie snapped. She was caught up in his riddles and he was wearing out her patience.

'You do your job, Inspector,' he said. 'Just do your job and leave me out of it.'

* * *

'Mike O'Brien is next on my list.'

Lottie watched O'Malley walk sluggishly up the hill, away from the train station. She didn't think he had it in him to be a murderer. But he was a deeply wounded man with a scarred past. Anything was possible.

'You're going to let O'Malley go, just like that?' Kirby said.

'I've nothing to hold him on,' Lottie said. 'Plus I don't think he has the strength to strangle a kitten let alone three people.'

She checked in with Lynch while Kirby turned the car.

'Shit,' she said, finishing the call.

'What?' he asked, switching the wipers on full.

'No sign of Sean. But they're contacting his friends again and also their parents. I need to find him.'

'Wait till they finish checking out his friends.'

'And Lynch can't locate O'Brien,' Lottie said. 'He's not at home or at the gym.'

She followed O'Malley's progress. He crossed the canal bridge and disappeared under the yellow hue of the evening streetlights. He seemed smaller somehow, as if the weight that anchored him to an unstable ground all his life had suddenly become embedded in a mud bank. She doubted he would ever be cut free to sail with the wind at his back.

She silently wished him luck. He would need it. So would she.

CHAPTER 100

It was dark. 'Pitch black', his mother called it. Sean felt Jason's soft breaths against his shoulder. He was cramped, needed to piss badly and had no idea how long it was since the man had left. Jason stirred.

'You awake?' Sean asked.

'Yeah. What's going on?'

Sean shifted and stood up, trying to loosen the rope from his wrists. 'Who is that weirdo?'

'I'm not sure, but I've seen him before. Oh, this is all so mad.' Jason remained slumped on the floor.

'Come on, bud. You have to get moving or we won't be able to do anything.'

'What can we do? Nothing, that's what.'

'I'm not giving up that easily. We have to get out of here.'

'Not a hope,' Jason said.

Sean twisted and turned. Eventually he loosened the rope and it fell away. He edged his way around the room in the darkness until his hand reached the knob on the door. Twisted, pulled and pushed. It was steadfast. He moved further along, feeling the walls. Found the second door. Same result. And no windows. There had to be a way to escape. He felt deep into his combat trousers and pulled out his knife. At least he had a weapon.

'I have a knife,' he said.

'What you going to do with that? Kill yourself?'

'Don't be a shithead. Come on. Two heads are better than one. We have to think.'

'I've no energy to think.'

Sean made his way over and kicked at Jason.

'I can't do this without you.'

'Do what?'

Sean thought for a moment. There had to be something they could do.

'At least help me. You're the one with the brains.'

'I'm not so brainy to end up in this mess,' Jason said.

Sean sat down on the cold floorboards and took out his phone. It was dead. He fingered the knife. Would he have the balls to stab the man? He wasn't so sure.

'Please . . . think,' he whispered. 'We need a plan.'

Jason pulled himself into a sitting position and Sean cut the ropes binding him.

'Okay. At least we can go down fighting.'

Sean passed the knife to Jason.

'Swiss army?' Jason asked, feeling one sleek blade.

'I've never had a chance to use it. Before now.' Sean took back the knife and flicked out the various blades. 'We could do some damage with this thing.' He opened the longest blade and slid home the others.

'I'm with you so,' Jason said. 'We still need a plan.'

Sitting in the silence, Sean slipped the weapon back into his pocket. 'A war plan.'

CHAPTER 101

Bishop Connor glanced at Mike O'Brien sitting on the edge of a gold-filigree-legged chair. O'Brien looked weary, eyes small and black. He, on the other hand, felt good.

'Where is Rickard? He should be here.'

'He's not answering his phone,' O'Brien said.

'Planning permission is approved,' the bishop said. 'Dunne kept his part of the bargain, now we need to ensure Rickard keeps his.'

'I put my neck on the line for this.'

'Tom Rickard is a man of his word. You will get your money.'

'His bank balance is a mess.' Mike O'Brien raised his head.

'What do you mean?' Bishop Connor jolted up straight.

'I've been massaging the figures for months, sending bogus returns to Head Office. It was part of the agreement with Rickard. I don't know how much longer this can go on before they discover the manipulation, start asking awkward questions and demanding repayment of his massive debt.'

Bishop Connor shot him an angry look. 'I need my money too. Why isn't he here? What can be more important at this stage of our plans?'

O'Brien shrugged his shoulders.

'How soon can Rickard's company start hauling down that monstrosity of a building?' Bishop Connor was anxious to be rid of the physical reminder that had caused him so much trouble over the years.

'There's a waiting period for objections. A month or so I think. Could be longer.'

'What? Another month?' Bishop Connor's cheeks flared fluorescent red. He picked up a glass of water and swallowed it in a single gulp.

'That's the system,' O'Brien said. 'And the building cannot be demolished. It's on some Protected Structures Register.'

'You know what I mean. It would be nice, though, to see it all crumpled into the ground.'

'It's difficult to bury secrets, isn't it?' O'Brien looked up from beneath heavy eyelids.

'When that place is gone, all ill goes with it. And it will be a fantastic place when it is finished,' Bishop Connor said. One hundred and twenty hotel rooms and an eighteen-hole golf course. Lifetime membership. And St Angela's history buried. Forever.

'That's if he has the money to do it,' O'Brien said.

'I hope you're not serious.'

'Like I said, Rickard's company is sitting on a stack of loans. If even one bank calls in its share, the whole thing will collapse and Rickard will be bankrupt.'

Bishop Connor hit the redial button.

'Rickard, we could do with you at this meeting. Things need explaining.' He then held the phone at arm's length looking at it, his face curling into itself with anger. 'He hung up on me.'

'I just want my money.' O'Brien rose to leave.

'Where are you going? We are not finished yet,' Bishop Connor said.

'I think I am,' O'Brien said. 'I honestly think I am.'

CHAPTER 102

Tom Rickard disconnected the call as Melanie came down the stairs and placed a suitcase in the hall. He looked at his wife, silently questioning.

Arms folded, she stood on their ridiculously expensive Italian marble floor and stared back at him.

'Where are you going?' he asked.

'*I'm* going nowhere,' Melanie hissed through closed lips, her make-up and clothes immaculate.

'But, Mel . . .' he began.

'Don't you Mel me. I smell her, you know. Every time you come home from your soirees. Our son is missing and I've had enough, Tom. Enough!'

Rickard sighed, buttoned up his coat.

'This is it so?' he said.

'You made your bed so go lie with your dog.'

'But Jason . . . we have to find our son . . .' He gesticulated his arms about wildly.

'You drove my baby away. Go.'

She pushed past him into the living room, the echo of her high heels deafening him. He looked around at all he'd worked for and saw emptiness. He'd lost everything. He picked up the suitcase and pulled the door behind him with a soft thud.

He drove away, leaving his wife and life behind. He had to find his son.

* * *

Mike O'Brien did not like the way the meeting had ended with the bishop. He drove erratically around Ragmullin. Was he hoping to get arrested for dangerous driving? He didn't know. He didn't know who or what he was any more. He was lost. More lost than ever before in his life and that was saying something.

Tom Rickard had ruined everything. But wasn't it his own fault too? Being bullied by the bishop. He should have remained strong in the face of that adversary. But he knew he had never been strong. Weak and manipulated – that's what he was. The carbon beneath the diamond, according to Lottie-fucking-Parker. We'll see, he thought, shrugging resolve back into his bones.

He parked outside the developer's house. All the windows blazed light out on to the snow, turning it yellow. What could he say to Rickard? That he was sorry? For what he did, for what he was about to do? No! He was through with being sorry.

He was going to stand up and be counted. It was time for him to come out from the shadows.

Gunning the engine, he drove away.

He would leave his mark.

* * *

Bishop Terence Connor ran his fingers through his hair. The meeting confirmed what he already knew. Rickard was going to screw him.

He marched from wall to wall, bare feet on plush carpet, leaving footprints in the deep pile. He had come too far to lose it all now. He wasn't about to let things slip away without a fight. There was too much at stake. St Angela's owed him.

He put on his socks and shoes. Pulled on his coat.

A cold edge, deep within his bones, told him it was going to be a long night.

He warmed up the engine of his car before driving through his automatic gates and into the pelting snow.

* * *

The four walls were starting to fall in on top of him. Derek Harte clawed at his throat. Water, he needed water. He needed to get out of here.

He'd already had five years in prison and he didn't want to spend a minute longer in it. He'd said goodbye to that life. Metal crashed on metal, doors opened and closed, keys rattled in locks, laughter and crying, shouting and screaming. His life was made up of bad choices. Starting with his bitch of a mother, whoever she might be. He hoped it was Susan Sullivan. Because she was dead and he wouldn't have to look for her and kill her.

'Let me out of here,' he screamed at the walls. 'Let me out . . . out . . . out.'

He curled into a ball on the floor and screeched at the injustice that was his shit of a life.

* * *

Patrick O'Malley looked at the canal for a long time. The cold ice cracking in places, solid in others. The streetlights, casting shadows and shapes through the falling snow.

He craved a drink, just one, a sip – no more than that. Two days without alcohol flooding his veins. And he felt worse than he'd ever felt. No, that wasn't true. The worst time of his life was the night of the Black Moon. He'd never known such terror as then. The memories flashed and dimmed. Fitzy screaming for his life. With his freckled nose and bright hair. Brave boy. A little hero. O'Malley could see the face clearly now and a spark pricked at the back of his brain. He thought of the photo the inspector had shown him. Was it Fitzy? Was the boy in the photograph the same boy buried under the apple tree? He shook his head. He couldn't be certain, but thought it might be.

Another image appeared on the shining ice of the canal. Susan, James and himself, looking out of the window as his little broken friend, Fitzy, was dumped in the clay. He closed his eyes. The memory flickered like a frame-by-frame movie. The men with their shovels, cracking the hard earth to make way for the young soul.

He opened his eyes and the scene remained there, a vivid vision. Suddenly, he could see the faces of the two men reflected in the ice, floating up from his subconscious. And the terror returned, stronger and more violent than before.

He needed a drink.

But first, he decided he would tell the detective lady everything he knew.

CHAPTER 103

Lottie was talking on her phone. She walked up and down the steps of the Garda Station.

'I know, Chloe. I'm doing all I can,' she said, clawing at her hair. Where was her son?

'But Mother . . . Mam . . . please . . . you need to find him,' Chloe cried. 'He's my only brother.'

'He's my only son.' Lottie choked down her panic. 'I'll find him.'

She hung up and rang her mother to go sit with the girls.

She was on the top step when she noticed Tom Rickard leaning against his car.

'Is your son missing too?' Rickard walked over and looked up at her.

'None of your business,' Lottie replied, turning to go inside.

He grabbed her sleeve, pulling her towards him. 'Now you know what it feels like.'

Instinctively, Lottie drew out her other arm to hit him. He didn't flinch but caught her wrist and shoved his face into hers.

'Find my son,' he said, and let her go.

'I'll find him.'

'You do that, Inspector.' He walked away, slowly and deliberately. The wind carried his voice. 'You do that.'

She watched as he hauled himself into his car. She watched as he drove down the road. She watched until the red tail lights disappeared in the distance.

And a coldness clutched every sinew of her heart, descending over her entire being. She had felt the same chill the morning Adam died, though that morning the sun was reaching high in the sky. Tonight the heavens were black and the ground frozen as another shower of snow fell softly to earth.

'Inspector?'

Lottie turned on the step to see Patrick O'Malley trudging along the icy footpath.

'I've something to tell you,' he said.

And he told her what had happened on the night of the Black Moon.

CHAPTER 104

After parking his car at the rear of the chapel once again, he let himself in through the side door. He hoped the boys had slept. He had plans for them.

He carried a plastic bag with crisps and soft drinks. Youngsters lived on trash. He beamed his torch along the corridor and shadows jumped back at him. Birds flapped angrily above his head and he longed for the day when this place would be a heap of dusty rubble. He hoped the two boys would sate his appetite. Quickening his step, he relished his rising excitement.

He unlocked the door and entered. The first blow caught him on the side of the head and as he fell, he saw the glint of a knife flash before his face. Then darkness.

* * *

'What do we do now?' Sean screeched. They dragged the stunned man into the room.

Jason kicked the prone figure in the ribs with his bare foot.

'Shit. That hurt,' he said and limped away.

'Stop freaking out,' Sean shouted, wondering just what type of a gobshite Katie had got herself involved with. 'We'll tie him up.'

He pulled together the ropes that had bound them. As he tugged, he felt a blow to his abdomen and was hurled against the wall. He dropped the knife. Blinking rapidly, he saw the man rise up, swivel and punch Jason under the chin. Jason fell unconscious to the floor.

Sean cowered against the wall as the man hit him in the face, picked up the knife and staggered towards him. He thrust the weapon against Sean's throat.

'Smart arses.' He nicked Sean's skin with the blade. 'That's what you are. Little fucking smart arses.'

The man lowered the knife quickly and sliced it at Sean's stomach. Then he kicked him hard in the same spot.

Sean roared. Blood seeped through his clothes, down on to his jeans. His fingers found the wound. It wasn't deep but he felt faint. He heard voices, far away in the distance, and struggled to keep his eyes open. White stars floated in front of him.

'I think it is time you and your imbecile friend entertained me.' The man wiped the knife against Sean's jeans, flicked it closed and secreted it in his pocket. 'I will be back in a while.'

He stood up, kicked Jason, then left the room, his soft footsteps echoing along the corridor.

Pain inched through Sean's body. He gagged and blood eased out of the corner of his mouth, the copper taste choking him. Tears flowed down his cheeks as he inched in the dark toward the plastic bag on the floor. He tore at it and pulled out a can. Snapping it open with trembling fingers, he drank, fuelling energy into his throbbing body. He hauled off his hoodie, yelping with each movement, and held it tightly to his wound. It wasn't as deep as he'd first thought. Attempting to stem the flow of blood, he bunched the makeshift dressing inside his waistband, tying the sleeves around his hips.

He continued to cry. Loud, terrified sobs.

No one was going to find them.

They were going to die.

He collapsed back on to the cold ground.

CHAPTER 105

'Can't you drive any faster?' Lottie asked.

Kirby floored the accelerator and skidded. He righted the car and clamped a cigar between his lips.

'We can't be sure he'll be there.'

'From what O'Malley's told me, I think Jason's being kept there and I know who abducted him.'

'Bit of a leap of the imagination, isn't it?'

'If I'm wrong, I'm wrong. Hurry up.'

She was sure she knew who Brian was. He must have been tipped over the edge because of something to do with the development of St Angela's. And he'd targeted Rickard by taking Jason. She was still trying to figure it out when her phone rang.

'After a lot of wrangling with the service provider, we've triangulated Sean's phone GPS,' Lynch said.

'And?' Lottie gripped the edge of the seat. Please God, at least let Sean be all right.

'Well, it's a wide area. From the hospital to the cemetery and around the back of the town. About four square kilometres.'

'See if you can get them to pin it down more. Thanks.' Lottie hung up. 'He is grounded for life,' she said, but she couldn't stop the dread in her voice. Could Brian have taken Sean too?

'He's fine. Don't you be worrying. Probably off having a few cans with his friends,' Kirby said.

'He is only thirteen but I'd take that at this moment,' Lottie said.

'That GPS area . . .'

'What, Kirby?' Lottie twisted to look at him.

'It includes St Angela's.'

Lottie opened her mouth to speak but nothing came out. Had something awful happened to her son?

'K . . . Kirby . . . faster.' And she started to cry, uncontrollable sobs breaking from her body. She'd lost Adam, she couldn't lose her son too.

St Angela's loomed up through the darkness.

Kirby pulled up beside Lottie's abandoned car. She quickly studied the black windows, her eyes drawn toward the little chapel, to the side of the main building. She recalled what O'Malley told her about the priest and the children and candles and whips. Dear God.

She blinked. Was that a light flashing in one of the windows? She sat up straight. A flash, then another. Someone walking with a flashlight?

'Look. Kirby. Up there. Do you see a light?'

He was out of the car before her, heading for the steps. She jumped out and skidded on the ice, coming to a halt behind him.

'Looks like someone with a torch,' he said.

'Come on.' Lottie ran up the steps.

She furiously felt in her pocket for the key, found it, and shoved it into the lock. As they entered the doom of St Angela's, she felt all the sinister foreboding she supposed the young Sally Stynes must have felt so many years before.

* * *

The man was back, dressed in a long white robe. Sean would've laughed if he hadn't been convulsed in agony.

'What are you doing?' he groaned, watching the man wrap a rope around Jason's waist, hauling him to his feet.

Jason staggered, but remained standing, eyes like glass. Sean was dragged upright, his feet tearing on the floor, the rope was curled around his wrists and pulled tight. He was tied up, behind Jason.

Sean swayed with dizziness. He suddenly felt like a little boy. He wanted to be at home, playing his crap PlayStation. He didn't need a new one. He'd tell his mam, his old one would do just fine. Niall would fix it. He knew his friend could. Yeah, he'd ring him to come over with his tool kit and together they'd make it work. He'd help out around the house, no complaining. Empty the dishwasher, hoover the floor, clean his room. He promised himself, he'd do all those things, just to get out and feel his mam's fingers running through his hair, holding him close. He wouldn't cry. No. But he did. Sean Parker cried and he didn't care.

'Shut up, you wimp,' the man growled and flicked the torch up and down the walls as he dragged the two boys behind him along the corridor.

'Oh, no,' Jason muttered.

'What?' Sean whispered through his sobs, each step shooting pain through his stomach.

'Oh no . . .' Jason began, his voice fading.

'Oh no, what?'

'This t-time . . . he . . . k-k-kill . . . me.'

'This time?' Sean asked. 'Was there another time?' It hurt to talk, but he wanted to know what Jason was talking about.

Sean pulled him round and witnessed feral fear in the other boy's eyes, causing his own heart to miss a beat.

The man chanted, a slow menacing mantra and led them in a procession, down a stone staircase and into a small chapel. A blaze of candles threw light out and upwards. Above the altar, a rope hung suspended from the rafters, a noose knotted at its end.

Sean's anguished sobs echoed through the cold air.

This was not good.

Not good at all.

* * *

'Ssh,' Lottie said, standing still on the stairs, in the hallway.

'I said nothing,' said Kirby.

'Shut up and listen.'

They listened.

'I thought I heard a scream.'

'I heard nothing,' Kirby said. A noise boomed down towards them. 'It's only a door banging.'

Lottie ran up the stairs, two steps at a time.

'No. Before that . . . I heard a scream. There's someone here.'

'Sure we know there's someone here. The flashing light told us that.'

'Kirby? Shut up.'

At the top of the stairs she looked along the corridor. She could see nothing in the darkness. No movement. No sounds. Only Kirby's laboured breathing from the exertion.

'Singing. I hear singing or chanting or something,' Lottie whispered.

'With all due respect, Inspector, I think you're hearing things.' Kirby stopped to catch his breath.

Flinging him a filthy look, Lottie crept along in the direction of the sound. Maybe she was imagining it. Maybe not. She was going to find out. With or without Kirby.

'Wait for me,' he said, his body struggling to keep up with his voice.

She sighed, wishing for the hundredth time she had Boyd behind her, not Kirby.

* * *

Sean's hands were still tied.

The madman unbound Jason and careered him ahead. The boy stumbled towards the altar, fell and the crack of his skull against marble sent a shock wave through him.

Shoved into the front wooden pew, he tried not to think of his pain. He looked around. There had to be an exit. An escape route. At least he'd stopped crying. He needed to be in control. That's what his mam preached about her job. Be in control of the situation.

The chapel was a warren of alcoves and wooden confessionals. He couldn't see an exit door. He had to take the man out. But he had no way of overpowering him with his hands tied. Think. Think fast. His brain was blank. His breathing quickened as suffocating terror built up in his chest. He tried to still his breaths to a slow even pace. He tried counting them. He couldn't. They tumbled out of his mouth, one on top of the other, until his eyes watered and snot ran down his nose.

He allowed himself a glance towards the altar. And knew at once he shouldn't have. All the virtual games in the world couldn't have prepared him for the scene being played out before his eyes. Bile rose in his throat and he was sure he would be sick.

The man was looking straight at him, a curved upturned crest of pale lips, eyes reflecting the candle light and his hair streaked damp against his scalp. He'd looped a rope around unconscious Jason's neck, deft fingers tightening the noose. Sean watched as he untied the end of the rope from the front pew and pulled, hoisting Jason into the air. He restarted his chanting, low and laboured as he heaved him upwards. Sean looked away, stifling vomit in his throat.

Out. He had to get out.

When the soles of Jason's feet were free from the ground, the madman tied the rope around the pew, tugged it secure and his incantations intensified.

* * *

Lottie tracked with her hands, up and down, and all over the wall at the end of the corridor. Kirby tried too.

'It's definitely chanting. Coming from here. But I can't see a door,' she said.

'There's no way through,' he panted.

'There has to be. This is where I saw the lights. The windows . . .'

She realised she couldn't have seen anything from this location. It was the end of the corridor. She mentally conjured up the number of windows again. She ran frantically along the length of the corridor and back again, counting. She remembered Rickard's plans and the odd sequence of windows.

'There's a room blocked off,' she said.

She tried the door beside her. Locked. Kirby shouldered it and it splintered open. She stepped in. To her right, three windows. She shone her phone light around and saw a second door.

'This is it,' she whispered to Kirby.

The scent of burning candles wafted towards her when she turned the handle. A flickering light highlighted a stone staircase. Turning to Kirby, she placed a finger to her lips. Creeping silently forward, she peered over the banister into the pit below.

Lottie stifled a scream. Kirby placed a hand on her shoulder.

'What am I looking at?' he whispered.

'Madness,' Lottie said, as she watched the man she knew pull a noose round Jason Rickard's neck.

And then she saw her son.

CHAPTER 106

Sean heard a noise at the top of the stairs. He froze. Someone else was here. He tried not to look around. Didn't want to do anything that might warn the murdering bastard, but instinctively he turned his head and stared straight up into his mother's white-eyed terror. A strangled whimper escaped his throat. The man turned and also looked up.

His mother tore down the stairs and Sean knew this might be his only chance. Ignoring his oozing wound, he charged out of the seat toward the altar. Unbalanced with his hands bound, he stumbled and fell.

Rather than loosening his grip on the rope, the man tightened it. Jason's eyes bulged as he began to strangle.

Scrambling to his feet, Sean aimed his shoulder at the man's midriff. He met with taut muscles and an arm locked around his neck, securing him. He heard his mother thundering down the aisle, screaming, running toward him until she came to a stop a metre away.

* * *

Lottie halted her run. The bastard had Sean. She fought for control.

If she made any sudden movement, her actions could be fatal. Her heart thumped and banged in her chest, so loud she could hear it pulsing furiously in her ears.

Professional. She had to be professional or God knows what might happen to her son. A knot wrenched in her ribcage, squeezing like a vice-grip. Goosebumps threatened to tear her skin to shreds. A violent fear erupted within her and she prayed to a God she no longer believed in. She prayed to Adam. She prayed, and then she spoke.

'Let the boys go,' she said, 'Brian.'

She inched forward as Mike O'Brien recoiled at the mention of his birth name. Still, he held on to Sean and tugged the rope, tearing the last remnants of life from Jason. The boy's head slumped sideways. The rope held fast.

Locking eyes with her son, Lottie silently vowed, *A few more minutes, son.*

'Very clever, Inspector. I have unfinished business here. Do you wish to watch?' O'Brien's voice rose and fell in a singsong.

Lottie fought against the war battling within. She must be calm and logical. Glanced at Kirby. He had drawn his semi-automatic pistol. Too dangerous to use it with the boys captive. She scowled at him. He slipped the gun back into his side holster. Stemming a lurch of nausea as O'Brien's arm tightened around Sean's neck, she wanted to rush forward, to drag her son away from the madness.

Dredging up all her training she calculated her distance from O'Brien. No visible weapon, though she knew the long robe could conceal just about anything. She willed a resolute calmness into her voice.

'You don't have to do this, you know,' she said. 'You *are* Brian. I know what happened to you in here. It was wrong, but you can make it right. Release them. It's not going to solve anything if you hurt them further.'

She edged closer.

'Inspector, it will make *me* feel better if I do what I intend to do. You cannot stop me,' O'Brien said, his voice high and strained, white knuckles visibly tightening around Sean.

He's strong and fit, Lottie reminded herself. She laboured to stem the urge to rush him, to grab his steely grey hair and yank it from his head.

'How can it make you feel better? You're a grown man, these are two helpless children,' she pleaded.

From the corner of her eye she saw Kirby circling slowly to the right.

'I was a helpless, abandoned child and no one helped me,' O'Brien snarled.

'I'll get you help. It's not too late. Let them go.'

He laughed. Lottie flinched as the cruel sound reverberated throughout the acoustically designed chapel. Kirby was almost level with O'Brien on the steps.

The laughing continued, uncontrollable, demonic strains to her ears. She needed to silence it. Her son, his face red, eyes streaming. Then she saw the blood, seeping from his abdomen.

Distraught with anguish for Sean, Lottie recalled what Patrick O'Malley had told her about Brian. Had he really killed a defenceless baby? Had he been instrumental in the death of Fitzy? Why had he killed Sullivan and Brown? What madness lurked, yet to be awakened, within his soul? She couldn't find any answers as terror prowled through her veins. She desperately fused her thoughts back to the scene she was witnessing.

'Let them go?' O'Brien questioned, his voice high and hysterical. 'Perhaps I will let one go and allow you to watch as I destroy the other.

Who will you choose, Lottie Parker? Who is the diamond and who is the carbon? Will you save your son and let this other boy die before your eyes? What do you say to that, Madam Inspector?'

'I say you're totally insane!'

Lottie lost her last thread of control. She stepped forward. O'Brien edged backwards, still clutching Sean around the neck. The swish of his cloak fanned the candles lining the altar steps. A small flame caught the bottom of Jason's jeans and began to smoulder.

'You can't kill both of them,' she said. Jason could already be dead. He was so still, his face purple, tongue protruding. 'Let them go. I promise, I'll help you afterwards.'

Struggling for the appearance of outward calm, she called up her years of experience into this one moment.

'You know nothing of the torment I've suffered,' O'Brien screamed. 'Don't even try to imagine it.'

Keep him talking, divert his attention away from Kirby.

'Why Susan and James? Why did you kill them?' Another step forward.

'You think *I* killed *them*? Why would I?'

His shrill voice filled her ears. She stole a glance at Kirby. He was five metres from O'Brien, level with him on the wide step.

O'Brien inched backwards, grabbed something from the altar, his cloak flapping open, displaying nakedness beneath, a crisscross of old scars on his chest. The steel of a knife glinted in his hand. Lottie caught a glimpse of the tattoo on his leg. Deep and dark.

'They had that tattoo also. What was it for?' She had to stall him. Kirby was getting closer.

'God-almighty-Cornelius-Mohan told us we were tarnished with the blood of the devil and he had to mark us for life. To keep the demons away. Hah!' A piercing cry went up from him. Lottie recoiled as his hold tightened around Sean's neck.

'He invested evil spirits into our souls; it was his way of owning us. He was the devil incarnate.' The voice was a high-pitched, unnatural whine.

He pulled Sean upright by the neck. Lottie could see the whites of her son's eyes rolling in his head.

She jumped forward, Kirby moving at the same moment. She grabbed for the knife, but O'Brien's hand swooped down and the blade sliced through the padding of her jacket, cutting into her upper arm. Ignoring the pain, adrenaline strengthening her resolve, she continued her assault. Raised her other arm, elbowed the man's throat, pushing firmly until he released her son. The boy collapsed. Kirby raised his large booted foot and kicked O'Brien square in the chest.

O'Brien fell backwards and a whoosh of flame swept up behind him. Quickly she grabbed Sean. Kirby picked up the knife, cut through the rope and pulled Jason from the noose.

Lottie lashed out with her foot as O'Brien rose from the fire and connected with his torso. He fell into the candles, his burning cape igniting further as he outstretched his arms, flailing against the blaze. His flesh crackled. Screaming, raw and inhuman sounds, O'Brien batted wildly, fanning the flames. He dragged himself to a kneeling position, stood up in a wave of orange and yellow light, tearing at his burning robe, his hands on fire. His skin was already sizzling, oozing, slipping down his body. He fell back into the inferno.

On her knees, consumed with the smell of fried human skin, Lottie dragged Sean along the ground, crawling away from the blaze.

'I didn't kill James and Susan, or Angelotti, I didn't,' the voice from hell screeched as O'Brien twisted and turned, trying to quench his burning flesh. 'Cornelius Mohan, yes I did that bastard in.' He screamed in agony and was engulfed in smoke and fire.

Kirby had his phone in one hand, shouting frenzied commands, while hauling a lifeless Jason to his shoulder. Lottie hugged her son to her breast and undid the rope binding him. Kirby slapped wildly, quenching the fire on Jason's jeans. She only moved when Kirby steered them towards the stairs.

'We can't leave him there, like that,' she said, glancing back at the man dancing around like a wound-up ballerina in a jewellery box of fire. Kirby tightened his grip on her hand.

'Shoot him,' she shouted.

'He's not worth the waste of a bullet. Come on,' he said. 'Now!'

Lottie followed Kirby, Jason secure across his wide shoulders, and she clutched Sean around the waist, dragging him up the staircase with her. On the top step she allowed herself a backward glance. The man was ablaze, his skin a melting slime. He sank downwards, his screams dying as the inferno swelled out towards the wooden kneelers. Thick black smoke choked the air.

Her son was safe. That's all Lottie could think of in that instant. Her son was safe.

She didn't look back again.

She heaved Sean along the corridor, down the stairs, through the hall and outside. She dropped to her knees on the frozen steps, her son in her arms. She welcomed the cold air, coughing up smoke from her lungs, and remained there, statuesque, until the wail of sirens stole the silence of the night.

* * *

31st January 1976

Sally kept her eyes open all night long; the night of the Black Moon, Patrick called it.

She listened to the night-time sounds, to the soft breathing of the other girls in her room, to the scratching in the skirting boards and the ceiling. She imagined grotesque shapes dancing in the moonlight, belts and candles swaying toward her and away from her, like some obscene ballet. She heard babies crying in the nursery but no footsteps hurried to soothe them. They were alone. She was alone. And the night seemed to go on forever.

She didn't know what had happened to her baby; she didn't know why Fitzy had died; but she vowed there and then, that one day, however long it took, the truth would be revealed. She would remember for the rest of her life.

She lay awake as the first light of dawn broke through the window with the moon just a shadow in the sky.

DAY NINE

7th January 2015

CHAPTER 107

The first orange rays of dawn crested through a snowy horizon beyond the hospital walls while the nurse monitored Sean's vital signs, as she'd done every twenty minutes for the last five hours. Contented that her patient was stable, she nodded to Lottie.

'The doctor will be here in a minute, but Sean is doing fine.' The nurse left.

Lottie kissed her son's hand and forehead, and gently traced her finger over his eyes, telling him over and over she was sorry.

Watching the IV tube bleeding life into him, she counted each drop as it dripped downwards. One, two, three . . .

Sean's eyelids fluttered. Lottie's internal anger had caused her fingers to linger on his eyes. Removing her hand, as if it were scalded, she wondered how much longer could she go on causing her children pain.

The door opened. Boyd stood there wearing a navy cotton dressing gown, neatly tied around his narrow waist. His face, still bruised and pale, was grave. Lottie dipped her head and he was at her side.

'You shouldn't be in here. They'll throw you out,' she said.

'Let them,' he said, and gently kissed the top of her head. 'Ugh, smoke.'

'Feck off, Boyd,' she sobbed.

'It's okay to cry.' He rubbed her shoulder.

'No, it's not. I've failed him. Failed my son, my family. Jason too.'

'You saved Sean.'

'Yeah,' she said, unable to screen the scorn from her voice, 'but what about Jason? I should've figured it out sooner.'

He didn't answer. She pushed him away.

'You look terrible,' she said.

'So do you,' he said, pointing to the wound on her arm. 'The murderer, did he have a bruise and a limp?'

'He does now. You better go.'

'I'm getting out of here, anyway.'

'What?'

'You've too much to handle and I'm here like a spare prick watching soaps on the television. You need me.'

She didn't object. She needed Boyd, even if he was like something out of *The Walking Dead*.

As the door closed behind Boyd, Lottie let her fingers linger for a moment on her son's face before the nurse returned with the doctor and hustled her out.

* * *

Superintendent Corrigan paced the corridor, Lynch and Kirby behind him. No sign of Boyd.

'Inspector Parker,' Corrigan said, clamping a hand on her shoulder.

Lottie didn't know what to say, so she said nothing.

'The bastard is barely alive and needs to go to the specialist burns unit in Dublin. He'll have to wait until this snowstorm abates. Air ambulances are grounded,' he said.

'He's still alive? Lottie asked, incredulously.

'Prognosis is not good. Eighty per cent burns.'

'Good,' Lottie said. 'And St Angela's?' She was avoiding the question she knew she must ask.

'The fire was contained to the chapel. We'll seal it off as a crime scene when the fire crew are done.'

'Jason?' she asked, eventually.

'You know you were too late.' Corrigan shook his head. 'Feckin' shit luck.'

Lottie swayed. She'd already known Jason was dead. Just needed it confirmed.

'At least we have our murderer,' Corrigan said.

'I'm not so sure,' she said, hesitantly. Hadn't O'Brien told her he didn't kill Susan or James or indeed Angelotti? He had no reason to lie. Especially as he had admitted to killing Father Cornelius Mohan.

Kirby steadied her as the Rickards appeared at the other end of the corridor. Corrigan moved toward them. Tom Rickard stared straight through her before taking Corrigan's sympathetic handshake. Lottie allowed Kirby to steer her in the opposite direction.

'Can I have a word, boss?' Kirby said.

Leaning against the wall, Lottie nodded.

'I know this isn't a great time, but I have to tell you . . .' he began.

'Spit it out, Kirby.'

'Moroney, the journalist . . .'

'Go on.' Somehow, she knew what he was going to say.

'That stuff he reported about James Brown being a paedophile, well, I might have said something I shouldn't have.'

'Ah, Jesus, Kirby. What did you say?'

'Moroney overheard a conversation about what we found in Brown's house. He rang me for confirmation. We were up to our necks in reports and stuff, so I might have agreed with what he said, to get him off the phone.'

Lottie shook her head. At least now she knew the source of Moroney's information. She had been wrong to suspect it might have been Lynch. Probably a genuine mistake on Kirby's part. At least she hoped so. Deciding to let it go, she said, 'Don't let it happen again.'

Kirby exhaled and tapped his pocket for a cigar. 'Thanks boss.'

'And you did well with O'Brien.' It was the closest she could come to a compliment in the circumstances. She watched Kirby stroll off down the corridor as Lynch joined her.

'Sean? How's he doing?' she asked as they walked.

'He'll recover. In time,' Lottie said.

Tom Rickard's eyes. She didn't want to see that look again any time soon. She'd found his son, like she'd said she would; but she'd failed him in the worst possible way.

Lynch said, 'Kids always turn out fine.'

'And what the hell does any of us know about it?' Lottie muttered. She kept on walking.

CHAPTER 108

Rounding the corner, she bumped into Father Joe standing at the nurses' station.

'You're a sight for sore eyes,' he said, flicking a strand of hair from his brow, breaking into a sad smile. But Lottie read sorrow in his eyes. Welcome to my world, she thought.

'Joe.' He was holding a bulky A4-sized envelope. Tiredness creased his face like crumpled linen. 'What are you doing back home?' she asked.

'How's Sean?' he asked, ignoring her question.

'Good,' she said. 'No. Not good. God, I don't know.'

'I'm sorry, Lottie.'

'Everyone is sorry. What good is sorry?'

'I'll come back later.'

'Don't bother,' she cried. 'I don't want to see you again. My son almost died. And it's all my fault.'

'Nothing I say can make any difference at the moment,' he said, lowering his head.

'Then why are you still here?'

He handed her the envelope.

'I paid a visit to Father Angelotti's office. I got this.'

'What is it?' She turned the envelope over in her hand, still bristling.

'Look at the return address.'

'James Brown. He sent this to Father Angelotti?' She noticed the postmark. 'December thirtieth. The day he died.' She questioned with her eyes. 'But Father Angelotti was dead by then.'

'Brown mustn't have known that.'

'I don't understand.'

'All I know is Father Angelotti's staff were getting ready to return it, so I volunteered to take it with me. I caught the next flight home.'

He took a sheaf of papers from his inside coat pocket and handed them to her.

Lottie arched an eyebrow. 'What are these?'

'I went back to Father Umberto's place, looked through the records again and found more information that might be of interest to you.'

'I haven't time for all this now,' she said, leaning against the wall.

'I know,' he said, his shoulders drooping.

He shoved his hands into his pockets, turned and walked down the cluttered corridor, leaving her standing alone.

She watched him until he disappeared behind the closing elevator doors. Her anger evaporated; in its place an intense loneliness settled.

CHAPTER 109

'What's in the envelope?'

Boyd leaned against the wall, outside Sean's door. Fully dressed, looking like a corpse.

'What the hell? Boyd? Are you serious?'

'You need help and I'm it.'

'You're half-dead,' Lottie said. 'Go back to your room. I have the team.'

'The envelope?' he repeated.

'I haven't opened it yet.' She turned it over in her hand. 'James Brown posted this to Father Angelotti. Joe brought it from Rome.'

'Joe? How cosy.'

'Boyd?'

'What?'

'Don't start.'

'I've missed you, Lottie,' Boyd said.

'I missed you too, you daft man, and now I need to check on Sean.'

Voices echoed from the elevator. Katie and Chloe ran forward, tears streaming, arms outstretched. Rose Fitzpatrick hurried up behind them. Lottie smiled a weary thank you to her mother.

Her family, bruised and damaged, but complete.

* * *

With Sean awake at last and comfortable, his sisters either side of the bed holding his hands, Lottie could contain herself no longer. She tore open the envelope and read James Brown's words. They jumbled up inside her, flitting about like an image from Alice in Wonderland's mad tea party, then merged into a cohesive picture without the Mad Hatter. Now she had the full story, scripted in Times New Roman, imprinted firmly in the forefront of her mind.

She had to talk to Patrick O'Malley again. Before it was too late.

CHAPTER 110

She should really be with her son and the girls, but her mother told her to do what she had to do, then come back.

Sitting at her desk, Lottie felt totally at odds with herself, but at least her son was safe with his granny entrenched in his room, taking control as usual. But for once, she was glad of her mother's help. Conflicted though she was, Lottie knew she had to end this case. Afterwards, she would make the space to spend time with her children. Sean needed her, Katie needed her and even Chloe, in her own obstinate way, needed her. As for Rose Fitzpatrick, Lottie knew her mother was a survivor, with or without her. For the first time, she acknowledged the grief and trauma her mother had endured. It couldn't have been easy for her. She had battled through it all. Now she must do the same.

Kirby dropped a Happy Meal on her desk.

'Lunchtime,' he said.

Lottie glanced at the clock. So it was. She yawned and couldn't remember when she'd last eaten or slept. A false energy was keeping her going so she didn't stop to think about it.

She read through the copies Father Joe had given her.

'Boyd, I think I know how Derek Harte, James Brown's lover, became involved in all this.'

He sat on the edge of her desk. She welcomed his easy familiarity and at the same time she hoped he wouldn't keel over.

'Right, Sherlock,' he said. 'Explain.'

'He's a wrong number.'

'You can say that again.'

'Seriously Boyd, look at this.' She pointed to an entry on one of the ledger pages. 'The reference number attached to Susan Sullivan is AA113.' She lifted up another copy. 'So look at the records for the babies and check reference AA113.'

Boyd scanned the page and found the number. 'It says Derek Harte.'

'But that number was changed.'

'How do you know?'

'Look at it carefully. You can see where the ink was rubbed away and a three put in place of a five. I believe this was changed intentionally. Someone didn't want the true identity of Susan Sullivan's child discovered.'

'So, Harte wasn't Susan Sullivan's offspring after all,' Boyd said. 'Looking at it, I can understand how Father Angelotti made his mistake. But who is her child?'

Lottie pointed to the correct reference number and Boyd stared, his jaw dropping.

'Are you serious?' he asked.

'Unless someone tampered with the other numbers, I'm very serious.' Lottie shook her head wistfully. 'It's so sad.'

'Does he know?' Boyd asked.

'I don't think so.'

Boyd rubbed his hand over his scarred neck and said, 'So all these people were killed to keep this fact a secret?'

'That's part of it.'

'What's the rest of it?'

Lottie pulled the old file out of her bag. She picked up the photograph of the young boy with the wry smile, freckled nose and crooked shirt collar. 'This is the other reason.'

'The missing kid?' Boyd asked.

'I think so.'

'Are you going to wait until I go on bended knees to beg for the answers?'

Lottie smiled. She had really missed Boyd.

'His mother reported him missing in early 1976, having put him in St Angela's months earlier. The Church authorities branded him a runaway. He was never found.' That was enough information for Boyd for now, she thought.

'So what does James Brown's information confirm?'

'James Brown and others witnessed a murder in St Angela's, perpetrated by Father Cornelius Mohan, aided and abetted by Brian. And when James and Susan threatened to expose it, they were murdered to keep the fact buried.'

'Okay. Let me get this straight. Mike O'Brien, originally called Brian, was coerced by Father Con to take part in some sick ritual which resulted in the death of a boy, nearly forty years ago.'

'Yes,' Lottie said.

'So who is the kid in the photo?' Boyd asked.

'Not now, Boyd.'

'Lottie, I've read the file.'

'Then why ask stupid questions? Let's talk to Patrick O'Malley,' Lottie said, closing the file. She shoved it back into her bag.

'But we know O'Brien was the murdering bastard,' Boyd said, once again rubbing the scars on his throat.

'He only admitted to killing Father Con.'

'Yes. And he half-killed me too. He didn't admit to that, did he?'

'No, but I believe someone else murdered Father Angelotti, Susan Sullivan and James Brown.'

'I'm lost now, Lottie.'

Lynch rushed into the office, hair loose, flying around her face.

'We looked everywhere. There's not a sign of O'Malley.'

'He can't just disappear,' Lottie said. 'He's out there somewhere.' She turned to Boyd. 'Think. Where would O'Malley go? His past has come back to haunt him. Where would a tormented soul go?'

'Back to the source of his torment?' asked Boyd.

Lottie sprang out of the chair, wrapped her arms around him and kissed his cheek. 'You're right. Come on.'

'If you say so,' he said with a grimace. 'Next time you hug me, mind my wounds.'

'Next time?' She winked at him. 'I'll drive.'

She checked in with her mother at the hospital. Sean was doing fine.

Dumping the Happy Meal in the bin, Lottie followed her team out the door.

CHAPTER 111

In daylight, St Angela's had lost its sinister ambiance. It was only a rambling old building with doors and windows. But Lottie knew it shielded the secrets of horrific brutality behind its concrete and stone. She'd read the insanity in Cornelius Mohan's faded notebook and followed the story in James Brown's envelope. She'd discovered the cover-up in the Rome ledgers. And witnessed its legacy reincarnated last night. For what? Torn lives and damaged souls. Bodies buried but the living carrying the burden. That's how she'd felt at Adam's grave a few short days ago. Now she fully understood what she'd been thinking then and a crushing sadness settled in her heart.

Taking a deep breath, she walked over to the figure leaning against a scarred, bare tree.

'They did a good job of saving the rest of it,' Father Joe said, nodding toward the building.

The site was almost deserted. The fire crews had rolled up their hoses, slid ladders on top of truck roofs and departed from the site. A couple of gardaí manned fluttering crime scene tapes. Burning stench hung in the air, but the smoke was gone and smouldering embers remained. The chapel walls were singed black, windows shattered, the roof caved in. But the main structure of St Angela's endured, unscathed.

'Pity the whole place didn't burn to the ground,' he added.

'What are you doing here?' Lottie pulled down her hood to get a better look at him.

'I felt drawn to it. After all the lies.'

'Joe . . .' she began.

'Don't, Lottie. Don't say anything.'

He pushed away from the tree. She placed her hand on his arm.

'Did you see any sign of a vagrant? Patrick O'Malley. We're looking for him.'

'Just the place for vagrancy,' he said. 'Bishop Connor is nosing around.'

Lottie beckoned to Boyd. Lynch and Kirby brought up the rear.

'Bishop Connor is here,' she said. 'O'Malley must be too. Spread out and look for them,' she said. 'Not you, Boyd. You look like you're about to faint.'

'I'm fine,' he said, averting his eyes from Lottie holding on to the priest's sleeve.

She dropped her hand, shrugged her shoulders and headed into the walled, snow-covered orchard, outside the cordoned-off area. Boyd trudged behind her, Father Joe at his side. Lynch and Kirby crossed the frozen lawn and hurried left around the back of St Angela's.

It was Lottie's first time inside the small orchard enclosure. In the lifeless winter it was barren, trees shredded bare, the ground swathed in a white sheet of purity. She truly believed there was nothing pure in this place. Evil stalked every crevice in its walls and bodies lay uneasy in unmarked graves. She glanced upwards at the window, where three sets of terrified eyes had witnessed atrocities no child should have to observe or comprehend.

Shadows spread at the base of the trees and the sun struggled to find its place low in the grey afternoon sky. At the furthest corner of the orchard, she saw them. Two figures. Silhouetted marionettes, twirling around each other, leaving streaked snow in their wake.

She put a finger to her lips and inched forward.

The puppets ceased their dancing, interrupted by birds fleeing as a flock from the branches.

O'Malley swung round and looked directly into her eyes. Blood poured from his cheek and a blue nylon rope lay useless around his neck.

Bishop Terence Connor turned slowly and dropped the other end of the rope.

'It's all over, Bishop Connor,' Lottie said. She wondered at his audacity to attempt committing a crime metres from gardaí. He must surely be mad.

'Over?' Bishop Connor shouted. 'Over? Not yet.' He stood with his arms reaching to the heavens. 'It is over when my God tells me.'

'You're finished.' Father Joe stepped up beside Lottie.

'You!' the bishop exploded, pointing his finger towards the priest. 'You are the cause of this.'

'Me? You're insane,' Father Joe said, voicing Lottie's thoughts. 'All those people are dead. For what? To cover up St Angela's abusive past?'

He opened his hands, palms upwards. 'How could your God could allow this?'

'My God? He is your God too.'

'That's where you're wrong.' Father Joe tore his clerical collar from his neck and flung it into the snow, where it blended with the whiteness.

'Blasphemy. I did all this for you,' Connor roared.

O'Malley started toward him. Lottie silently urged him to move away from Connor. She remained by Father Joe's side. Boyd edged forward, nearer to O'Malley. The vagrant knelt in the deep snow, bloodied and unmoving.

'She was your mother, you know,' Bishop Connor said, a smile slowly creasing his face in a sinister mask. 'Susan Sullivan.'

Father Joe lurched forward, hands outstretched to grab the other man's throat. 'You're the lowest of the low,' he screamed.

Lottie grabbed the tail of his coat before he touched Connor.

'Susan Sullivan,' Bishop Connor repeated, taking a step backwards. 'Yes, Joe, you are her son. She never found out. I sent the records away to Rome, having first altered them. I put out a false trail. Father Angelotti helped there, unwittingly I might add. Once that Susan Sullivan started her meddling, I knew she would stop at nothing to uncover the truth. I only wanted to protect you.'

'You're lying,' Father Joe cried.

Lottie's heart shattered into little pieces for him. The only time he had had contact with his mother was the day he was born and the day she died when he had administered the last rites as she lay at his feet.

'You are the bastard son of a paedophile priest and a girl barely out of childhood.'

'Liar,' Father Joe whispered, shaking his head, trying to make the vision disappear, but Lottie knew it would remain with him forever.

'I would've known by my birth certificate if I was adopted.' His voice was broken, a million pieces of shattered glass.

'Back then,' Connor sneered, 'the nuns, Father Con and I, we made sure there was no time-wasting with adoption certificates. With the babies we dealt with, their birth certificates appeared to be the genuine article but we maintained details of the original births in ledgers.' He tried to move forward, but his feet sank deeper into the snow.

'You changed the reference numbers,' Lottie said. 'Why?'

'Because I could. And because Susan Sullivan wanted to know who and where her bastard child was. I had to protect him.'

'Why kill Father Angelotti?' Lottie asked, stalling him.

'Because Angelotti was going to reveal the truth, once he'd discovered his mistake. He had realised the records had been changed so he organised a meeting with Brown to get him to talk to Susan. Of course I offered to drive him to see how things would pan out. Brown never showed and I took my chance. I had hoped Brown would get the blame. Unfortunately the weather didn't help there.'

Father Joe shook his head again. 'I can't believe what I'm hearing.'

'It's a fact. I lived my life for you. I spared you in St Angela's all those years ago. I placed you with a good family. Spent my life covering up for the Church.'

'And you covered up a boy's murder,' Lottie said.

'I did what I had to do,' Bishop Connor said. Suddenly his shoulders drooped.

Lottie knew he had lost his fight.

'Why kill Susan and James?' she asked.

'They were blackmailing me. Wanted to expose the secrets I'd worked all my life to keep buried. I had to stop them. I couldn't afford it any more.' He laughed cynically. 'If I had known Susan Sullivan was already dying of cancer perhaps none of this would have been necessary.'

Convinced she was staring into the eyes of the devil himself, Lottie said, 'You concealed the abuse of children. You moved Father Cornelius Mohan around, allowing him to commit further abuse in new parishes. Babies, never making it out the door of this place, throwing them into unmarked graves. A young boy beaten to death behind these walls and unceremoniously buried here.' She waved her hand around the enclosure. 'Somewhere.'

'You can't prove anything.' His eyes challenged her.

Lottie held his stare, counted to nineteen before he looked away. Lynch and Kirby, weapons drawn, unnecessarily, took up positions along the wall behind the bishop and O'Malley.

'And why does one boy's death matter so much to you, Inspector Parker?'

'It matters to everyone,' Father Joe said. 'Especially to those you murdered to keep things secret.'

Lottie pulled at his sleeve to shut him up.

'You are a discredit to the collar you wear,' Bishop Connor spat.

'No, I'm not,' Father Joe said. 'But you are.' He inched forward. Lottie pulled him back.

O'Malley broke from Boyd's grip, leaped upwards and lunged at Connor's shoulders, knocking him into the snow. Lottie hauled up Connor as Boyd grabbed O'Malley.

'I saw you with my own eyes,' O'Malley said, blood spluttering from his mouth. 'From those windows up there. Me and Susan and James. We saw you throw poor Fitzy in a hole under a tree.' He pointed wildly around the orchard. 'And you'd been in the chapel. We'd seen you do nothing when he screamed and cried. Brian and Father Con beat him until he was stripped bare of his skin and what did you do? Absolutely nothing. You could've stopped it.'

Boyd dragged O'Malley away from his tormentor.

'You murdering bastard,' O'Malley shouted at Connor. 'But you didn't get me.'

Lottie snapped handcuffs on Connor. All his arrogance had disappeared, leaving a dead blackness in his eyes.

'My brother,' she whispered in his ear. 'Eddie Fitzpatrick. What did you do to him?'

'Buried him. What else could I do with his broken body?' He scanned the orchard with a swift head movement. 'Here. Somewhere here.'

Lottie slapped him hard across the face. He didn't flinch. If anything, his eyes dimmed, murky shadows clouding them over.

'Your family abandoned that boy,' he sneered. 'Your father shot himself with a bullet through his mouth; your mother threw a grieving ten year old behind these walls and walked away. And you . . . you . . .'

'I was four,' Lottie murmured.

'And why did your mother do that? The lovely upstanding Catholic Rose Fitzpatrick. I'll tell you why. Because your brother was a thieving, good-for-nothing tearaway. And the widow couldn't stand the added shame of the boy ruining her life. So she had him locked away.'

'Shut up,' Lottie cried.

'Ask her, you ask her.'

Lottie's tears dampened her cheeks and a soft flutter of snow fell to earth. His words had hammered home things never spoken aloud in her family. Things her mother should have told her. And she still wasn't sure if she'd found what she had lost all those years ago.

Boyd's hand slipped into hers.

EPILOGUE
30th January 2015

'Charlotte Brontë, that's who you were called after.'

'I know, Mother,' Lottie said. 'You told me numerous times.'

Before this she couldn't get her mother to talk about her brother or her father. Now, she couldn't shut her up. Rose had explained to Lottie that Eddie was an awful handful after their father committed suicide. She had despaired of what to do about him until, on the advice of the parish priest, she placed him in the care of St Angela's for six months. And then he disappeared.

'And poor Eddie, we called him after—'

'Edward Rochester. *Jane Eyre*,' Lottie said. 'I know.'

But she didn't know anything any more.

The digger operator held up his hand and switched off the machine. It was getting dark and Lottie didn't know if he'd found something or was quitting for the night.

She moved away from her mother, leaving her standing with Chloe. Katie was at home minding Sean. They were not doing too well, either of them. The Rickards had buried Jason five days after he died, in a private ceremony. None of Lottie's family were there. The Rickards didn't want to see Katie. The girl couldn't understand it. Lottie could. Boyd had bought Sean a PlayStation 4. It was still in its box, unopened. She'd got him a new hurling kit; he'd thrown it under his bed.

Now she was struggling to keep her family intact. Her children needed her more than at any time since they'd buried their father. They were son and daughters, sisters and brother. Lottie knew how the hasty action of a mother could change that dynamic for ever, and she couldn't afford to make a mistake, not where her children were concerned.

In her job, she still didn't know if there would be any disciplinary action regarding her flight to Rome and her handling of the murder investigations. Superintendent Corrigan was reluctant to apologise for his actions in shielding the bishop and was avoiding her. But for now she was on paid leave. Work could wait.

The sky leached grey into black, and night was descending before the day had succeeded in fulfilling itself. Lottie felt the same.

A spotlight directed a shaft of light into the three-foot-deep hole. She knew it was time.

The new moon glinted in the dark.

The Black Moon.

Maybe the bad omens were behind them. Maybe not.

She stood on the edge of an abyss wondering where she would find the inner strength to walk away. But Lottie Parker never walked away.

She noticed Father Joe standing at the wall, by the archway. Jeans and black polo-neck sweater under his big jacket. He was taking a sabbatical. His whole life, he had unknowingly lived a lie, and now he grieved for his dead birth mother, whom he had never known. He looked lost, a deep sadness shading his eyes. Lottie waved, then dropped her hand as he walked away. Suffering for the secrets of others.

This reminded her again of her own family secret which this case had awakened. Her brother's yellowing missing person's file in her drawer; she could never again deny it. And she was proud of his heroism. O'Malley had told the story, painting Fitzy's – her own brother's – time in St Angela's in big bold colours. Her mother had cried for days.

Lottie sensed Boyd falling into step beside her. She felt his hand resting on the small of her back, soft and comforting.

'It will only be bones. You don't have to look, Lottie.'

She glanced up at the dark windows, then she walked closer to the unmarked grave beneath the bare apple tree, highlighted by the radiance of the crescent moon.

'Oh, but I do,' Lottie said, peering over the mound of clay. 'I do.'

A LETTER FROM PATRICIA

Hello dear reader,

I wish to sincerely thank you for reading my debut novel, *The Missing Ones*.

I'm so grateful to you for sharing your precious time with Lottie Parker and company. I do hope you enjoyed it and that you will follow Lottie throughout the series of novels.

In order to get through the darkest days of my life when my husband Aidan died following a very short illness, I began writing this novel. I filled notebooks with lines and lines of words, which at the time I thought of as therapy. But the more I wrote the more I realised that, with a lot of hard work, I could shape the words into a book. And I did. It hasn't been an easy journey but I think I'm getting there!

All characters in this story are fictional, as is the town of Ragmullin, though life events have deeply influenced my writing.

I do hope you enjoyed reading *The Missing Ones*. I'm a little embarrassed to ask but if you liked it, I would love if you could post a review. It would mean so much to me.

You can also connect with me via my blog, which I endeavour to keep up to date, or on Facebook.

Thanks again, and I hope you join me for book two in the Detective Lottie Parker series.

Love
Patricia

www.patriciagibney.com

 @trisha460

patricia.gibney1

ACKNOWLEDGMENTS

Writing a novel is a personal journey, and I could not have reached my destination without the support and encouragement of many people along the way.

Firstly, I want to thank you, my reader, for taking the time to read *The Missing Ones*. Without you my writing adventure would be in vain.

To the Bookouture team, in particular my editor Lydia for initially telling me she loved my novel and then for taking me on. Thank you for believing in me.

To my agent, Ger Nichol of The Book Bureau, for signing me up. That first email Ger sent to say she was halfway through the book and couldn't wait to finish it filled me with the self-belief to think yes, I can be a published author!

The Irish Writers' Centre is an invaluable resource. The courses and tutors are excellent and I have made life-long friends through it. Arlene Hunt, Conor Kostick and Louise Phillips have assisted in developing my potential and my writing skills through their courses. Also Carolann Copland of Carousel Writers' Retreat, everyone associated with the Irish Crime Fiction Group and Vanessa O'Loughlin of Writing.ie. Thank you.

Niamh Brennan for her advice, wisdom and eagle eye when critiquing my work in progress. And of course for all the texts and emails encouraging me when I was flagging. I value your opinion greatly.

Jackie Walsh for accompanying me to crime writing festivals and writing holidays. Niamh and Jackie have become great friends, writing buddies and sounding boards for plot development and building confidence in my writing.

Teresa Doran, Liam Manning and Padraig McGovern, for listening to me reading first drafts at our weekly Write 1 group.

Tara Sparling for reading the manuscript.

Alan Murray and John Quinn for advice on policing matters; any mistakes are entirely my own. In order to help the story flow, I took many liberties with police procedures.

Antoinette and Jo, for always being there. Best Friends.

My sister Marie for being by my side through all that life has thrown at me.

My sister Cathy and brother Gerard, family is everything.

My mother and father, Kathleen and William Ward, for believing in me and helping me throughout my life, especially the most difficult times.

My mother-in-law, Lily Gibney and family.

My children, Aisling, Orla and Cathal. You give meaning to my life. I love you so much. And the newest member of our family, my baby granddaughter Daisy, is proof that life is full of surprises.

Aidan, my dear husband, whom I miss deeply, encouraged me to follow my dream. He would be so proud today and I wish he was here to share this moment. Much loved. Always in my heart.

Read on for the beginning of The Stolen Girls, the next book in Patricia Gibney's Detective Lottie Parker series.

PROLOGUE

Kosovo 1999

The boy liked the peacefulness of the creek, midway between his home and his grandmother's. Despite the roar of water flowing down the mountainside, it was quiet today. No gunfire or shelling. He looked around as he dipped the bucket into the spring water, making sure he was alone. He thought he heard a car in the distance and glanced behind him. Dust was rising from the twisting road. Someone was coming. He hauled up the bucket, spilling the water. The screech of brakes and the sound of loud voices propelled him to run.

As he neared home, he dropped the bucket and fell to the ground, lying flat on his belly, gravel tearing into his bare skin. He had left his shirt hanging on a rusty nail sticking out of a concrete block back where he was working with Papa. They'd been trying to mend the shell damage on his grandmother's house. The boy knew it was futile, but Papa insisted. At thirteen, he knew better than to argue. Anyway, he had been happy to spend a day with Papa, away from his chattering mother and sister.

On elbows and knees he crawled over the dusty roadway into the long scrub grass at the edge. Only a few yards from his house, but it might as well have been a mile.

He listened. Heard laughter, followed by screams. Mama? Rhea? No! He pleaded with the sun in the cloudless sky. Its only answer was a burning heat on his skin.

More rough laughter. Soldiers?

He inched forward. Men were shouting. What could he do? Was Papa too far away to help? Did he have his gun with him?

The boy crept on. At the fence, he parted the long brown grass and leaned in between two posts.

A green jeep with a red cross on an open door. Four men. Soldier's uniforms. Guns slung idly across their backs. Trousers around ankles. Bare buttocks in the air, humping. He knew what they were doing. They'd raped his friend's sister who lived at the foot of the mountain. And then they'd killed her.

Fighting back his useless tears, he watched. Mama and Rhea were screaming. The two soldiers got up, straightened their clothes as the other two took their places. More laughter.

Clamping his teeth onto his fist, he choked down sobs. Shep, his collie dog, barked loudly, circling the soldiers hysterically. The boy froze, then jumped, cracking his front tooth against bone, as a gunshot echoed up against the mountain and back down again. He let out an involuntary cry. Birds shot up from the sparse trees, merged as one, then flew in all directions. Shep lay unmoving in the yard beneath the makeshift swing, a tyre Papa had put up on a branch when they were little children. They were still children, but they didn't play on the swing any more. Not since the war.

An argument broke out among the soldiers. The boy tried to understand what they were saying but couldn't avert his eyes from the naked, dust-covered figures, still alive, their screams now muted whimpers. Where was Papa?

He stared, feeling hypnotised, as the men pulled on surgical gloves. The tallest one extracted a long steel blade from an old-fashioned scabbard attached to his hip. Then another one did the same. The boy was frozen with terror. Watching transfixed, he saw the soldier crouch behind his mama and drag her up against his chest. The other man grabbed eleven-year-old Rhea. Blood streamed down her legs and he quelled an urge to find clothing to hide her nakedness. Weeping silent tears, he felt powerless and useless.

One man raised his knife. It glinted in the sun before he drew it downwards, slitting Rhea from her throat to her belly. The other man did the same to Mama. The bodies convulsed. Blood gushed and spurted into the faces of the abusers. Gloved hands thrust into the cavities and tore out organs, blood dripping along their arms. The other two soldiers rushed forward with steel cases. The bodies dropped to the ground.

Wide-eyed with horror, the boy watched the soldiers quickly place the organs of his precious mama and sister into the cases, laughing as they snapped them shut. One took a marker from his pocket and casually wrote on the side of the container and another turned and kicked out at Rhea. Her body shuddered. He looked directly over towards the boy's hiding place.

Holding his breath, eyes locked on the soldier, the boy felt no terror now. He was prepared to die and half stood up, but the man was moving back to his comrades. They packed the cases into the jeep, jumped in and with a cloud of stones and dust rising skywards, drove back down the mountain road.

He didn't know how long he stayed there before a hand clamped down on his shoulder and pulled him into an embrace. He looked into a pair of heartbroken eyes. He hadn't heard the frantic running or the frenzied shouting. The vision of the disembowelled bodies of Mama and Rhea had imprinted themselves as a photograph in his mind. And he knew it would never fade.

Papa dragged him towards the bodies. The boy stared into his mother's eyes. Pleading in death. Papa took out his pistol, turned his wife's face into the hot clay and shot her in the back of the head. Her body flexed. Stilled.

Papa cried, big, silent tears, as he crawled over to Rhea. He shot her too. The boy knew she was already dead. There was no need for the bullet. He tried to shout at Papa but his voice was lost in the midst of the turmoil.

'I had to do it!' Papa cried. 'To save their souls.' He pulled the two bodies, and then Shep, into the house. With determination in his steps he hurriedly emptied a jerry can of petrol inside the door and threw in a lighted torch of dry reeds. Picking up his gun, he raised it towards the boy.

No words of fear, no movement. Yet. The boy was immobile until he saw Papa's work-stained finger tremble on the trigger. Instinct caused him to run.

Papa cried out, 'Save yourself. Run, boy. Don't stop running.'

Looking over his shoulder as he went, he saw Papa turn the gun to his own wrinkled forehead and pull the trigger before falling back into the flames. They ignited in a whoosh of crinkling, falling timber.

The boy watched from the fence as the life he had known burned as bright as the sun in the sky. No help came. The war had caused everyone to fend for themselves and he supposed those living in the other houses along the road were hiding, terrified, awaiting their own fate. He couldn't blame them. There was nothing they could do here anyway.

After some time the sun dipped low and night stars twinkled like nothing was wrong. Without even a shirt on his back he began the long, lonely trek down the mountain.

He did not know where he was going.

He had nowhere to go.

He did not care.

Slowly he walked, one foot in front of the other, stones breaking through the soft rubber soles of his sandals. He walked until his feet bled. He walked until his sandals disintegrated like his heart. He kept on walking until he reached a place where he would never feel pain again.

FRIDAY NIGHT,
8 MAY 2015

Ragmullin

CHAPTER ONE

It was the dark that frightened her the most. Not being able to see. And the sounds. Soft skittering, then silence.

Shifting onto her side, she tried to haul herself into a sitting position. Gave up. A rustle. Squeaking. She screamed, and her voice echoed back. Sobbing, she wrapped her arms tight around her body. Her thin cotton shirt and jeans were soaked with cold sweat.

The dark.

She had spent too many nights like this in her own bedroom, listening to her mother's laughter with others in the kitchen below. Now she remembered those nights as a luxury. Because that wasn't *real* dark. Street lights and the moon had cast shadows through paper-thin curtains, birthing the wallpaper to life. Her dated furniture had stood like statues in a dimly lit cemetery. Her clothes, heaped in piles on a chair in the corner, had sometimes appeared to be heaving, as the headlamps of cars passing on the road shone through the curtains. And she thought that had been dark? No. This, where she was now, was the true meaning of pitch black.

She wished she had her phone, with her life attached to it – her cyber friends on Facebook and Twitter. They might be able to help her. If she had her phone. If only.

The door opened, the glow from the hallway blinding her eyes shut. Church bells chimed in the distance. Where was she? Near home? The bells stopped. A sharp laugh. The light flicked on. A naked bulb swayed with the draught and she saw the figure of a man.

Backing into the damp wall, scuffing her bare heels along the floor, she felt a tug on her hair and pain pinpricked each follicle on her head. She didn't care. He could scalp her bald as long as she got home alive.

'P-please…'

Her voice didn't sound like her own. High-pitched and quivering, no longer laced with her usual teenage swagger.

A rough hand pulled her upward, her hair snarled round his fingers. She squinted at him, trying to form a mental picture. He was taller than her, wearing a grey knitted hat pierced with two slits revealing hostile eyes. She must remember the eyes. For later. For when she was free. A thrust of determination inched its way into her heart. Straightening her spine, she faced him.

'What?' he barked.

His sour breath churned her stomach upside down. His clothes smelled like the slaughterhouse behind Kennedy's butcher's shop on Patrick Street. In springtime, little lambs succumbed to bullets or knives or whatever they used to kill them. That smell. Death. The cloying odour clinging to her uniform all day long.

She shuddered as he moved his face nearer. Now she had something to be more frightened of than pitch-black nothingness. For the first time in her life, she actually wanted her mother.

'Let me go,' she cried. 'Home. I want to go home. Please.'

'You make me laugh, little one.'

He leaned towards her, so close that his wool-covered nose touched hers and his sickly breath oozed through the knitted stitches.

She tried to back away but there was nowhere to go. She held her breath, desperately trying not to puke as he gripped her shoulder and pushed her to the door.

'Stage two of your adventure begins,' he said, laughing to himself.

Her blood crawled as she hobbled into the barren corridor. High ceilings. Peeling paint. Giant cast-iron radiators snatched up her faltering steps with their shadows. A high wooden door blocked her progress. His hand slid around her waist, pulling her body to his. She froze. Leaning over, he shoved open the door.

Forced into a room, she slipped on the wet floor and fell to her knees.

'No, no…' She swung around frantically. What was going on? What was this place? Windows sheathed in Perspex kept daylight at bay. The floor was covered in damp heavy-duty plastic; the walls were streaked with what she thought looked like dried blood. Everything she saw screeched at her to run. Instead, she crawled. On hands and knees. All she could see in front of her were his boots, caked in mud or blood or both. He hauled her up and prodded her to move. Rotating her body, she faced him.

He pulled off the balaclava. Eyes she had only seen through slits were now joined by a thin, pink-lipped mouth. She stared. His face was a blank canvas awaiting a horror yet to be painted.

'Tell me your name again?' he asked.

'Wh-what do you mean?'

'I want to hear you say it,' he snarled.

Catching sight of the knife in his hand, she slithered and slipped on the blood-soaked plastic before falling prostrate before him. This time she welcomed the darkness. As it glided over the tiny stars flickering behind her eyes, she whispered, 'Maeve.'